THE WIDOW

of

WALL STREET

THE WIDOW

of

WALL STREET

A NOVEL

RANDY SUSAN MEYERS

ATRIA BOOKS

New York London Toronto Sydney New Delhi

ATRIA BOOKS

An Imprint of Simon & Schuster, Inc.
1230 Avenue of the Americas
New York, NY 10020

First Atria Books hardcover edition April 2017

ATRIA BOOKS and colophon are trademarks of Simon & Schuster, Inc.

For information about special discounts for bulk purchases, please contact Simon & Schuster Special Sales at 1-866-506-1949 or business@simonandschuster.com.

The Simon & Schuster Speakers Bureau can bring authors to your live event. For more information or to book an event, contact the Simon & Schuster Speakers Bureau at 1-866-248-3049 or visit our website at www.simonspeakers.com.

Manufactured in the United States of America

10 9 8 7 6 5 4 3 2 1

Library of Congress Cataloging-in-Publication Data

Names: Meyers, Randy Susan, author.
Title: The widow of wall street : a novel / Randy Susan Meyers.
Description: First hardcover edition. | New York : Atria, 2017.
Identifiers: LCCN 2016021400 (print) | LCCN 2016029193 (ebook) | ISBN 9781501131349 (hardcover : acid-free paper) | ISBN 9781501131363 (softcover : acid-free paper) | ISBN 9781501131370 (ebook)
Subjects: LCSH: Capitalists and financiers—Fiction. | Married people—Fiction. | Stockbrokers—Fiction. | Wall Street (New York, N.Y.)—Fiction. | Domestic fiction. | GSAFD: Love stories.
Classification: LCC PS3613.E9853 W53 2017 (print) | LCC PS3613.E9853 (ebook) | DDC 813/.6—dc23
LC record available at https://lccn.loc.gov/2016021400

ISBN 978-1-5011-3134-9
ISBN 978-1-5011-3137-0 (ebook)

To Jeff, who owns my heart.

"Truth is the only firm ground to stand upon."
—ELIZABETH CADY STANTON

THE WIDOW
of
WALL STREET

CHAPTER 1

PHOEBE

November 2009

Phoebe never hated her husband more than when she visited him in prison. The preceding nightmare of ordeals—eleven hours hauling a suitcase by bus, train, and cab, her muscles screaming from the weight—were the coming attractions of the misery she faced the next day.

She arrived at the grimy hotel close to midnight. Without sleep, exhaustion would lengthen every minute tomorrow. After wrestling her luggage to the bed, Phoebe thumbed through a small stack of folded sweaters, hoping they would withstand the raw weather. So many never-envisioned experiences: riding a dingy Greyhound bus; drowning ramen noodles in a hotel coffee maker; choosing clothes to wear to Ray Brook Federal Correctional Institution—and then envisioning her choice through her husband's eyes.

Each month, Jake became more of an albatross, and yet, even now, through tooth-grinding anger, Phoebe found herself still seeking his approving smile and the satisfaction of soothing his melancholy.

Phoebe worried how long she could, would, continue making the long trip to this prison in upstate New York. One hour farther and she'd be in Canada. To stop visiting required strength she hadn't yet found—loving and worrying about Jake had been her default for too long—so she agonized about everything from prison conversation to the choice between wearing a cardigan or crewneck sweater.

"Why won't you stay longer?" She dreaded hearing those words Jake repeated every visit. "Other wives come Saturday and Sunday, not for a measly few hours."

She'd stare just as she had before. Silent, hoping her eyes might express the command she couldn't speak: *Screw yourself, Jake.* Her husband, once a titan—a god—now whined like a child.

What she said: "A few hours is plenty."

What she didn't say: *Two days would kill me.*

What he said: "Getting out after three hours must be nice."

What he probably meant: *I hate you for being free.*

What she said: "Staying here must be hard."

What she didn't say: *Leaving is deliverance from you.*

Then she'd change the topic—a difficult task with a world of off-limit issues: The kids. Jake's guilt. Her lack of money. Her not knowing this man; this fraud of a husband who steamrolled over her desperation to unravel the tangled skein of their past.

She held up first a soft white turtleneck, and then a subdued blue cardigan, and finally a camel-colored blazer. Jake liked her to dress sharp. Even in prison he demanded that she reflect well on him. How ironic. Yet, after building her life on pleasing Jake—even after him swindling her and everyone else in his life—she couldn't shake the habit of following his orders.

Phoebe also needed to please her other husband, the new authority in her life—the Federal Bureau of Prisons—and adhering to the prison's rules for visitors meant dressing to its standards.

"Visitors are held to a dress code before being admitted into the institution."

Stark divisions outlined her life. Before, she would wander through the highest-end stores clutching fabric from an old Caribbean-blue dress, a shade that brightened her eyes, to match that color in a sweater. After . . .

"Visitors wearing transparent clothing, dresses, blouses or other apparel of a suggestive or revealing nature, halter tops, short shorts, miniskirts, culottes, or excessively tight fitting clothing will not be admitted into the institution."

Too tired to concentrate, she placed her wardrobe choices on the extra twin bed. In the morning, when she knew the temperature, she could make her decision. And November temperatures in the Adirondack Mountains often fell below freezing.

After brushing her teeth and covering her face with motel lotion, she carried her laptop to bed. Her closest relationships were with her sister and her Mac; lately she had started Googling "average life of Apple laptops." Imagining life without her electronic connection petrified Phoebe. Thoughts of spending almost two thousand dollars for a replacement provided equal amounts of panic.

Messages from frightening strangers stuffed her Gmail in-box. The distraught and inflamed found her no matter how many times she changed her email provider. Her encrypted email account—Hushmail—the sole communication method she managed to keep private besides her cell phone, contained only one new message, from her sister. Deb wrote daily, always cheerful. Today a long-ago picture of the two of them climbing on iron monkey bars in a Brooklyn playground accompanied her note.

No word from the kids. Occasionally, Kate sent updates about Amelia, Phoebe's granddaughter. Noah wrote monthly emails filled with agony and anger.

After dashing off a quick note to Deb—"Everything is fine! Weather holding up—more tmw"—she opened Etsy, her online Xanax. Phoebe daydreamed of having an anonymous work life there, building friendships with a community of crafters who appreciated one another only for their dedication to the perfect quilt or ceramic mug. She could sell handmade recipe books devoted to cupcakes. At night, as she struggled toward sleep and fought against memories—and giving in to sleeping pills—she invented pen names: Mimi Appleby. Yoshiko Whisby. Gianna Gardner.

Phoebe tried holding back, but finally, pressing her lips hard together, unable to resist, she opened PrisonMessages.com. Within moments, she found herself captured by Karlgirl's question: "Would you be angry if your man showed off your sexy pics?"

Phoebe couldn't conceive of any man wanting photos of her, sexy or otherwise, but still, she slipped into the world and wondered about Jake in that situation.

The man she thought she'd married would have gouged out the eyes of any man trying to see her naked. Today's Jake would likely sell pictures of her to the highest bidder.

Like a man vowing to stay off porn sites, she slammed her laptop closed.

Ten minutes later, Phoebe reopened it, and then unwrapped a packet of peanut butter crackers as she waited for the machine to come fully alive. She munched as she scrolled through the topics: "Prison Weddings." "Legal Help." "Loving a Lifer." On and on. She never visited "Execution Watch" or "In Memoriam"—the latter full of tributes to those who died in prison—but she lurked in chat rooms, reading, trying to learn something about Jake's world.

The women she followed were Mrs.25Years, Nick'sOne, and JimmysGirl, all experienced guides to prison protocol. From them, she discovered that underwire bras set off alarms and precipitated a guard's too-familiar hands feeling you up. Phoebe dreaded seeing someone mention Jake. "Guess who my man saw in the yard!" Prison-Messages.com shackled you to your her husband by name and deed.

She clicked "Loving a Lifer," despite knowing that her love for Jake died more each day. After his confession, Jake had morphed into that awful relative attached to your flesh like a parasite; one you were forced to care for because he lived on your family tree.

She scrolled down the forum, reading titles.

Thread: "What bonds you to your lifer?"

If her daughter could see her, she'd fold her arms and ask, "Exactly, Mom. How can you continue choosing him over us?" Phoebe would again beg Kate to understand why leaving Jake alone, pummeled by a world's anger, seemed like kicking him as he lay on the ground.

At the time, Phoebe hadn't thought that she'd chosen Jake or rejected her children, not while the mash of shame, confusion, and loyalty roiled. She hadn't known how to abandon him. Her son and daughter had their spouses, their children, and each other. Jake could lean only on her. She became his security blanket. He became *her* prison.

Thread: "I am exhausted."

Yes. They were all tired, facing their angry men on visiting days. Tired of their men's locked-up desperation boiled with resentment, these overly sensitive men offended by their need for women living on the outside. They exhausted their women, these men.

Thread: "Need topics for talking with my man on the phone."

Conversation with Jake required only audible nodding from her.

Thread: "What are the best traits of your lifer?"

Inexhaustible stores of love dust sprinkled the screen. Despite having committed crimes so awful they had received life sentences, these men still inspired their women to enumerate their good qualities. Had they forgiven them their murders, their rapes, their thieving?

Jake swore that no singular moment had marked the beginning of his thievery, but he was lying. Everything began somewhere. He hadn't slipped into his Byzantine plot. His had been no banana peel of a crime.

And now he talked about the guys. People imagined prisons as all fear and knives, but the truth didn't unfold so tough. They cooked. They shared books. They were his goddamned buddies.

Phoebe longed for her children. Deep, visceral want threatened to topple her each morning. Antidepressants, antacids, and shame sustained her.

· · ·

The cab driver didn't acknowledge Phoebe, except for nodding when she asked for Ray Brook Federal Correctional. Maybe he was being polite, accustomed to allowing psychic space to sad women visiting locked up men, but more likely, she disgusted him. She recognized the expression: the shock of detection and the scowl.

You.

Her.

The face of Jake's crime. Wife of the demon. Even if she dyed her hair, wore sunglasses, dressed plainer than an Amish woman, someone shook his or her head as she passed.

The prison loomed. The cab stopped.

Tipping the driver worried her. Too little, and he'd despise her. Too much, and he'd hate her for giving him tainted money.

She paid the thirty-five-dollar fare, adding six dollars. Wind hit as she stepped out and faced the cold colorless brick of Ray Brook. Already she'd curled her hands into fists so tight that they ached.

Her entire marriage had been a battle against being known only as Jake's wife—now she feared the battle could be over for good.

Phoebe had become two almost-spectral things: a widow to a living man, and a childless mother.

Part 1

———

THE EARLY YEARS

CHAPTER 2

PHOEBE

August 1960

"You're not going to that party, young lady. You're too young, and he's too old. Case closed."

Phoebe ignored the shrill threat penetrating her bedroom door and concentrated on building layers of rosy pink lipstick. She disappeared inside her reflection, coloring each millimeter of her lips, and then pressed her mouth against a tissue. Finally, she dipped her finger in a blue container of Pond's loose face powder.

Her mother banged on her door. "Your father's on his way up."

Tap powder on upper lip.

Tap powder on lower lip.

"He's removing the lock from this door and it's going to stay off until you prove yourself to be trustworthy. Mark my words."

Tissue.

Powder.

Lipstick.

Phoebe repeated *Seventeen* magazine's advice three times. She smiled at her image, tilting her head, trying to capture her more attractive side. *Seventeen* swore that the angle a girl presented determined her degree of desirability. When she first read the article, she'd run to the mirror, magazine in hand. Now the words were etched so deep that she could recite them:

For most girls (whether it be for taking terrific photos or making a great first impression) one side of the face looks better than the other. Angle that side toward the camera—or the boy whose eye you want to catch.

Not sure of your best? Use a sheet of paper to cover one side of your face and then the other and choose the half with more upturned features (such as the corners of your eyes or lips). If you can't decide, pick your left side, the more visually pleasing for most faces.

Phoebe's sister, Deb, laughed when Phoebe asked her which side was Deb's best. Despite being two years older, Deb, an actual seventeen-year-old, read *National Geographic*. Deb didn't require the safety of makeup. Family and friends all called Phoebe the pretty one, but instead of giving her confidence, their praise necessitated that she maintain it daily. How could she not, when almost everyone but her mother so valued her appearance?

Phoebe peered into the mirror again. Left. Definitely prettier. The moment Jake entered, she'd turn that side toward him.

"Do you hear me? Are you alive in there?" Her mother's Brooklyn accent assaulted Phoebe's ears. Lately, Phoebe enunciated her words with such care that her parents asked if she had a sore throat and did she need a lozenge, for God's sake? "Are you planning to spend the rest of summer vacation in that room?"

Phoebe wondered if her shirt were the right shade of blue.

"If you're not out in three minutes, your father's taking the door down.

"Red!" her mother yelled. "Get the toolbox!"

Like so many Brooklyn men, her father kept his neighborhood name, Red, despite that his hair had faded to more of an autumn-leaves color than the strawberry blond it had once been. When Phoebe wished aloud that she'd inherited his hair, her mother snorted, "You want to look even less Jewish than you already do?"

Phoebe dialed up the radio volume. Deb always tried to teach her to just do what her mother said, but her sister didn't understand.

Nothing Phoebe did resembled anything their mother wanted, a fact made evident by her relentless harangues:

"Stop teasing your hair into a rat's nest! Are you a streetwalker?"

"Maybelline should name that lipstick Evening Blood! You look like a vampire!"

"Your room is filthy. You think you'll catch a husband with those habits?"

She caught her mother's anger on a daily basis. Lola Beckett didn't like Phoebe—not the way she adored Deb. Her mother and Deb matched, with their curly brown hair, curves, and practicality bred into every cell.

"Our little shiksa girl," her mother called Phoebe, with her straight, near-black hair and the eyes her father had christened California blue. Her wire-skinny body also aggravated her mother. After preparing cottage cheese and Jell-O for Deb and herself, she slapped extra-thick peanut butter on slabs of buttered rye bread for Phoebe, who then nibbled at half the sandwich before throwing the rest in the garbage. Phoebe planned to stay skinny. Jake admired her thinness, seeing her tight body as his win.

Her father gave his trademark three sharp raps on the door. "Pheebs, don't drive your mother crazy. Come on out, honey."

"Don't 'honey' the girl," her mother said.

"Let me handle this, Lola." He knocked again. "Enough, Phoebe."

Hi, Jake, Phoebe mouthed at the mirror. She opened her eyes as wide as she could without appearing crazy, mimicking the magazine models who appeared so thrilled with life.

"He's holding the screwdriver," her mother warned as Phoebe unlocked the door so quickly her mother almost fell into the room.

"Jeez, Mom. What's going on with you?"

"Lose the tone, missy. I'm protecting you."

"From what?" Phoebe widened her eyes at her father.

"Don't look at Daddy when I'm talking. You're getting too serious with the boy." Her mother blew out cigarette smoke disgustedly. "Not a boy. Almost a man!"

"He just turned eighteen, Mom." Phoebe placed her hands on her hips.

"You're only fifteen. A child."

Phoebe blinked away tears of anger—afraid her mother would no-tice forbidden mascara dusted on her lashes. "He makes me happy!"

"Happy." Her mother spit out the word as though repeating some-thing corrosive. " 'Happy' only means one thing at his age. I don't trust him."

"Deb met Ben at fourteen, but you act like he's perfect."

"Ben is a mensch. Smart and good."

Daddy put a hand on her mother's arm. "Lola, sweetheart, he is a go-getter."

Phoebe smiled, but before her glee grew all the way—she had found a go-getter!—Daddy swiveled back to her with stern eyes. "Your mother's right: you're too intense with this guy. He steamed up your glasses. Or you steamed his. Either way, neither of you is thinking straight. We want you to be a good girl, Phoebe. Promise us—"

The doorbell rang before Phoebe could hear the guarantee that her father wanted to exact from her, but she'd have promised every star in the sky to end the conversation.

"I promise to be perfect. Always!" She grinned, not worrying which direction her face pointed. A father loved you from every angle. A mother's job, Phoebe supposed, was judging you whatever the viewpoint.

"That's my girl," he said. "We can trust you, but your mother wor-ries."

"Just don't think about anything serious." Her mother spoke faster as Phoebe backed toward the stairs, desperate to race down and greet Jake. "Your life is in front of you. You're bright and talented. You can do anything, go anywhere. Don't throw anything away."

No more fighting tonight. Freedom beckoned.

"Do I look pretty?" She almost sang the words as she pirouetted for her parents.

"For goodness' sake, Phoebe," her mother answered, "you're never anything but pretty. You think beauty's the solution, but in truth, your gorgeous face is the problem."

Even beauty could be a curse in her mother's world.

. . .

"What a looker you are." Jake brought Phoebe closer and hummed the melody of the Drifters' latest hit in her ear before murmuring a few words of the song. "This magic moment, when your lips are close to mine."

All around, couples swayed in the dim light of Jake's friend's finished basement.

Jake tightened his grip, and she leaned against his broad chest. He towered over Phoebe, preventing her from peeking over his shoulder to see if Helen saw them dancing. Last night she and Helen had spent an hour on the phone, trading time being in love. First Helen talked Alan, Alan, Alan, then Phoebe babbled Jake, Jake, Jake, until they'd nibbled every morsel of their sumptuous elation.

Secretly, Phoebe thought Jake tons more exciting than Alan, who'd planned his entire life by sixteen. Just about every girl in Erasmus Hall High School would pick Jake's sardonic humor and tough-guy looks over Alan's nose-to-the-grindstone personality.

Jake planned to conquer the world. Phoebe believed him capable of anything. Except, perhaps, being a doctor. Or a dentist, like her father. She laughed against his starched shirt.

"What's so funny?" He tucked a strand of hair behind her ear. "Cute ears. Like little shells. Did someone spin you out of gold?"

"I'm imagining you as a doctor. You don't have the patience for patients."

"Very funny. Measuring me as husband material? Are you planning on marrying a doctor?"

She drew back. "Whoa. My parents warned me about going too fast."

"Your parents don't like me?" Jake's wounded look touched her.

"Don't be silly. How could they not like you? They barely know you."

"So why are they worrying about you going too fast?"

"I'm only fifteen."

"Years go by in a flash, as my father reminds me every day." He pressed his hand against her back. "You won't always be young."

Phoebe frowned, not enjoying being yanked out of their magic moment. With his words her skin dried up, her shiny hair fell limp and drab, and her taut waist expanded enough to require a corset. "Good work finding the world's most not-romantic thing to say."

"Hey! You may not always be young, but you'll always be gorgeous. You're a thoroughbred. You won't let yourself go. When my mother married my father, he considered her a babe. His hands could span her waist. I wonder if you're small enough."

Jake circled Phoebe's midsection with his hands and squeezed. She sucked in until her stomach hurt, even knowing that he'd exaggerated.

"Now my father would have to hire a guy to help hug my mother all the way around." His crooked grin shot sparks straight through her despite his appalling words.

"Meanie! What a way to talk about your mother."

"Ha. She says worse about my father and me. Anyway, you've seen her, right?"

Sadly, yes. Phoebe and his parents both turned up to watch Jake lead the swim team to victory a few weeks after she and Jake began dating. Helen had nudged her and nodded in the direction of an overweight couple.

"Jake's parents," Helen had whispered.

Phoebe tried not to stare, but temptation hung heavy. Compared with Mr. and Mrs. Pierce, her parents were Tony Curtis and Janet Leigh. Her father kept trim and immaculate, his thick red hair always close cut, shirts ironed taut. Her mother girdled her body into submission, arranged her curls to flatter her wholesome, round face, and never left the house without swiping on her Royalty Red lipstick.

Jake resembled his father, but only in the broadest terms. Mr. Pierce drooped as though someone had vacuumed out his muscle, leaving only the doughy parts. His arms dangled like a monkey's, making him appear shorter than Jake, even though he matched him in height—both of them nudging six feet, though losing out on the final half inch. But where his father wilted, Jake gleamed with rugged ambition and virility.

Even now, at the beginning of summer, Jake had become toasted-delicious, with a lifeguard tan matching his broad swimmer's body, which narrowed at the hips. Sun streaks coppered his thick russet-brown hair. A cleft divided his chin. Rough skin and heavy-lidded eyes saved him from being a pretty boy.

Jake's mother had worn a housedress to the competition; the sort worn by women who lived in ancient apartment houses complete with basements perfect for murder. Phoebe's mother described living in those dingy brick buildings as having tickets to a tiny bit of hell.

"Not even an elevator! You know who lives in those places?" she'd ask. "Lazy people who don't care how their children grow up. Remember, girls, never let your husband come home to a messy wife."

That bit of Mom's wisdom seemed worth taking. After all, her parents still held hands. Daddy's smile when he looked at her mother wrapped their whole family in love. At night, Phoebe could hear them giggle from their bedroom.

Jake twirled her in a circle, almost lifting her off the ground. "Once upon a time, my mother combined the looks of Jayne Mansfield and Jane Russell in one woman—though personally, I go for the Audrey Hepburn type. Now my mother's Sophie Tucker. Catching my father when she did was a good move for her."

"You make marriage sound horrid. Like a game."

He raised his dark eyebrows. "The game of love, baby. Everything in life is some sort of contest, and everyone wants to be a winner." He squeezed her close. "You and I, we'll always win."

. . .

Phoebe slowed her steps as she and Jake approached her house. She almost tiptoed; if she made the slightest sound, her mother would be out on the porch before Jake's lips touched hers.

Two weeks before, when she had come home from a date with scraped red cheeks, beard burn showing on both her good and not-so-good sides, her mother had lectured her for forty minutes on the fate of girls who got mixed up with boys who didn't control themselves.

"Listen, Phoebe. No one ever blames the boy when something

happens. You better believe girls always wear the mistake. You'll be the one taking care of the results, and you can take that to the bank."

Jake's energy traveled at the speed of light, gathering friends and followers as he sprinted. He worked two jobs, but being miserly didn't come with his hard work. Every time she turned around, he opened his wallet, whether buying burgers for the entire crowd or buying her a teddy bear that she had thought cute.

"Do you know how lucky you are? Look at this." He spread his arms wide as though to hold the wide, leafy street. Buckingham Road resembled a miniature world. Walk one block away, and congested Brooklyn returned: people jostling into one another as they raced to the subway, hurrying from the candy store to the delicatessen to the Chinese laundry, everyone rushing like the tide at Coney Island. Molecules pressed in, all the breath, all the words flying out of people's mouths.

In fourth grade, Miss Leanza had said that almost 8 million people lived in New York City. Sometimes Phoebe thought they all converged on Church Avenue.

Buckingham Road offered an oasis. An island of green divided it in two. A median of trees and grass lifted her street into something majestic.

Jake reached for her. A magnetic pull slammed them together. Since meeting Jake, she understood why her mother made such a fuss over Phoebe's comings and goings. Without the rules of convention, Phoebe would crush her lips to Jake's until they consumed each other.

He pressed against her. The sensation of wanting him closer, an arousal as agonizing as it was exhilarating, left her confused and breathless.

"Okay. Okay." She pushed him away, excitement slowing her speech. "My mother will come out any minute."

He walked her to the doorway, stopping for one more clench before they stepped on the porch. "Which window is yours?" he asked. "I want to imagine you curling up in bed."

She pointed to the corner of the second floor. Her room overlooked the lush greenery. Sometimes, when her mother's criticisms piled up and Phoebe began to see nothing but wispy hair and pimples in the mirror, she would stare out the window and imagine an amazing future when her life gleamed so bright that even her mother's words couldn't hurt.

For now, she had Jake.

CHAPTER 3

PHOEBE

November 1963

"Come on, Pheebs. What's the big deal in missing one class? You're in college, not the army."

Phoebe tuned Jake out, shuffling notes as she sat cross-legged on her bed.

"All the other girlfriends will be at the party," he said. "Show up for me, okay?"

Phoebe gritted her teeth as Jake begged. "I told you. I'm not cutting class. My paper's due."

The only way he'd please her at this point was to leave and let her finish writing "What People Think of the Poor." He deserved credit, though. He'd helped her with the assignment, distributing her questionnaire to twenty of his Brooklyn College fraternity brothers and forcing them to fill them out. He'd even answered one himself, surprising her with some of his responses—quick and pointed; Jake was not typically one to indulge in pontification.

Q: To what degree do you think the poor are responsible for their own plight?
A: The rich will do anything they can to keep what belongs to them. Thus the poor must claw at the rich to get theirs.

Q: Which of these aphorisms do you think best describes your attitude toward the poor in America?

    1. God helps those who help themselves.

    2. The poor must pull themselves up by their bootstraps.

    3. The meek shall inherit the earth.

A: Number 1!!! Everyone's got to grab their own prize. No one hands over money.

Jake peered over her shoulder, reading the questions aloud as if seeing them for the first time. "'Is society responsible for fair wages?' 'Can people be expected to rise above their parents' societal place?' You bet I'm rising above my parents' place. Not that it's a long leap." He gave a lopsided grin. "But I plan to pole-vault to the top. For both of us."

Phoebe reached back and patted his shoulder, his dense muscle almost distracting her determination to make this paper perfect. "I question plenty in this world, but your success never makes that list."

"You're the best thing that ever happened to me." He lay back and laced his fingers behind his head. "Plus, you're so damned smart. You can go all the way. As much as you love books, you can get your doctorate. Teach college. Together we can do anything. I'll make sure of it."

He rolled over and traced the outline of her knee. "Our kids will be terrific, you know. We'll give them everything we never had."

She hardened herself against his dreams. "Rising in status and the size of a paycheck isn't the only proof of worth," she said. "What about people who want to help other people? Or those who devote themselves to the arts? Or teaching?"

"Like you?" Jake draped an arm around her shoulder. "People like you need people like me to support your do-gooding. So come to the party."

"You're relentless. And I don't mean that as a compliment."

"Class is more important to you than me?"

"No. Class is more important to me than your frat party."

"Everything at City College outweighs anything at Brooklyn College?"

"To repeat. Going to class trumps your Christmas party. Why are they celebrating in November, anyway?"

"Everyone's gotta be with their family during the holidays. Anyway, we're not having a Christmas party. We're celebrating Hanukkah."

"You're a rabbi now?"

"And being in Manhattan has turned you into the Queen of England? Too good to go to my party?"

She hated when he twisted her words, as though going or not going proved her loyalty to him. "How about if I take the train straight to the frat house after class? So I'll only miss—what? An hour or two?"

"Fine. Whatever you want. Have it your way."

With a bare brush of his lips as a good-bye kiss, a bit of punishment masquerading as affection, he left. Jake was a two-headed coin. On one side lived the rough-sexy guy who knew how to both protect her and accept that he needed her—the guy who took her on magic carpet rides. On the other side was the man who bared his teeth when he didn't get his way. She adored the first; the second wearied her.

She inched the front door closed, fighting her craving to slam the wood to splinters, knowing her mother would race in and ask, "What's wrong? Are you mad at Jake?," her voice betraying the truth that she hoped to hear about a problem in the relationship.

If her mother were Catholic, she'd be lighting daily candles at Holy Innocents, bribing God with her piety, praying for His intervention, that He would force Phoebe to dump Jake.

Which, at the moment, tempted Phoebe more than she wanted to admit.

From the day she received her acceptance letter, Jake had acted as though Phoebe attending City College of New York instead of Brooklyn College portended treachery against him, her parents, and the entire borough of Brooklyn. For Phoebe, being at the relatively more sophisticated CCNY made her impatient with Jake in ways she'd never been—reacting against the same traits in him that had impressed her a mere few months ago. Whereas before he seemed like the go-getter that her father had admired, now, especially compared with her brilliant sociology professor, his ambition seemed uncouth. When they were out with others, Jake squeezed her hand every other second, seeking squeezes back as admiration for something clever that he had said. Conversely, listening to her professor lecture about class differences in America made Jake's glib talk seem thin as waxed paper.

Monday through Friday, breaking up seemed the best course; come the weekend, feeling Jake's shelter, knowing she'd caught the love of the guy that every girl wanted and every guy admired, she shoved those thoughts away. Walking through the world with Jake meant half the work was already done. He cleared the way for her.

The downside of those weekends was their going-all-the-way arguments. She didn't want to sleep with him. Not yet. The more he pushed, the tighter she locked her legs against both of their cravings.

"Are you afraid that I won't respect you?" he'd ask. "I damned well worship the ground you walk on! I love you. You know I'm marrying you, right?"

Soothing her with talk of a wedding didn't help. Despite his sway over her—even after three years of dating, his touch thrilled her—getting married seemed like a final chapter in a life that she hadn't yet led. Why the rush to marry him? To marry anyone? Sex sealed a deal she didn't want at the moment.

Yet saying no was hard. Whatever "physical chemistry" meant, they certainly owned the formula. Wanting him had never presented a problem, but she'd fallen in love with college, too. Recently, the City College of New York brought the roses to Phoebe's cheeks. She skipped off to her Introduction to Sociology class as though running to meet her lover. Poli-sci class met her with a hug of newness. In high school, she had done okay—she was especially good at taking tests—but the distractions of Jake's attentions, along with staying on top of her clique, had distracted her from studying. Now education drew her as though it wore the sexiest cologne on earth.

Being smart and writing reports, getting good marks—that didn't satisfy her anymore. Phoebe wanted to be learned. School left her just about breathless.

. . .

The next day, on the subway ride from Church Avenue in Brooklyn to 135th Street in Harlem—a long, soporific ride—Phoebe faced up to another reason for the roses in her cheeks and her motivation for never missing an Intro to Sociology class.

Professor Robert Gardiner.

Phoebe rolled the name around as she walked onto campus, entered his classroom, and chose a seat two rows from his desk. When he smiled, she beamed back. She slipped her pen and pencil from her bag and pulled out her notebook. She was cool and ready.

Professor Gardiner had most definitely not come from Brooklyn. For the first few weeks of class, Phoebe hadn't wanted to speak for fear of sounding like a parody of a Brooklyn girl, all *dese* and *dose*. At night, she whispered to the mirror: *cahn't*, instead of *caint*, and *cahfee* in place of *cawfee*, until she went too far and sounded like Katharine Hepburn. Jake spotted the changes right away. "Stop putting on airs," he'd ordered.

Life became complicated. Phoebe spoke in a manner she thought sounded educated when outside Brooklyn, and then reclaimed her accent as she exited her neighborhood subway stop.

"Today we'll jump ahead and study deviance and crime," Professor Gardiner announced.

While her Jake was no shrimp—he almost touched six feet—Gardiner topped him. Sun-colored hair hung in his eyes. When he spoke about pioneer social worker and suffrage activist Jane Addams and the settlement house she helped found, he sounded as reverent and impressed as Jake did when talking about Mickey Mantle and the Yankees.

Each quiet word Professor Gardiner uttered provided depth and clarity. Like Phoebe's father, her professor understood the worth of being good. Unlike her mother, who shook her head in frustration and muttered "Enough!" when Phoebe's father dropped a coin into the cup of every beggar they passed. (Though she knew her mother secretly admired Daddy for his generosity—as she did everything.

To her mother, Daddy was a minor god.) Phoebe stared trance-like as Professor Gardiner lectured. His strong, straight white teeth impressed Phoebe the dentist's daughter, and his blinding smile screamed fourth-generation American—he looked like a sexy portrait of Jesus.

She scribbled down the golden nuggets of information that Gardiner provided, resentful of others—mainly girls—who were similarly engaged in doing so. She wanted him to be only *her* discovery.

As he turned to the board to write down the key events tying the Industrial Revolution to changes in social conditions and crime, the door opened. A panting woman wearing a too-long skirt clutched a clipboard to her sizeable chest.

"Professor Gardiner." She huffed out a teary breath before continuing. "I need you in the hall, please."

Without a word of apology for the interruption, she left. Gardiner held up his hands, signifying "I don't know," followed her out, and the whispering began.

The girl next to Phoebe put a hand to her chest. "Maybe someone in his family died. Or it could be an emergency for one of us."

Chills shot through Phoebe. What if her mother had suffered the heart attack that Mom always worried about? Or Daddy? Hadn't her mother mentioned that his color seemed off yesterday? Work would drive him to an early grave, her mother always said. As Phoebe imagined her father in a hospital bed, or worse, Professor Gardiner returned, frowning and colorless.

"We have some bad news."

A waiting silence came over the room.

"I . . ." He stopped and closed his eyes, pressing his fingers to his brow. "President Kennedy has been shot."

A collective gasp sounded.

"He's dead?" asked a rumpled young man from the back of the classroom.

"I'm afraid so." Professor Gardiner walked to the front of his desk and sat on the worn oak. After a moment of quiet, he crossed his arms and spoke. "Mrs. Treisman—she's our department secretary; such a kind woman—suggested I dismiss everyone. So you can be with your families. But—"

Competing thoughts swirled. Where were her parents? Deb? Was Jake at the fraternity house? Who had shot the president? Their handsome, brave President Kennedy. Had a war begun in America?

"—I don't think you should go, though. Not immediately. Of course you want to be with your loved ones, but rushing to the subway might not be the best idea. Not right away. Certainly, if you need to go, do so. Only you know your family circumstances. But if you can, let's take a few minutes together. Let this settle in."

A few students stood, nodded at the class, and then left, books held tight.

"Anyone have a transistor radio?" Professor Gardiner asked after the door closed.

Two students raised their hands.

"Bring them up front. Let's tune them to the same station, shall we?"

One guy, wide and hefty, the other built low to the ground, like a wrestler, carried their small radios to the professor. Phoebe's nerves buzzed as the group set up the radios on the professor's desk. Static-filled voices vied for primacy until they both hit the sound of Roger Mudd reporting from Washington.

With his voice came reality.

They wept as they listened. Professor Gardiner radiated calm. When Mary Alice Haverstraw actually started sobbing, gulping between ragged breaths, he patted her back, leaning down and whispering secret words.

She hated Mary Alice. In Phoebe's family, her nickname would have been Sarah Bernhardt—the name her mother coined for whenever she thought Phoebe became too dramatic. After the hundredth time of being compared with some old actress, Phoebe had learned to hold her tongue. Hey, she'd love to weep like Mary Alice, but being a spectacle was a sin in the Beckett home. Any time that she or Deb whined, their mother reminded them that Daddy listened to people in awful pain all day, and he didn't need more agony when he got home—as though their father treated leprosy, when, in fact, he injected Novocain the minute a patient opened his or her mouth.

After wiping away a few escaped tears, Phoebe caught Mr. Gardiner's eye. Without a hint of her usual reserve, she blurted out her thoughts. "Losing President Kennedy feels like a lifeline slipped away," she said. "Everything seems dark. Frightening. Who's Lyndon Johnson, anyway?"

No one paid the vice president attention—at least no one who grew up in her Brooklyn neighborhood. A Catholic president was as close to a Jewish one as they'd get in their lifetime.

"President Kennedy represented a bridge to a world where you couldn't imagine how your relatives might end up in an oven," Phoebe continued, before realizing she sounded like a Sarah Bernhardt minus tears.

Professor Gardiner didn't seem disgusted by Phoebe's sentiments. He walked over and sat in a blessedly empty seat across from hers, squeezing her shoulder—not as good as getting the slow sympathetic pats Mary Alice got, but welcome. His cool hand comforted Phoebe. His long fingers could have conducted a symphony.

"You're right," he said. "John Fitzgerald Kennedy represents . . . represented a new generation. We will mourn, but the world won't go backward. The changes the president brought will remain."

A calm and measured cadence—with none of the staccato wiseguy sounds so endemic to Brooklyn boys—colored his words. His voice carried the sound of Manhattan private schools; a man who illuminated the workings of the world. "Your observation captures all our feelings, Phoebe. Thank you."

Fear of the future mixed with a shameful shiver of delight at Professor Gardiner's admiration. The possibility that he might think her wise brought a never-before-experienced satisfaction. By the time Professor Gardiner dismissed them, he and the sainted dead president had merged into one beacon of light.

· · ·

Three weeks later, Phoebe handed in her last Introduction to Sociology paper before Christmas break, this one on "Corporate Responses to Poverty."

"Ready for the holidays?" Mr. Gardiner asked when she approached.

"Almost." Phoebe searched for a witty line. Her energy had been spent angling to be last to place her report on his desk. Now, as she faced him, new concerns jumped forward. Her dry mouth might breed anything from bad breath to stuttering.

He meant Christmas; they'd celebrated Hanukkah over a week ago. Even in New York, non-Jews assumed that everyone spent the days before Christmas wrapping presents and drinking eggnog, when, in fact, her family would be eating a luxury spread from the delicatessen for Christmas Eve dinner: a platter of lox interspersed with silky sable and golden white fish. Chocolate-covered grahams—made even more delicious with the addition of a layer of jelly between the sweet cracker and the thick hard shell of chocolate. Blackout cake from Ebinger's, the best bakery in Brooklyn. Chopped liver. Egg salad. Rare roast beef sliced thin. Fresh rye for her grandfather. Honey cake for her grandmother. Bialys for Deb.

Religion didn't rule her family, but her parents respected the altar of heavy Jewish cuisine, making up for their lack of Christmas festivity with food-packed silver trays.

"My grandparents are coming over," Phoebe said.

"Ah, so you do mark the occasion. Thought I put my foot in my mouth for a moment."

"We don't have presents or a tree," she said. "Blintzes and bagels— that's our rejoicing."

"I know bagels, but I'm a little vague on the blintzes."

"You never ate blintzes?" Maybe she lived in too homogenous a neighborhood, but his unfamiliarity surprised her. "Something delicious is in your future."

He leaned back and put his hand behind his head. "Perhaps you'll introduce me to the custom. Expand my sociological knowledge of cuisine." His crisp blue shirtsleeves, rolled up two perfect times, revealed golden, fine hair on his arms.

"How are you still tan?" she asked.

He laughed, and she blushed at her stupid boldness. "I play tennis until I slip in the snow."

She pictured him and his wife batting the ball back and forth, their classic gold wedding bands reflecting the sun—a woman so exquisite that even a drop of cosmetics disturbed her flawlessness. They likely spoke about Proust in bed.

Jake read Mickey Spillane and Ian Fleming.

"I always thought missing out on the brightness of the holidays must be sad."

"We light candles for eight nights," Phoebe said.

They remained silent for a moment. Professor Gardiner doubtless pictured a dingy menorah in her shtetl-like home, compared with an evergreen crusted with ropes of lights and shimmering with ornaments placed before a brownstone's fireplace.

He grabbed her hand. "I apologize for insinuating that Hanukkah is any less important than Christmas." His warm skin sent sparks through Phoebe. She wanted to run her fingers over and around his knuckles, caress the light hair on his wrist.

"Black hair with blue eyes. A stunning combination. You're magnificent," he said. "You must hear those words constantly."

"Not really." Why had she lied? Jake complimented her on everything from the sheen of her hair to the curve of her cheek. She strained for memories of Jake's generosity to offset Professor Gardiner's charged touch. The gold bracelet he'd bought Deb for her birthday. How he challenged her mother or anyone else who dared to be unkind to her. Distributing her questionnaires to his buddies.

She forced herself to see a vision of Mrs. Gardiner. "Your wife is lucky," she said. "Your talent for praise is outstanding."

His smile disappeared. "Presently, she's not appreciating many of my talents." He dropped her hand. "We're apart at the moment."

At the moment. What did he mean? A week of breathing space? A few steps from a divorce attorney? How old was he? Thirty, at the most? She could almost touch her eighteenth birthday.

"You should try blintzes sometime," Phoebe said. "I think you'd like them."

"Yes. I think I would."

. . .

In February 1964 Rob Gardiner tasted his first blintzes at Katz's Deli. Running into anyone Phoebe knew seemed unlikely in this no-frills room, crowded with yellow-topped Formica and chrome tables. People from Brooklyn didn't trek to Manhattan—not even to the Lower East Side, which was just across the Williamsburg Bridge—for food that was already available around the corner.

Between bites, they exchanged life stories as though gifting each other rubies and gold. Now Phoebe knew that Rob had married without thinking—caught up with, as he said, "the will of the crowd." She bent her interpretation of his hazy words to meet her wont: Professor and Mrs. Gardiner, an ill-matched couple, joined in haste, ecstatic at separating.

Over the next few months Rob and Phoebe moved from Rob tasting his first blintz at Katz's to him introducing her to Chinese-Cuban restaurants, along with the hushed Cloisters in Upper Manhattan. The Cloisters' stained glass, sculpture, and medieval manuscripts in the midst of acres of greenery seemed impossibly exotic just an hour's drive from her house. That the subway traveled there—a place so quiet, so not related to Brooklyn—astonished her.

They first kissed in the shadow of a worn tapestry hanging on a wall. Elation at being in Rob's arms swirled with overwhelming guilt toward Jake. Wrong, so wrong, what they were doing, but true love had arrived.

She and Rob should marry in the Cloisters, surrounded by the hush of cool walls covered by ornate fabric. Phoebe conjured up a June ceremony, her body draped in yards of white eyelet with a form-fitted top. Tiny pearl earrings would be her only adornment until Rob placed a burnished gold wedding band on her finger.

Now, two months later, with breaths of warming April air drifting through the open window, she sat on the edge of Rob's desk in his small office. Dusk obscured the campus; they'd only allowed themselves the luxury of meeting at school in darkness.

"Can you sneak out for dinner?" Rob ran a finger down the nylons covering her leg—the Hollywood gesture turning her inside out. "What say you?"

"My parents will go crazy if I don't get home soon." She tamped down thoughts of Jake, coming at eight to take her to see the new Stanley Kubrick film, *Dr. Strangelove or: How I Learned to Stop Worrying and Love the Bomb*. Not her choice, but when she suggested seeing a *Black Orpheus* rerun down in the West Village, Jake said, "Why stop there? Let's go see Shakespeare, m' lady," as though seeing a Brazilian foreign film was a joke.

Each weekend, Phoebe meant to break up with Jake, but she couldn't find the courage to destroy him. And, she knew she'd miss him. Spending time with Rob brought shivers of excitement and fireworks under her breastbone. If sensations were made visible, sparkles would emanate from her head. From her skin to her soul, her sensitivity grew until being touched had become exquisitely painful.

Weekends with Jake provided a welcome calm, where she could sit back and let the world wash over her.

"I can't say good night yet," Rob said.

She swung out her leg from the edge of the desk where she sat. Electricity ignited, but they couldn't touch, since Mary Alice or any hungry coed might appear in an evening burst of need. "Me either."

Rob spun the air between them with his finger. "Do you feel the energy?"

She nodded, unable to speak.

"Ripening air." He gazed up as though reading the wall. " 'This bud of love, by summer's ripening breath, May prove a beauteous flower when next we meet.' "

"Shakespeare." Phoebe imbued her guess with authority. "*Romeo and Juliet?*"

"Brooklyn turns out quite learned girls."

"You'd be surprised what Erasmus can teach."

"The priest?"

"The school." She didn't admit her ignorance of Erasmus High being named for a priest. Keeping up with Rob took work.

He traced her hand resting on his desk, running his index finger over each of her nails. "Winsome," he said of her pale polish. "Opalescent."

Phoebe closed her eyes against the blood rushing up her legs. He worked his way to her forearm with the softest of touches.

"I want to be alone with you." He held out his hand and drew Phoebe from her chair. Before opening the office door, he peeked out and checked in both directions. After a moment, he nodded. She tipped her head forward as though the CIA spied on them.

He left the room first. A few moments later, she followed, ten paces behind. Paintings of horses lined the hall. Rob slipped into a door at the end of the corridor and began climbing the staircase, Phoebe following.

When they reached the uppermost floor Rob's patrician fingers touched her shoulder and turned her left. He reached around to open a door, slipped past, pulled her inside and latched the lock behind them. In the dimness, she made out a broad conference table, oak chairs with wide arms, and a worn brown couch.

"Where are we?"

"Wait," he said. He led her through another door to a wrought iron staircase that coiled up to another floor. She climbed the steps behind him. Cold curlicues along the railing bit into her palms. At the top, he pushed hard against a heavy door that opened to a steeple. Wooden beams crossed the ceiling, circling a huge brass bell. The walls surrounding them were chest high. The campus sprawled before them.

"I give you the tower." He swept out his arms as though offering her a palace.

"We're allowed up here?" She tiptoed to the edge and surveyed the paths filled with people.

He came from behind and enclosed her, covering her hands with his. "We're invisible."

"What if somebody comes up?" Flashes of want overwhelmed her.

"I locked the door below."

"What if someone wants to come in?"

Rob ignored the question and pressed his lips to the back of her neck. She arched back, catching the scent of Muguet des Bois perfume rising from her heated throat. He touched her breasts, first with tenderness and then with ownership.

"So small to be enclosed in an iron circle."

"Cotton."

"Cotton like iron."

"Small?"

"Small as in wonderful. Small as in *bijou*, delicious and perfect." He spun her and teased open a button on her blouse. She began to stay his hands and then stopped. Rob was no high school boy, no college kid, not a member of the Church Avenue softball team. First, second, third base—you didn't play those games with professors.

"I adore you." He held his hand inside her bra, the not-so-iron barrier, and ran his hand over a now-bare breast. "You are the satin of youth, and I must possess you. We are in the very wrath of love."

CHAPTER 4

PHOEBE

May 1964

"Again?"

Her mother's question followed her from the kitchen as Phoebe raced into the downstairs bathroom. She fell before the toilet, raised the seat, and vomited. Tears leaked as she pressed the heels of her hands against her forehead. She'd thrown up every morning for the past week. Waiting for her period had become her constant occupation.

She washed her face with cold water, careful not to splash her blouse, and dabbed her skin dry before turning to go back to the breakfast table. Her mother stood outside, arms crossed, blocking Phoebe's path as she tried to leave the bathroom.

"Again?" her mother repeated. "Still you're going to tell me you caught a bug? Whose bug is it?"

"I just don't feel well, Mom."

"Do I look stupid? You don't feel well at exactly eight o'clock every morning? You're lucky your father leaves early for work."

Lucky why? Her mother conjured her father for anything related to the body or emotional state of her daughters, using him as a cudgel to crack them open.

"You'd better tell me how much weight you gained at camp, Deb," she'd say, "or I'll ask your father." As though her father's den-

32

tist eyes could weigh Deb with one glance. And yet her threat often worked. Neither sister wanted Daddy drawn into their battles with Mom.

"The cafeteria food is awful. Maybe I have food poisoning."

"And last month the food tasted perfect, right? Now, *voila*, you're a delicate flower?"

Phoebe erased all expression until her face became a blank slate. "It's the cafeteria."

As she walked away, her mother threw out more words. "You better pray that's the case. And if it's not, you make sure to talk to me first."

Phoebe kept walking.

Her mother caught up with her and grabbed her shoulder with a mobster's grip, forcing Phoebe to turn and face her. "I mean it. You're barely eighteen years old. The smoke from your birthday candles still hangs in the kitchen. You need me, daughter of mine."

. . .

Phoebe slid her tiny gold locket back and forth on its thin chain as she waited at Katz's Deli for Rob. She'd lied to her parents, to Jake, and even to Deb, about the heart, telling them the necklace had come from Helen (and swearing her best friend to secrecy).

"You can't put my picture in there," Rob said when he gave her the present. "At least not yet. But simply wearing it will bring me close."

He planted kisses on her bare shoulders as he placed the almost weightless chain around her neck.

Everything would work out.

I love you. I love you. Rob had vowed his devotion countless times.

Her parents would adjust. Being Jewish meant little to them. Her cousin in Great Neck had married an Italian girl, and they attended the baby's baptism bearing pink-wrapped presents six months after they'd gone to the church wedding.

Jake would explode.

Phoebe worried the edge of her wool sweater, soothing herself by pressing her fingers hard against one another.

She'd break his heart, but she had no other choice. Tears leaked at the idea of never seeing Jake again, his pain, imagining him with another girl, but she couldn't have two men.

Confirming the pregnancy was step one, but that meant solving two mysteries: how many weeks before a test would work, and who would give her an exam without her parents finding out.

She prayed that Rob would offer answers.

Her stomach churned. She searched for the ladies' room, just in case, hoping the queasiness signaled only nerves.

Rob walked in wearing a sports coat and a wide smile. Blood rushed from her head so fast that she knew her skin matched the white of the chipped mug in front of her.

After a not-so-furtive glance around, he pecked her on the forehead. His chaste lips brought heat back to her heart, even if the rest of her was still made of ice.

"Tea?" He cocked his head to the side as he examined her cup. "I thought you were a coffee person."

"My stomach's been off," she said. "My mother served tea with tons of milk and sugar when we were sick."

"No milk there." He pointed to the dark liquid, the tea bag sunk to the bottom of the cup.

"I grew up." Dairy nauseated her these days.

"So you did." Rob's smile became tender. "So you did."

He picked up the smeared menu, studying the plastic-wrapped paper, looking proud of his newfound knowledge of Jewish delicacies. "Can one eat blintzes for breakfast?"

"Any time of day is fine," she said. "They're like pancakes: breakfast, lunch, or dinner."

"I ate a bowl of Wheaties at six." He weighted his gaze with significance. "Writing."

Together they worshipped at the altar of Rob's novel. The first few pages immediately revealed his worship of J. D. Salinger, but in a good way, she told him—and she believed what she said. He wrote as Salinger would have written if Salinger had composed with more heart.

Salinger had children, right?

"How about we share a plate?" he asked.

"A plate of what?"

"Blintzes, of course. Where are you this morning?" Only after studying her face did he reach for her hand. "Whoa! You're cold."

"I'm freezing." With those words she began chattering so loud she heard her teeth clicking.

"Phoebe, are you sick?" Rob rushed around the table and sat in the empty chair beside her.

She squeezed her eyes tight against tears. "I—I can't eat any blintzes."

"Forget the blintzes!" He moved the glass sugar pourer to bring her hands closer. He covered them with his own, sharing his heat.

"My period is late," she whispered. "Two weeks."

Rob dropped her hands. She twisted her tiny locket, twirling until the chain would twist no more, then unfurling the necklace and starting over. Perhaps she'd put a picture of Rob on one side and the baby on the other.

"You can't be pregnant. I used a condom every time." He offered this as though arguing an irrefutable point of logic.

"They're not infallible."

The ancient waiter arrived carrying his small green pad and nub of a pencil. "Order?"

"Coffee. Just coffee," Rob said.

The old man shook his head and left.

Her hands trembled as she reached for him. "We need the name of a doctor where I can go."

He drew back, leaving her hands in the tundra of the empty table, and crossed his arms over his chest. "I hear Mexico is the place."

"Mexico?" She struggled to make sense of his words.

"You can get what you need there. Easy."

"Why would I go to Mexico for a pregnancy test?"

"Don't act ignorant." The waiter placed a mug before him, halting Rob's words for a blessed moment. She built a tower of wrapped sugar cubes until he covered her hand. "Stop."

"Mexico?" she asked again.

"You're serious, aren't you?" He lightened his coffee, stirring the liquid until small riptides appeared. "Girls take care of these problems with doctors in Mexico."

She cocked her head in confusion until awareness came, and she realized what he meant. A ragged cry emerged unbidden.

"What the hell were you asking for when you said you needed help?"

"What I said," she whispered. "Where to go for a pregnancy test."

"Aha. So you're not sure that you're . . ." He rested his elbows on the table and laced his fingers. "Can't your girlfriends tell you?"

"It's hardly something I want to ask about."

He nodded. "Of course. You don't need to spread rumors and such."

"Rumors?"

"You can hop down and get put right. Nothing's public this way." He gazed off to the side as though receiving information. "No. Not Mexico. Wrong place. Sorry. Puerto Rico is what I meant."

"Maybe I'm not pregnant. I'm not very late." Protective instincts kept her from telling him about her morning bathroom sessions. Her sore breasts were no business of his.

"The sooner, the better." Rob clipped off the words as though talking to a student seeking advice on whether to major in sociology or political science.

Phoebe shivered. "We need to figure this out. First we'll get the facts and then think about what's ahead."

"Can I ask what you mean by 'what's ahead'?"

Did Rob work at speaking as though he were the fucking Prince of Wales? Impatience replaced fear. "Can we end the polite charade, please? I think I'm pregnant, and if I am, well, we'll be parents."

Rob shook his head. "First, I'm not going to be anyone's parent. Second, are you crazy? You're my student. Do you want me to lose my job? Are you trying to ruin my life?"

"Rob—"

He held up a hand. "I'll help you find out where you can go in Puerto Rico." His eyes darted around the restaurant. "If need be, I'll ask my father for money."

. . .

Rob became a stranger. She didn't ask for anything again. He didn't offer. In class he treated her as though she were invisible.

After two weeks spent praying he'd become the man with whom she had fallen in love, class again passed in a haze of her stares and Rob's snubs. Each time she raised her hand, he disregarded her waving arm so pointedly that Phoebe wondered if everyone noticed his deliberate refusal. Rob picked Mary Alice to speak about typhoid management in the late 1800s, even though containing infection had been Phoebe's topic in the most recent paper assigned.

Five minutes before the end of class—Rob glanced up at the clock on the wall and nodded at the 3:55 time—he put down the chalk and brushed off his hands.

"Okay," he said. "I'm handing out your papers. They represent almost half of your semester final mark. Let's hope you gave your best efforts." Campus wisdom thrummed with the rarity of an A from Mr. Gardiner, much less an A+.

He took a stack of papers from his briefcase and walked into the first aisle. The perfectly aligned pile he carried reminded her of his damned organization skills. Each of their rendezvous had been timed to the minute, with precise snacks laid out in the borrowed apartment. Two glasses for the half split of wine and a plate with crackers, cheese, and grapes always appeared, as though an assignation maître d' had arranged their trysts.

Only the first time did she ask why they were meeting at his mythical friend's house and not at his apartment—though the question tortured her every time she arrived at the anonymous Jane Street apartment in Greenwich Village.

"Since your wife moved out, why don't we go there?" she'd asked.

A pained expression covered his face. Rob shook his head as though ridding himself of memories. "Ah, bringing you to where I lived with . . . it would seem wrong. Iniquitous." He breathed out the sigh of a million beleaguered men. "But if going there is so important . . ." His sentence trailed off in an implication of the pain and humiliation such a request would engender. Oh, but he would bring her to his home if forced.

Phoebe now faced the realization that he'd likely never left his wife. She was third in line to receive her paper.

Abrams.

Abrams earned a soft "Excellent."

Ahern.

Rob returned Ahern's paper with a raised eyebrow and a clipped question as to Ahern's interest in pursuing legibility lessons or, barring that, would he consider the purchase of a typewriter?

Beckett.

He placed Phoebe's paper on the desk. "Good work, Miss Beckett." A stoplight red A+ screamed from the title page. Underneath the grade he wrote a comment in his sophisticated half-cursive, half-printed handwriting: "Excellent analysis. You understand all the inherent problems. You'll go far."

Rob had nailed one thing in his comments. Phoebe understood. She finally understood.

. . .

Phoebe paced the nap off the rug waiting to be with Jake the following weekend. While he hadn't been absent from her life, she'd avoided being close, claiming anything from exams to clusters of migraines to avoid being alone. They'd been as intimate as always, which meant staying above her beltline and his, but as infrequently as she could manage.

Now, as her waistline expanded, her mother scrutinized her morning till night. Now, when being thin meant so much, food beckoned like water in the desert. All week she'd forced herself to be calm until Sunday, when she found her moment.

As everyone readied to leave for a bris out in Hempstead, Long Island, hosted by her aunt Ruth, Phoebe feigned a migraine—one requiring cold cloths and hot tea. When Jake showed up at the house in his suit and tie, her impatient-to-leave mother sent him up to her bedroom.

There she lay, freshly showered, dusted in Cashmere Bouquet talcum powder, wearing a black silk slip as though about to be covered by her dress, with the sheet arranged around her almost bare shoulders.

He knocked on the open bedroom door. "Your mom sent me up to get you."

Phoebe imagined them all waiting at the foot of the stairs, her mother's arms crossed impatiently over her emerald-green dress, the one she rotated with her cornflower-blue shift for afternoon occasions.

"My head is pounding," she said. "Driving would kill me, but I don't want to keep you from going."

"And miss witnessing someone snip your cousin's son's schlong? I can manage. I'll study and be your nurse, okay, princess?"

She lay on her side in a boudoir pose, the thin covers draped just so, crossing her arms to make cleavage with her hormone-inflated breasts.

Jake brushed his fingers over her arm, lightly, but with intent. "I'll get my books."

"Tell my parents you're staying with me."

Phoebe shut her eyes when he left, trying not to cry. Sounds floated up. The front door closed. Her father started up the car. The front door opened. Footsteps came closer.

Tears flooded her cheeks.

"Pheebs? Honey? What's wrong?" He stood in the doorway. "Should I stop your parents? Do you need your mother?"

"No. No. Just you." She wiped her tears. "I only need you, Jake."

He lay beside her, stroked the swell of her hip, the curves of her body, first slowly and then with rushing intent.

As though enchanted, her body responded. She wondered if it was wonderful or awful how she had turned from Rob with such speed.

Who cared? Rescue beckoned.

She matched Jake, bone for bone, skin to skin. Made for each other. Whereas with Rob she had watched her every move, needing to prove her worth, with Jake she became unconstrained until she understood Helen's wide-eyed chatter about orgasms. Phoebe thought her best friend had been exaggerating when she described in embarrassing detail the wonder of sex.

Rob's touch brought pleasure, but perhaps she'd been more excited by the idea of someone like Rob than by the actual Rob.

With Rob, she sighed.

Jake made her scream.

Afterward, he didn't question the lack of blood. Jake understood tampons and afternoons at Catskill hotels spent horseback riding. He cradled her as though holding a crystal doll, stroking her back with a steady, soothing hand.

"How's your headache, Pheebs?"

"Better."

"Are you okay otherwise?" Jake tucked his head a bit, gesturing "down there."

She cupped his rough chin. "I'm quite fine."

"So what's with all the jokes about 'Not tonight, I have a headache'? Seems like we found a miracle cure."

"You're my miracle." Truth, she now knew.

"I love you, Phoebe." Jake appeared astounded at his luck; the warmth she showed after a season of remoteness. "I'll always take care of you."

"You're too good to me." She bit her knuckle, willing to rip her flesh to keep from crying.

"You make me whole. I need you by my side. You balance me. Forever, right?"

"Forever," she repeated.

"Consider this my unofficial proposal, Pheebs. You won't believe what will follow. I swear I'll make this place seem like a pauper's house."

After the awful things she'd done, Jake would save her. Phoebe swore to God she'd never hurt him again for as long as she lived.

CHAPTER 5

PHOEBE

Jake and Phoebe spent every night together, most often driving to Jones Beach on Long Island, the most secluded place in their universe. Phoebe didn't believe that Jake had come to her a virgin, but his intoxication with her was obvious. In an unfortunate moment of introspection, she connected the dots between Jake, her, and Rob. The truth resembled an analogy from a comparative literature paper.

Phoebe was to Jake as Rob was to Phoebe.

With Phoebe, Jake jumped a class.

She knew that the more frequently they made love, the more believable her pregnancy would be, but exhaustion saturated her every cell. Tonight she'd rather read in bed than see Jake. Perhaps this was a by-product of her condition, but who in the world could she ask?

Her mother's determined footsteps, the creak of a knob turning, and muffled words, signified Jake's arrival. A vague discomfort at the base of her spine—she'd felt it twanging the moment she woke—became progressively worse when she walked.

"He's here!" her mother shouted up the stairs, as though Jake didn't deserve being called by name.

"I'll be right there."

The other night, she'd asked her mother directly, "Why don't you like him? He's graduating college. He works hard, and he's good to me. What else would I want?"

Her mother ignored the question, staring a hole through Phoebe's midsection and then frowning. "Your father says I should leave it alone." Phoebe had walked away without a word.

Jake would soon be her unwitting savior. Her mother should embrace him as the Messiah. Every time Phoebe turned around, she caught her mother studying her middle as if expecting a tiny grand-child to leap out and shame her.

Scribble-filled papers—Phoebe's invented formulas as she attempted to figure out how soon before she should spill her secret—covered her desk. She tossed them in the trash, all the while praying that Jake possessed no aptitude for menstrual math.

After seeing her wan face in the mirror, Phoebe added another layer of bright red lipstick. As her middle thickened, she wore ever-livelier shades, despite the pale, almost white, lip colors that had sprouted as though a zombie cult had invaded fashion. Overnight, anyone with style sense had stopped wearing red lipstick, but Phoebe needed to wear something fiery enough to stomp out all else about her.

She threw a windbreaker over her untucked blouse and stood soldier straight, sucking in her gut, trying to hide the bump as she squinted at the full-length mirror hanging on the back of her door. Disgusted by her image, Phoebe ripped off the thin jacket and pitched it on the bed. Who wore a coat in 79-degree weather?

"Phoebe!" her mother yelled. "Are you coming down? Did you hear me call?"

She opened the door. "One minute!" she screamed and then clicked the lock.

Ridiculous clothes crowded her closet, one more form fitting than the next, as though she were Brigitte Bardot and not some foolish knocked-up Brooklyn girl. She flipped the hangers until she reached a navy blouse dark enough to minimize her size.

Phoebe drew on another layer of lipstick and walked downstairs. Her mother glued her eyes to her stomach. *Why not put on a searchlight and make sure everyone stares, Mom?*

Jake hadn't mentioned marriage since the first time they had made love, and Phoebe would rip her teeth out before she let herself be the one who broached the topic. The words needed to come from his lips; be his idea. She'd be indebted to him forever, but if he sensed even a hint of her desperation, the world would be permanently uneven between them.

Leading with her gleaming mouth, beaming wide enough to show all her father's hard work in ensuring her perfect smile, she went to Jake.

. . .

Seeking lovemaking positions in Jake's Plymouth Fury meant choosing between working around the stick shift or using the backseat, which translated to a toss-up between awkward discomfort and twisting like a pretzel.

Jake came in a shudder. Phoebe, seized by a cramp, clutched his shoulder, almost tearing his flesh with her nails. Over his head, she saw the starry Long Island sky, the black asphalt of the parking lot. Gritty sand and cold ocean water lay in front of them.

Another wave of pain hit, and she dug harder into Jake's back.

"Whoa! Good that I made you happy, but, um, you're ripping my skin off." He placed a hand on top of her curled fingers, gently trying to unfurl each one. "Pheebs?" She remained rigid. "You okay?"

"Something's wrong." Too much rushed out from where she usually dabbed herself clean with a few tissues.

"What? What is it?" He began pulling away, but she tugged him back, frantic not to acknowledge the pain and mess. Spasms of cramps overcame her, and she held him harder.

Jake lifted himself above her, looking at where they were joined. "Let's see," he insisted.

She let go, put her arms behind her on the seat cushion, and curled forward, peering at the wetness on her stomach. Even in the darkness it appeared to be blood.

"Oh, Jesus." Jake grabbed a towel he kept for cleanup.

"Something's wrong," she whimpered.

"We're going to the hospital."

"No! Take me home. It's only my period." Hope and alarm collided. He stopped for a moment. "How—"

"I don't know," she lied. "My mother will understand."

Jake hesitated, but he'd landed in a problem belonging to the tribe of women. Unless she exsanguinated in front of him, he'd never bully her about this. Going home, she'd get away with calling this a heavy period, even if her mother knew the truth. Marriage could again become her choice.

Jake broke every driving law in New York State racing back to Brooklyn. Phoebe remained curled in her seat, praying that if she stayed immobile her body might remain in quiescent limbo. The ride passed in a moment yet took a hundred years.

Jake supported her as they staggered up the walkway. He leaned on the bell, not letting up until her father answered and took Phoebe into his arms.

"Lola!" her father screamed up the stairs.

Her mother galloped down, her hand on her chest, prepared for the worst. "Oh my God! What happened?" Her eyes met Phoebe's. Understanding passed between them as her mother glanced at the bloody towel clutched between her legs. "Come. Bring her to the den. I'll put blankets down."

"Are you crazy?" Phoebe's father asked. "She needs to go to the hospital. Now."

"We can wait one minute, Red." Her mother peered into her father's eyes. "Let's keep this here if we can. Do you understand?"

Her mother obviously hoped for the same thing as Phoebe: a flow of heavy menstrual fluid, a hot water bottle for cramps, an aspirin for pain, bed rest, and then pushing the incident behind them.

"We're taking her to the emergency room." Her father's tone ended the conversation.

Jake propped her up on one side, her father held the other. Step-by-step, they led her out. Her mother ran ahead, clutching blankets and towels gathered in some instant house sweep, lining the backseat with the piles of fabric as Phoebe approached.

"Stop worrying about the seats!" her father yelled. "We're getting in."

Her mother dropped everything wherever it landed and backed away, clutching her throat as he lowered Phoebe into the car.

Fear swirled as Phoebe imagined what lay ahead. Coldness overtook her. Jake slid in next to her. His shirt absorbed her dripping tears.

"We don't have to go, Daddy." Her words shook with her chills and chattering. "Please. Mommy can take care of me."

Her mother swiveled from her husband to Phoebe. "Daddy's right. I'm sorry, honey."

Her father drove down Church Avenue until taking a sharp left turn when they reached Ocean Parkway.

"Where are you going?" her mother asked.

Blood leaked faster. How much before she died? Pain shot through her back.

"Coney Island Hospital," said her father.

"Why not Margolis?" her mother asked, naming their family doctor. "You should have called him."

"He's not in his office at this hour and we certainly can't wait until tomorrow when he's there."

"It's a heavy period," her mother insisted. "She needs extra pads, not a hospital."

"Enough, Lola. Nobody in this car is stupid." Her father stopped for a red light, drumming his fingers on the steering wheel as traffic sped across the road. He glanced in the rearview mirror. "Hang on, sweetheart."

Jake drew her closer. "I'm here for you. Always."

Her mother muttered in the front seat. Phoebe caught one word: pig.

Moments after pulling up to the hospital emergency entrance, her father ran in and came out with two attendants wheeling a gurney. She clenched against screaming as they helped her on the stretcher, waves of cramps engulfing her. Jake's hand scorched her icy one, but Phoebe kept squeezing.

They wheeled her into the bright, cold emergency room. She squeezed her eyes against searing lights as they rushed her to a curtained area. One nurse blocked Jake and her parents from entering the compartment. Two others peeled away the towels, skirt, and underwear in a mess of coagulated and fresh blood. Rusty stains covered her thighs. Wavy streaks of red lined her calves.

A doctor walked in and without preamble peppered her with questions. "What do we have here? When did this start? How far along are you?" His high forehead shone like the black stethoscope hanging around his neck.

"I—I don't know. I never took a test."

"Good God. You girls. How long since your last period?"

His face blurred. The nurse packed something between her legs, spread by the force of stirrups. An aluminum lamp hung down low to put a spotlight on her splayed body.

"I'm not sure," she lied.

"Take an educated guess."

The nurse repeated Phoebe's whispered answer: "Two months." Phoebe prayed her family and Jake had been hustled out of earshot.

"Is your husband here?" The doctor picked up her left hand, on which she wore her modest sweet sixteen ring: an amethyst stone set in silver.

"I'm not married."

"Her family is in the waiting room, Doctor." The nurse squeezed Phoebe's ankle as she spoke.

The doctor stationed himself between her legs and then pulled away the packing, poking with a rubber-gloved finger as though testing for doneness. He examined the mess staining the cotton. Phoebe's cramps slowed.

"Looks like early fetal material. Did you expel anything into the toilet or anywhere else?" he asked.

She shook her head, afraid that speaking would bring tears. And she'd rip out her eyes before she cried in front of this awful man.

He peered lower, bending before Phoebe, who now realized that humiliation had no endpoint. "Bleeding appears to be lessening. Nothing we can do now. You lost the baby, of course. Must be a relief to you. All's well that ends well, eh? The nurse will clean you up and let you know what warning symptoms to watch out for."

"I'm going home?" As much as Phoebe had resisted coming to the hospital, now she didn't want to leave. She wanted cleansing and sleeping without seeing her father's disappointed face, her mother's angry one, and the confusion and guilt covering Jake's. Unless she got the guts to tell the truth, he'd believe in his ultimate sin forever.

CHAPTER 6

PHOEBE

Rising and falling voices woke Phoebe. Her mother's strident tones pounded like jackhammers. The soothing words her father spoke indicated his prevailing patience.

A veil of grogginess hung heavy. After pressing a hand to her pounding head, Phoebe forced herself to turn toward the clock. Seven in the morning. Shards of nightmares clung. Everything felt sticky and sore. She put her hand down exactly where she didn't want to touch. Gritty dried blood covered her inner thighs, but at least the thick pad from the hospital had held up. A wide piece of cotton batting backed by plastic sheeting lay beneath her. The nurse had slipped her the folded packet as though giving her a consolation prize. Congratulations! You lost your virginity, the man you loved, and every shred of dignity, but you get to go home with this blue bed pad.

"What kind of girl did we raise?" she heard her mother yell. "Rushing out to God knows where night after night and spreading her legs for that—for that nothing schmuck."

"Quiet, Lola. You'll wake her."

"Good." Her mother's voice rose. "Our daughter should be awake and lying in the bed she made. Everything's been handed to her on a silver platter. I'd kiss my parents' feet if I'd been given half of what we gave her. College. Beautiful clothes. Whatever she wanted, we gave her, and she lets a nothing knock her up."

Phoebe needed to pee but didn't want her parents to hear her get up. The patches of dried blood itched. Grime covered her. She longed for a shower, but more, she wanted to hear her parents' conversation.

"What bothers you so much about him?" her father asked.

"The apple never falls far from the tree. Look at his mother and father. Thieves. Dreck."

"Them, not Jake. He's a hard worker. His brother, too. Jake wants to be a lawyer."

"Lawyers. Pure like the driven snow, right?" Her mother laughed. "Probably getting his degree in case his parents get arrested again."

"Come on, they weren't arrested."

"The FBI came to their house!"

"One of my patients said they had a business problem."

"A business problem? How very modern." Her mother huffed. "His father put the so-called business in her name. What a coward. Is this who you want for your daughter?"

. . .

Before lunch, Jake arrived carrying white tulips. Phoebe, showered and numbed by a pain pill, lifted her hand in a weak wave.

"How are you?" Jake wrapped his fingers around her forearm. "My poor baby. So pale."

Phoebe stared at the ceiling. "I'm okay. They told me to stay in bed for a few days." Never leaving the achingly clean sheets on which she lay seemed like the perfect remedy.

"I'm sorry. For this." Jake looked as though someone had punched the young right out of her. "For getting you into this mess."

Waves of her sins—of omission, of commission—attacked with a thick physical presence in her throat and weighed down her muscles. "You never pressured me."

"You kept saying no, and I kept asking. Now see what happened." He waved a hand around the area of her hips. "Your mother thinks I'm a mass murderer. Your father probably considers me a putz. I blew it."

Phoebe brushed away his words. "They're upset with me. My mother doesn't want me giving up my chances. Throwing away my life." The steady ache in her pelvis and a vague and unexpected thud of loss for her baby left no room for careful talk.

"Throwing your life away how?"

"On you." Phoebe brought her knees to her chest, trying to soothe the pain persisting through the large white pill.

Jake's guilty expression tortured her. She looked away and examined the room of the child she'd been, all pink and white, as though she were born to be a confection. A Hostess Sno Ball of a girl. Peel away the top layer, and underneath she remained spongy and sweet.

"Being with me is throwing away your life?"

"It's your family. My mother thinks they did something illegal. Did they? I don't care if it's yes or no. Honest. I only want to figure out what she's hammering my father about."

"Your father hates me, too?"

"My father's on your side."

Jake's shoulders sagged. "At least there's that."

Phoebe thought of his family—his parents' apartment. The Pierces' ancient cabbage-rose pocked rug murmured failure and depression; her own family's spotless white carpet saluted her father's earnings.

Their cramped rooms screamed Nan Pierce's inability to turn away anything, no matter how cheap or ill-made. Her outdated wardrobe matched her hairstyle and beaten, bitter expression. Every one of Ken Pierce's features pointed to the ground. Phoebe didn't know exactly what he did for a living; they all referred to his job as "something with the *Daily News*" and then let it go.

"What happened with your parents?" Phoebe asked. "What should I tell my father if he asks?"

"After their store failed—paint—they decided to do investments."

"Do investments how?" The word *investments* conjured up nothing. Other than putting money in her savings account—the same one her parents had opened for her when she turned sixteen—she never grasped the fine points of anything about business. Her mother always riffled the *Times* until she came to the financial section, which was filled with print so fine she used a special pair of glasses to read the words. Every morning, Phoebe's father said the same thing: "You can't study stocks day to day, Lola. It's a cumulative thing."

"How will I know the trend if I don't watch?" A true product of the Depression, her mother guarded each dime and watered coins into dollars. Rules drove her parents. "Save regular, no matter what you earn!" "Pennies can turn to fortunes!" "Do right, and right will come back to you!"

"They opened a small brokerage, but they didn't register with every one of the million places asking them to cross every *t*. No big deal." Jake shrugged.

"Did they go to jail?" The thought of his parents in prison terrified her.

"Christ. Of course not. They got fined. They lost the business. Their lives fell to shit. Guess what the upshot will be?" Determination covered his strong face: that combination of rough and handsome, so different from Rob's patrician features.

Jake's dark sexiness had become once again what she wanted in the man she loved. Anything reminiscent of Rob repelled her.

She took his hand and squeezed. "What?"

"I'm gonna prove them wrong," Jake said. "Your dad won't need to defend me like some idiot son. I won't need anyone's protection. You'll see. Everyone will see."

He cupped her chin, forcing her to stare straight into his eyes. "I love you." He reached into his pocket and took out a blue leather box, snapped it open, and took out a ring. He grabbed her left hand, went down on one knee, and held out the chip of a diamond as though holding a prize before a queen. "Marry me."

CHAPTER 7

PHOEBE

September 1968

Phoebe beat two eggs with fear and venom, certain that each circle of her fork brought her closer to becoming her mother. Smack in the center of the supposed youth revolution, she felt more middle aged than buoyant.

Marriage at nineteen meant this: four years later, only twenty-three, she'd been tossed into the world of matrons. Their apartment was spitting distance from her parent's home. *Glamour* and *Mademoiselle,* formerly studied for tips and hints, now read like anthropology texts, leading her to wonder if she'd been relegated to *Ladies' Home Journal.* At the beauty parlor, she pored over *Vogue,* hungering for a microshort Twiggy haircut. Two minutes later, inspired by another cover girl, Jean Shrimpton, she vowed to grow her hair long, letting it flow over her shoulders and leave behind the common pageboy swinging around her chin. Geometric, Mary Quant–like, and miniskirted, that's what Phoebe yearned to be, but she feared she'd married herself to the tedium of twin sweater sets from Macy's, doomed to be part of a dying history just when she wanted inclusion in the great wave of change all around. The wave of influential British designers could open a path away from the tedium of Brooklyn fashion.

Her job, which she loved, Jake considered a holding pattern before motherhood, considering her work inferior both for the location and her low salary. Tutoring immigrants in the ways of New York and working with their kids held less weight to her husband than helping out at his office—which she did on Saturdays. His business bored the hell out of her, though his energy for finance infected her at least enough to become mildly interested by association.

Phoebe slipped a plate of scrambled eggs and bacon in front of Jake. Even as she served him, he kept his eyes on the *Wall Street Journal*. She cleared her throat, crossed her arms, and finally, when the first two actions failed, smacked him in the back of the head. "I'm not offering maid service, buddy."

He ran a hand over her behind. "A little French uniform wouldn't hurt."

She rolled her eyes. "Would a short skirt elicit a please and thank-you?"

"Probably not. But my eggs sure would get cold." He pulled her to him and planted a noisy kiss to the side of her lips.

Phoebe doubted it, seeing his eyes latch back on the paper. She grabbed the *New York Post* and took a minute bite of melba toast. Don't lose your Audrey Hepburn, Jake reminded her until she yearned to chop his words with onions and force-feed him with the mix. "Delicate and dark—that's my style," he'd say.

Sometimes when he left for work early, she ate a bagel. Afterward, she did jumping jacks and a hundred sit-ups. Not this morning, though. No bagel. No sit-ups. Seconds after choking down a piece of the crumbly cracker, she raced to the bathroom, turned the sink taps on full force, the running water a sound barrier, and then threw up. Not that Jake would notice—not unless she vomited in front of him.

Marriage rendered her a shade more invisible each day—until Jake wanted sex, and suddenly she became 3-D. Those nights, instead of turning on his bedside lamp and studying tiny numbers, he'd run a hand down her arm and enumerate one of her charms:

"Damn, your skin is satin and cream. I want you so much."

"You're the entire package, baby, and just as gorgeous as the first day I met you."

They still clicked like magnetized dolls. Phoebe dissolved during lovemaking, but the rest of the time, she became hypervigilant, agree-able in everything from the scent she wore to keeping the house free of dust and clutter. Her original guilt played a part, almost crushing her. Sometimes she considered revealing the truth of her lost baby, hoping the inevitable battle would bring them closer. More likely, the truth would destroy her place in their relationship, and their balance of marital power would teeter until she'd hit a permanent bottom.

Sometimes the reality that she had married too young slipped past her denial. Marriage meant feeling shackled at a time when the world seemed to be cracking wide open for women.

In either circumstance, she forced herself to remember Rob's cold face at the news of her pregnancy. With that memory, she embraced Jake with gratitude. When swimming in the brew of love, resentment, and indebtedness overwhelmed Phoebe, she'd note the ways their marriage had succeeded. Despite her mother's pleas for an immediate grandchild, Jake had pushed her to graduate from college. After taking the stockbroker's exam, he had started his own company, Jake Pierce Equity. Phoebe gained bragging rights as Jake hustled success at JPE from almost nothing. Her uncle Gus gave him cheap rent in his ac-counting office in the Bronx, but Jake had built everything else alone. Each time Phoebe saw Uncle Gus he'd grab her upper arm, pull her close and whisper, as though it were a secret, "He's got some head on him, that man of yours. Smart as a whole college."

Business rolled in so fast, he'd drown if she didn't help him on Sat-urday, paying his bills and typing up lists of the stock trades he'd made that week. Yes. Exactly as he'd predicted, Jake began to tear through the world. He strutted. She smiled. When he became too in love with himself or worked crazy, long days, her sister's advice helped Phoebe clamp down on the scathing words dying to escape.

"Remember?" Deb would ask. "Don't you remember how Mommy nagged Daddy—how we hated it? Treat Jake like the man he is."

. . .

The best hours of Phoebe's week began when she arrived at the Mira Stein Settlement House on Rivington Street, on the Lower East Side.

If it wouldn't drive Jake nuts, she'd add Saturdays to her Mira House schedule. Her title was program associate, which meant she filled in wherever needed, getting involved with every age group. That Monday, when the exercise teacher didn't show, Phoebe ran the senior workout class.

"What should I do?" she asked her boss, the assistant director. Energy shimmered off Trixie, who never searched long for an answer.

"Just make them move. Gently. Easily. You'll think of something."

Phoebe set up a circle of battered metal folding chairs. Elderly men and women, all over eighty, held on to the raised backs, kicking up their heels, marching in place, and bending side to side. All while "The Beat Goes On" played, the walking bass-line perfect for the exercise. Introducing them to Sonny and Cher gave her a kick.

In the afternoon, she settled in with the after-school kids, who stretched toward her like neglected plants too long in the shade. For a few hours, they got to play intricate games of make-believe and draw giant Ferris wheels, instead of caring for younger siblings or translating their parents' symptoms to overworked doctors at the Orchard Street Clinic.

"Mrs. Pierce, help me!"

Phoebe ran to Anthony, who stood by the sink covered with clay. She turned on the water and rinsed the grit off his skin and on to hers. Then she washed them both clean until his hands were again pale gold. The boy hugged her, leaving proof of his affection with wet handprints.

"I love the days you come," he said.

"And you're the sunshine of my week."

Tomorrow she'd welcome the members of Cooking for English— the highlight of working at Mira House. She'd proposed this class after spending months proving herself as a program assistant—even including the cost of the Cooking for English materials; a donation from her softhearted father. The idea sprang from a chance encounter with a mother who'd brought a jar of perfect borscht as thanks when Phoebe didn't complain about the mother being late picking up her child. The gift of food generated the most animated conversation she'd had with any mother at Mira House. Clarity came: use food to bridge the cultures, exchanging recipes for knowledge of New York.

Her students taught her dishes and customs from their home countries: Russia, China, Hungary, Korea, and many others. She tutored them in English, the rules of rent control, and every other trick they needed to live in New York.

. . .

Phoebe stirred the beef in wine sauce in careful circles, determined to keep the roux from getting lumpy. She'd learned the dish watching her mother make it twice a month but still couldn't get the liquid to the silky consistency her mother produced, where the merlot married the broth, flour, and touch of butter until it seemed as though Julia Child had visited the Beckett family.

Tonight Phoebe planned a perfect dinner. Water boiled, ready for the egg noodles. Baking powder biscuits punched out in flawless circles covered a cookie sheet and waited for the oven. Russian vegetable pie cooled on the counter. All his favorites.

Devil's food cake decorated with two tiny rattles—one pink, one blue—waited, secreted in the back of the fridge.

As the stew thickened, the phone rang. Inevitably it would be Deb—also married and a supper maker now—or her mother. This was the hour the three of them prepared dinner and called back and forth.

She didn't miss a circle of stirring as she reached for the phone. "Hello."

"So, answer me this one, okay? When do we get to stop taking care of your mistakes? Daddy told me everything."

"Mom?" Phoebe put the receiver in the crook of her neck and searched the table for her cigarettes. "What are you talking about?"

"Your genius husband didn't tell you?" The click of her mother's lighter traveled through the wire as she lit her own cigarette. "What's the noise banging behind you?"

"The radio."

"What station is that? Screeching cat sounds?"

"I'll turn it down."

"Not down. Off. I can't hear myself think."

Phoebe shut off the music, reflexively obedient to her mother's demand.

"So, did he tell you?"

"Did he tell me what?" Phoebe dipped into the pot and sampled a bit of sauce. Almost perfect. Velvet smooth.

"How he lost everyone's money?"

Phoebe sighed, deliberately loud enough for her mother to hear. Who should be called Sarah Bernhardt now? "He lost whose money?"

"Are you listening? Jake needed Daddy to bail him out. He didn't tell you before he came to us begging? What kind of marriage are you in? I'm aware of every single thing Daddy does. Do you even know who Jake is?"

Phoebe didn't bring up the money while they ate supper. Jake seemed oblivious to her silent serving, probably grateful she didn't beg for a Walter Cronkite–free dinner when he flipped on the small television on the kitchen counter. As he listened to the news, she searched for ways to approach the subject, until finally, while clearing dirty plates, she blurted out her anxiety.

"My mother called," she said. "Fuming. Why didn't you tell me about the loan?"

"What are you talking about? And for the love of God, when *isn't* Lola fuming?"

Phoebe squeezed dishwashing liquid in the sink. "Don't play dumb."

"Since when are my work issues any of Lola's concern?"

"When you ask my parents for money."

"The money was between your father and me." He stood, picked up the silverware, carried it to the sink, and dropped in the knives and forks, looking pleased when they clattered off the dishes.

She clutched the edge of the counter and tried not to scream. After counting to twenty, Phoebe spoke in a calm and even tone. "So what happened?"

"Nothing. It wasn't a big deal. A cash crunch, that's all."

"My mother said you needed Daddy to cover your clients' accounts."

"Your mother's always made it pretty damned clear that she doesn't like me."

Phoebe pressed her lips together, returned to the table, and sat across from Jake, her hands clasped on top of the bright-yellow tablecloth. "You lost clients' money?"

"I didn't lose anything. An investment went south. Normal stuff."

"Why did you have to cover something normal? I don't understand. They invested. Isn't it their risk?"

"This is so not a big deal." Jake picked up his crumpled napkin and smoothed the wrinkles. "There's a time and a place in business to show losses, and this was neither the time nor the place. You don't understand."

"Then explain it to me."

Jake grabbed a pad and pen from the junk drawer, flung it on the table, and dropped back into his chair. "Okay. Watch and learn, baby." He drew a black line with a Flair pen, creasing the paper as he bore down. "I'm giving you the easy version."

She worked to concentrate. Numbers and the whole world of investment sent her thoughts to her plans for Mira House the next day.

"There are two sides of my business." Black ink dotted the white notepad as Jake jabbed at the left side of the paper. He wrote "JPE" across the top in letters so thick they shouted off the page. "This is the brokerage. Think of it as plain old vanilla."

Phoebe tried to stay engaged. "For which I type up orders, right?"

"Exactly. Joe Blow calls and orders ten shares of XYZ stock, and we make the transaction for him. He sends us money. We send him the stock. Got it?"

Her mother probably blew this whole thing up. Phoebe snuck her hand in his and squeezed, looking forward to his expression when he saw the rattles on the cake.

"This side . . ." He jabbed at the paper. "This is *The Club*. The investment advisory I told you about. People give me money they want to invest, and I make the decisions what to buy. Then—"

"This is the business you have with Uncle Gus?"

"No!" He held his palms out again and took a deep breath. "Sorry. It just drives me a little crazy. Gus acts like he owns part of the Club, but all he does is send some clients my way. After that, he's out of it. I don't even let him keep the books. He only tracks the brokerage. For which I pay him fair and square."

"Why not the Club books?"

"What I make for the clients is nobody's business."

"Doesn't he send you them?" she asked.

"If I send your sister to Dr. Klein, does it mean he should tell me how much she weighs?"

"Good point." Phoebe pointed to the paper. "Okay. Make it crystal clear."

Jake gave an authoritative nod. "Short and simple." He labeled the right side of the paper "Brokerage." "Once more: this is the stock-trading business, the brokerage. Here, in Jake Pierce Equity. I buy a stock and sell it ten minutes later for a few pennies more. If I misjudge or don't move fast enough, I lose. Sometimes I purchase stocks 'cause I know someone wants it; sometimes because I think it's a good price and I can find someone who wants it. I don't make much profit per sale. It's about volume—making lots of sales."

"And if you buy a stock nobody wants?" Phoebe asked.

"I own it, and I take the bath." Big-shot teacher was Jake's favorite role, even with an audience of only one. "Sometimes I sell it for less than I paid."

"And we take a bath," she said.

"Trust me, I'll do all the worrying. Now, on the other side, we have the private investments. The half that Uncle Gus christened the Club."

When he wrote "Club," the paper tore a bit. "This is where I build up slow and steady. Unlike the brokerage—where I am basically a middleman—here I play a long game. We want these customers for life. I invest their money in stocks and bonds that I choose and get a small percentage of their gains as my fee."

"And if they lose?"

He grinned. "Then I earn a pretty small fee, eh? Bottom line? With

JPE, I buy with the intention of selling right away. I'm a broker. The government sets the rules of the game. The Club is different. I'm the advisor and the manager. I make the decisions. I write the guidelines. I choose, invest, and hold the funds for the clients. I send them statements each month. The first clients were the ones your uncle brought in."

"Are you gonna do it every time a price goes down? Cover the losses in this club? Are you running a business or a charity?"

"I'm not going to fail. Ever. Soon I'll make more money in a year than your father makes in ten. This was just a blip at a bad time."

"You know I want us happy more than rich, right?"

"We'll be both." He rose and offered his hand, bringing her into his arms. "I'll earn damn castles of joy. Our lives will be magnificent, baby."

"I don't want my mother calling and driving me crazy. You have to warn me if you go to my father. It put me in a terrible position."

"It won't happen again. I've got this. Maybe I should have told you, but, Pheebs, this investment should have been a sure thing. It was a one-in-a-million mistake."

"So why didn't you tell me?"

He sank into the sling chair. "Haven't you ever been embarrassed?"

Phoebe sat across from him. "But you could tell my father?" She rubbed the chrome and leather sofa arm, shaken, thinking of the cake hidden in the back of the refrigerator, the rattles ready to break her news. This man she thought capable of anything, the man about to be her baby's daddy, it terrified her to think he could end up like his loser father.

"I needed to be sure I could fix things before we spoke." He rose from the chair as though trying to escape.

Everything they'd bought resembled showroom furniture: modern and hopeful, Danish and sleek. Everything had to be perfect. Jake hated things out of place and insisted on a hand in everything. Even her perfume had to be Jake approved. Muguet des Bois, her scent since high school, had become tiresome, but she still smelled like seventeen and lilacs because Jake hadn't yet sanctioned something new.

Wait until this place matched Deb's, with baby mess everywhere.

Charlotte wasn't even crawling yet, but she'd overtaken every room in Deb and Ben's apartment.

He paced the perimeter of the room until Phoebe stood in his way and placed her hand on his arm. "I don't want you to trust my father more than me," she said.

"It's not trust, honey. Your father knows business; he understands how things can slip away if you don't pull them right back."

"My father's not J. Paul Getty, he's a dentist. Twenty thousand is hardly chicken feed. You know he tells my mother everything. She probably called me before you even closed the door at my parents' house."

"Enough." Jake imprisoned her upper arms in his hands. "You're married to me, not your mother. If I screw up, I'll make it good. Red is my father-in-law, and if I want to ask him for money, I'll do it. If you don't trust me, we can't be a team."

He released her, traced the lines of her face, and then smoothed her hair. "Don't worry. I know you trust me. You'll never regret it. We're going to end up the greatest team the world has ever seen. I'll give you everything you've ever wanted, Pheebs."

"What I want most is . . ." She stopped. What *did* she want most? "Honestly, all I need is for us to do three things in this world: take good care of our family, do good work we can be proud of, and concentrate on bringing out the best in each other."

"Hold that thought." Jake went to the hi-fi console they'd inherited from Phoebe's parents and flipped through a stack of LPs. "Ah. Here it is."

He held up *The Genius of Ray Charles,* the album with the song that played for their first wedding dance and the one that they always pulled out to mark the end of squabbles. He placed the disc on the turntable and set the needle on the track.

As the first bars of the old standard "It Had to Be You" spilled through the room, Jake bowed from the waist and held out his hand. Phoebe took his hand and joined him. She leaned against his chest, feeling under her cheek the still-starched front of the shirt she'd ironed that morning, taking in the big-band brass over Charles's bluesy voice.

She breathed in the very Jakeness of her husband: the warm, mossy smell of Aramis cologne, the lime tonic he used to control his thick hair, and the inky smell he brought home from the office. He brought her closer. She felt him hard and pressing against her.

"Is it still safe?" He nodded toward the bedroom.

"How did you know?" she asked.

He tipped up her face and kissed her with a new depth of love and gentleness. "Roses in your cheeks and rattles on the cake."

"You peeked!"

"I hate secrets," he said.

"Unless *you're* keeping them." She ran her hand down the muscle in his back. "And yes. It's safe. It will be safe for a long time."

"You're sure?"

Memories of her miscarriage probably worried him. After all, they'd been making love when it happened. "I talked about it with the doctor," she said. "He said there was no reason to think the two were connected. Losing the baby and . . . what we were doing."

"Still and all. I'll be gentle." He spun Phoebe to the right and then gently dipped her. "Everything important is right here in my arms."

CHAPTER 8

JAKE

October 1968

"You believe this schmuck's luck?" Jake stabbed at the *New York Times* that covered his desk. He moved over the wax paper from his thick pastrami sandwich to read more of the article.

"Fucking Onassis. More dough than God, and he gets Jackie Kennedy? The guy looks like a frog. Money makes you rich and handsome, huh? Listen to this, Gus: *The thirty-nine-year-old widow of President Kennedy, two inches taller than her new husband, stood beside the sixty-two-year-old multimillionaire during a thirty-minute ceremony and gazed intently at the officiating Greek Orthodox prelate.*"

Gus made a vague humming sound. The old guy wouldn't stop working unless you stuck needles in his arm. His thick black glasses appeared welded to his pale face. Half the time, his hair pointed toward heaven, since he raked the grey with every stroke of his pen. Jake loved the guy, but he was a mess.

Of course Jackie gazed at the minister—anything to avoid seeing the shrunken old man she'd have to screw later. "He must be the luckiest asshole on earth."

Gus concentrated on his oversized adding machine, punching numbers as the white tape spewed out paper coils marked with inky blue numbers.

Jake made a sound between spitting and a raspberry. "It just shows. Nothing matters except a huge bankroll. You can be a gnome, you can cheat your way to the top, but if you have the dough, the *Times* will cover your wedding as though you're Prince Charming."

"So, what's the lesson?" Gus's rabbinical expression reminded Jake of Hebrew school; that mix of Socrates and soul diving. Jake had hated Hebrew school.

"Money trumps all. Think I'll make it the company logo."

Gus took off his glasses and rubbed the bridge of his nose. "I know you're joking, but listen to me, kiddo. Here's what's more important than your bankbook: your reputation. Shortcuts always come back and bite you in the ass."

"Doesn't seem as though Onassis has been hurt."

"Sometimes the hurt doesn't show. It's on the soul. In the end, you answer to God, and I imagine He charges a high price."

Each time Gus brought up right and wrong, Jake wanted to pop him one. If anything, Jake bent like a pretzel to dot each and every *i*. The feds had made a lifelong impression when they took his parents for questioning. Look around their office—it was he who practically ironed the paperwork to make it perfect.

When he was an old man like Gus, he'd sit around and pontificate. But this was his time to build his life and dazzle the world.

"Money might not send you to heaven, but having it is a hell of a lot easier than the alternative." Jake refolded the newspaper to its original shape and gathered the wax paper from his sandwich. He brushed crumbs into his tissue-covered hand and threw it in the trash. Each time Gus threw apple cores and sandwich remains straight into the basket, Jake redoubled his vow to be in his own office by this time next year. Someplace classy. He'd dance naked in Times Square before renting a shit office like this Bronx dump. The place hulked in the shadow of the elevated train—a pigsty where the gloom hiding the dirt and overflowing trash cans was the only positive.

"Are you worried about Onassis being a prick or that you won't end up being like him?" Gus ripped off the white adding machine tape and stapled it to a sheaf of papers.

"Nobody becomes Onassis without being a prick." Jake picked up a copy of the *Pink Sheet* to check stock prices. Like everyone else in the business, he pored over the daily publication for quotes on companies that traded over-the-counter. Smart people could make plenty on OTC stocks.

"Are you ready to go down that road?"

Jake flipped the bird. "Already walking."

Gus dismissed him with a wave. "Big talker." He winked and flashed a pure-white grin, showing off the perfect dentures provided by his brother the dentist, Jake's father-in-law. "But a smart one. You have dollar signs where the rest of us have corpuscles."

Despite chafing under his lectures, Jake relished Gus's regard, basking when Gus treated him as a cross between family and the goose laying golden eggs. Jake churned out profits as though he manufactured them for the clients. Sure, vinegar got mixed in when Jake's father-in-law covered his one mistake, but that was two months ago. He'd worked seven days a week to climb out of that hole.

Red was a hell of a father-in-law. He never even hinted to Gus about the problem once it was fixed. Lola? Another story. Same as ever, his mother-in-law always acted like a bitch. Now she scrutinized him with narrowed eyes, waiting for him to fall again.

Neither Gus, nor the friends and family he brought into the Club, knew a thing about his fumble. They never suspected that their holdings almost disappeared. Thanks to Red, they continued to believe that Jake spun gold.

Who did he hurt? Nobody. Club members got their profits. Red got paid back. Climbing out of his personal financial hole would be his last step in erasing the setback. Barely worth worrying about. He'd end up on top of the world, and he'd play it straight. Not like the shit his parents had pulled, running a brokerage without a license. Every neighbor had come outside and watched those asshole federal agents drag away his parents.

Covering the losses was genius. He took his knocks paying interest to Red but kept his clients. His hot streak returned in no time, and he'd juggle twenty-four hours a day, seven days a week to keep all the balls in the air.

Genius. He laughed at his own bullshit. He'd stayed up half the night until he figured out how to manage the crisis. One night he had to sit up until four in the morning, heartburn and stomach pains hit him so hard. Another night he woke in tears, in the midst of a dream about being paraded in front of neighbors. Phoebe might have known if he hadn't declared that his head was so stuffed from sinus problems that he woke up sniffing because he couldn't breathe.

Jake tapped his financial bible with an index finger every morning: *Registration and Regulation of Brokers and Dealers* by Ezra Weiss. He bought the book the day it was published, read every word twice, memorized what he needed, and then gave the text a place of honor on his desk. Occasionally, he stared at the author's photo, imagining his own picture—though as a *New York Times* bestseller, not the author of a dry text. He'd already come up with book titles:

Pierce Investment Strategies: Secrets to Success!

Pierce Invested: Strategies to Millions!

Wall Street Pierced: How One Man Beat the Stock Market!

The last line electrified him. He wondered if *Pierced* would work as a title. The cover—he doodled iterations as he spoke on the phone—he imagined vivid gold with a dense silver title. Somewhere there'd be an artistic black dollar sign, with smaller versions on the spine and back cover.

Unless the dollar sign gave a cut-rate appearance.

At the right time, he'd ask Phoebe. Matters of taste were her specialty, though he worked plenty learning about the best of everything. Once a month, he broke his tedious commute and exited the train in Midtown. He strolled Madison Avenue checking out how big shots dressed, stopping in Brooks Brothers, where he rubbed suit fabric between his fingers and lingered over briefcases, choosing what he'd soon acquire. Until he could afford the best, he waited, carrying his papers in his old college gym bag. Who cared how a guy in his twenties carried his shit to the Bronx?

He read the *Wall Street Journal* daily, and subscribed to *Forbes* and *Architectural Digest*, along with *House Beautiful*, *Gourmet*, and *Vogue Paris* for Phoebe.

His wife turned heads already, but for his plans, she needed to add a little sheen. Less Brooklyn, more Manhattan. Phoebe would make beautiful children. A daughter with her Snow White skin and delicate features, or a son with her brains and his balls, and life could be perfect.

Fuck it, he loved the hell out of her.

Crisp piles of money, scorching nights of sex, and silver-framed photos of a flawless family defined Jake's endgame. Tons of dough. Tons.

Men climbed over one another these days for over-the-counter and initial public offerings, convinced that every OTC stock and IPO would be the next Ma Bell. Every Tom, Dick, and Harry thought they were next in line to be a millionaire. Jake might as well be the one to sell them the chances to hit the jackpot.

Phoebe wrote down every brokerage trade, but details about the Club he kept private. Jake didn't need to be answering questions about that pot of cash. As long as the Club's clients got their statements, it was nobody's beeswax how he used the money it generated. If it took a few days to catch up on the buys he claimed to have made, so be it. Eventually he followed through. Cash flow required an elastic touch.

Gita-Rae, his first hire—though he shared Gus's assistant, Ronnie Gallagher—provided his missing puzzle piece. He could only afford her part-time; her hourly rate would astound Gus. But she kept secrets like a sphinx. She was no genius, but she wasn't a dummy. Shrewdness, that's what Gita-Rae excelled in, and a head for numbers.

Money was her god. Growing up, she'd lived in the apartment next to Jake's and also attended Erasmus High School same as him and Phoebe, although they hadn't traveled in the same crowd. At fifteen the two of them discovered sex. Gita-Rae was boney as hell and flat-chested, but nobody gave a better hand job. Her dirty-sexy looks screamed *bedroom*. They lost their virginity to each other, though they never touched now. His need for her skills for the Club exceeded her carnal pull.

The Club might not be the main attraction of JPE, but it gave him a bigger thrill than boning Gita-Rae could. Private investment funds didn't need to be opened to the public, and they weren't strangled by regulations. No one got in without an invitation. *His* invitation. Gus told him people whispered about the Club, asking how they could join.

"Any new clients?" Jake called across the room.

"Don't be so impatient," Gus said. "I don't know how you stay on top of the clients you have now."

"Wake up, Uncle. Now's the time. Can't you see dollar bills falling from the sky? It's like pollen in the spring, leaves in the fall—you only need to sweep up the piles. Everyone's wallet should be bulging."

"What goes up must come down, boychik."

"You think Onassis lives by that weak-sister philosophy?" Jake wiggled his eyebrows.

"Live by his philosophy when you have his bank account."

"I'm thinking like a wealthy man starting now. Think rich, be rich."

"Big heads are the first thing to bring men down. The ego takes away your balance, and whomp, you tumble over like Humpty Dumpty."

Gus might produce clients, but, Jesus, he depressed Jake.

Thank God for Ronnie Gallagher, who lived and died by numbers. Gus had brought the young accountant into the office fresh from school a few months ago. Each week, Jake paid for a few more of Ronnie's hours to have him report directly to Jake. The kid's skills were crackerjack. More important, he didn't spend his time lecturing.

Patience and details weren't Jake's strong suit. Worker bees like Ronnie and Gita-Rae took care of the small stuff while he added bricks to his base. Jake planned on being a millionaire before he hit thirty. When the baby came, they'd live in a house, not some crummy apartment, where just by sniffing the air you knew how much garlic Mrs. Lynchowski threw in her soup and whether she served sweet or sour pickles.

Anyplace where your neighbors didn't hear every time you farted.

Jake read real estate ads the way that some men read girly magazines. He'd already shoved plenty into his secret bank account, earmarked for their house, which he didn't touch even when he borrowed the money from Red. His father-in-law could afford it.

Jake's path led straight up, and nothing would stop him.

. . .

A week later, he circled house ads as he drank his first cup of coffee. As Phoebe grew larger, Jake worried. Imagining his future house soothed him. He could draw the place he wanted for his flawless family. Phoebe would bounce right back from her pregnancy—he hated seeing her tight body stretch out. No way would he let a fat wife drag him down. Wrapping his arm around her waist brought him top-notch pleasure. Other guys' eyes opening a bit wider when they saw his doll of a wife almost gave him a hard-on.

If he expected her to be perfect, he needed to provide the right place. They should have already moved someplace where Phoebe could breathe in sweet fresh air and eat farm-fresh food. He wanted her healthy and happy.

"Is breakfast coming anytime this year?" Jake held up his coffee cup. "I need to be at the office early. I gotta get outta here."

"You work for you. What are you going to do? Dock your own pay?" Phoebe flipped a piece of French toast.

Egg-soaked challah browning in butter might be the scent of heaven. God, she cooked like a French chef, soaking the bread overnight until the slices expanded to twice their size.

"Did you tell Mira House you're leaving?" he asked.

Phoebe piled the French toast on a blue plate, ignoring his question.

"Did you?" he repeated.

"There's no reason for me to quit so fast." She reached into the fridge for syrup and butter, carrying the bottle of Log Cabin to a pan of hot water.

"No reason? I don't like the idea of you traveling on the train while you're pregnant. Especially now, when it's getting cold and you could end up slipping in the snow."

"Snow? It's only October."

"October in New York. Anything can happen. Sixty degrees today, twenty tomorrow. Plus, you need to be fair to them—the settlement house."

Phoebe placed the plate before him; it was flanked by the warmed syrup in a china creamer and pats of butter on a small glass dish. "Fair?"

"The more time you give them to find a replacement, the better." He took her hand. "They'll be heartbroken, but I need you here."

When she shook him off, he pointed to her belly. "We both need you. And I got plenty of work to keep you busy but safe."

Pregnant and working in a slum—Christ, she'd make him look like a loser. How were people going to trust him with their dough if they thought he needed money so badly he sent her to work in a ghetto? Plus, memories of that night in the hospital never left him. If need be, he'd be careful for both of them.

Just shut up and for once do what I tell you. That's what he would have liked to say.

"I'll curl up and die from boredom in that dusty office," Phoebe said. "The two of you yakking about every article in the paper, not to mention having to listen to Uncle Gus's stupid jokes. It's torture."

Torture? His spoiled wife wouldn't know discomfort unless the devil himself grabbed her by the neck.

"This won't be for long, honey. I got plans. We're going to be living someplace fantastic by the time you're in the delivery room."

"I'm fine living here," she said. "I can't stand being stuck behind an adding machine."

Pinched, pursed, her face folded into a suspicious expression that mirrored her mother's—the face Jake hated. Fine. He wouldn't pressure her anymore on helping at the office. He'd get Gita-Rae to come in an extra day if it meant marching down the street wearing a sandwich board to attract more clients.

"Okay, Pheebs. I don't want you worrying. Just stop working in that ghetto and concentrate on the baby. I'll manage the rest."

. . .

Jake's phone rang minutes after he stepped into the office.

"All morning it's been like this," Gus said.

"Picking it up was too hard for you?"

"Do I look like a secretary?" Gus held up his hands. "You want to be a big shot? Act like one. Hire your girl full-time."

"I thought you were my girl." Jake grabbed the phone on the third ring.

"You wish," Gus said.

"JPE." Jake stuck up his middle finger. "Jake Pierce speaking."

"Jakie! Just the guy I wanted. It's Eli. Eli Rosenberg. Gus's cousin."

He wedged the receiver between his chin and shoulder, gestured as though making a writing motion, and then pointed to the receiver, mouthing "Eli."

Gus threw over a pencil followed by a pad. Eli—Gus's wife's cousin—held hot-ticket status. Not only did he invest $15,000 in the Club, but he also brought in three others with as much.

"What can I do for you?"

"Already done, buddy. Heck of a return. Couldn't be happier."

Happy? Hell, the man should be ecstatic. Eli and his family realized over 25 percent returns in the Club last year when the S&P 500 did about 16.5 percent—he'd pulled a fucking miracle out for them all, picking winner after winner. Some of his clients needed to be educated to understand just what a big deal that was—beating Standard and Poor's index of the country's top companies.

"Glad to hear you're a satisfied customer."

Finding Dippin' Donuts just as the company went public placed the huge cherry on the sundae of his ride of perfect picks. Again Jake felt the rush of calling it right, following his hunch that the good old

USA was ripe for breakfast on the road. He put everything available into Dippin' and never regretted the move. Hell, he even bought some for him and Phoebe.

"More than satisfied, big guy. You did it. We're cashing in on top."

French toast flipped in his stomach. "What are you, crazy? The ride's just begun."

Eli laughed. "I bet lots of people said those words the day before the Crash. Hey, pal, I'm sixty-one. I'm not looking to be Midas. Comfortable works just fine. So thanks, you did well by us. We made money. You made money. Everyone's happy. Now send us all checks. We're investing it in a house. A place in the Catskills."

"Us? Who do you mean by us?"

"The cousins. They'll be calling later. We're going in together and buying an empty bungalow colony in Loch Sheldrake. Making it a family place. Four cabins. One for each of us and one for guests. We'll have a lake, a couple of rowboats. Come up with your pretty wife. Bring the whole *mishpocha*."

Fuck him and fuck his *mishpocha*. Like Jake gave a shit about bringing his family to visit Eli at some pissant farm. He added up Eli's and the cousins' profits and almost croaked. Between the four of them, he'd end up paying out close to $150,000. A fucking fortune. You could buy ten houses for that money. This move would bankrupt him.

The Club didn't come close to having cash like that on hand. When Dippin' Donuts hit the high-water mark, Jake cashed in to make a killing on another stock, borrowing a little Peter to buy some Paul. He used a personal float once in a while, when hot stuff was ripe for the buy, when his bills were due and it worked—as long as the Club clients didn't act like assholes.

Jake planned to put it all into the clients' accounts and keep it neatly zipped, buy all the stocks timely as Big Ben, just as soon as his client base solidified. For now, he moved it in and out. Another year or two, and then he'd have it all under control.

You gotta keep it all straight and clean, Jake.

Of course, Red. Believe me, I learned my lesson. I feel like a schmuck.

He'd almost lost it when Red clapped him on the shoulder like a real father, as though Jake were someone the world could count on, not some loser like his dad.

Hey, kid. You caught an ambition attack. Hustling is good. Being a hustler, though? Stay away from that, son.

Jake wouldn't ever ask his father-in-law for money again.

Whatever it took, he'd make this right.

CHAPTER 9

JAKE

Jake held up two ties, placing one and then the other under his chin. "Solid or striped?"

"Solid." Phoebe nodded at her empty teacup. "One more? This cold has me knocked out."

"Knocked out and knocked up. Sad combo, baby." He put a hand on her forehead. "You feel warm. I think this is more than a cold. You're staying in bed. One tea coming up."

As Jake headed to the kitchen, he chewed his tongue to release any gathering irritation on having to do one more thing before leaving for work. Even the stupidest of husbands knew enough to brew a cup of tea for an eight-months-pregnant wife without complaining. Jake prided himself on taking care of Phoebe way beyond what he'd seen growing up. His parents had lived as though in bordering countries where treaties prevented all-out war but allowed repeated skirmishes. Early on in his marriage, Jake had vowed that his children would grow up surrounded by love, money, and opportunity.

After relighting the flame under the still-warm teakettle, he grabbed a clean cup. Memories of his parents refilling the same sticky one all day turned his stomach. How could anyone drink out of a dirty mug?

Evidence of last night's meal filled the sink. Poor Phoebe could hardly lumber to the stove and back. Jake folded up his sleeves and tied on a red apron. While the water boiled, he washed the dishes, and then scrubbed the counters and put away the remains of breakfast: a carton of Wheaties, a bowl, and the yellow butter dish from Phoebe's toast. Even scanning the morning papers had become difficult with her laid up in bed, but he saw the most important headline of the day: *PEACE-TALK HOPES BOLSTER MARKET; Stock Prices Show Advance for Third Consecutive Day.*

God loved him.

History worked for him.

Heebie-jeebies shivered down his arms as he pulled a fresh tea bag from the Tetley box, releasing the dusty odor. Back home, wrinkled, dried-up tea bags wedged into stained tin cups littered his mother's kitchen counter. She had rotated them, convinced that she could pull six more ounces from even the most desiccated. Even a whiff of tea had made him sick since childhood. Now he could hardly stand to leave the tea bag in long enough to make Phoebe a strong brew, but he forced himself to let it steep until the water darkened to the tongue-turning tannic mess that Phoebe preferred. Once the liquid appeared sufficiently murky, he added sugar. Lately she asked for two heaping teaspoons.

His wife had craved sweets since the day the rabbit died—although, in truth, he didn't know the exact date of her pregnancy test. Lola's constant gifts of sugary shit didn't help. Last week, his mother-in-law had brought a bakery bag stuffed with chocolate chip cookies and blueberry muffins, and then yesterday she gave them yet another Ebinger's blackout cake. Both her daughters would be bigger than houses if Lola's will prevailed. Deb still carried half her pregnancy weight around her gut despite having dropped the baby months ago. Her husband didn't seem to care, though. Ben still stared at her as if she hung the moon and the sun to boot.

Well, good for him. Ben could afford having a blimp for a wife, the happy-go-lucky schlemiel. How much elegance did a biology teacher at Stuyvesant High School need? The guy had yapped for hours at Sunday's dinner about how life would change when Stuyvesant turned coed next year.

Good luck, buddy.

Married men with pregnant wives lived in horny hell these days.

Hemlines rose every day—soon the fabric would barely graze a girl's ass. Breasts of every size bounced free. Silky hair swung in all directions. Business took all his focus, and having a not-in-the-mood Phoebe sapped his concentration; sex kittens taunting him everywhere made life a bitch. Just to cover his nut, he needed to work harder every day—not having relief in the bedroom killed him.

Jake had learned a few lessons since starting JPE.

One: stocks that go up, come down.

Two: you can't rely on clients. They want their money. They want perfect records. They strut around when they win—with amnesia about who made the win—and throw fits when they lose.

Three: you always need more clients.

Four: stay loose.

He needed sex for number four, but since being pregnant, instead of reaching for him, Phoebe begged for Vanilla Wafers, Tetley Tea, and lemon Italian ices from the place down the street—hell to get home before they melted. After she had passed the six-month mark, he maybe got a pity hand job once a week, and that only took the edge off. He took care of himself in the morning shower. When he'd married Phoebe, he'd sworn he wouldn't be a cheater. A cheater was a lowlife. Totally without class.

Tea sloshed as he carried the tray with the overfull mug and plate of dry toast into the bedroom.

"Toast! I didn't even have to ask." She beamed as though presented with a platter of gold. Making Phoebe happy was so easy that he felt like shit for not doing it more often.

"Least I can do while you're cooking Popeye in there."

"Olive Oyl."

He set the tray on the bed and put an ear to her belly. "I hear a boy."

Phoebe stroked his head. "Do you honestly care?"

"Not one bit." He lay against the mound of his child again, thrilled with the oceanic sounds. His son or daughter formed in his wife, and he vowed to do anything to build them perfect lives. Make them proud.

"What's happening with the real estate agent?" Distress sounded under her casual words.

"The guy said we're reaching too broad. We need to concentrate on one area."

"How are we supposed to choose?" She placed a hand on her mound of a belly as though protecting the baby from evil house brokers skulking in the bedroom corner. "We've only ever lived in Brooklyn."

"Your cousin lives on Long Island. You know her neighborhood. You like where she lives." Phoebe got so jumpy when they talked about moving, you'd think leaving Brooklyn would kill her. What had happened to the girl who adored City College?

"At least in Brooklyn, my mother will be around to help. Your mother." Phoebe blew on the tea before taking a sip.

Jake snorted. "My mother? Forget it. Your mother and Red can drive out wherever we are. Or I'll pay for a cab."

She rolled her eyes. "Big shot rolling in money. You're too hard on your mother. She's gonna be a grandma."

Jake held up his hand. "Logistics will be my department. My parents will come out plenty—don't worry."

"How far will we have to go to afford what you want? I don't want to be stuck in some New Jersey cow town."

"No money talk. That's my problem—you need to rest between Popeye and that cold."

Phoebe struggled upright and swung her feet to the floor. "Rest? The place is a wreck."

Memories of her miscarriage kept him from agreeing; from tearing his hair out at the state of the apartment every time he came home. He spent nights scrubbing after she passed out from pregnancy exhaustion.

"I promised Deb to help with her baby." She tried to stand. "I need the practice. I'll take a shower and then go over to my sister's house with my mother."

"No. Take the breaks while you can." He helped her to her feet. "I'm not letting you take a shower while you're alone in the house. Not while you're running a fever. I'm calling your mother to come over. Meanwhile, I'll stay here."

"Jake—"

He put a finger to her lips. "Shush." Looking around and seeing no robe of hers—not surprising, as they were so behind in laundry; nor could she fit into those tiny silky things she wore before pregnancy—he grabbed his flannel robe and draped it over her shoulders.

Their undersized bathroom steamed up in moments. Like so many Brooklyn apartment house bathrooms, theirs had small black and white tiles and white subway tiles with impossible to clean grout doomed to forever dinginess. Jake sat on the closed toilet, listening to Phoebe wash. He couldn't resist peeking through the place where the shower curtain parted, watching her gleaming belly jut out from her tiny frame. Her breasts had grown; the once-rosy nipples were now brown. He'd thought that her gravid body would turn him away from her, but instead it brought forth strange combinations of lust and worshipful love. She carried their child. They were family.

The water stopped running. He handed Phoebe a towel through the shower curtain. She'd become modest as she grew larger. When she pushed back the metal rings on the rod, he helped her climb over the lip of the tub and then placed a second towel over her shoulders and a third one on her head. He pressed down on the towel, feeling the vulnerability of her hair flat against her scalp and the bumps of her head under his fingers.

If he knew phrenology, would he learn anything new about his wife? Secret pockets of history and futures could be available through the ancient science.

And if she ran her fingers over his head, maybe she'd love him less.

She leaned against him as he dried her back. The thin cloth drank up the moisture too fast. He'd buy thick, absorbent towels for the infant, for her. Next time he went to Madison Avenue, he'd make a side trip to Bloomingdale's and visit its linen department. Find out who made the very best.

. . .

Jake pulled out his ledgers: thousands of dollars separated the pivotal figures—how much he owed and how much was due.

Acid ate holes in his gut. Milk, his drink of choice these days, hardly touched the flames. He'd borrowed from loan sharks to cover what Eli and his asshole cousins had forced him to pay out. Their *gonif* interest rate was killing him. They were all thieves.

Jake hustled. He and Phoebe went to winter-fucking-wonderland weekends in the Catskills, dined with school connections, and attended fraternity reunion events. Warding off the stink of desperation, which killed any deal, took subtlety. Every function required planning. He coached Phoebe to drop hints about his success and demurred when approached directly about his investment fund. Groucho Marx became his mentor, as Jake took on the comedian's tag line: Who wanted to join a club that would accept them as a member?

As Gus's contacts dried up, Ronnie Gallagher tapped into his network: a vast sea of Irish families with full bank accounts. Jake paid him per client, and they both made out. Money in, money out. He couldn't ingest enough Rolaids or milk as he raced to keep the in above the out. The Club stopped being fun. His days morphed into a cruel cycle of chasing profit. Expending new client funds to oil the machine—paying staff, saving for his house, buying supplies—meant putting off more and more trades until a mountain of chits piled up.

But, hey, who cared if he bought the stock this week or next, or the following month, as long as everything added up in the end? Money was money. Gita-Rae didn't give a shit, thank God. The woman demonstrated genius in creating perfect statements, taking Jake's information—the date he had purportedly purchased the stock—entering it as though the sale had gone through, and using some Byzantine coding system to track it.

Menus of investments weren't offered at the Club. He didn't have time for bullshit. Go somewhere else if you want to pick stock. Meanwhile, the brokerage arm of JPE built up a reputation as the place where you made a trade for a few pennies less.

Soon he'd stencil "Jake Pierce Equity" on a door in Manhattan. Like Goldman Sachs, he'd make a family kingdom. The giant investment firm made its bones with promissory notes. Jake would find an equal for JPE. Something spectacular. Something new. His brother swore that the next wave of wealth and information would roll in on a surge of computers. Theo, five years younger than Jake, had inherited whatever brains traveled through their family, getting his doctorate in math and computer science, baffling his parents, who couldn't understand what computer science meant or why Theo studied in Indiana, of all places.

Idiots. Neither his mother nor father could pull together an ounce of insight between them. Indiana State University attracted the best in the new field. Meanwhile, Theo, deep in college debt, had only Jake as his safety net. On top of buying all Theo's books and supplies, he sent him a weekly allowance.

"Hey, buddy, wake up over there. Check your messages." Gus gestured with his chin at the small shelves labeled "Jake," "Gus," "Ronnie," and "Gita-Rae." Gus held the folded *New York Times*—every section, from the look of it—as he came out of the can. Jake bought his own newspaper every day to avoid touching the shared copy. A private bathroom topped the list of his future office must-haves.

"Gallagher's been acting like your secretary all morning." Gus grabbed the yellow notes that filled the overflowing mail slot and threw them on Jake's desk.

"Call Billy." "Call Billy, ASAP." "Call Billy minute you get in!"

"You take these?" Jake yelled across the room. Ronnie glanced up, pencil in hand, as he entered figures on his green analysis pad.

"Yeah. Billy called."

"I can read, jerk. Is something wrong?"

Ronnie shrugged. "Dunno. He sounded happy to me."

Jesus. The guy did fine in his arena: keeping records, keeping his mouth shut. Ask him to step two feet outside his home court, and he flattened. Ronnie sure as shit didn't know that Jake used day-old copies of the *Pink Sheet* that Billy, his old Brooklyn College buddy, pinched from Bach Investments. Just as important, Billy kept his ears open—listening in on Bach's top brokers for the best trades and passing on the information.

He dialed fast.

"Bill Mazur, Bach Investments."

"Jake."

"Jake! Gonna make you a happy, happy man. Remember when I told you to buy into Cinema Right Films' limited offering?"

"CRF? The television station offshoot?"

"Yeah." Billy took a loud drag on his cigarette. "Did you do it?"

"I did." Jake doodled dark lines on the corner of a message sheet.

"Did you buy big?"

Jake turned the pages of his books, searching for the number. "I went my limit." And actually bought it.

"Good man. CRF is breaking out big today. Now I got another one for you. A technical business. *Capisce?*"

"I understand technical." Jake would call his brother for anything he found confusing.

"Write this down. Omdex. The company's gonna go public and it's gonna be big. I gotta go. Buy now. You'll owe me."

Visions of houses danced in front of Jake. Out of their stinking apartment and into a place with a damned lawn. His in-laws, his parents—they'd all see their grandson take his first steps on green grass owned by Jake. "How big?"

"Fucking huge."

Success pooled deep in his groin.

By the end of the day, all signs pointed to a home run. *Thank you, Billy.* At the market's closing bell, a boatload of profit that he intended to turn to cash was pulling into port.

"I gotta do some celebrating!" he yelled to Gus. "Champagne style."

"Unless you invested some hidden fortune of your own, it's the clients who'll be lifting the champagne glasses. How much did you make on your cut?"

Classic Gus, just like Phoebe's whole family: always cautious, always putting a little bump in your road. *Watch out! Don't get so excited!* Jake gave his father credit—he'd lost a ton, but at least he'd been willing to play the game.

"There's enough for everyone," Jake said.

"Go easy on the celebrating, kid," Gus said. "One day doesn't a millionaire make."

"Millionaire? I'm aiming for billions." Jake winked, as though he were kidding, gave his crooked grin, and tipped an imaginary hat. "I'm off to buy a dozen roses for Phoebe. Careful enough for you?"

Jake steered his boring beige Chevy Caprice, Phoebe's choice, toward FDR Drive, heading to the real estate agent with the glossiest *New York Times* ad. Screw the White Plains broker who'd hauled him all over Westchester and Long Island and came up with nothing worth showing Phoebe.

Jake made the first visits and saved the cream for her—not that any had risen up yet. He couldn't give her first looks. Without him narrowing down the choices, they'd get stuck in some oversized ranch house like her sister and Ben. Phoebe lived under the curse of growing up beautiful and middle class. Life came too easy for her. People who never needed to stretch rarely reached for the stars. Jake pushed for both of them.

Rothschild Realty's office appeared polished with sunshine and honey. The knockout owner who stood for a handshake may as well have modeled Herb Alpert's *Whipped Cream & Other Delights* album cover: all tall and tan and lovely. Though not so young.

"Georgia Rothschild," she said.

"Any relation?" he asked.

"I like to keep my clients guessing. Welcome. I'm picking out prime properties for you."

They exchanged a few flirtatious comments and then she turned back to flipping through her listings, stopping at one and nodding, marking the page before moving on, leaving him to check out this real estate broker with the tumble of bronze hair falling over broad shoulders until she looked up.

"So. They've been taking you to Long Island?" She leaned back and lit a cigarette. "You know the Island's for beginners, right?"

"What kind of beginners?" He stretched his legs out full.

"Beginners to nowhere. Why not jump right into the middle, eh?" She slammed the property book shut. "Not all of Long Island is a snooze, but the ones you can afford are. And getting to Manhattan from the Island is hell on earth. You work in Manhattan, right?"

Jake ignored her question and asked his own. "Where's the middle tracking to the top? The top with kids?" he asked.

"Greenwich. Connecticut," she shot back. "A fast ride to Manhattan. A decent train. Plus, Greenwich is small, especially compared with Long Island. Saying you come from Long Island could mean anything: a millionaire on the Gold Coast, a total nobody from Levittown. Say you're from Greenwich, money's always in the conversation. Come on. I'll show you."

. . .

Jake slipped into Georgia's white Chevy Camaro, a low rider as sleek as Georgia. They were a coordinated pair—down to the baby-blue interior matching her eyes, which he bet she ordered for the impact.

"Nice car," he said.

She offered an enigmatic smile, stretched her magnificent legs, and let her skirt ride up her thighs. Damn, how was she so tan in the middle of May? Jake didn't hesitate to feast his eyes as Georgia sped up toward the New England Thruway. Frankie Valli's "Can't Take My Eyes Off You" pumped from an eight-track car stereo sound system better than any Jake had ever heard. He imagined a life of fast cars, spring-tanned women, and a bulging wallet. All that and his perfect family.

Georgia pulled into the driveway of a small stone house. Oak trees filled the yard, making the house next door nearly invisible despite the homes being within yelling distance. Carpets of yellow tulips bloomed in a dense border.

"Not bad, right?" she asked. "The first time I saw this house, I pictured red shutters and a red porch. Barn red."

Jake imagined wide red planks replacing the black painted ones and planters filled with a profusion of yellow flowers, white Adirondack chairs, and terra-cotta stepping-stones, looking like a spread from *House Beautiful*.

"Come on." Georgia turned off the engine. "We're on a move-fast schedule, cause I'm gonna show you every house in town near your price range." Sex emanated from her half-smile. "Close enough, at any rate. I bet you're a fast climber."

Jake pegged her as near forty. Could even be forty-five, but hot. Old enough to want him simply for fun. He flexed his shoulders after rising from the low car.

"I'm not gonna play games with you, Mr. Pierce. Truth? I'm showing you the best first. Not the cheapest. Not the one I think you should buy. You look. You decide. This house will sell itself. The place only came on the market this week and won't last long." She waited a few beats. "Death in the family. Kids don't want the house, only fast money."

Jake spent his days selling, fast-talking, slow-talking—whatever the mark needed. He saw through Georgia's "I don't care what you do, because I know this is a winner" line. *You don't buy it—no problem. Someone's waiting right behind you.* Jake sold that way too. He recognized the approach, but despite his knowledge, the tactic almost succeeded.

Almost. He hid his interest like a pro.

"Let's see what we got here. After, we'll check out the rest. I'm in no rush." He walked in front of her, keeping his shoulders wide.

. . .

After seeing a colonial, a split-level, and some modern monstrosity, they landed at a spread on the Long Island Sound that appeared to be way out of his price range.

The minute he saw the place, he craved waking to a water view.

"What's up with this?" he asked. "Apparently you didn't start with the highest priced after all."

"True. This house is way above your ceiling."

"Why bring me here?" They sat in deck chairs on the broad white terrace, feet up on the railing. Salty early-evening air settled over them. Georgia's legs gleamed in the soft beach light. Sexy as hell.

"You wanted to see a house on the ocean. I figured you meant one for sale."

"Good point." The house toppled way over his ceiling price.

"By 1931, Greenwich's per capita income topped every town in the area. Could be you're not ready yet."

"You sell via insult method?"

She swept her hand in front of them. Gold and sapphires flashed. Perfume wafted; the scent of expensive hovered in the breeze. "Don't knock it. I don't do badly. Not one bit."

Jake started doing figures in his head, wishing his brother were here with his calculator of a brain, though nobody could figure the price of this place down to an affordable number. Then he thought about all the gains he made that day.

Not your money, boychik.

He estimated his take on the 20 percent.

Nowhere near the down payment. But with today's hits, the Club account sat fat, happy, and at his disposal.

Not his to take, but surely his to borrow.

"Listen," she said. "I'm sorry for bringing you here. My mistake. This isn't an entry-level place."

He maintained an impassive expression while inwardly cringing at her humiliating words. Treating him like a dumb Brooklyn kid—sure, he knew what game she was playing, but screw her. Screw her for thinking she could bullshit him.

Jake rose and leaned on the railing, his back to the ocean. He circled her brown ankle with his large hand, able to fit it all in. He ran his fingers up the line of her calf, the inside of her thigh, stopped, and went back down again. Then he traced his steps back up.

Georgia put her head back. Opened her legs a little. Then a bit more, as his hand traveled. Her hands clenched as she shifted lower in the chaise lounge.

"You cheated before?" Her words came out breathy.

"Who said I'm cheating now?" he asked.

"You're gonna."

"Nah. We're not going all the way."

Georgia laughed. "All the way? Are you sixteen?"

His hand went higher. "Nope."

Fuck her.

Blowing him wouldn't be wrong. Fellatio wasn't infidelity.

Only a blow job. That's all he'd take from Georgia. Just to make sure he could concentrate for the rest of the week.

Part 2

BUILDING AN EMPIRE

CHAPTER 10

JAKE

May 1970

People swarmed over Wall Street that Friday. Students covered the Federal Hall National Memorial steps. Yesterday the National Guard had killed four students at Kent State University during a Vietnam War protest in Ohio. Today, throughout the nation, protesters aimed their signs at President Richard Nixon.

A crying shame, those killings. Nobody but college kids and a few grandmothers trying to stop the war. They actually expected to make a difference with their marches? Ah, what the hell. Who else did the world have now? Such a ragged piece of history America inhabited. Vietnam had thrown the economy in the tank. Thank God things were quiet on Theo's campus, but, Jesus, tragedy was as possible in Indiana as Ohio.

Nixon didn't help matters, the bastard, calling these kids "bums," while he sent their classmates to be killed in Vietnam. Nixon. His shifty eyes told the whole story of his character. Meanwhile, business was going to shit all over the country.

"Okay, buddy, here we go again. Although my hope is shrinking, the way you're rejecting everything." Georgia's breathy delivery took the sting off her dismissive words. "Only two more before we reach foraging level. You've crossed off every property within a mile of your desires."

"Ah, I believe in you." He let his eyes travel her body. "Do your magic and pull a rabbit from a silk hat. My faith in you is limitless."

"Can the sweet talk." Georgia lifted her hair off her neck and twisted it into an approximation of a ponytail. Perspiration dotted her hairline. Her clothes clung to her back even though the temperature hadn't topped sixty degrees. Tramping all over Wall Street clearly took a toll. She wore heels, which must have made walking even harder, plus her dress seemed like a long sweater. Sexy as hell—and he appreciated the effort—but not meant for hiking. A whiff of pure Georgia spun with her perfume wafted his way. His suit wasn't exactly air-conditioned, but he'd taken off the jacket and rolled up his sleeves.

"That last place could have met all your criteria." She wrapped her hair with a rubber band pulled from her huge leather bag.

"Could have? Have you ever known me to do 'almost'?"

"What's wrong with subdividing? Or operating open space for a while? Two private offices should be plenty, right? One for you and one for your brother when he joins you."

"You running an office-consulting business on the side?" Jake asked. "Stick to finding me the floor plans I want. I'll decide what works. Don't worry. Your commission will come."

"Don't get testy, sugar." Georgia reached out for his arm, but he pulled back before she made contact. New York sometimes became Main Street USA. You never knew who watched.

He tuned her out as she babbled on. Duplicating his imagined future offices might not be possible yet, but Jake would be damned if he'd start out far from the ideal. Dough pumped in from both sides of JPE. Greenwich generated so many connections that he'd hired three brokers and rented space from the medical supply business next door to Uncle Gus. A waterfront address helped, despite the monthly payments killing him. Location defined you.

Gita-Rae's new assistant, a tough-nut kid, kept the flow going between the brokerage and the Club. Charlie Marshal had barely scraped his way out of high school—similar to Gita-Rae—but his instinct and brains beat every college boy Jake hired.

Dragging Phoebe all over New York and Connecticut resulted in boatloads of Club members—but he paid a price. After going with him to every dinner-dance and fund-raiser in town, Phoebe nagged for quiet dinners, just the two of them and two-year-old Katie. When the hell was he supposed to have time to work? Gita-Rae might be smart, but she needed guidance. Only Jake could decide when and if to make a buy, versus making the illusion of having purchased stock for the Club. Not that he wouldn't make good on all those buys; eventually he'd make the whole enchilada right. But right now he simply had a cash flow balancing act.

A hundred tasks needed his attention every day between running JPE and pressing the flesh. Nobody but he could play the role of Jake. Thank God Theo would be working for him come July. Jake planned to plop all the brokerage details on Theo's plate.

Attracting money required burnished bait. JPE's public face required luster and the brokerage provided that and respectability. Every day, the brokerage attracted more corporate clients, especially when Theo popped in to take the helm during his time off from school. His brother had perfect pitch for knowing the company's coming technical needs when it came to anything computerized—both with managing their stock offerings and making improvements in how they managed the business end of JPE.

Theo needed an office. Solomon Azouley, the second broker hired, deserved one. Not only did he bring smarts, sophistication—something Charlie lacked—and education, but also Solomon measured a man in five seconds.

Plus, Sol—the nickname Solomon preferred—was black. Jake's secret weapon, Sol. Clients, whether from the brokerage or the Club, heard the name Sol and figured him for Jewish. In fact, Sol's father was Jewish, which explained how Sol slung Yiddish with the best of them, but to his ignorant clients, Sol appeared only as a massive black man who intimidated the hell out of them. Jake loved watching them react. He swore that some clients signed on just to show how open-minded they were.

He knew Sol from high school, but they'd lost touch until an Erasmus reunion, where Jake discovered Sol not only had brains and a brokerage license, but also he was money hungry as hell and not squeamish about the occasional shortcuts. The JPE team was shaping up nicely, especially with Charlie and Sol providing the perfect duo for managing the handshakes needed between the brokerage and the Club.

He needed to house the Club's inner workings somewhere private for two reasons: to keep them separate from the straight-laced types he planned to attract for the brokerage and to give them privacy for machinations that the Club's patina burnished.

Sometimes he wished he'd never started the damned club, but he was in too deep to stop now. If Jake could write checks and buy out every client, he would. He'd concentrate on building the best broker-age in New York City.

He shook away the thoughts. The funds he'd need to first straighten out the Club and then close it down meant earning a mountain of money. Soon. In due time, he planned to be aboveboard. Meanwhile, he'd keep the balls in the air.

"Let's move," Jake said to Georgia. "It's almost noon, and I want to see every office available in the area."

. . .

"What do you think?" Despite this being the fourth office suite they'd visited in just two hours, Georgia managed to sound as excited as though she'd never turned a key before. They stood just inside the main area of the third office space to which she'd brought him. Light poured in through wall-length windows, wavy glass showing the age of the building, along with the scuffed floors. No problem. Wood could be buffed and shined. He paced the large room, figuring that fifteen desks would fit, making a trading floor possible.

Jake liked the look of the place immediately. "I think this." He pulled Georgia in for a long kiss. "You did good."

He crossed his arms and took a walk around. For the Club office, he pegged a room well away from what would be the brokerage. Halls separated the space from the other areas. An arched window with multiple diamond-shaped panes dominated the rectangle; he pictured Gita-Rae holding court.

Four private offices would be sufficient for now. Furniture left behind by former tenants helped—the pieces were good enough to use, at least in other people's areas. He'd take the largest office, an oversized square with built-in bookcases—he liked that classy touch. A good paint job would cover the apartment-house beige on the walls. He stood at the bank of windows and gazed out.

This might actually work.

Georgia wandered in. "Impressive, right?" She sat on the massive oak desktop, resembling a teacher's desk in a school for giants.

"Not bad."

"You're gonna take it, right?" she asked.

"Oh, yes. I'm gonna take it." Jake crossed the room as he spoke.

She leaned back, tossing her hair over one shoulder.

He unbuttoned her dress, pulling down the soft fabric until her arms were trapped in the sleeves. Then he pushed her back on the sun-warmed wood.

Yes. This would work.

He pulled up her silk slip. Thank God for the private bathroom off his office-to-be. Phoebe's nose worked like a hound dog. Soon after meeting Georgia, Jake had bought Pheebs the largest bottle of Joy perfume made and told her to set aside the Muguet des Bois. Having your women wear the same scent made life easier.

. . .

Weeks after moving, unpacked cartons were driving Jake nuts, though Gita-Rae prevented the place from resembling a gypsy bazaar by hiding them in the Club zone, where nobody but the authorized went.

Only Charlie could carry out boxes without question, though he sometimes brought Vic, another Gita-Rae guy from the neighborhood, to help him. Vic had made his way, like Sol and Jake, through college and became a broker—but where Sol had traded a Brooklyn state of mind for Manhattan, Vic still conveyed a cocky hood aura. Vic and Charlie would always be Brooklyn guys. Neither minded hauling a few boxes.

Charlie was shrewd, but Vic had real brains along with street smarts. When Gita-Rae had difficulty figuring out the price for back-dating a sales figure—making it look as though the buy had been made at a certain value, or even that it had been made at all—Charlie approached Vic, and he never asked shit about the why. Everyone understood cash flow, especially someone like Vic.

The four of them were his pipeline from one end of JPE to the other: Sol to Vic to Charlie to Gita-Rae and back again. And Jake paid them well, handing out fat checks weekly along with the occasional thick envelope holding a few hundred-dollar bills.

Now Jake entered the Club offices in search of particular books for his built-in bookcases. Gita-Rae crouched, pushing boxes to one side or the other, instructing Charlie how to rearrange the remaining ones.

Gita-Rae, his office queen; he'd genuflect before her if she asked.

Phoebe, in short, wasn't as thrilled with her.

"She wasn't exactly a star in school," she had reminded him when they first moved to Greenwich—when post-baby lack of sleep and leaving Brooklyn conspired to make her a real bitch. Finding things to pick at became her new hobby during those months. She'd been rocking Katie when she'd taken the swipe at Gita-Rae. The disparity of Phoebe's Madonna-like appearance and her hard-edged observation repelled him. Jake didn't expect or want a shrinking violet—he appreciated Phoebe's sharp wit—but bitchiness reminded him of Lola.

"Gita-Rae grew up where I did. I need a reminder to keep me in check," he'd said. "And bottom line: she might seem a bit crude, but she's in the back room. The important thing is she's a hell of a smart gal."

Real bottom line? Gita-Rae might be clever and cunning, but those qualities rolled around Wall Street like cigarette butts. Knowing how to keep her mouth shut made her number one. Sure, she'd been a fuckup at school, stuck not even in the commercial track but in what they called "general"—the New York City Public School system's way of labeling you a loser. Idiots. Gita-Rae was as shrewd as they came, but books didn't float her boat the way they did Phoebe's.

It was money that made Gita-Rae smile.

The New York schools had also labeled Charlie an underachiever. Perhaps his square edges couldn't be filed down to fit into the system's circles, but he knew how to obey upward when it suited him—and how to snap the necks of those who needed a reminder that Jake ruled this place.

"Ready for a break from decorating?" Jake asked, looking down at Gita-Rae.

She put out her hand. Jake pulled her up in one swift motion. "Funny guy," she said.

"Hey, I'm not the one rearranging boxes."

"No. You're the one who throws hissy fits like a little girl when things aren't perfect," she wisecracked.

"Ah, who else could boost my ego like you?"

"What can we do for you, boss?" Charlie asked.

"I need the box with the *Encyclopedia of Economic Models*. Find both sets: part one and part two. Leather bound."

"Beautification project?" Gita-Rae asked.

"Not the point," Charlie said. "What you show is who you are. Who you become."

"Suck-up. Watch out. Jake will measure the inches our chairs are from our desks if we let him." Gita-Rae used a garish orange letter opener pockmarked with fake rhinestones to open a box marked "Jake's Books."

"I leave you alone, don't I?" Jake said.

"Only because our space is off-limits to anyone and everyone."

True. No way he'd allow that ugly thing that she held to be seen in the brokerage area. After putting up with the dust, overflowing trash and filthy bathroom at Gus's, along with the subway soot floating in, Jake's offices would be a showplace. Only deep black and pure white would be allowed, mixing in some steel grey like Phoebe wanted. As much as Jake hated to admit it, her eye was sharper than his.

"So find the books, but first—" Jake considered how much to say in front of Charlie. "First we need to get the statement material ready. Between new clients and moving, we're gonna be squeezed."

Gita-Rae nodded, stealing a glance at Charlie before responding. "It's getting to be more than a one-woman job."

"What about your assistant? Nanci with the *i*?"

"She types what I give her. It's not like she has a brain."

"So you hired someone brainless?"

"I hired a terrific typist who's smart enough to do what I tell her and dumb enough to not care what she does. Money's all she wants."

Everything had a price tag, including blindness. People like Nanci, Gita-Rae, and Charlie? Jake guaranteed they'd never leave. Nobody would pay them like he did.

"Can Charlie help?" Jake asked.

Charlie stepped forward. "Whatever you need, boss."

"We're gonna need more time from Vic," Gita-Rae said. "I can't keep up with pricing everything."

"I thought Vic helped you already." Jake cocked his head. "You been bullshitting me?"

Her answer—a deep cigarette laugh—irritated him.

"What? I'm funny?"

"Boss, I wouldn't know where to start if I wanted to bullshit you. I'm just happy if I can keep in check. I just didn't want to overstep with Vic. Give him too much Club work." She glanced over at Charlie. "I keep everything on a need-to-know basis, just like you want."

"Send him to me," Jake said. "We'll talk."

He left without another word. God bless Gita-Rae. She knew him. His business motto contained one simple sentence: "No one knows everything."

Except him. And only one balance of power worked: him on top.

How long since he had really made any buy for the Club? Three months? Four? Soon every penny would be in order, but at the moment, his bills devoured him, and he needed every new client's money just to keep afloat. The brokerage did well, but not well enough that he caught up with all the bills. Their gorgeous house sucked out more money every day. Georgia forgot to mention how sea breezes brought wood rot along with the scent of salt, or how many people it took to landscape a spread like theirs. The cars he needed to impress. The memberships.

Only fresh client money could feed the gaping maws of his business and life, but fuck it—rules didn't grow an empire. Who else but Jake Pierce kept everyone's portfolio going during three years of a bear market? Word of mouth spread plenty when the whispers said that the Club's returns held when the Dow fell 36 percent. But Jake woke at two, three, four in the morning, adding numbers, smacked by the gargantuan figure he'd need to get everything straight and to buy the stocks and bonds listed as already bought.

He kept a secret ledger—written in code—with every stock trade he purported to have made, numbers that Gita-Rae gave him. As the numbers added up, the mountain of money necessary for client payouts became higher.

His glee at the thought of arranging books on his shelves dissipated as he opened his office door. After placing the pile on his desk, he reached in his pocket for the ever-present Rolaids to calm his sour jitters. Then he rummaged in the back of the top drawer for a pack of M&M's.

He made sure the brokerage stayed 100 percent on the level. The feds only kept watch on that end of the business. The Club, which he ran as a private group, might as well use Monopoly money as far as how much they looked. Not that it mattered. In just a month or two, everything would be on the level. The market would work for him. What went down must come up. As long as he tracked it, he'd be okay. Reality would match his numbers. At that point he could fold the Club.

This whole setup was temporary. As soon as Jake had enough stashed away to make sure his little girl—and the son he knew would follow—never wanted for anything, and he could look out for his parents, get them out of that awful apartment and buy them a decent car, and ensure that Phoebe could stay home and take care of the kids just like her mother did, then he'd be satisfied. He'd get more clients while he also made killer buys in the market. Solomon could help figure out what was hot.

He had to keep his reputation—the greatest juggler, the perfect stock picker—intact.

Jake closed his eyes and pictured the Club straightened out with all the books in order. The imagined perfection calmed his heart. All he needed was a little time and some rest.

. . .

That night, he tiptoed into his baby girl's room to make sure she was breathing. He guessed all parents did that once in a while, even when their baby was almost two—like Katie. They always seemed younger when they slept.

He'd look at her tiny back moving up and down and feel his heart crack down the middle. Nobody ever prepared him for the sucker punch of love you felt every time you saw your kid sleeping. Sometimes she'd wake. When she did, she never cried—she smiled and lifted her arms to him. He'd swing her up easy as peeling a banana. She'd hold on like a koala, as though he were her world.

Sometimes, like tonight, he absolutely needed to hold Katie, even knowing that Phoebe would have his head for rousing her. He slipped his hands under her, her body warm under the Dr. Denton footed sleeper. Phoebe and Deb called them footies, and, truly, there was nothing in this world better than the sight of his Katie and her cousin Charlotte in their footies, running down the long hallway and out to the deck to stare at the ocean water lapping in the Long Island Sound. At that moment, it felt as though Jake had personally invented the sea for his family and then conjured up the moon to make shadows dance on the black water.

Katie settled her head into the crook of his neck, her soft curls tickling his nose. He carried her into the bedroom, where Phoebe slept, and laid his daughter next to his wife. The two of them found each other like kittens as they slept, Phoebe curling around Katie.

Jake washed up and put on his pajamas. He climbed in, and between him and Phoebe, they made a Katie sandwich. His wife opened her crystalline blue eyes and, after shaking her head in the tradition of wives everywhere—*Oh, Jake*—she reached over Katie and stroked his arm.

"She's beautiful, right?" Jake kissed the top of Katie's head, inhaling her milky smell, feeling as though he'd fight an army to protect her. "I mean, all babies are cute, I guess, but she's extraordinary."

"All parents think that about their kids," Phoebe whispered. "Especially when they're asleep." She ran a finger over Katie's curls and then took Jake's hand. "But yes, she's very special."

"My girls," he said. "My two extraordinary girls."

CHAPTER 11

PHOEBE

August 1970

"Play!" Katie's piercing voice drilled into Phoebe. "Play now!"

She took a long breath before answering her daughter. God likely wired two-year-olds with grating voices so that parents couldn't ignore them, and then added shots of big-eyed lovability to prevent those same parents from throwing them into traffic.

"Lower your voice, honey," Phoebe said. "Mommy needs to get dressed, but if you're a good girl I'll let you play with something special." Phoebe handed Katie a powder puff and a closed lipstick cylinder, confident Katie didn't possess the motor skills to uncap the tube. "Pretend you're going to a party. Just like Mommy."

Katie grabbed the forbidden treasure and then raced away, crouching from view so the prizes wouldn't be taken from her. Phoebe had to finish dolling up before Jake rushed in—her babysitting mother in tow—ready to take a three-minute shower, step into a fresh suit, and leave.

"Katie pretty, Mama?" She fluffed whatever particles of powder remained on the puff over her face and made a moue of her lips.

Apple.

Tree.

Katie.

Phoebe.

"You're the smartest, strongest little girl in the world." She and her still-best-friend, Helen, prayed that their daughters might grow up with a greater lust for doctorates than wedding rings. Jake rolled his eyes at the tiny trucks and sturdy blocks Phoebe bought, but she wanted her girl to reach for everything.

Katie stamped her foot as she continued tugging at the lipstick cap.

"Say 'pretty,' Mama!" Katie imitated Jake's stubborn inflection down to a frightening degree. "Katie is pretty!"

"Yes. You're pretty. More important, you're smart, and you're strong."

Katie shook her head as though educating her mother had become a full-time job. Phoebe resumed matching her face to a recent *Vogue* cover, trying for a similar wash of a monochromatic complexion contrasting with focused drama on the eyes.

Left to her own devices, she went for simplicity, but Jake insisted she "gussy up" when they went fishing for clients—an expression she despised. Each time he said the words, her lips curled in till she felt the blood leave, imagining herself a sharp-hooked liar reeling in a guppy.

Phoebe assured her husband daily that she understood the psychology he used to grow the Club side of JPE. At first, she'd been insecure about her ability to follow his orders, but he reminded her that they were creating a family business. Doing her share meant building interest for him. He'd schooled her in how to present the Club: always talk about JPE in a sideways manner, subtly working the conversation to the topic—as though the words popped out despite yourself. Eventually, she had not only gotten good at the game but also enjoyed her performance.

"Jake hates when I reveal anything about his sideline," she'd murmur. "He does love the science of investment. Sometimes I think the Club's more for him than anyone else—he finds the work fascinating, playing around with formulas and strategies he's devised. He won't even tell me the details. He calls it using the Pierce Principles for his secret sauce."

Followed by:

"Don't mention investing to Jake. He won't talk about the fund, he only does—"

At this stage in the conversation, Jake mandated shaking her head as though discouraging them.

"Look, it's better if you just give me your phone number, and I'll have his girl get in touch if you really want. Trust me, he's not going to talk to you directly about this," she'd say. "Anything else—he loves talking about boats since we moved to the ocean—but not this. You'll hear from his girl, and she'll give you a yes or a no.

"Just between us? Sometimes I think the decision is all about what mood he's in when she approaches him."

The "girl" translated to Gita-Rae, and what she did with the information, Phoebe didn't know or care. Supposedly, Phoebe's routine increased the client base mightily, and in the end, her act helped everyone:

Jake got more clients.

The Club made more money.

Clients benefited from Jake's principles.

Nobody lost money with the Club. Steady soup beat a sizzling pan every time, Jake said.

"Bring Mommy the lipstick, honey." Phoebe examined herself. She'd rimmed her eyes in deep chocolate, separated her lashes into fans of black with tips of gold, and burnished her skin with illuminators until her complexion appeared suffused with pale incandescence. Still, no matter how lovely the effect, she doubted the result was worth an hour of her time or wrestling with Katie.

"No," Katie said. "Mine."

"No, honey. Not yours. Mine." She leaned in closer to the mirror and shook her head. Sparkly gold earrings reflected her shine. Phoebe practiced a sensuous smile, appreciating her sexy image. Black waves spilled over one shoulder; she'd grown out her Jackie O bouffant. Too bad they weren't going to a hotel instead of the country club.

When she listened to her friends, Phoebe realized she didn't have much company in her attitude toward the bedroom. Just last week, Helen had admitted that between her daughter's constant demands and working, she never felt like having sex. Not Phoebe. Jake's success excited her, which in turn frightened her. She saw how his stupid crooked grin attracted women; how they brushed up against him. The aura of money drew them.

"Give me the lipstick, Katie. Now!"

Katie threw the heavy tube, hitting Phoebe in the thigh. Yes, two-year-olds had been put on this earth to test you.

Thank God for her mother providing breaks as often as she did. Lola might drive Phoebe nuts, but Jake and Phoebe trusted that Katie would live through the hours spent with Grandma Lola. The child's safety with Jake's mother? Not such a given. The last time they had left Katie with Nan, they had returned to find his mother sprawled out asleep in front of Johnny Carson while Katie rearranged cigarette butts in the ashtray.

They'd never invited Grandma Nan to babysit again, limiting her time with Katie to family functions—all of which were now held at their house.

Because they had the biggest house.

Because they had the water view.

Because being in Brooklyn depressed Jake.

Helen's mother's funeral had been their last trip back together, with Jake's attendance in question until the last minute. Phoebe had been ready to take the train and drop Katie at Lola's house, but after finding out how many of the old crowd would show up, Jake decided to go.

She'd like to think Jake wanted to please her, but driving down the Hutchinson River Parkway, he'd instructed her, once again, on dropping hints about the Club.

. . .

"Guess what he talked about the whole drive?" Her mother stood in her hallmark inquisition pose, arms crossed over her chest with her chin thrust out.

"Murder? Mayhem? Sex? Tell me, Mom. What offended you?" Phoebe glanced up the stairs, anxious for Jake's appearance.

At what point would her mother be proud of Phoebe's choices? Dear Lord, they stood in a house on the fucking water. Neither she nor Jake had passed the age of thirty, and they had the money to spend for a Tabatabai Tabriz rug in their huge family room. For Lola's last birthday, Phoebe and Jake had given her an Ebel watch.

"Be careful with that tone, missy. Someday you'll be on the other side, and that voice will bounce right back at you." Her mother tipped her head toward the living room. "God and your daughter are listening."

"God should worry about more than my jokes."

"Trust me, he worries. About everything and everyone, including your husband. All Jake talked about during the ride—with me stuck in the backseat while his buddy sat up front like a king—was who owned what boat and who had a driver and who bought what house."

The "buddy" was Ollie Howard. He and his wife—not Phoebe's best friend, by any measure—lived next door. Of course, "next door" in Greenwich hardly meant sugar-borrowing close.

"Plus, he made me take the train from Brooklyn to his office."

"So you said. Twice. He offered to pay for a cab, Mom."

"What? Your father and I can't afford a taxi?"

"What's your point?"

"My point? A son-in-law looks out for his mother-in-law. You think Daddy would ask Grandma—may she rest in peace—to schlep into Manhattan by train? Or to take a filthy taxi with some stranger yakking at her the whole way?"

Phoebe put on a concerned expression as she waited for her mother's motor to run down.

"What kind of men cackle over boats like women over jewelry?" Lola touched her fingers to her temples as though trying to contain her shock at the men's antics.

"I very much doubt Ollie or Jake cackled." Phoebe took hold of the banister and once again glanced up the stairs.

"Oh, trust me. They cackled like witches. Your husband has you wrapped up like a mummy. Jake said this! Jake did that! Did you start your *knippel*? Must I remind you every week?"

"Again with the *knippel*. Does it seem like I need to hide cash?" Phoebe gestured around the house, sweeping in the oversized windows highlighting the view. The foyer where they stood could fit Deb's Brooklyn kitchen, dining room, and living room. Why did her mother think she needed to keep a cache of money like an old woman in a shtetl?

Phoebe's mother kept her own *knippel* in an old white pot on top of the cabinets. She'd showed the girls her hiding spot at the same time she whispered the secret passed down from mother to daughter each generation. Deb had been sixteen at the time, Phoebe fourteen, when they learned about the custom of women keeping a secret stash of money.

"Listen to me," Mom had said. "You know I love Daddy."

But? Mom's wisdom was usually prefaced with a *but*.

"Daddy's a good man—the best man—but he trusts everyone too much," she said. "I worry about you girls. You need to keep your eyes open. Don't be a schlemiel."

The implication being that Daddy was a schlemiel and people took advantage of him. Deb and Phoebe would nod—unwilling to risk their mother's cutting remarks—and then go in their room and pinky swear that they'd never be pinched and distrustful like that. They wouldn't knock down their husbands or roll their eyes behind their backs.

Nevertheless, hide dollar bills they did. Mom made them absolutely swear, on her grave, may they rot in hell if they disobeyed, to always have their own money. No woman should be so dependent that she can't buy a loaf of bread, a bottle of milk, or go to the beauty parlor without a man's goodwill.

Phoebe hoarded a bit of cash as she'd promised, but irritation at her mother's attitude toward Jake kept her from admitting it.

"I've told you this a hundred times. The future is shrouded. Nobody can lift that veil. Look, your father is an angel. Truly, sometimes I don't know how he puts up with me. Who needs to hide money less than me, right? But my mother told me to make a *knippel*, and so I did. Thank you, God, in the end, I used the *knippel* to surprise your father with a cruise to Jamaica, and not a divorce lawyer like some woman after her husband beat her half to death."

"We can afford ten cruises, and Jake would never hurt me. So we're okay on all fronts." Phoebe crossed her arms and rolled her eyes.

Katie began crying, but Lola blocked Phoebe from rushing to her.

"I'll go. You wait here for your wonderful husband. Who, no, I don't think will beat you. He's not the type. But marriage means watching out for all sorts of troubles. Sure, you think he's the greatest thing since sliced bread, but trust me, he's the sneaky kind. When I turn out to be totally off the mark, a blessing on your head."

. . .

A shocking ring of color circled the dance floor. Bright yellow linens decorated with psychedelic orange daisies concealed the wooden tabletops. Fuchsia glass jars of deceptively simple zinnias—from the most expensive florist in town—served as centerpieces. The staid fund-raising committee had chosen the Broadway show *Hair* as the theme, honoring the wildly popular musical as it worked overtime to attract a younger crowd.

Perhaps in reaction to feeling ancient at twenty-eight in this Age of Aquarius, perhaps wanting to catch Jake's eye, Phoebe wore a stoplight-red halter dress slit almost to her waist, in direct contrast with most other women in the room, who chose flowing faux-hippie fashions. The slash up the side along with staggeringly uncomfortable high heels showed off her shapely legs.

"Don't forget to talk to Joan Frankel." Jake lifted a light-colored bourbon and water from the gleaming bar. After finishing the drink, he locked fingers with her. "And by the way, I'd love to take you to bed right this minute. That's just how steamy you look. Anyway, Joan's husband's loaded, but he won't do a thing without her. He owns a chain of tire stores."

She didn't want to let go of his hand. "So I look okay?"

Jake eyed her from top to bottom, backing away and crossing his arms as though taking in the entire view. "Like I said: sexy as all hell. Red's a good color for you. The dress is almost perfect, but it's cut a little low. Not for me. I love provocative. Money likes conservative."

"Are you in charge of making the next Mr. Blackwell list for best dressed? How about I dress like Queen Elizabeth? Should I carry a little white handbag and wear pink lipstick?"

"Phoebe. You're more beautiful than any woman here. Which

would be fantastic if you were working on the men, but it's the wives you're after tonight. But make sure you wear that dress next time we go dancing."

"When's the last time we went out dancing?" she asked.

He raised his eyebrows and held out a hand. Sometimes Phoebe forgot just how sexy he could be. "How about right now?"

Phoebe looked at the dance floor where a few brave couples were already twirling around. The band had just begun a song she loved. The vocalist almost sounded like Dionne Warwick as she trilled the first notes of "This Girl's in Love with You."

She could feel eyes on them, felt the power of being a steamy young couple. He placed his hands on her lower back as they swayed together, then he led her with a strong hand, spinning her out and then back as though he were Gene Kelly.

"We still got it, eh?" He nibbled at her neck.

"Jake!"

"Let them all eat their hearts out. Every guy here wishes he were me."

When the music segued into Sly and the Family Stone's "I Want to Take You Higher," an impossible rhythm for slow dancing, they walked off the dance floor hand in hand.

"Okay. It's Harry Frankel I want to work with us," Jake said. "Ollie asked his wife to make sure we were sitting with the Frankels. Get the seat next to her."

Ollie's wife moved the women of Greenwich around her social chessboard as though they were pawns to her slightest and largest desires. How Poppy Howard managed the rare feat of being a second wife with first-wife clout was the Nancy Drew mystery of Greenwich, though being a former model and a graduate of Rosemary Hall and Radcliffe didn't hurt. Nor did being the daughter of a top Hollywood producer. Even old wealth swooned in front of movie money. If she wanted Phoebe and Jake at the Frankel table, that's where they'd be cutting their sirloins.

"Your wish, my command." Phoebe headed to the table by the band, enjoying the satiny feel of her dress brushing her skin.

Joan Frankel held a caramel-colored drink. A backup waited on the flowered tablecloth. From the deep color of the liquid, she took her drinks neat.

"Joan?" Phoebe leaned to kiss the woman's powdery cheek. "What a pleasure to be sitting with you. We don't have a minute to speak at exercise class."

Despite being twenty years older than Phoebe, Joan's leather mini-skirt barely covered her overly tanned thighs and, ignoring the heat outside, she wore a short blue-dyed fox jacket over a satiny top. Bumps of gold and diamonds hung from and wrapped her.

"I didn't realize you were sitting here." Meaning the Pierces' place in Greenwich's pecking order wasn't particularly high. "Your husband's quite a dancer."

"Ah, you know men," Phoebe said. "Every now and then we can drag them out on the floor, right? I'll probably be waiting another five years."

Joan laughed. "I know exactly what you mean."

"Men. Anyway, you look terrific, Joan. Blue fur—how incredible!"

In fact, Joan appeared to have dipped her money in glitter and hung it on random body parts.

A faint smile materialized, highlighting the woman's spectral bleach-lightened mustache. "Harry surprised me with this last week. I couldn't wait to wear it."

"Of course! My God, it's fabulous." Especially perfect if Joan took up stripping. "Are you living at the gym? I can't bear being next to you." Phoebe patted her imperceptible tummy bulge before settling beside Joan. "I feel enormous next to you."

"Darling, you have a little one at home. I never left the house when mine were tiny. You're adorable."

Phoebe stroked the hideous fur jacket. "Oh, this is gorgeous! Did Harry pick it out himself?"

Joan laughed. "What an idea! Of course not. This beauty came through the art of the question-hint."

"Question-hint?"

"You young girls always need schooling. Listen. If I'm reading a magazine or newspaper and see something I like—I found this in a

Bergdorf ad—I point and tip my head a bit." Joan aimed her viciously long red fingernail at a napkin in demonstration. "Then I say, 'Harry, do you think I can carry this off? Am I too old?' Do this enough, and he's bound to pick up on a few things."

Phoebe feigned a sad expression. "Jake spends every second at work. By the time I've washed the supper dishes, he's half asleep. We don't talk enough for me to hint about anything."

"He's at his burning-ambition stage. I remember it all too well." She patted Phoebe's hand.

"Sometimes I think my husband cares more about making fortunes for clients than making me happy." Phoebe sighed.

The other women at the table turned toward them.

Phoebe pulled up a gravelly imitation of Jake's voice, infusing her words with irony. " 'Bottom line, Phoebe, my job is working for the clients—growing their funds steady and upward.' I swear, if his accounts dip one day out of the month, he's impossible to live with. Thank God that's a rare occasion."

"What does he do, your husband? If you don't mind my asking." The woman on the other side of the table spoke with a sugary Southern drawl. "I'm, by the way, Suzy Ramsland."

The name pinged.

Ramsland Insurance.

Suzy's breasts spilled out from her Saks-version peasant blouse.

A female-only table until the meal began wasn't unusual. Greenwich dinner-dance culture put the men at the bar drinking and fetching cocktails for the wives while the women held court at the table, complaining about husbands and comparing their children's accomplishments.

"He runs JPE. Jake Pierce Equity." Phoebe gave a self-deprecating laugh. "Actually, he owns it. Jake would kill me for talking. He thinks I'm bragging when I do, and, God, he hates attention."

Joan waved away Phoebe's concerns with a flash of gold. "Don't worry. Nobody's here but us chickens! If we listened to every little thing our husbands said, we'd probably all be home scrubbing toilets, and they'd be here with twenty-year-old hookers."

"Smoking cigars," added Suzy. She snorted and added, "Or having their cigars smoked."

Suzy's caustic observations soothed Phoebe. If they accepted Suzy, maybe Phoebe could become a member of this not-so-old-money group. She should let go of her unease at talking up the Club. Obviously these women enjoyed the spoils of wealth, and if Jake did nothing else, he made people rich.

"Spill," Joan said.

"Mostly JPE is a garden-variety brokerage." Phoebe gave an exaggerated yawn to show just how boring she found the conversation. "But he has a quiet little investment club on the side."

"A mutual fund?" Suzy's inflated breasts belied a sharp brain. Eyes gave away smarts every time.

"Not really. It isn't open to the public. It's almost like he considers the Club his hobby." She leaned in and whispered, "Jake has come up with some sort of investing recipe. He jokes about his secret sauce. I couldn't explain the method if you tortured me. It doesn't bring those once-in-a-lifetime insane returns, but he always brings in a steady up. Always. I don't know how he manages."

"What kind of 'steady up'?" Suzy asked.

Phoebe shook her head and held out her hands. "I know I'll get this wrong. That's probably why I shouldn't say anything about this. Jake barely accepts new clients. He doesn't want aggravation. He likes beating the system with smart caution, loves getting profit for people, but he despises them trying to pick his brain."

"I don't care how he makes the money." Joan lifted her glass toward her husband, looking the very picture of cognitive dissonance to Phoebe, this man she usually saw at club dinners wearing the most conservative of suits. Now Joan's husband, shaved to the pink, and rotund, stood at the gleaming bar wearing bell-bottoms and a tie-dyed headband. "I just care about the profits. So what are we talking about?"

"Promise me you won't repeat this, or I'm screwed." Phoebe spun her heavy-bottomed glass in circles. "It probably won't even sound like a big deal to you. Ugh. I built this up too much."

"Enough!" The fourth woman at the table, shaped like a mouse with similar coloring, surprised Phoebe with her deep, throaty voice. "We'll be the judges."

Phoebe gave a cautioning glance around the table. "He says the last few years have never been lower than ten percent. And never higher than twenty. This is no get-rich scheme. For goodness' sake, I don't even know how I began talking about this. Shhh! The guys are coming."

Joan put her head close to Phoebe's. "Do you play bridge?"

Part 3

—

LIVING THE DREAM

CHAPTER 12

PHOEBE

June 1980

The black Town Car glided down Sixth Avenue with the slickness of money. Each week, Phoebe debated taking the train—her stated preference—versus arguing with Jake who insisted on sending a car as though she were made of sugar and angel wings. Debating with him left her so limp that by the time she arrived at Mira House she needed a strong cup of coffee before leading her Cooking for English session.

In truth, the train drained her, though she'd never admit it to Jake. The subway improved marginally after Edward I. Koch had become mayor two years ago but she remembered her mother nagging her to turn around her rings so that the stones didn't show, and besides, dragging in supplies by the commuter rail and then subway was a lot of work to prove she hadn't lost her edge. She liked to think of herself as retaining the girl who rode the subway from Brooklyn to Harlem, traveling up to City College every day. The girl who caught the eye of the coolest professor on campus.

Older and wiser, Phoebe could now appreciate what a liar and louse Rob Gardiner had been, while also smiling at the bit of rebelliousness she'd shown by sleeping with him. She didn't, however, welcome the other signs of aging. Faint lines around her eyes signaled she was five years from forty. The fifty sit-ups and leg lifts she'd added to her morning run at six o'clock barely kept gravity in check. One of the many reasons she'd returned to work was her desire to wake up her mind along with her muscles—both of which had slackened since having children.

Jake and the kids were wary of the energy Phoebe gave to Mira House, her closeness to the staff—basically everything that removed her from the center of their lives. She'd spent since forever fully concentrating on the kids, him, and socializing for the sake of the business, but this year, with Katie going into seventh grade and Noah entering fourth in September, Phoebe's choices were leave the house or choke. In September, despite Jake's grumbling, she'd revived her Cooking for English classes.

Katie and Noah didn't want to relate to her in that constant way of little kids anymore—but they wanted her there and available at all times. Like a lamp. Perhaps you didn't need to turn it on every minute, but you sure as hell wanted to know that the moment it got dark, you could. Maybe Phoebe was fooling herself, but teaching children how to fend for themselves every now and then seemed part of the parenting job.

She didn't worry that much about Katie. Her daughter retained the same stubborn self-concern she'd always had, though thankfully, as Katie grew older, Phoebe had managed to build up her empathic side. After registering her in a horseback-riding academy that mainstreamed special-ed students into their programs, Katie's view of the world widened. Both she and Noah attended a session of day camp at Mira House each summer to offset their idea that all children vacationed at oceanfront resorts. More important, they discovered a world where popularity and worth were measured using scales other than money and blondness.

Noah's problem had never been a lack of empathy for others. If anything, he soaked up the world too readily, feeling the pain of everyone he met. Phoebe hoped that his not having her immediately accessible all the time might build up Noah's resilience.

Jake wanted her to somehow be at the ready for him every moment while still being interesting and relevant to his potential clients. One day he'd be praising her commitment to what he called "the halt and

the lame," as though she were Jane Addams, and the next day pout if she couldn't go to the movies with him. She'd thought that after being married for so many years, he wouldn't be so needy of her company. Instead, it often felt as though it was only when he was alone with her that he could relax.

Last week, during their Phoebe-taking-the-train-versus-being-driven argument, Jake joked, "Maybe you should be teaching social studies on Long Island, like your sister. At least I wouldn't have to worry about you being on the subway."

At the moment, teaching sounded heavenly. Years ago, Phoebe had tired of enticing people into the Club. Sumptuous houses, designer clothes, and precious jewelry were still just houses, clothes, and jewelry. Jake's work talk brought on near comas of boredom. Within two sentences of listening, she zoned out. The words—*the split, the spread*—floated like threads of DNA, another topic beyond her visualization.

Phoebe liked subjects she could visualize, such as the sociology Rob had taught her years ago. Class differences continued to fascinate Phoebe. For instance, her beige linen pants—so simple against the limousine upholstery. Nobody at Mira House would guess what she'd paid for the pants she'd bought at Saks. Just the idea of spending that much constituted a leap up the hierarchy of earning potential. They wouldn't suspect that her striped bateau-neck shirt represented a day's salary for a typical Mira House employee.

Mira House kept her connected to the girl in love with Rob: the Rob she'd thought he'd been. She mostly kept her memories of him hidden, unwrapping them on nights she couldn't sleep. When she saw the 1973 film *The Way We Were*, with Robert Redford and Barbra Streisand as two star-crossed lovers, she realized Rob had been her short-lived Hubbell Gardiner. Sometimes she wondered what became of him. Mostly she was grateful that she hadn't married him. Hindsight said he would have treated her like crap.

The car pulled in front of the settlement house. "I'll be about three hours," she said, leaning forward.

"Of course, Mrs. Pierce. I'll be here." Leon, Jake's driver, patted the *Daily News* on the passenger seat beside him.

"Please. Don't wait for me." She checked her watch. "Just be back at around one."

Sympathy tinged Leon's smile. "I don't think so. Mr. Pierce would go wild if I just left you here."

"It's not like you're dropping me off to wander in the desert for forty years." She knew Leon would win, but she still tried to gain her freedom. "I've been coming here since I was twenty. I know my way around."

Again, Leon smiled. "Right," he said.

Right. Stated in the correct tone, *right* meant "I hear you, and I am now going to ignore you in the most polite way possible."

She gave up and opened the door. At least Leon had recently given up that fight. Ever since Ira Henriquez, Mira House's newly hired director, had noticed Phoebe alight from the car via the chauffeur's politely offered hand, she had refused Leon's help. Ira hadn't said anything, but his eyes had widened at the sight of the limo, and his hello held a laugh. Not that Ira would ever be unkind. He didn't seem built for anything but menschiness. Every woman at Mira House fell half in love with Ira's mix of honorable and humorous soon after he took the reins.

Phoebe arrived for Cooking for English at least an hour early so that she could set up the kitchen. She often felt less the teacher than the one learning. Not only were some of the clients older than Phoebe, their offered wisdom went in all directions. She rarely said this aloud, not wanting to sound like a liberal cliché, but for God's sake, they'd been through far more than she'd ever experience. How could they not be as much teachers as students?

Her teaching assistant, Eva, tall, slender, her dark skin always complemented by lipstick the color of bittersweet, offered only small details, but her parents escaped from Rwanda in 1963, when Eva was only eight years old, during a wave of violence against the Tutsi. They were barred from returning, but Eva had made trips to bring out her family left behind. That alone meant her survival skills surpassed Phoebe's by light years. She and Eva were slowly building a tentative friendship; that Eva held Phoebe's former title and job—program assistant—added another layer of connection between them.

Staff and students took turns picking recipes. Today happened to be Phoebe's week. After a complicated cooking month that included spicy *doro wat* chicken stew from Ethiopia, peanut rolls from Cameroon, and *banh xeo*, a sort of Vietnamese pancake, she wanted to lighten up the class with cupcakes. Most of them envisioned her life as a confection anyway: light, sweet, and fluffy, a giddy existence—which in comparison with their lives was more than true. Strawberry shortcake cupcakes seemed the perfect choice.

Flour, eggs, sugar, and other ingredients lined the chrome counter. In the fridge, heavy cream chilled. Baskets of the freshest, largest berries available in Greenwich sat on the cooling board. Eva put out equipment as they readied for the students.

The door squeaked open.

"I'm first, yes?" Adina was always first. Phoebe suspected that she came so early and eagerly to escape her five children.

"First, and a most welcome sight." Eva's English—she also spoke French and Kinyarwanda, sounded musically clipped. "Help me put out the mixing bowls, please."

By the time they had laid out bowls in a line, accommodating seven students plus Phoebe and Eva, the others had arrived.

Linh hesitated in the doorway. She struggled with her husband's rages, which were followed by his fear of arrest. He prostrated himself before Linh, weeping at his shame at the position and his fear of being arrested, as he begged for her forgiveness, having heard of how the American police could interfere with anything they wished—even the relations between a husband and wife. Linh dreamed of college. She pretended that Cooking for English ran twice as long, giving herself time to study in the library.

"Here," Zoya, the oldest woman in the class, said when she saw Linh. "Come in, come in. Beat the eggs. Build up those skinny arms."

Zoya fancied herself third in command after Eva and Phoebe. She barged in each week as though docking in a grand harbor. Russia left her with a hatred of authority, a dismissal of Communism, and fear of starving.

Linh, sylphlike to Zoya's bulk, grinned with her lips pressed together, hiding her missing tooth. Phoebe tossed in bed some nights, fixated on how to have her father repair Linh's smile without insulting her or playing favorites. Other nights, she stayed awake wondering why she wasn't fixing every one of her Cooking for English students. "Give *me* the money, instead of the synagogue's building fund," she should tell Jake, but she knew his answer. Jake's generosity expected payment, usually in the form of investing the organization's funds. Without his explicitly demanding this tit for tat, somehow it always evolved once the connection was made.

Linh nodded and took the whisk Zoya held out. Phoebe allowed only basic kitchen implements. She wanted the women to be able to duplicate these recipes at home—though baking cupcakes seemed an odd skill to offer no matter how much English they learned along the way.

"I wanted to beat eggs." Adina, who faced off with Zoya for the role of Queen of the Stove on a regular basis, crossed her arms over the apron covering her plain brown kurta. "Linh can measure flour."

"*The* eggs," Eva said. "You *want* to beat *the* eggs."

"You can prepare pans," Zoya said, as though the jobs were hers to extend. Zoya would do well anywhere from prison to the Pentagon. "Or you can whip the cream if you need the work hard."

"Hard work, not work hard," Eva corrected.

"I don't care," Linh said. "She can do it. Anyplace is a good job."

Phoebe began to correct Linh's grammar, but Zoya got her advice in first.

"Don't let them push you." Zoya pointed both forefingers at Linh. "Fear is your entire problem. Everyone becomes your boss."

"Nobody is bossing anyone." Eva put up her hands and stepped into the cupcake war.

"We're a team," Phoebe added.

"Ha. America is all about sharing, right?" Zoya laughed. "Like everyone is kindergarten children."

"No. Like we in Cooking for English are all in a place where we respect and help each other," Eva said. "And the proper way to say it is: *It's like everyone is a kindergarten child.*"

Zoya and Adina rolled their eyes as the rest of them divided the tasks written on the board.

"Acting like brats never helps." Eva's soft voice managed to dominate the room anytime she spoke. Despite being breathtaking enough to model, all Eva desired was educating herself, earning as much as possible, and then someday perhaps returning to Rwanda when peace prevailed.

"Thanks," Phoebe said. "Sometimes teaching adults is odd."

"It's not easy being a stranger in a strange land, eh?" Eva's grin telegraphed something coming. "We starved in our countries, and our parents sacrificed, so we could come here and learn how to put cakes in cups."

"In America, big problem is stopping eating," Zoya said. "That's why they learn to make tiny 'cup' cakes. Perhaps I become famous for a Russian diet plan. Stand in line for your food."

"Americans want to have cake and eat too." Linh laughed as she beat the eggs. She repeated her words in Vietnamese. "Did I say the words right?" she asked another Vietnamese woman in the class, who nodded yes.

"We can show before and after pictures." Zoya moved her hands from showing far apart to close together. "We make pictures of women turning skinny from standing on line for long enough."

"American women do love makeover stories." Phoebe handed out cupcake tins to be oiled.

"What is 'make over'?" Zoya asked.

"It's when we work to become better versions of ourselves," Phoebe said. "With makeup or diets."

"Where is money in the makeover?" Yen, a newcomer, asked. "Cash makes only difference in becoming new you."

Phoebe began to speak about inner beauty and peace until she realized if she weren't the teacher, they would all yell "bullshit!" if she said those words. "I guess money is the true agent of change."

"Yeah," Zoya said. "Money buys almost everything."

"It doesn't buy happiness," Phoebe said.

"It doesn't buy unhappiness," Zoya said. "Better to be unhappy with money than unhappy without."

"Paychecks are what we need. Not sugar." Yen scooped a hollow in the cupcake as she spoke and stuck in a strawberry. "Will learning to make cupcakes buy our children clothes? Send them to college? Heaven isn't cupcakes."

"Heaven is not cupcakes. What a perfect name for an article." Eva stood to her full six feet and lifted her arms. She spoke in a deep voice, as though imitating God. "They needed help, and I sent them cupcakes."

"My people," Linh said, continuing with the godlike delivery, "you will be like the Americans. Sweet and stupid."

"Or, if the cupcakes fall, you will be flat and mean. Also an American," Zoya said.

Linh glanced at Phoebe, seeming to judge if she were angry. Phoebe grinned and laughed to show how not-angry she was. If Phoebe and her family had been forced to uproot and live in Vietnam, eat strange foods, learn new languages—if Jake suddenly had to work as a dishwasher rather than wearing thousand-dollar suits—they'd probably blow off steam in more ways than making fun of sticky rice balls.

More than anything, a fat savings account would help these women. Businesses made the difference for her family back when they arrived from Romania, right? Her great-grandfather peddled hats up and down the East Coast before opening his store. She'd mentioned this, her immigrant grandparents, to the women in class. They knew she'd come from humble beginnings and moved way up. Of course, they had no clue of how far up the ladder she'd climbed with Jake. They didn't know that Jake could make more in a day than many of them made in a year. Maybe more.

"We should be selling these." Phoebe spoke with deliberation as an idea formed.

"Selling them to who?" Eva held up one of the finished products. The luscious twirl of white frosting surrounding the perfect plump berry half-buried in the white cake appeared like a jewel. "Like children with lemonade?"

"No. Like Mrs. Fields." Phoebe imagined it all at once: aprons, boxes, and window fronts like jewel boxes.

"Who is Mrs. Fields? Does she work here?" Linh asked.

"It's a cookie," Zoya said. "Very expensive cookie."

"Sold by a very smart woman," Phoebe said. "On her way to being a very wealthy woman."

"And we can get rich with these cupcakes?" Linh asked.

"Maybe we can."

. . .

First she discussed the idea with Helen; a conversation she considered the equivalent of trying out a show in Boston before taking it to Broadway. Helen being Helen—always busy, usually working, and a huge fan of managing two tasks with one motion—they walked as they talked. Helen worked close to the United Nations, so they speed-walked along First Avenue until they reached Sutton Place, an area cushioned with wealth, and continued uptown on York.

Helen exchanged her trademark spectator pumps for Nikes before their walk, though she still wore her favored royal-blue suit. Phoebe, always small next to Helen, now felt like a child. Her friend worked out daily, building her arms to a female version of Herculean strength. As she strode, her calves almost burst the pantyhose containing them. She held herself straight as the buildings surrounding them. The hair that Helen had formerly tortured into a tight bun now waved over her shoulders.

"Slow down," Phoebe said. "Are we in a competition?"

"Aren't best friends always in a bit of a contest?"

"Only when one's a lawyer." Phoebe skipped a few steps until she was even with Helen. "Remember when we were in high school, and all we did was compare Alan and Jake?"

"And now we complain about them—"

"I don't complain about Jake that much. Do I?"

"About the same as all women moan about their husbands."

"You hardly say anything about Alan."

"Ah, he's a steady guy. Not much to whine about, so you won that particular contest, eh?" Helen put up her hands. "Enough with the men. That's not why you wanted to talk, is it? Or is something wrong at home?"

Did Helen look hopeful? Phoebe suspected that Helen's opinion of Jake could be better. "Home is fine. I want to run an idea by you. A business I'm thinking about. What do you think of me and the women of Mira House becoming the Mrs. Fields of cupcakes?"

"Your Cooking for English women?"

"Exactly." She explained all the details she'd worked out: from having the women buy in through sweat equity to using as many local ingredients as possible. She envisioned a women-owned, women-supported business.

"So you're proposing a high-end product will benefit your immigrant students. Sort of like soaking the rich to build up the poor. I love it. But what does Jake think?"

Phoebe looked away as she answered. "I haven't told him yet."

"Are you afraid he won't approve?"

Phoebe knew from Helen's tone that her friend was convinced that Jake would try to stop her.

"Because, if you want my opinion," Helen said, "I'd worry more about him taking it over. Absorbing it."

"Why would he want a cupcake store?" Phoebe asked.

"Sometimes I think Jake wants everything."

"I'm only going to ask him for start-up funds. I helped him enough to have earned the investment."

Helen twisted her head to the side. "Most certainly, honey. But you know Jake. I don't think he tracks debts the same way as other people."

· · ·

Three weeks later, Phoebe served her idea to the family along with angel food cupcakes topped with summery lemon frosting—confections to show off the product and to sweet-talk funds out of Jake.

"Seriously?" Jake laughed. "You want me to invest in cupcakes?"

"No, I want you to invest in me. The women I work with and me. Smart women who only need a break."

Noah and Kate looked from Phoebe to Jake and back again.

"Umm . . . I think it sounds cool," Noah said.

Phoebe wished Noah took on a role other than mediator in the family. He reminded her of Deb, but he lacked her sister's protective armor.

"Thank you, Mr. Business," Jake said.

Phoebe clenched her hands under the table. Jake's answer to Noah's sensitivity was intended to toughen up their son, believing that was the only way to help secure his future. "Thank you, honey."

Noah shrugged, either pleased at her appreciation or acting cool for Jake. The older the kids got, the harder it was to read them.

"This is my plan: I work with Eva—she's my assistant at Cooking for English—as my partner. She's smart, calm, and organized, with an incredible head for numbers. Then I thought I'd pick the two students most likely to help make it a success. Zoya, the woman from Russia, because she's brave and—"

"You need to be brave for cupcakes?" Jake asked with amusement.

"You need to be brave to throw yourself completely into a business. You know that. Zoya had the guts to face down the Russian bureaucracy. Plus, her energy level amazes me. And she loves money." Phoebe sent Groucho eyebrows to Jake. "You should appreciate that."

"How about the second one?" Noah asked. "What's her specialty?"

"Linh's funny. Which is an important quality when things get rough. She's artistic. And she's the best cook in the class."

"It sounds kind and caring—like everything you do. But do you expect to make money?" Jake asked.

"Look at Mrs. Fields and Famous Amos. Niche brands are taking off. I expect to make enough, eventually, to donate to Mira House. This won't support them, but it can help. More than that, I'm looking for Eva, Zoya, and Linh—and others someday—to make decent salaries. Maybe buy-in with an ownership program. As we grow, and need more employees, we'll always hire from Mira House."

"I won't lie. I'm impressed. That's a lot of planning for a short time," Jake said. "You want to weigh in here, Katie?"

"Not really." At twelve, Kate often spoke like such a know-it-all that she seemed a Jake replica.

"But I want to hear your opinion," Jake said.

"You only want to hear opinions if they match the ones you think are right." Kate placed a second cupcake next to her half-eaten first one. "These are delicious."

"I doubt they're low calorie." Jake took a second one for himself.

"And I doubt it will show up on my body like it will on yours," Kate said. "You have an old metabolism. I don't."

"Ah, but you need to worry about catching a man. Not me."

Phoebe glared. "Kate doesn't need to worry about anything except keeping up her terrific grades and doing her chores."

"You don't need to defend me, Mom. Dad's kidding. God. Don't be so hard on him." Kate rolled her eyes. "Let's get back to cupcakes. Finally—something interesting in this family. Noah is right. It does sound cool."

"Wow, I came up with something cool. Did you hear, Jake?"

"You're always cool to me, hon." He stretched out his legs and crossed his arms across his large chest. "Have you written out a business plan?"

"Some. We're still working on it. The nutshell is this: What better way to help the women I work with than building a business with them? We could be the first of a kind. A Mrs. Fields, begun and run by women who had to leave their own countries."

"Backed by my money, which I hand over like a big present?" Despite Jake's needling words, he seemed interested. He had his business gleam in his eyes.

"You hand over plenty now."

"That's because I get tax deductions."

"We can set it up as a nonprofit! It can go through Mira House. These women got so excited today. We spent the whole time planning and coming up with ideas. We even have a name."

"So you've given this actual serious thought? Besides a cute name?"

"I'm so serious, you can take it to the damned bank." Phoebe folded her hands on top of the table. "And you're going to be part of it. I've been there for your business. Now you can be here for mine."

"What's the name, Mom?" Kate asked.

"The Cupcake Project. At first, we had Cupcake Heaven, but this combines serious and sweet. Eva, Zoya, and Linh came up with it."

Noah pulled himself up as tall as possible. At ten, he was always the shortest in his group. "I think Cupcake Project's a great name."

"Me too." Kate stuck her tongue out at Jake. "You're being mean. All you want to do is make money. Mom wants to make the world better."

"Okay, okay. You show me the written plan, then I'll look at how I can help out."

Jake might think he kept his soft spot for the kids' opinion of him hidden, but anyone with a heart saw it. Phoebe rose, walked around the table, and gave Jake a kiss. He needed to bluster, but he'd come around.

The Cupcake Project.

Finally. Something of her own.

CHAPTER 13

PHOEBE

As far as Jake knew, the Cupcake Project bubbled low. During the past five months his support came in waves, first praising new recipes and then peppering Phoebe with nervous questions about how he or the family could survive without her constant attention. Phoebe veiled the gritty parts of the work, hoping to slide as much as possible past his radar.

The previous evening, after dinner, he'd given in to his reservations. "Who's going to take care of your business when we're out of town?" After the question, he had grabbed an oversized cupcake covered with pink peppermint frosting and dusted with crushed red and white candies. "What about when I want to go out for dinner or a movie? What's the plan if there's an event where I need you?"

"Who takes care of JPE when *you're* away?" she asked.

"Honestly? Sweetheart, we can't compare JPE to the Cupcake Project, can we?" He shook his head and laughed.

At night, sleep eluded her as she planned ways to run a business around Jake's schedule, the kids' school, and their myriad Greenwich community activities. Her parents weren't getting any younger. Nor were Jake's.

Still, and he couldn't deny this, Jake's interest in Phoebe had renewed with her concentration on the Cupcake Project. Last week, he'd pointed to an awning idea she sketched and then stilled her hand with his.

"How about using cooler colors? Literally. Ice cream shades, but better. Pink and green is too girly." He motioned for her to rise and then sat in her chair. "You don't want to limit your customer base to women and children." He held his hand to his chin. "You don't want the place to seem like Baskin-Robbins. We gotta make the store upscale. Blue. Sky blue and white. With touches of yellow. French country-looking."

"I can picture that!" Phoebe wrapped her arms around him from behind as he sketched rough pictures, dazzling her with visions. They worked well past their usual nightly news routine until they fell on each other, burning off heat so searing that the sex, unlike their usual weekly lovemaking, reminded her of when they first discovered each other's bodies.

At that moment, Phoebe believed she could have it all.

. . .

Cupcakes covered Phoebe's butcher-block counter. Linh, Eva, Zoya, and she had spent the day testing recipes and now taste-tested for what they'd include in their first Cupcake Project lineup. They batted ideas all day: seasonal menus, specialty items, which would be the regularly featured cupcakes versus cupcakes of the month.

One thing they never wavered on: knowing that Greenwich would be the perfect place to open the shop. Storefront rents seemed almost reasonable compared with New York City. The commuter rail would make an easy commute for them, and Phoebe could be within reach for the kids and Jake. In a few years, Kate and then Noah could work at the Cupcake Project.

"So? What do you think?" Zoya held up a cupcake frosted in a perfect swirl of caramel and chocolate.

"Magnificent looking," Eva said.

"Tastes even better." Zoya offered the cupcake to Eva, who leaned over from the end of the table where she was making concentric circles of red, white, and blue sugar for a batch of Fourth of July cupcakes and took a small bite.

"Oh, that's heaven," Eva said. "Though by now, my palate is sugar deadened."

"Me, me!" Noah said. "My mouth is alive!"

"You already tested a Ginger Heaven," Linh said. "Can he have another, Phoebe?"

"What the heck. Eventually he'll get tired of them, right?" Phoebe wiped her hands on a red-striped apron and glanced at the clock. Five. She loaded baking tins into the dishwasher and then wiped smudges off the copper backsplash.

Jake and her mother were due at six thirty, giving her just enough time to shower and make dinner for the kids and Lola. The chicken marinated. A fresh rye loaf waited for slicing. If she and the kids worked hard, they could whip the place into shape. At one point in the not-too-distant past, she'd have chosen a wine for dinner, her tool for shaving away Jake's irritation, but he'd recently become a teetotaler. She tried to remember when he'd stopped completely but could only recall a gradual cutback from a few cocktails after work, to one, to a small glass of wine, to nothing. "I lost my taste for the stuff," he'd say.

She considered her formerly flawless nails: only flakes remained of the eye-bleeding red she'd applied two days ago. Add repainting nails to the list of chores to be done before leaving for some temple dinner with Jake.

"Mom, listen to my idea." Kate jumped down from the stool where she'd been shaving chocolate for Eva. "Listen, everyone listen!"

"We're all listening," Zoya said.

"We make aprons, in all sizes—including ones for kids—and sell them at the store. People will buy them for their daughters and their granddaughters."

"You should make them for boys also. Boys bake," Noah said.

"I'll draw designs," Linh said.

"We can do T-shirts also." Kate twirled in excitement. "And little notebooks and other things."

"Maybe we'll be the new Hello Kitty," Phoebe said.

"We should invent Cupcake Kitty!" Kate said.

"Two Cupcake Kitties—a boy and a girl," Noah said.

"Is that your goal, Noah?" Jake's unmistakable voice boomed. "To be a kitten boy?"

Jake stood in the entrance to the kitchen, Lola behind him. The same lines around the eyes and initial grey hairs that had aged Phoebe—every sign engendering another purchase for her arsenal of antiaging products—added another level of gravitas and attraction to Jake. His middle had broadened, but so had his back and shoulders. He looked more imposing each year.

"Why not just buy him a rhinestone tiara, Pheebs?" Jake smiled as though he were making a joke and then examined the kitchen with a theatrical expression of shock. "We're zoned for factory work now?"

"You're home early," Phoebe said.

"I planned on taking my wife for a glass of wine before we went to the synagogue dinner. Who knew I'd be interrupting the Sara Lee sweatshop?"

"I told you we were working here today," she said.

"You did?"

"I did."

Frozen expressions spread through the room. Zoya was the only one who didn't appear about to curtsy.

Lola pushed in front of Jake. "Are these the extraordinary women I've been hearing so much about? Finally I get to try one of these temptations. What do you recommend?"

Phoebe's hand shook as she grabbed a caramel chocolate cupcake and handed it to her mother, grateful for her presence. Lola helped soak up those moods of Jake's that Phoebe absorbed in seconds. The older Phoebe became, the more she appreciated her mother's wisdom and the more she saw the beauty of her parents' marriage. They might not experience the same highs as she and Jake, but at this moment, Phoebe would sacrifice those to lose the lows.

"We'll straighten up in here," Eva said. "Go put on your finery."

"I need to drive you to the train first."

"Don't worry, honey," her mother said. "I'll call a cab for them."

Jake peeled off three twenties and laid the bills on the counter. "This should cover the fare."

The taxi's meter wouldn't rise above ten dollars. Phoebe squeezed the sponge hard enough to feel her nails through the cellulose as she attempted not to scream at Jake's need to smooth his every move with cash.

. . .

"You embarrassed me." Phoebe's words came after a long silence during which she'd showered and dressed.

"Coming home to the international house of baking isn't my idea of fun. For God's sake, this is my home." He picked up the paisley tie Phoebe had placed on the bed. His burnished leather belt offered a rich contrast with the silk mauve bedspread.

"Those are my friends. My coworkers."

"Seriously, Pheebs? They're not your friends; they're your project. They make you feel good about yourself. You're their Lady Bountiful. We can write a check and bring the same result."

For the second time in an hour, she used tricks against crying: Biting her tongue just past the edge of pain. Squeezing every muscle in an isotonic feat of unseen rigidity. She smelled a fight coming, but she wasn't in the mood for backing down. "The Cupcake Project is the opposite of charity. This project means dignity. Work."

He pulled on a fresh white shirt. "That's not the issue. I feel as though you're half here. You're ignoring the kids—"

"Ignoring? The kids love this. They're spending more time with me than with their friends."

"They love being able to eat sugary crap whenever they want. What are you teaching them?"

"About helping people. Hard work."

"You're in another world half the time," he said. "I feel as though we're losing you, baby."

Again, she felt twisted in confusion. Did he think she was always going to be here tending to any need he and the kids had at any given moment?

Jake tightened his tie. "You complain about your mother watching you and Deb like a hawk, but she cared a hell of a lot. You guys were number one for her. I want the same for our kids. For me. You're the best wife and mother in the world, Pheebs. You hold us together. Don't let go."

. . .

Two weeks later, tangy ocean air rushed through the open windows. Indian summer had slipped in. Phoebe lifted the covers to slide out of bed.

"Wait." Jake put a hand on her arm and pulled her toward him. "Why are you jumping out of bed?"

"It's early," she whispered. "Sleep."

"It's not sleep I want." He brought her down to the cave of warmth their bodies made. He slipped his hand between her thighs. "It's you."

"I want you also, but—"

"But you're running away from me to work. I know. Because I'm a bastard." He rolled her to her back and raised her hands above her head. "I'm sorry. We can't lose this time, or someday we'll regret it. This life might not always be ours," he whispered.

Jake sounded scared, as though they were back when she was in college, and he'd wanted her to stay with him in Brooklyn. He lifted himself above her, his still-muscled arms on either side. "You keep me together."

After, he fell back asleep, and she tiptoed downstairs. As the coffee brewed, she sketched out a menu board. More important projects needed attention—a budget, an ordering system, and the many other tasks to divide up between her and Eva as business managers—but designing with colored pencils invigorated her. Writing up lists of people to approach for funds? Not so enjoyable.

Women people.

Jake didn't know, but Phoebe's intent was to eventually fund the Cupcake Project without him, to make it a woman-owned business, funded by women, for the benefit of the women served by Mira

House. Helen thought it might interest *Ms. Magazine*, with the magazine listing it as an ethical investment.

An hour flew by while she worked during the quiet early morning. Jake and the kids would be up soon. After planning breakfast in her head—slow-cooked oatmeal—she checked on her list of donors to approach, beginning with Helen. Helen had a load of money but Jake still refused to take her and Alan into the Club, because Alan's law office did work for Fidelity Investments. "He'll be hocking me for details. I know the type." Jake repeated the same bullshit anytime Phoebe mentioned them joining.

Phoebe and Helen maintained their closeness despite Jake's and Alan's enmity, agreeing that husbands were an entirely different breed of humanity. If women let the success of their friendships rest on their menfolk, there'd be nothing but lonely women out there.

Helen had lots of rich corporate clients. The only break she took for each of her kids' births was three months. Her mother, who lived with them, virtually raised Helen's three daughters, and the arrangement worked. Helen's commitment to women's rights had brought her all the way to serving on the board of the National Organization for Women. If Phoebe didn't ask her to invest, she'd feel insulted.

Everything about the Cupcake Project delighted Phoebe. From the moment she'd slipped Betty Friedan's *The Feminine Mystique* from her mother's nightstand a month before Phoebe's high school graduation, she'd believed there had to be more to life than marriage and children. Two lines from the book remained wedged in her memory: "It is easier to live through someone else than to become complete yourself," and "The only way for a woman, as for a man, to find herself, to know herself as a person, is by creative work of her own."

First Mira House, now the Cupcake Project, and soon, she hoped, like Jake, she'd travel in boardrooms. Boardrooms of her own.

· · ·

Phoebe kicked off her too-high heels and rubbed her instep. "Thank God that's over." The awful country club they'd visited for cocktails receded in the side mirror view. If Trinity Chapel in Manhattan married Stonehenge and then birthed a faux Guggenheim in a frightening version of modern meets caveman, the result would be that building.

"Want to go to the movies?" Jake asked.

"Are you kidding? I can't wait to take off this dress. We can watch something at home."

"Come on. It's only eight. We'll go to the movie theater at the mall in Stamford. I'll buy you a damned sweat suit at Saks on the way if you want to be comfortable." He placed a hand on her thigh and squeezed. "I need this right now. A little escape."

She looked at him as though he'd grown a second nose. "Jake. Really. It's too late. We can watch a movie on TV."

"I want to relax in a big dark theater. Do you think these nights are fun for me?"

"They're sure not *my* idea of a good time."

"They're not supposed to be fun. They pay for being able to have our lives." Jake opened the heating vent. "I need a break."

"Let's have a true break." She squeezed his knee. "Seriously. We can ratchet everything down and make our lives simpler."

"Really?" He pulled off the exit for the mall. "You think it's that easy? Boom, we ratchet it down? Are you ready to give up your project?"

"We're not out nights and traveling for my business."

"You don't have a business, baby. Cupcakes? You have a charity masquerading as a business-to-be that I'm underwriting."

Jake could turn mean in one second. She felt as though he'd slapped her. Their marriage undertows, these hurricanes of love disassembling, were impossible for Phoebe to follow. When Jake spoiled for a fight, he'd twist through any road to spew out his mood. If she simply remained still, the storm passed, but immobility brought another kind of poison.

"Fine," she said. "Hide your checkbook. I don't need you."

"Oh? And just exactly how do you plan to pay for opening your bakery? Selling your jewelry?"

Phoebe looked at the upgraded engagement and wedding rings that hung too heavy on her small hands. She wished. Trading these oversized jewels for a leaded glass window for the Cupcake Project would thrill her. She drew dream windows from memory, based on an art deco storefront she'd once seen in Harvard Square in Cambridge, Massachusetts.

"I'm getting investors. Four are already lined up. Ethical investors."

Jake pulled the car over to the side of the road, slamming the brakes as he parked in a shallow inlet of sand surrounded by weather-dried rosebushes. He captured her wrist with a grip that bordered on painful. "What the fuck is that supposed to mean?"

Phoebe went rigid. "I didn't mean anything. Calm down."

"'Ethical investors'? You didn't mean anything?"

"I meant approaching groups of women who pledge to invest in programs designed to do good. Like organic farms. Windmills. Or businesses to help immigrant women."

Jake's hand loosened.

"What did you think I meant?" She curled her toes till they ached to keep from crying, from screaming.

"Nothing."

"You didn't mean 'nothing,' Jake. You almost broke my wrist."

He took a series of deep breaths. "Why didn't you just say yes to the damned movie? Then this wouldn't have happened. You do this to me all the time. By the way, I don't want you begging for money, making me look like a cheapskate. Just let me know what you need. Do you hear? I'll pay for it."

War raged in her chest. Swears bubbled up. *Screw you, Jake.* Cravings to bolt from the car, march away, and never return, filled her.

"What do you think it will look like—asking strangers for money? Did you think of how it looks?" He took her hand and held it softly. "I'm sorry. I didn't mean to scare you."

Phoebe ripped a ladder up her stockings as she raked her legs to keep hateful words at bay. "Not everything is about you. Not everything is about the business."

"No!" His face became so red that Phoebe worried about a stroke or heart attack. "Everything is about the business! How we live, how we walk, how we talk. We're selling dreams, for God's sake! Do you understand? Nobody is funding this but me."

She didn't understand. Phoebe really didn't understand a word of his reasoning except this: his dreams would always trump hers.

CHAPTER 14

PHOEBE

Phoebe had learned to use silence and smiles to ensure the maintenance of both her marriage and the Cupcake Project since the inception of her business almost a year ago.

She slipped her hand in Jake's as they left the movie theater after seeing a sneak preview of *On Golden Pond*. "Think that will ever be us?" After speaking she considered how abnormal it was to ache for a relationship of a couple nearing the end of their lives, even one played by Katharine Hepburn and Henry Fonda.

His odd chuckle sent shivers through her. "Sure. I can be a bastard right to the end. But if we're living nice and quiet at that age, then miracles actually do come true."

"Why would a quiet life be a miracle? I don't need a mansion overlooking the Riviera."

His laugh sounded strange. "Wish for the mansion."

She pulled away her hand and crossed her arms. "Did you go to the doctor? Is there something you're not telling me?"

"Take it down a notch. I'm gonna be forty, not eighty."

"Do they know what's causing the pains in your chest? The rest?" Phoebe wasn't a fool. Men could die before they turned forty. Twice this month, Jake woke with chills, panting, and with his heart racing. She'd begged him to go to the doctor, calling him at work every day to drive home her point.

"It's nothing. Come on." He pulled her close and nuzzled her neck. "You smell good. I like this new perfume. Let's go for a walk. Doctor's prescription. Then we'll go home and screw. My prescription."

She pushed him away. "Waking up at midnight clutching your chest is not nothing."

"So you'll miss me when I'm gone?"

"Seriously. Did you go?"

"Okay, okay!" He raised his palms. "Enough. Yes. I went."

"And?"

"And I didn't want to tell you. I have maybe a year to live. Two, if I'm lucky. Two months if you're lucky."

Phoebe closed her eyes and shook her head. "Tell me what she said."

He brought her close for a hug. "You care."

"You have doubt?"

"Trust, but verify," he said.

"Spill." They reached the quiet road leading to Greenwich's Bruce Museum, where they often walked after seeing a movie. Though they'd only been inside the building once, they felt a certain ownership. Films were Jake's escape—the stroll afterward, hers.

"She was baffled how a man nearing forty could be so extraordinarily vital, so exceedingly handsome. So sexy."

"If you keep this up, you might die before we get home."

"Okay, no big deal. Apparently I have the disease of the day."

"Diabetes?" It ran in his family. His mother and all her sisters were on insulin.

"Honestly, do I seem five hundred years old?" He tried to give her a theatrical kiss, but she pulled away.

"Do we need to play twenty questions before I get an answer?"

"Heebie-jeebies. Sleeplessness, sweat, the pounding heart, the pain in my arm—all symptoms of panic or anxiety attacks."

"Did she test your heart?" For heart disease, she could lower his salt, cook low fat, and force Jake to adopt whatever measures the doctor suggested. "What do you do for these attacks? Does she think you should go to a shrink?"

"I'm sure she does," he said.

"And? What are you going to do?" Just last night, Jake had woken drenched in sweat and shaking. When she asked what she could do, he shook his head, looking so stricken she thought he might cry. Finally, still silent, he left and turned the shower on full blast. When she'd tried the bathroom door—worried his heart would give out while she did nothing—it was locked. He'd answered her knocks with only a muffled "Go away."

"Good question," he said. "I'm gonna walk it off like an athlete."

"Very funny."

"I'm not making a joke. Play in the big leagues, pay the price."

"She can't give you anything?"

"What? Valium? Taking drugs are your first reaction?"

"It's not my only thought, but it's an answer."

They made a second pass around the wooded museum property and then headed back down toward Steamboat Road. She knew the chance of his taking a mind-altering drug was slim. These days, Jake not only didn't drink, he worshipped sobriety the way others genuflected before God. Phoebe tried to trace his path from the usual teenage beer and pot binges, to social cocktails, to becoming the King of Temperance, but like so much in marriage, Jake's drinking changes were incremental. She imagined that his odd Calvinism extended to prescription drugs.

"I have two choices, Pheebs. Live with it or drive it out with exercise. We'll install a gym, okay? Hell, we can both use it." He reached over and pinched her midsection. "Is that a chocolate cupcake I feel?"

"Screw you." Now Phoebe lusted for Breyers cherry vanilla. Not scooping out a big bowl for him and one anemic spoonful for her, but eating the entire gallon.

"Sorry," he said. "You're still the prettiest girl I've ever seen."

"Is that why you feel such a need to shoot me down?"

He put an arm around her waist. "I don't know why I do half the things I do."

. . .

Phoebe, Eva, Linh, and Zoya sat in silence, stunned by the reality of being in the actual store of the Cupcake Project, waiting to open the doors for the first time. This, their opening party, was timed for an after-school launch. Based on Jake's advice, invitations containing a golden ticket for a dozen free cupcakes a month had been sent all over the community: the wealthy wanted something for nothing as much as the needy. Maybe more, as so many of them got rich by being cheap bastards.

Noah and Katie, already excited at being allowed to miss a day of school, investigated every inch of the place, narrating as they explored.

"I adore this!" Katie held up a pearly-white notebook with a stylized triptych of blue-glittered cupcakes on a lemony background—their logo. "Can I have one? Please, please, please!"

Phoebe offered her a ten-dollar bill. "Here. You'll be our lucky first sale."

"I'll write notes during the opening." Katie skipped to the register for Linh to ring her up. "We'll have a permanent memory of the first of the countrywide chain of Cupcake Projects."

"Since you'll be our historian, we should throw in a pen." Linh plucked a sparkly blue marker from a pottery jug on the counter.

Impulse buys were scattered around the shop. Business had initially brought friendship to the four of them; then they had fallen into the frenzied first stages of friend love. Phoebe took care not to show how much she preferred their company to anyone else's, including that of her husband. In her proudest moment of wrangling Jake, she had convinced him to support a fund-raiser for Mira House—with the proceeds earmarked for giving women internships at the Cupcake Factory—flattering him until he threw his full business weight behind the event. They had raised over $500,000. Better yet, he had invested the money for Mira House, along with its capital fund. Now Mira House was a member of the Club.

Zoya polished the bakery's antique golden oak floors until sunlight glinted off the wood. After trying out wrought iron stools, they decided comfort should reign. They wanted a place that parents and children would seek out. White paper on rollers covered square tables with mason jars of crayons plunked in the middle. The padded chairs, with oilcloth seats the color of lemon ices, had rungs where short legs could rest.

Their coffee machine was so massive it required two men for delivery and set up. Airy low-fat angel food cupcakes, along with "Skinny Kisses"—chocolate chip meringues with a whisper of sugar overdosed on vanilla—would draw in the thin sweet-desperate women of Greenwich.

Blue ribbon with yellow polka dots waited to be curled around gift boxes. Smaller orders would go into Provence blue bags with yellow circles.

An old-fashioned jukebox anticipated sugary fingers holding quarters. Songs from Frank Sinatra, Blondie, Pat Benatar, Michael Jackson, and Devo were chosen to satisfy all tastes and ages.

Jake had promised to leave work early to be there for the opening. Deb would bring their parents from Brooklyn.

"Mom?" Noah stood in front of her, solemnity shading his eyes.

"What, baby?"

"You really love this store, right?"

She didn't think Noah would ask if she loved the store more than him; her sensitive boy skewed in other directions. At ten, he fretted over small beach creatures. Last weekend, he spent the afternoon guiding crabs back to the surf until Jake went to see why Noah had been crouching on the sand for hours.

"What the hell are you doing scavenging there all day?" Jake had yelled down from the deck, causing Noah to lie and say he was searching for coins.

Jake worried that Noah's soft side would lead to poetry or painting. "Who cares?" she'd finally asked when his sputtering about their son's time helping her bake became unbearable. "He can spend his life throwing pots on a wheel if that's his passion."

Jake had puffed up like a bullfrog until she'd thought he might actually physically explode at the idea of his son becoming a ceramicist.

"He's coming into the business," Jake had declared.

"You need to get over yourself, my darling." Phoebe turned to leave, but his determination to have the last word was stronger and faster than her stride.

"He needs to learn to be a man."

"He's ten."

"He's my son."

"And mine." She'd lowered her voice. "Let him be himself. Come on, honey. Let's see you relax for a few minutes. Why don't we join him and see what's so interesting."

She'd managed to jolly Jake into an old Brooklyn College sweatshirt and onto the beach, where Noah went from stiffening up to showing off, once he saw that Jake was interested in his rescue operation.

"You see," Jake had said, as though coming down to the sand had been his idea. "This is what it's all about. Being able to walk down the stairs and be right here on the beach as a family."

Phoebe leaned against him, his wide shoulders protecting her from the wind behind them. "When we were kids, Noah, a trip to the beach was a huge deal," she explained. "Packing sandwiches. Packing up the car. Walking for miles over hot sand to get a space to put our blanket. See what Daddy has given us?"

Katie snuck up behind them. "Am I invited?" She and Noah skipped down to the shoreline. Soon the two of them were working together to build a rescue-the-crabs roadway.

Brilliant sun warmed them enough to combat the March wind. Phoebe left the comfort of Jake's protective arms long enough to run upstairs and make egg salad sandwiches—harkening back to the ones her mother used to bring to Coney Island. When she returned, Jake lay back on two elbows, looking more relaxed than she'd seen him in too many years.

Remembering that day, Phoebe planted another seed for her Noah. "Yes. I do love the Cupcake Project. Remember, as an adult, you'll spend almost as much time working as with your family. Maybe more. Make sure you choose work that makes you happy, my darling boy."

. . .

By six o'clock, women, children, and a sprinkling of men packed the bakery. Phoebe's parents kept squeezing her hand and grinning. "See, this is what I always wanted," her mother said. "For you to use your head. Where's Jake?"

"Lola, he runs a huge business," her father said. "Anything could happen."

"Stop apologizing for him, Red."

Phoebe held up her hands. "He'll get here when he gets here. Drink some champagne and have fun."

Deb steered Phoebe from their parents, throwing back an apology as she did. "Sorry, guys. Eva is looking for her." As they walked away, she whispered, "I'll run interference with them. Don't worry."

"Have I appreciated you enough all these years?" Phoebe asked her sister.

Eva circulated with glasses of champagne for the adults and cherry-studded ginger ale for the kids. Phoebe grabbed an overfilled glass and drank it fast. Jake's absence felt deliberate. She turned when the bell tinkled over the door, opening for another guest. Ira Henriquez smiled, looking thrilled to see the crowd. She knew that as the Mira House director, he'd be happy—but his joy emanated from their growing closeness.

"Phoebe!" Ira grabbed her in a bear hug. He gestured around the room. "Damn. You're a miracle."

She pointed to Eva, Zoya, and Linh in succession. "If there's miracle status to hand out, it belongs to all of us."

The previous night, she'd put up the three of them in the swank local inn, despite their protests, wanting a good-luck dinner together. Linh's husband would never have let her out for the entire night—his suspicions were always at red alert level—so Eva and Zoya had cooked up a story of Phoebe screeching that she needed all of them working through the night to ready the bakery.

By the second glass of wine, they'd become almost hysterical laughing as Linh imitated her husband swearing. She'd risen to her full five feet, making her eyes angry threads as she spat a mix of Vietnamese and English through her lips. "Who is supposed to watch kids and cook? My mother? That white witch thinks she owns you. *An Cu Cua Toi.*" Linh dropped character and lowered her voice. "That's what he said. Which means you should eat his cock."

"Would that be worthwhile?" Zoya asked.

"Ptui!" Linh imitated gagging. "Like licking a wriggling worm."

Now Phoebe grinned, remembering the night. Ira smiled back, seeming to mistake her mirth as happiness at seeing him.

"I brought the entire board of directors," he said. "We rented a van." Ira bit into a cherry chocolate cupcake. "Jesus Christ. Heaven on earth."

Zoya popped up between them, opening her arms wide and leaping on Ira, who protected his cupcake by holding it above his head. Jealousy flashed through Phoebe—her infatuation, she prayed, remained well hidden from the world. Hell, every woman in Mira House was half in love with Ira. Combine his cowboy aura with his seeming ability to rescue an entire town and—abracadabra—the perfect man.

A buzz went up.

Jake walked in.

Ira turned. "Seems like someone important just came in."

"My husband." Phoebe remembered they'd never met, Ira and Jake, and she wasn't looking forward to the encounter. They knew her from such different angles.

"The man behind the woman?"

"The man who financed most of this operation."

"Introduce us so I can thank him."

Together they walked toward Jake. Her husband's hug reminded her how men read each other like jungle animals. If Jake had a ruff, it would have doubled in size.

Ira put out his hand. "We owe you a debt of gratitude."

"For giving over my wife?" Jake grinned.

"Jake believes in the chattel theory of marriage," Phoebe said.

"Humor. Love's favorite servant," Ira said.

"Is that a quote?" Phoebe asked.

"Just made it up," Ira said.

"A humanitarian plus a poet." Jake clapped Ira on the back. "You deserve the gratitude, I'd think. Sacrificing so much for so little."

"Little? Hardly." Ira cocked his head and studied Jake. "My work's not measurable by a gold standard, but I sleep well at night."

"Thank goodness for men of mammon to support saintly works."

Zoya insinuated herself between Ira and Jake and clapped their broad backs. "The two big shots finally meet." She caught a glance at the four of them in the mirror. "We look good, huh? We should all go out sometime."

"Who knows, maybe we will," Ira said. "We'll celebrate as we look back at the beginning of the Mira House fortune. Created by Phoebe. Brought to life by Mira House. Invested with Jake."

CHAPTER 15

JAKE

April 1986

Compared with New York, Cambridge in April looked bucolic—at least from where Jake waited for Gita-Rae's call. Outside the limo, students, professionals, and even the street people moved at a leisurely pace that made New Yorkers resemble overwound toy soldiers.

Jake enjoyed saying "My daughter's at Harvard," but the kid better think twice before thinking she could settle here. Living in New England was fine for college, but she'd be back in New York when she went to graduate school.

He planned for both the kids to work at JPE. Only in the brokerage side, of course, until he got caught up at the Club or shut down the entire pain in the ass. Keeping that garbage from Phoebe and the kids, now and forever, was his top priority.

Jake glanced at his watch: 10:01. Gita-Rae was late. Phoebe would kill him if he didn't return to the restaurant before the food came. He reached for his worn brown notebook, identical to the hundreds he kept in a locked drawer in his home office, each used for only one purpose: tracking the Club funds. Every page was divided in two and then labeled in his own hand:

Cash In: Funds brought in with new accounts.
Cash Out: Withdrawals by clients.

All written in unintelligible shorthand.

Each morning, he checked his personal account balances—some in his name, most in a joint account with Phoebe, some in just Phoebe's name—against the Club account. Their personal savings were spread between Fidelity and three banks.

Jake monitored the in and out more often than he shaved—which was a feat, because his beard grew so thick that he needed two shaves a day.

Two things let him breathe: checking the numbers with Gita-Rae and making sure his father had enough tasks. He couldn't stand picturing his old man slouched in front of the boob tube. Jake kept him busy; made him feel worthwhile. He wrote out a list of senior centers where his father could pass out business cards. Not Jake's—ones from Gallagher & Graham.

Ronnie Gallagher, no longer the green young assistant he was for Uncle Gus back in the Bronx, had formed the bookkeeping partnership of Gallagher & Graham, also known as G&G. They fed more clients to the Club than anyone—though lately, the Cook and Baylor Equity Fund in New Jersey showed promise for bringing in the horsey set.

The shrill ring of the mobile assaulted him.

"Ready," he said.

"Good morning to you." Gita's sibilant release of smoke brought her essence through the static-ridden connection, as though her particular mix of acrid tobacco, coffee, and Opium perfume ran through the air.

"Let's do this fast." Jake held up his thin-tipped pen, ready as always to fit as much as possible on each page. "I need to charge this damned phone already."

"First, the good news. Louie Klein's secretary called. He's putting in another 125K. Apparently some guru is looking at a downturn—in the middle of everything skyrocketing, this wizard's playing Chicken Little—and Louie's shoving more into the Club for safety."

"We have great affection for wizards, and we love Louis to death." Klein, his largest Club member, treated Jake like family. His vast fortune came from *Guance Rosee*, his exclusive line of skin care and makeup. Women shelled out for the overpriced products, unaware the popular lipsticks—*Ciliegie, Peonia, and Viola*—carried nothing from Italy but the name. Klein chased every dime. When Uncle Gus, his childhood friend, introduced Klein to Jake, he said, "Ask Louis to show you his first nickel."

"Here's the bad news. Three of G&G's biggest fish decided to invest in some start-up company. They took out everything."

A familiar cold swept through him. "How much?" He girded himself. Tomorrow he'd start on a game plan. Write an outline to put everything in order. No more bullshit. After he paid his clients the amounts shown on their statements, he'd shut down the Club. Concentrate on the brokerage. Fuck it. This arrangement had gone way past the sell-by date.

"A blip compared with everything else."

"How much of a blip?"

"Five hundred K."

Jake covered the phone's mouthpiece. *Fuck, fuck, fuck!* "Thanks, Gita-Rae. No big deal, but glad you're tracking it, darling." He knocked the tips of his fingers against his upper chest, right in the center, where Phoebe said anxiety rested.

"Always earning my keep, boss."

Everyone in the ghetto up on the thirty-seventh floor believed that he sat atop alps of cash, which, of course, was Jake's intention. On the downside, Gita-Rae assumed a withdrawal of $500K meant no more than an accounting entry.

What did she think of the daily tally he insisted upon? Did she gossip about the numbers with Charlie? Not with Nanci—Gita-Rae prized keeping her distinction of boss lady. She considered Charlie a peer, notwithstanding his raise in stature since Jake named him the company's chief financial officer.

Despite the swanky new offices that JPE had occupied for a year now, the Club staff still rolled around in a dusty pigsty, believing they had one up on the straitlaced brokers and management above them on floor thirty-eight. They played by different rules, locked away in their clubhouse, thinking that Jake allowed this because they knew the real deal. They thought he exploited some ultimate irony of investment. While feeder fund managers talked about his secret strategies of buying in and selling out with a razor-sharp timing particular to Jake's spectacular system (believing him a virtual savant of investing), the Club staff understood that the seeming investments he made—the ones listed on statements—were made possible by wedding a brilliant computer program to his staff's slog work. The statements represented nothing more than numbers on paper. They assumed his transactions were made outside the realm of acceptable—thus needing padding between reality and public information.

Some of their guesses about where the money rested traveled to his ears: Swiss bank accounts that allowed singular interest rates available only to a chosen few; treasure chests of illegal doubloons growing in value at an unprecedented degree; or maybe secreted stores of oil, ready to be uncovered when a depleted world would pay quintuple the rate.

While they crowed at the piracy they imagined him pulling off, they never doubted that the provenance of growth existed—that a pile of cash, wherever it might be hidden, grew each day. This he knew, because to a man, they invested with the Club themselves, devoting a portion of their princely salaries and bonuses to their own Club accounts, convinced of the safety, if not the legality, of their bottom lines.

Jake vowed he'd catch up and make it whole. He just didn't know how or when.

"Okay. Got it," he said to Gita-Rae. "Call Ronnie at G&G and also Cook and Baylor's girl."

"Cynthia?"

"Whoever. Give them a message: April is now our bonus month. A four percent incentive kicker for all new accounts over 200K. Solomon can put in the proper bullshit language to make it kosher."

Jake hung up, secure in Solomon's way with words and Gita-Rae's dogged follow-through. He scribbled down the numbers Gita-Rae had given him and then dialed his father. His mother answered with her usual whine of a greeting.

"Ma, I need to talk to Dad."

"No time for even hello?"

"I'm on the mobile phone, with maybe five minutes left."

"Fancy-pants family on the move. How are the kids? Are you enjoying the trip? I don't care, but your father should occasionally see a piece of the world out of Brooklyn."

"Ma, I bought you a car."

"How far do you think I'll drive with your father and his shaky hands?"

"Put Dad on. Phoebe's waiting for me."

When nothing else worked, citing Phoebe made the difference in shutting down his mother. His wife induced subservience, likely the worship of beauty dressed by money.

"Jakie?" His father sounded tired. "You need something?"

"Gita-Rae has a new list of senior centers. She's gonna set up some presentations for you to give. Put on your good suit. Bring us new clients."

He heard his father growing taller. The old man loved doing the act and believed every word he said.

Jake returned to the table with thoughts of needing to make up 500K thrumming like a curse. He barely heard the kids and Phoebe's words as he tried to process the number. When Phoebe's hand came to rest on top of the *New York Times*, pulling down the page to see him just as Jake began reading the second paragraph of the story, his heart was racing. He pressed his lips together and flicked her hand away.

"Are you going to read throughout the entire brunch?" she asked. "First you're out there on the phone and now the paper? This trip's about Katie. What went on out there? Your mood was fine before you talked to the office."

"I'm here! Should I gaze into Kate's eyes every second?" He turned to his daughter. "No offense, honey."

"It's okay, Mom," Noah said. "Nobody cares if Dad reads the paper."

Jake wasn't blind. He frightened Noah—sure, he knew that—but the boy needed toughening. He wanted his kids resilient, not babied into a life spent as a rich man's children. Especially Noah. Kate's moxie never failed her. Jake didn't alarm her—which annoyed him or amused him, depending on his mood.

Jake shook the *Times* back into crispness. "I gotta stay on the ball. Remember what happened to Steve Jobs last year. They threw him out of Apple, his own company. That's why you don't go public. The poor *schmendrick* poured his life into his company and they booted his ass out. Remember this when I'm gone."

"He brought Apple public to get megabucks for expansion. That's how he went from rich to insanely wealthy." Kate tapped the tabletop. "But he still wanted control, which you lose once a board is in place, right? He lost the fight. That's business, Dad."

Ah, the assurance of youth. One year at Harvard and she could analyze Apple and Steve Jobs.

"Correct, my Harvard genius. This is what I'm paying the bills for. But nothing is more important than control. You go public, you give it up."

"We know your strategy: One, keep the money in the family." Kate made an invisible checkmark.

"Two, keep the power in the family." Noah made a second and more dramatic checkmark.

People groveling at the office meant nothing. This, his family, was everything.

"Three, keep the most power for yourself," Phoebe said. "You never fail there."

"Complaining?" Jake held up her hand and rattled the collection of bracelets. "You want diamonds *and* power?"

Kate lifted his wrist, turning his hand to see the time displayed on his Patek Philippe. "You have both. Why shouldn't Mom?"

"We all do fine in this family." There were worse things than his drawer of watches. Opening the dresser to his velvet tray of neatly lined gold and leather soothed him no end. Matching a timepiece to his suit, strapping it on, and shooting his cuffs marked the beginning of his day.

He lifted the ugly brown mug to drink the last of his coffee. How had they ended up at this place? Pewter Pot. The big teapot hanging outside and the dark wood and waitresses in frilly aprons were meant to make them feel as though they were visiting Ye Olde London instead of Harvard Square. Fat chance with street kids hustling for change everywhere and others begging you to support everything from AIDS research to homeless veterans.

Jake folded the paper and handed it to Phoebe, who stuffed it in her straw bag. "You'll find out what working for your money means this summer. See what you think about me and Steve Jobs after sweating your way through the jobs I have planned for you on the brokerage floor."

"I keep telling you, I'm going to Southampton," Kate declared. "Uncle Theo said I'd be doing him a favor, keeping an eye on the kids."

"Babysitting while you bake on the beach? With the partying going on there? No way. Between the drugs, the alcohol, and the rich boys looking to get laid, anything could happen. Sleep with someone these days, and you're taking your life in your hands."

"God, Daddy. I want to help Uncle Theo and Aunt Ellen watch the kids, and you have me dead of AIDS. Don't you trust my judgment at all?"

"*You* I have faith in. In the Hamptons, I believe nobody. You'll work at the brokerage and drive in with me."

Kate slapped the table. "I don't want a job with you. I don't even want to go to the Hamptons. You know what I want? To be at Mira House. I just knew you'd flip out. Ira said I could work at the summer camp."

"After I said no, you called Ira?" he asked Phoebe.

"Having options is never a bad thing." She stabbed a piece of pancake. "We never decided anything for certain."

"Mom said I could be a junior counselor," Noah added. "Kate and I could take the train in together."

"Or they can go in with me," Phoebe said. "I've been thinking I need to spend more time there."

Jake bet that Ira would love that. "Why don't you just devote every minute you have to the halt and lame? Oh, wait. You do."

They had set him up. Put forth the Hamptons and then he'd say okay to the Lower East Side? He didn't slave so that his kids and wife could grime away down there while he came home to an empty house. He'd be damned if the three of them went off to save the world with cupcakes and basketballs, while he looked like Scrooge counting money in the back room.

"Of course they're going to hire the kids. You practically support Mira House," Jake said.

"That's not the point." Phoebe did her angry-finger thing, tapping on her thighs, probably pretending she was drumming against his head. "They should learn life outside Greenwich and the Hamptons; outside the entire money world."

"Forget it, Mother Teresa. They don't need to learn poverty— what's required for the future is that you understand my business. You want to help more, then why don't you really help? Of course you should give. Jesus, bring my checkbook, I'll write any number you want. But the kids stay with me." He turned to Kate. "You're not going to Uncle Theo's. He never should have asked you without checking in first. You're coming to work with me. And you?" He looked at his son. "I'll get you a job at the marina. That's that."

CHAPTER 16

JAKE

October 1987

"Zip, please."

Phoebe turned her back to him, peering over her shoulder. The gaping zipper revealed velvety skin curtained by black satin. Ownership, love, and admiration smacked into a collision of desire as he ran his finger from the hollow of her spine up to the fine hairs escaping her stern bun. In the hotel mirror, he saw the abstract painting, a slash of red and black, juxtaposed against his delicate wife.

The doc should have prescribed sex instead of pushing Prozac, although right now he could use both. His jaw was tight as the Tin Man's before the oiling. Tonight he'd throw his Hail Mary pass, a chance at salvation in a world gone mad with new technology. Hooking potential Club members on the notion of guaranteed steady returns became difficult when men believed any computer-connected stock was bound for Microsoft glory.

Jake hated thinking how much he'd have if he'd actually bought shares during Microsoft's initial public offering. Twenty-fucking-eight dollars per share on offering. Now, after splitting and rising ad nauseam, a share was worth $143. He'd be up fifteen million if he'd made the trades he purported.

Fuck it. His ass could be in the gutter just as easy. Might as well gamble in Vegas as play the market. Life would smooth out with his new legitimacy plan.

Staying positive meant concentrating on the future. Look at the brokerage, running like silk over glass. Theo kept a tight lid on the staff at JPE. Solomon added the gravitas. Where other firms let their guys go wild, Jake screwed the lid tight: no flash, no fucking in the stairwell, no snorting coke in the men's room. No goddamned dwarf tossing. Some of the stories he'd heard—Jesus, his sins were the least of the Street's crimes.

Hell, last year *Asset Magazine* had declared JPE the best-kept secret on Wall Street, the broker's brokerage—the high-tech king straitlaced enough for your grandmother. His secretary had blown up the article, framed it in brushed steel, and placed the image front and center in the lobby where people entered.

If he'd written it himself, the piece couldn't have been better. Plus, they had only whispered a mention of the Club: "Pierce's powerful under-the-radar investment arm is almost impossible to join—rumor has it that entry requires being vetted by a hush-hush cadre of those in the know, whom nobody can identify. One source called it 'Jake's toy,' where he gets to mix his ingredients for investments only available to preferred clients."

After the article hit the newsstands, potential clients begged for Club membership, but he remained distant, ensuring that they believed only pushing the proper buttons opened the gate to Jake's magic castle. Now every asshole with a computer wanted to play day trader, forgetting that what went up also came down. Meanwhile, the Club's daily cash in and cash out drifted further apart, and he needed an infusion.

He slid Phoebe's zipper up and then teased the tab back down. The scent of Poison rose as he massaged the tight muscles. Poison brought Bianca to mind, but perfume was the only connection between his wife and his current plaything. Blond wasn't simply the color of Bianca's hair; her aura, her personality, every word she spoke matched the buttercup shade of her curls. Bianca's giggles, her chatter about everything and nothing drove him insane, so the little time they spent out of bed, the television usually blared in the background.

When Bianca pouted about the sex, followed by Chinese food

delivery, followed by a movie popped into the VCR, the routine he'd established, he reminded her of the rewards with which his habits came. She'd mope for a moment or two, but then snuggle beside him and gaze at the newest trinket he'd picked up at some hole-in-the-wall jewelry store.

Jake didn't fool himself. He'd gone from swearing that he'd never cheat, to Georgia, to a variety of one-night stands, to regular "dates" with Bianca, but at least it never meant anything but sex. Emotionally, he and Bianca shared nothing. Hell, look at the two women side by side: Phoebe's strictly classy appearance, taut, toned, and sleek, outshone Bianca by miles, but sometimes you wanted a Twinkie instead of uncovering the layers of Baked Alaska. Bianca's bubble breasts would be hanging down long after Pheebs's still stood at attention, but playing with them now provided a heck of a treat. His poor Phoebe. No matter how many hours she spent exercising, she'd passed forty. Bianca's pliability, her satin finish, her expanse of unmarked flesh: it was her moment in time, and one he relished touching. No army of cosmetics and skin-care products lined her bathroom shelves.

"How about an early celebration, Pheebs?"

"I'm all dressed and ready." Even as she spoke those practical words, an aura of pliancy rippled toward him.

"So you are." He tugged her tight dress up and bent her over the bed. She arched up to meet him, and he pulled her closer, holding her hips, feeling the silk fabric slither over her skin, watching golden chains slip up and down her arm. Poison's heady aroma collided with the scent of roses on her dresser, and he drove into his wife with the force of screwing two women at once.

. . .

A large placard with his name and picture made the Waldorf Astoria Hotel ballroom entrance seem to rise and greet Jake in acclaim. His portrait took up half the real estate on the poster. Underneath his image, the words read "The Jewish Guardian of the Heart Fund Honors Jake Pierce, Advocate & Sustainer."

After his father's fatal heart attack two years ago, he'd donated a million dollars to begin the Kenneth Pierce Fund, under the umbrella of the Jewish Guardian of the Heart Fund. Jake's mother had died a month later, and he donated another two hundred grand but asked them to keep the name the same.

"I still can't believe you donated so much," Phoebe whispered as they entered the Grand Ballroom. "Are we really that rich?"

"We are, baby. This is our life." He swept his hand to take in the entire scene.

She squeezed his hand. "But you gave over a million? How in the world—"

"Don't worry. I put a pile of contributors together, that's all. Donating's an investment." If they thought you could drop a million, they'd throw ten million at you. If he'd given twenty million, they'd fall down on their knees, begging him to take their money.

"But still," she said. "So much."

"We're in a different stratosphere now." He analyzed the room to see who was there and where the money congregated. "I'm not a putz from Brooklyn anymore."

"You were never a putz." She laughed, her face lit with the glow of the room. "Okay, sometimes you're a putz, but very often you're a heroic putz."

"Thanks, baby." He lifted his chin toward a group he'd identified as being married to the room's biggest money. "Over there, you see those women? Go forth and bring me greedy wives. Then you can go talk to Deb and Helen. And thank me—I put them at our table and not the gold-encrusted wives."

"Putting on my Groucho glasses as we speak." She ran a hand down his cheek before walking away.

Jake pulled up his Club persona. Right about now, a drink would be perfect. He imagined the cool bite of Scotch and ached for the liquid like mother's milk. A few seconds later, the craving left. Most people thought he'd had an alcohol problem that he'd conquered with iron control. Some believed medical reasons kept him sober. Friends accepted his declaration of loathing the smell, since his mother self-soothed with booze more and more as the years went on.

The truth was none of the above.

In vino veritas.

Loose lips sink ships.

Jake headed to the polished mahogany bar, white lights marking the path to the booze. Longing rushed in again. He pushed down the hunger with a promise of having this shit over in another year or so. Then he could have a drink.

He'd be glad to close the door, though he wondered if he'd miss the kick of seeing the insane gullibility all around. Sometimes he felt like he was the victim. After all, Jesus Christ, who would have expected so many people—smart people, well-informed people, business people—to buy into the idea that anyone could keep building a fortune straight up? Life always came with downs, so who actually believed that Jake could perform the magic he said he could pull off? The educated ones, they had to know, wink-wink, what they were buying into. Otherwise, how could it have been so fucking simple building a fortune using his artless plan?

He clapped a hand on his brother-in-law's shoulder. "Hey, bro. Thanks for coming."

Ben hugged him. "Man of the hour! Congratulations. What an honor. You deserve every accolade. Honestly, I don't know how you manage these miracles."

Alan, Helen's husband, stood smirking on Ben's other side. Why Phoebe insisted he include this jerk in tonight's affair was beyond him. "From Flatbush Avenue to the Waldorf," Alan said. "We bow to thee."

Sarcasm and sour grapes laced Alan's words. He and Helen were in a small group of people blackballed from the Club. Phoebe brought it up repeatedly, how much Alan and Helen wanted to open an account with the Club, and just as often, Jake gave a flat no.

"I don't understand," she'd said only last month. "All of the family, all our friends, you let in. What's wrong with Helen? She's my oldest friend—my best friend."

"Enough with Helen and Alan already!" He'd stomped over to the kitchen cabinet and grabbed a handful of Sugar Wafers. "He works for Fidelity. What does he need me for? He lives inside the giant."

"Helen said they're so big, it's like having fifty million choices for dinner."

"I thought Alan was the big expert."

"He's a lawyer, not a stockbroker. They could really benefit from you."

"I told you before: he's a pain in the ass. Always asking questions. Always wanting to ask why I do this or say that. I don't need his bullshit."

"How can I keep saying no?"

"You don't have to. I just did."

"Will you at least explain the reasons to him?"

Jake had walked over to where she washed the dinner dishes and squeezed her shoulder with kindness. He wasn't a fool. Helen and Phoebe went back to grade school, and his refusal to let Alan and Helen into the Club embarrassed his wife. But worse would be letting them in; the combination of Alan's ferrety curiosity and his knowledge of financial legality with his oversized brain was lethal.

"No. Not wanting to talk to him is exactly the point, including not talking about his not joining. That he keeps badgering you just proves how I'm right."

She'd scrubbed a small pot. "I feel so weird. Everyone is a member except her. What do I say?"

"Tell her this, and say it's a secret you shouldn't be telling: the Club board doesn't allow members who have positions of internal authority at financial institutions. For reasons of security."

"Is that true?" Phoebe asked.

"I just said it, didn't I?"

"How come you never told me before?"

"How long before you realize how much I hate talking about business? Why do you think you, me, the kids, none of us has an account with the Club?"

Phoebe appeared puzzled. "What position of authority do I have?" Underestimating her intellect tripped him up every time.

"Oh, baby. Business is all about appearance," he'd said. "Can we simply drop this? Don't I get enough aggravation at work?"

Facing Alan's attitude tonight was proof he'd made the right decision. "And I bow back to you," Jake responded. "Phoebe says you and Helen bought a house out on the Island. Congrats. Sounds like both of you are doing terrific things."

"Chicken feed to you, eh?" Alan swept a hand over the room.

Jake clapped a hand on Alan's sloped shoulder. "Life is all about family, right? A beautiful family who loves you makes a good life. You're a lucky man."

CHAPTER 17

PHOEBE

Phoebe exhaled as she merged onto the highway. Even the massive trucks bearing down like dinosaurs on wheels didn't bother her. Being alone in the car for a blessed half hour, longer if the traffic stayed heavy, sounded excellent.

She headed to the Cupcake Project in Westport, Connecticut, which was managed by Eva. Linh was in charge of the original Greenwich shop; Zoya would oversee number three, getting readied in Westchester. They planned to open in a month, in time for Halloween. The three shops made a ragged triangle, with Phoebe linking the three points.

Two new stores in such a short time seemed a sure recipe for disaster, though after his reservations about the first store, Jake had pushed them like crazy. He had gone from being jealous of Ira and resentful of Mira House to acting as though the settlement house deserved historical treasure status and Ira was his best friend, including asking Phoebe to invite him to the award ceremony the previous week.

She hadn't.

Her worlds had already collided. Mira House invested all of its profits with Jake, taking out the money they needed for day-to-day operation and, with Jake's guidance, saving the rest for a long-range capital campaign. After Mira House had become Jake's poster child for what he called his long arm of charity, he had anointed himself the savior of nonprofits, with the Club representing the perfect stew of growth and safety. He forced Phoebe to step in anytime he couldn't fill a request to sit on a board. At this moment, her name decorated the stationery of a breast cancer research institute, a repertory theater, and a wild bird fund.

When juggling everything threatened to topple her, her link to sanity was inventing new cupcake flavors or updating menus. Katie called from college three times a week to talk over everything from papers due to how much her roommates drank at parties. Other friends couldn't pry a word from their daughters, while Phoebe lived every minute of Katie's life, including her romance with the boy she hid from Jake: a punk band musician. She couldn't be happier about Katie acting out; far worse would be getting involved with someone Jake thought perfect. He'd tie a bow around the pair before poor Katie knew the boy's middle name.

Noah grew from hiding on the beach with sea creatures to wringing himself inside out to earn Jake's pride. He ran track until he led the pack and debated until he hit the state championship.

Academically, he stood at the top of his class.

Socially, he could date any girl in the school.

Emotionally, only Phoebe could help Noah when panic attacks plagued him. Jake, with his obsessions about privacy, wouldn't allow therapy, insisting that anxiety was genetic. Jogging was Jake's version of a prescription.

Phoebe's solutions for Noah ranged from pathetic to terrible, including slivers of Valium, binging on VCR movies together, and, oddest and most soothing to him, trips to Brooklyn to hang out with her parents.

Jake leaned on her as though she were his personal crutch. An entire closet became devoted to her outfits for charity events and board meetings. Luncheons. He dragged her to the movies with each change of film at the local theater. She woke at five to exercise before getting Noah and Jake out of the house.

The Cupcake Project's success exceeded all expectations. Blessing or curse? Gig Baumer, their Jake-chosen accountant, swore that the taxes would break them, so thank goodness for Mira House. Being entwined with a nonprofit apparently saved their behinds. Gig took them under his wing as his own charitable arm. Phoebe couldn't understand a thing. Zoya nagged her to educate herself, but all the monies went to Gig, who parceled them out as needed.

. . .

As they wound down the tasks that needed completion before the shop opened, Eva handed Phoebe a batch of employee evaluations tucked neatly into one of their trademark yellow and blue folders. Then she brought two mugs of ginger tea to the table where they sat. "What's going on with you and Ira?"

Phoebe viewed Eva with suspicion. "What did Zoya say?"

"Why assume it was Zoya?"

"She's got the biggest mouth and the dirtiest mind. Ira and I are friends. Why would you even ask such a question?"

"We can see how close you two are lately. Inseparable. When men and women are 'just friends' "—Eva punctuated her words with imaginary quotation marks—"it's either because one or both of them is dead below the waist or they both find the other completely undesirable."

"We certainly aren't inseparable—gossip reigns here—but we are friends."

Despite driving all over New York and Connecticut, managing the business, and keeping up with the chores that Jake piled on her, Phoebe still went to Mira House on Thursday mornings for Cooking for English. After that came her only peaceful time of the week: lunch with Ira.

"Is that what Jake thinks?" Eva asked. "My man would find it weird if I 'ate lunch' "—again Eva used air quotes—"with a guy every week."

"Even if that man was part of your work life? In some sense your partner?"

Eva turned her head sideways and curled her mouth. "Oh, really? You're meeting Ira for work?"

"Not everyone's husband meets their every need. Honestly, Eva, the worry is much more about who Jake's lunch partners are than about who I dine with."

"Again?"

Phoebe dissected her fears about Jake's fidelity with only one person: Eva, her only friend who didn't either paper over Jake's faults or resent him for his success. "I just get the feeling. Truthfully, I almost followed him the other day."

"Followed him? Where would you pick up his trail?"

"That's the problem. He'd probably leave from work, but he won't be walking. Should I hail a cab and say 'Follow that car'?"

"You could get a private detective if you really want answers."

"That's the rub, eh."

"The rub?" Her puzzled air reminded Phoebe that Eva hadn't been born in the United States. Colloquialisms confounded Eva.

"Sorry, just a weird expression, meaning 'That's the problem.' If I knew Jake cheated—and I'm not saying he did—our lives would fall apart. Stop looking sorry for me. What? Do you think it's true?"

"Of course not. Why would I?"

Should she believe Eva's face or her words? "Did he ever come on to you?"

Eva's horrified look convinced her that Jake had never said an inappropriate word, but Phoebe knew the answer before asking. Jake, if he were to cheat, wouldn't play near their shared world. Her husband drew an inviolable circle around her and the kids, working overtime to keep two things from her: his work problems and whatever bad habits he knew she'd deem reprehensible. She pondered this as she drove, as she exercised on the rowing machine in the basement, doubting that Jake could be satisfied with watching old Westerns on TV as his sole recreation and release.

"It's my insanity, Eva. My suspicion bubbles up every few years. Your job is to remind me I'm nuts."

"Why would he cheat? Why would anyone cheat married to you?" Eva smiled. "Did I do that right?"

"I always think of the line 'Should I worry about my drinking?' Conventional wisdom says if you ask the question, you know the answer."

Eva grabbed a napkin from the counter and placed a cupcake on it. "Eat this. We just made them. Meyer lemon."

"Lemon?"

"To remind you even the sweetest life holds sour bits."

"Tutsi wisdom from Rwanda?"

"My horoscope this morning."

"Do you think our life is written out already, just waiting for God to unfurl it?" Phoebe asked.

"You mean do we have a predetermined destiny?"

Phoebe nodded before blowing on her hot tea.

"Reasoning like that indicates weakness. In my opinion." Eva straightened the pile of polka dot napkins. "If you think your future is fated, then you do nothing to keep danger away. You just lay there and let it wash over you."

Sometimes Phoebe blocked out how many sour bits of racial affronts forced her friend to pucker up each day. Some people pulled away their hands when she tried to give them change. They showed their shock at learning that Eva was the manager, not the counter help. Frosty reactions came from women walking the moneyed streets of Connecticut, as though Eva were there to mug them. Gentlemen slipped her their business cards, certain she'd happily meet them for an assignation.

"Call them out when it happens," Phoebe had suggested the first time Eva revealed the problem. "Ask them why in the world they're giving you their card. Loudly. Say this: 'You want me to phone you? Are you offering me a job?'"

"Nothing would make me happier, but I'll stick with quiet seething," Eva said. "The power dynamic rarely slides in my direction."

. . .

Ira waited at their regular table. Puglia Restaurant, an institution in Little Italy, brought memories of her meals with Rob at Katz's. The mix of locals and tourists recalled the deli, though it was fancier, with exposed brick and marble tables. Like Katz's, they pushed the tables close enough for patrons to examine their neighbors' choices with an intimate eye.

The first few times Phoebe and Ira ate together, she'd ordered grilled chicken, grilled fish, or the grilled vegetable plate. At their fifth meal, Ira pulled the menu from her hand and declared himself in charge of ordering.

"Any allergies?" he'd asked.

"No, but—"

He put up a hand to stem the words like calories and fat and told her to trust him, as though she were dining with an inverse of Jake: same style, different beliefs.

The simple dish of baked ziti with sausage the waiter placed before her that day had all but taken her to bed.

Now she traveled around the menu, moving from gnocchi to sautéed calamari with the ease of someone who'd never learned the language of Weight Watchers.

She squeezed through the narrow path to arrive at their table and kissed Ira somewhere between his mouth and cheek.

"You're here!" Ira still seemed surprised when she appeared each week.

She pointed to her wrist, tapping her watch. "Two o'clock."

They danced on a thin razor of attraction, held firmly within boundaries by never acknowledging their uncomfortable truth. Ira tried edging the conversation there, but only a few times. Phoebe blocked any mention of a "them." She had no need of marital tsunamis.

Safety lessons had come early in Phoebe's life. She could remind herself to stay within the lines simply by imagining who her first child might have been. All she wanted from lunch with Ira was sitting with someone who carried unrealized dreams about her.

"I ordered the *famoso*." He tipped his glass toward Phoebe, who clinked back with the familiarity of long-standing tradition.

She enjoyed knowing that people would peg them as a couple and think Ira had placed the wedding ring on her finger. This minor charade didn't give her pause. Walter Mitty romances she'd allow herself.

"Wonderful as always," she said after a sip.

Puglia's *famoso* "famous house wine" had become their tradition.

Ira insisted on paying for their meals. Phoebe, shying away from anything reminiscent of their unscalable bank account differences, ordered on the budget side, insisting that the house Chianti thrilled her.

"Truth time," Ira said. "Does Jake know about our lunches?"

And there went the applecart. Had Eva been prescient today? "I'd have no problem telling him. We work together. Aren't you rather like my boss?"

"Phoebe, I've never been your 'boss.' Don't hide there. I didn't ask if you would tell him. I want to know if you do."

"Why?"

"Trust me. I'm not breaching our walls. You intrigue me. Curiosity about your marriage is part of getting to know you."

"So you're not really asking if I tell him we have lunch once a week?"

The waiter interrupted, bringing amber glasses filled with ice water. "Ready to order?" They knew this prickly guy. What he meant was "Tell me what you want within five seconds, or you won't see me again for fifteen minutes."

"Spaghetti with meatballs," Ira said.

"Living wild, I see." Phoebe scanned the menu for something compatible with the combination of hunger and indigestion brought on by this cascade of upsetting conversation. Tums might be dessert. "Plain angel hair pasta with butter and a sprinkle of Parmesan."

The waiter left with a nod, indicating his lack of respect for their gastronomy.

"I upset you." Ira could interpret her lunch order. "Don't fret about what I said. You and Jake puzzle me. You're different when you're with him than when you're not, which indicates someone in the marriage is holding secrets." He pushed Phoebe's glass of water closer to her hand. "Drink. It helps cool your insides."

The icy liquid washed through, relieving the fiery nerves settling in her stomach. "Everyone acts differently when they're with their husband or wife." Even as she spoke, Phoebe knew she was wrong. Deb was Deb, and Ben was Ben, whether together or apart. Helen and Alan didn't change depending on the other's presence.

"No. They don't. God knows, in my marriage, we were at our worst as a couple. You, you're brittle with Jake, as though you're crafting how you present yourself. For him or you?"

"Why would I do that for myself?"

"To hide?" he asked.

Food arrived, bringing a welcome break from their conversation. Pasta lightly shined with butter would coat her insides so she could drink.

"What would I need to hide from?"

"That's exactly what I'm wondering. Sometimes you seem like you live in a corner of your life, your mind. You're an entirely different person at Mira House than you are with him."

"I'm the person Jake wants." With her stomach lined, she drank from her wineglass. "You're not married anymore. You're not a father. You don't know the price of a family."

"Do you?"

. . .

Ira's words continued to play as Phoebe mixed a crust for the chicken cutlets, speculating on possible truth. Sure, the nights Jake worked late were always welcome—but she thought all wives were a little more relaxed when their husbands weren't home, never allowing herself to think it might just be her and Jake.

Lately, Jake's base was jittery and tense. She never knew when he'd bark out news that they'd attend yet another night out with potential clients. Her dread had increased as Jake now expected her to wax on about the Cupcake Project's fiscal ties with JPE as proof of how much she trusted the Club. She hated using her business that way and could barely remember the new bullshit he tried to make her memorize.

"If the Club is so successful, why do you still need me shilling for you?" she had asked the previous week, genuinely puzzled. Financial advisors worldwide fed him clients—why did he still need her?

"You're the charity expert." He'd smiled. "And charities are my favorites."

"Why?" she asked.

"You feel good working with Mira House, right? Maybe I caught the bug from you. Seeing how we can grow their endowments means plenty to me and the rest of the staff."

Imagining Gita-Rae and Charlie deriving joy from helping non-profits rang false enough to make her laugh or cry. She stared at her husband, searching for answers behind his glaze of bullshit. Noah finally put her discomfort into words as they drove back from Brooklyn after visiting her parents, just the three of them, during Katie's college break.

"When it comes to understanding the Club, Mom, it's like he's swallowed the place, and the only way to get through would be to cut him open."

Kate laughed. "And don't try going up there to the thirty-seventh floor. They have business omertà. It's 'family' vis-à-vis Little Italy."

"You don't think there's anything wrong, do you?"

Both kids appeared puzzled. "What do you mean?"

She wasn't sure, but they'd worked there, and their reassurances would feel good. When she was around the Club staff, at parties and such, they belonged to that club that didn't want her as a member.

Gravel crunching in the driveway announced Jake's arrival. Phoebe ran into the powder room near the kitchen, opened the antique medicine cabinet hanging on the wall, and rummaged through the collection of lipsticks she kept in a red cocoa tin. After lining her lips with a youthful pink and smiling at the mirror, she retied the blue polka-dot ribbon on her low ponytail. She leaned closer to her reflection, turning from side to side, and then tipping her head up, searching for stray chin hairs betraying her. All clear, though her complexion appeared ashy. Somewhere below the sink, she'd stashed a bottle of Clinique moisturizer. There it was. She rubbed a small amount into her skin and topped it with a dab of blush.

Phoebe slipped back into the kitchen and placed the pan of breaded cutlets in the oven, listening to Jake's footsteps for clues as to which husband approached, hoping for the romantic version and dreading the man crackling with anxiety.

"What's for supper, pussycat?"

"Chicken cutlets." The scent of soap rose when she put her arms around Jake.

"Did you shower in the car?"

"I played racquetball late this afternoon. Where's Noah?"

"Probably out with his friends. Racquetball? Worn out?"

A familiar fizziness on her palate bubbled. She often wondered if her body released it to keep her from saying words she couldn't take back.

"Probably?" Jake asked. "Are you baking too many cupcakes to keep track of our son?"

"Our son is almost in college. I don't need to follow his every move."

"Is he coming home for dinner? Do you know that much?"

"He's studying at a friend's house tonight."

"What friend?"

"You sure go back and forth with your racquetball thing." She sliced the ends off fresh string beans. "What made you start up again? You haven't played in months."

Jake patted his midriff. "This. Started expanding."

He came close, grabbed a raw bean, and popped it in his mouth. Then he put one to her lips. She brushed it aside and kissed him, tasting peppermint and hidden happiness. "I can keep the chicken on low," she said. "We can take advantage of the empty house."

"I'm pretty hungry." He pulled back as she leaned on his shoulder.

This wasn't the shirt he'd worn when he left the house. He kept extra shirts in the office. For racquetball.

He put his hands on her arms. "Be glad I'm working to stay in shape."

"Are you having an affair?"

He chuckled. "This comes from racquetball? Not wanting to go to bed when Noah might come home any moment? Or are your girlfriends putting ideas in your head? Do you all have so much free time that you craft husbandly ghost stories?" He pushed her away and went to the hall. "When you see what I brought you, you'll feel like an idiot."

Phoebe followed, trying to imagine what he had. Jewelry meant he was sleeping with someone for sure. Sapphires or diamonds red-flagged a serious relationship, not just sex. How she knew this baffled her, but it felt true.

Jake opened his briefcase and drew out a bag from Bergdorf's. He handed it to Phoebe with a flourish. "I thought it was time for a change."

She saw tissue paper with yellow and white stripes and instantly recognized the wrapping and box. Giorgio. She'd gag if she uncapped it. The heady, thick scent smelled like a cheap woman trying for expensive. She tore the cellophane on the box in silence. She thought Poison overpowering and wore it only at Jake's insistence, but the overwhelming Giorgio made Poison palatable.

Phoebe couldn't put together Jake from Brooklyn with this man who apparently prowled the perfume counters of Bergdorf's until he found what struck his libido and then demanded she wear nothing else until he again became bored.

Phoebe unstopped the bottle and inhaled, trying to understand what kind of woman he wanted now. She'd dab it on sparingly before he came home.

"An affair?" He laughed. "My only affair is with you, Pheebs, and the only way I need to spice it up comes in beautiful crystal bottles."

CHAPTER 18

PHOEBE

Perhaps to prove how much he was not having an affair, Jake had almost attached himself to Phoebe that weekend. On Friday night, he even agreed to see *Cry Freedom* instead of *Robocop*.

On Saturday, they took a car service into Manhattan where Jake dropped her at Bergdorf Goodman's with his American Express and strict instructions to scorch the card while he worked for a few hours.

During their Saturday night meal with Ollie and Poppy, he draped his arm over her shoulders except when actively putting food in his mouth.

On Sunday, they actually drove into Brooklyn with Noah and had dinner with her parents at Peter Luger Steak House, her father's favorite place.

Three nights in a row, they made love, quite a record for a couple married over twenty years. "Is it the new perfume?" she'd asked at midnight on Sunday.

"All you."

She didn't believe him—if anything, it made her more suspicious, his need to show his devotion. Suspicion and actually wanting answers, however, turned out to be different animals.

What proof did she have? None.

Her qualms came from clean clothes, racquetball, and gossip about other women's husbands. She'd shake this off—Jake's addiction was money, not women. Where Ollie couldn't keep his eyes in his head, even with Poppy across the table, Jake acted nothing but appropriate.

When Phoebe was there.

No. No man could carry on a charade that well. She compared him with those she knew best: her father, brother-in-law, and Helen's husband. Jake fit in with their respect of family; not with Ollie, who pressed so close against her each time they hugged that she mentioned it to Jake.

He made a sound of deep repulsion. "I'll talk to him."

"Don't!" Why did she say that? Why did women feel a need to protect awful men from the truth of who they were; why were they afraid to have it revealed that they'd "told on him"?

"Do." He'd cupped her face. "No one cheapens my wife."

And though she'd rather he'd said that no one cheapens any woman, she loved his words.

Ollie never pushed himself on her again.

All weekend, no matter how hard she tried to push away the memories, Jake's vague answers looped. The comfort Jake bought with spa treatments and new clothes had a short shelf life.

. . .

Phoebe was shocked at the time when she woke on Monday morning. When Jake had left before six, she'd treated herself by calling in to the shop and leaving a message to postpone their meeting for a few hours, never expecting to sleep past ten.

Phoebe stumbled into the shower, skipping coffee and breakfast, knowing she could get both at the store. She calmed her anxiety that she might be late through a series of deep breaths. And of course, her inhalations carried the scent of expensive lemon potpourri sold by a tiny shop in town.

Money muffled Phoebe's world. The move from Brooklyn to Greenwich taught her what privilege meant. She had grown up in one of the best homes in her neighborhood, but walk a few blocks in any direction, and you ran into the shakier parts of life. Polished worlds such as Greenwich beveled the edges until you believed money shined up everything.

Perhaps people drank, screamed, and fell to their knees in the houses surrounding them but you never saw the pain. All of them worked overtime to make their lives more plush, wanting to reach the level of bliss they thought lived next door, where mounds of silk and gold buried sorrow and gloom and rows of evergreens screened away sound and sights.

Jake's rapaciousness never let up. When was enough enough? He didn't only want to consume, he needed to swallow the world whole.

. . .

Phoebe unlocked the door to find Linh, Eva, and Zoya crowded around a small marble table in the Greenwich store. "Am I that late? I'm so sorry."

"We got here extra quick." Zoya spat out the words.

"All of you?" Phoebe looked around. Everyone seemed edgy. "Is something wrong?"

"Are you okay, Phoebe? That is the question." Linh spoke in her properly learned English. Mira House had the same two ESL teachers for the past ten years, and neither seemed to believe in contractions.

"Why wouldn't I be?" Phoebe shook off her jacket with relief. No matter how fashionable the fitted apricot leather and squared-off shoulder pads seemed yesterday, today it resembled a space suit. Post-spa-treatment dizziness could be the only reason she had bought it. And no comments? She'd expected Zoya to touch the fabric the moment she arrived.

"Did you see the television? Listen to the radios?" Zoya picked up a napkin and dabbed her lips.

"I drove for all of five minutes. What's going on?"

"Where are you?" Zoya scissored her hands in front of Phoebe's face. "Living in bubble?"

"I rushed—"

Eva shook her head. "Don't answer. That's not our business." She poured a cup of coffee for Phoebe. "Sit down."

"You're scaring me."

"Did you talk to Jake since he got to work?"

"What's going on, for God's sake? Is there something I need to know?"

Eva turned on the radio they kept in the shop, tuning in until she hit the news channel. Phoebe tried to concentrate as phrases like *Dow plunges* and *market crashing* pounded over them.

"Listen," Linh said. "We don't know—"

"Call Jake and—" Zoya wove her fingers into a beseeching fist.

Phoebe quieted them with a gesture as she continued listening, highlights leaping out.

Are we re-experiencing 1929?

Slide continuing.

Expecting worse, much worse, by day's end.

Phoebe gave a silent prayer. She covered Eva's hands with her own. "Hey, this is old—well, old*ish* news. You know. It began last week. Jake says we're exactly where we want to be. Now that everything is dipping, the crap—his word, not mine—is washing out. The cream will rise to the top."

Coffee soured in Phoebe's throat as she put forth what might well be bullshit. She, in fact, had no understanding of what Jake meant, but his words had soothed everyone at dinner on Sunday. Her mother repeated his wisdom verbatim twenty minutes after Jake first said it.

Now three terrified faces watched her for assurance.

"Everything," Zoya said. "I put everything into the Jake thing."

"We all did." Linh's soft voice trembled. "Including my husband. We sent half his check every month."

"Half?" Eva twisted a bright gold ring round and round. "How do you manage?"

"Have you seen how many people live in their house?"

"Zoya," Eva scolded.

"It is true." Linh clasped her fingers. "We are saving to buy houses. Me. My sister. My parents will live with one of us."

"You'll get your house. I swear," Phoebe said.

"How can you promise?" Skepticism coated every syllable Zoya spoke. "Never a guarantee in business or government. Ask my dead husband."

The three women fell silent, hope falling from their faces. Phoebe imagined them reflecting on the circumstances that had brought them to New York. Her own great-grandmother had sewn jewelry and money in the hem of her coat before getting on the boat in Poland.

Linh looked up, tears trickling. "It is not your fault. We made the choices."

"You will be okay." Her heavy orange leather screamed "rich bitch liar!" from the back of her chair.

"How?" Eva said. "It would be impossible for us not to lose money. You read the paper. Jake may be smart, even a genius, but he's not a miracle worker."

"Wait. Let me talk to him tonight. I'll find out." Phoebe dug her nails into her arms.

Zoya bent and picked up the suitcase-sized turquoise bag she brought everywhere and rummaged until Eva exploded. "Are you mining for gold?"

"Does anyone think it is too early for beer?" Linh asked.

"Ah. Finally." Zoya pulled out a small marbled notebook, the kind children bought at the five-and-dime to track their homework assignments. She flipped the pages until reaching the last one with writing. "See. I report it down every time I get the statement. Here is what I think is my balance." She held up the white paper. "Nine thousand six hundred dollars. I save everything."

"That's a good amount," Phoebe said.

"Fuck you, good amount." She slammed down the book. "That is everything I own in world. It's nothing to you. Look at your coat. How much did it cost? Did you think about it? Did you wait for one minute before you bought it and think what else you could do with it? Did you wonder how many mamas in Mira House could buy twenty coats with what you spent? More?"

Linh brought up her knees and held them with her hands, making herself smaller. "Stop yelling."

Zoya took the book and shook it at Phoebe. "Coats! You think you are Eleanor Roosevelt when you're really Marie Antoinette."

Zoya's rage seemed a living creature, curling around Phoebe, snapping at her flesh. The ugly orange coat, boasted, screamed its price.

"You'll lose nothing," Phoebe said. "I promise. If I have to pay it from my own money, you will get it all."

CHAPTER 19

JAKE

Jake clutched Tuesday's *New York Times,* keeping his face somber until he hit the thirty-seventh floor. The headline burned his fingertips: "Stocks Plunge 508 Points, a Drop of 22.6%; 604 Million Volume Nearly Doubles Record." Exuding glee as the stock market tanked would be unseemly at best, but along with his shine from the Waldorf, as Wall Street lost, he gained. Skid marks would mark the road to his office as folks begged for the safety of the Club.

He loved slipping up the back staircase, used only by him, Charlie, and Solomon. Moving to this building uptown five years ago came with a long pleasure tail. The separation of a floor between his brokerage and the Club soothed him.

He unlocked the entry door and walked into the full throttle mess of Gita-Rae's domain. After saying a few hellos, asking after this one's son's college grades, that one's new house, he perched on the edge of Nanci's desk.

"How's your mom?" he asked.

Nanci's sigh held her mother's pain. Lung cancer was a bitch. Jake took her pudgy hand. "You're being strong for her. We're all proud of you."

Nanci shrugged. "I'm all she has."

"What about your brother?"

"Oh, God. You'd think he was still a kid. He hit forty-five last week, and you know how he celebrated?" She picked up a picture of her family in a red heart frame and drooped a bit more. "He went to Atlantic City and got drunk for three days. Meanwhile, I go straight to my mother's every night to make supper."

Jake pulled out his wallet and took out six twenties. "You get dinner delivered tonight. Something special. Make sure to buy flowers, from Phoebe and me."

Nanci made a gesture, as though pushing away the money. "Oh, Jake. You already do too much. Mom and I would never have made it this far without you."

"It's you who makes the difference to me. You and everyone here— you're the rocks of JPE."

Nanci stood and hugged him. "We love you. You're our hero!"

Hugging her back felt like squeezing a pillow, but God bless Nanci and all the rest of them. This dusty warren of offices acted like a tonic. After one last squeeze to her shoulder, Jake made his way to Charlie. After a perfunctory knock on the open door, he walked in.

"Read the paper?" Jake asked.

Charlie picked up a copy of the *New York Post* from the table behind him and rattled the paper. The words "Wall St. Bloodbath" spread in death-like letters across the front page. "I read it." He grinned wide, showing the full length of his Chiclet-huge teeth. "You won't be able to sign them up fast enough now."

"Solomon already got a call from the bozos at Cook and Baylor," Jake said. "I swear they fancy themselves British lords. Meanwhile, they're begging for more. No more having to sweeten the deal for them."

Jake couldn't stand those horsey-set assholes, acting as though they were doing him a big favor by throwing business his way. They were feeder funds same as Gallagher & Graham, fattening on his kickbacks like lice, while presenting themselves as Einsteins of Wall Street.

"Blood's in the streets," Charlie said.

"Fuck the blood. Marrow is showing." Jake took the leather guest chair. The guy's office appeared neat as his own, with stacks of periodicals on the side table lined up in perfect order. For someone who had barely finished high school, Charlie worked his ass off to keep up. He subscribed to every magazine and paper with a connection to finance, inhaling the words as fast as they arrived. "We have our work cut out for us. Get your pen."

Charlie kept notes in a small black leather binder. Jake thought of asking him the eventual landing for those small sheets of three-hole punched papers, but he filed the thought for future follow-up.

"The first thing we gotta do is put out the statements," Jake said. "Timing couldn't be better—we were set to mail them out tomorrow anyway."

"How do you want them to look?" Charlie asked.

Jake leaned back and stared at the ceiling. He crossed his ankles and ran over scenarios. A fast infusion of cash was important, but the endgame meant keeping to his script. "Smart, dexterous, edging on miraculous without going over the line. Conservative enough to appear almost bank safe, agile enough to move every second. And showing how we take full advantage of every computer assist out there without being ruled by machines."

These lines were nothing particularly new, but Charlie hung on to his words as though hearing them for the first time. He pointed to the three phones on his desk. "I turned off the ringers. Let them sweat a bit."

One phone was a direct line for big fish such as Louis Klein. Jake had already talked to him this morning—one of the few clients with whom he spoke directly about business. The second was for their feeders and corporate accounts. The last, Charlie used for nonprofits and foundations, such as the Jewish Guardian of the Heart Fund.

Jake tapped the paper. "Talk to Solomon, and he'll work on the numbers. All set?"

"Almost." Charlie picked up his Marlboros, worrying the box like a good luck charm, opening and closing the top, letting the sour odor of unsmoked tobacco escape. Only a disaster of tidal wave proportion would ever have Charlie smoking in front of him.

"I got to ask you something," Charlie said. "It's probably nothing, but I got a strange call this morning. A reporter."

"Reporters will be climbing up our ass with the news."

"Her questions were different."

"Different how?"

"She wasn't asking what or how we lost, but why we didn't."

"Charlie, everyone asks for the soup recipe."

"Sure, but she talked about running numbers to see how we do it—not like we were cheating; more like she wanted to analyze how we can have miracles in the midst of disasters."

"Give her the same line as always: it's not a public business, et cetera, et cetera. All true. We're just guides for these people. We're not even on the radar of government alphabet agencies."

"Something about her made me wonder."

Now Jake sat forward, leaning on his thighs. "What's up, Charlie?"

"Hey, you know me. I'm a believer. My cash is here same as everyone else in this office. I just wondered—"

"You wouldn't be human if you didn't think about your own wallet. Your family."

"Solomon, Vic—we talk sometimes."

He gave Charlie credit. The guy showed balls, coming to him like this. Staff had to wonder what the fuck he did with their cash, their paychecks, which they gave him like every other mark, using the Club and their Club profits like a checking account. They knew the statements were fiction but believed in the cash. They figured his scheme made them more money than stocks ever would, though God knows what plan they imagined.

"And?" He had to get out of there. Tension took over when he stayed in one place too long. He had to walk it off, buy a new shirt, a pair of cuff links, or a happy-ending massage.

"Where is it?"

Fuck him if he thought Jake would make this easy. "Where's what?"

Now Charlie went far enough to drag a cigarette from the pack and tap it against the ashtray. "The money. Where do you keep it?"

Jake stood. "You already know too much, right? Deniability is an important factor. It's my gift to you. Not that anything is illegal." He shook his head slowly and calmly. "Far from it. Your future's as safe as my grandmother's grave. It's just one of those simple plans nobody thinks of."

He walked to the door, turning before he left for a parting shot. "And that, my friend, is the last time we speak about this. Either you trust me, or you don't. Look around. Where the fuck do you think it all comes from? It's me. All me. This takes everything from me. I count on you to make the small shit happen. I'll make sure you and everyone else up here have the future of kings and queens."

Charlie pushed back his chair and also stood. "Forget I said anything. Jesus, we know. We all know the world is resting on you."

"And I know you all appreciate it. So go *shtup* everyone's accounts, including yours."

CHAPTER 20

PHOEBE

Phoebe pounced on Jake the moment he walked in on Tuesday evening, barely letting him put down his briefcase and take off his jacket. She followed him to the kitchen. Her anxiety about Eva, Linh, and Zoya had eaten at her since the previous day. Jake hadn't come home Monday night until long after she fell asleep, and then left before five this morning. He'd been in no mood to talk.

Now, by the time Jake finally walked in, all she cared about was getting his reassurance. Moments after flinging a plate of crackers and cheese in front of him, she began relaying the conversation she'd had with the women at the Cupcake Project and the promises she'd made.

He dropped a cracker, uneaten, on the table. "You said what?" Jake ran his hands through his hair. "Are you nuts?"

"They were almost hysterical. They can't afford to lose anything!"

"You don't do that!" Jake paced the floor, slamming his fist into his palm. "You *never* tell people you will cover their losses. Are you fucking nuts?"

"I can do whatever I please with my money. What better way to use it than helping people like Zoya and Linh? Eva?"

"Your money? Do you honestly think your cupcakes make a dime? Who do you think is underwriting this project of yours? Every penny of your business belongs to JPE in one form or another."

"These are my friends. Who need everything they have."

"People shouldn't invest what they can't afford to lose. Bottom line, if you need every cent, you stuff it under your damned mattress."

"Fuck you, Jake. Just because you can be a heartless bastard doesn't mean I have to follow you to hell." She wanted to strike him. For the first time, she understood how couples ended up attacking each other. Why weapons should never be at hand.

Jake bent with his hands on his knees, took a deep breath, and then straightened up and walked away.

She heard him at the liquor cabinet in the next room. Glass clinked. A bottle opened. He poured. A moment passed, and then he poured again.

He came back carrying what looked like undiluted Scotch.

"Here. Drink this." He handed her a glass. "Calm down."

"You had some?" she asked.

"A sip." He nodded as she drank. "Listen closely. One, we will be fine. We will get even more clients from this. Two, you never—do you hear me—never interfere with the business. Half of our friends and family are in the Club, and I do not want any one of them to think they can go to you. Not your mother or father, not your sister, and not your golden Mira House buddies. *Capisce*? This is mine. Only mine."

Jake's now-soft voice carried menace. Her heart raced as she wondered how she could keep her promise to her friends and keep her husband.

"Your girls will lose nothing. Not because they are different from any other client but because they have their money with me, damn it. Do you hear me?"

Jake being the only one in America able to deliver good news made no sense. She'd read the *New York Times*, the *Wall Street Journal*, the *Daily News*, and the *Post* while waiting for him to come home. Blood ran in the streets.

What magic did Jake possess? Could he be brilliant?

"When people question you, this is what you say: 'I shouldn't say this, but if it were me, I'd double down with Jake. He won't say a word, but he knows exactly how to play a down market. Whatever you do, don't sell. These are the times when people become wealthy.' Say nothing if you can't say that, but say what I told you, and you'll speak the truth."

For the first time, it seemed, Phoebe felt the weight of what people said about Jake: that he truly was a money magician. He could end up in history books, mentioned along with Peter Lynch and Warren Buffett. Being with him since she was fifteen limited her understanding. To her, he remained Jake from the neighborhood. But he was more. Perhaps even a genius.

"You truly are this smart, aren't you?" Phoebe whispered.

CHAPTER 21

PHOEBE

"Aunt Deb's crying. She sounds hysterical." Noah held out the phone toward Phoebe.

She grabbed the receiver, apprehension hammering. Ben's checkup last week had revealed blood pressure problems, high cholesterol, and weight gain—each one an ingredient for a heart attack.

"Is Ben okay? The kids?"

"Mom. And Daddy . . ." Thick sobs choked away her words.

"Deb! What happened?"

Ben's voice came from the background with the sound of the phone being transferred. "Phoebe, it's me."

"What's wrong?" Brittle cold invaded her chest.

"Are you alone?"

"Noah's here. Just say it. Tell me, Ben!"

"Your parents. They were in a car accident." He paused. His labored breathing and Deb's sobs panicked her. "Your father didn't make it. Your mother's in Bellevue."

Blinding pain pierced Phoebe's head. She sank to her knees, sucker punched by Ben's words.

"Mom! Mom, what's wrong?" Noah knelt beside her and took the phone from her hand. "Uncle Ben, what happened?"

The drive to the hospital took seven hours or seven minutes— Phoebe wasn't sure which. She'd locked her eyes on Noah's hands gripping the steering wheel, as she entered suspended animation: muscles contracted, balled fists, her heels pressed to the rubber mat as though moving the car with her inaction.

Bellevue Hospital's ancient systems and signs defied Noah's teenage parking skills. After the second time circling from the FDR service road to First Avenue and back again, Phoebe pointed out the window.

"Park there."

"That's a delivery entrance, Mom."

Park.

He pulled into the spot. "They'll tow the car."

"I don't care." This was the real power Jake bestowed. Having enough money to not give a shit. The car could explode moments after they walked away, and she wouldn't turn around.

Phoebe and Noah trekked through dingy hallway mazes to reach her mother's room. Not dirty, but unpleasant, and unbroken by reminders that life might be better than the grim interior of this hulking building.

Noah took her hand as they entered her mother's room. Ben stood in the corner, arms folded across his chest as he leaned against the radiator.

Lola lay in the bed closest to the window, forcing them to walk past her roommate, an ancient wraith of a moaning woman. Deb sat in a chair pulled close as possible to their mother.

Her mother's stillness frightened Phoebe. Traces of eyeliner on her closed lids were the only remnants of the face Lola showed the world.

Ben put a finger to his lips and gestured with his chin toward the corridor. The two of them walked out and leaned against the wall.

"How is she? Should we call a nurse for the woman in the other bed?"

"Deb already asked twice. This place is a zoo."

"Why'd they bring them . . ." Phoebe stopped. "Why did they bring her here?" Thick beige paint seemed designed to dull all senses, drown the urge to complain, muffle screams.

"Bellevue's the best for trauma," Ben said.

"What does she have?"

"A fractured pelvis."

Phoebe winced, imagining the bowl protecting her mother's innards shattered. "Are they operating?"

"We don't know yet. They're stabilizing her. She has an acetabulum fracture: a fracture of the socket of the hip. They manipulated it in the emergency room to get it back in place. Hopefully the procedure worked." Ben nodded at a passing nurse. "Meanwhile, she needs to be carefully watched."

"Should we transfer her?" Phoebe pressed her hand against her chest.

"Moving her in any way is dangerous. Right now they're stabilizing her enough to evaluate whether to operate. She's swollen. Contusions, you saw, cover her body. She lost three teeth. Her knees are three times their size."

"Has she spoken? Did anyone tell her about Daddy?"

"She was in shock when she came into the trauma center," Ben said. "So, no."

Deb came out of the room, her eyes red, wearing a wrinkled green cotton sweater and jeans. An orange elastic band held her thick waves in a messy bun. "Noah's watching Mom."

"What happened to Daddy?" Phoebe asked.

"He was already gone when they got here. A heart attack. He lost control of the car." Deb's words sounded dredged in a layer of Valium. A profusion of jewelry pressed against her skin when she took her sister's hand—her mother's engagement and wedding rings along with the oversized emerald ring Lola wore for special occasions. On her middle finger, Deb wore their father's gold wedding band.

"They were on the FDR. Your mother got tickets for a play," Ben said. "For his birthday. *The Phantom of the Opera.*"

Numbness left. Phoebe's chest ripped open. Visions of her parents—dressing for a night out, slipping into the Buick Regal that her father kept spotless, probably eating dinner out before the show—piled like photographs. She held on to the vision of her father alive.

Phoebe hugged her sister. "I'll sit with her. You and Ben get coffee. Or get outside for a few minutes." Bellevue's air surrounded them like a soup of infection and bleach.

. . .

Deep purple and black bruises covered her mother's face. Her hair, pushed away from the shiny unguents slicked over cuts and scrapes, frizzed in a brown halo. Grey roots that her mother would have covered with brown mascara peeked out.

Terror and grief fought for primacy as Phoebe sat watching her mother for the signs of danger the nurse had listed. Labored breathing. Hot skin. Swelling—though how could she see swelling through already swollen limbs? Noah fidgeted beside her, his healthy youthfulness no match for the claustrophobic atmosphere, the profusion of wires and tubes. He jumped on any request Phoebe concocted: a sandwich she'd never eat, magazines never to be read.

Jake appeared, late, apologetic, but lacking a clear reason for why he'd been out of touch. He wore a fresh shirt and smelled of a recent shampoo. Phoebe didn't care if he'd been at the gym or sleeping with every woman in Manhattan. He held her and murmured all the right things, but within thirty minutes of his pacing in and out of the room, repeatedly asking if he should arrange to transport her mother to Mount Sinai Hospital, she asked him to check on the likely towed car and take Noah home. Jake's already oversized energy had reached epic proportions since Black Monday six weeks ago. Being around him was unbearable now.

Phoebe turned her parents' rings round and round on her own thinner fingers until she asked for medical tape and wound it around the metal until the bands hugged her flesh. Deb had transferred the rings to Phoebe when she left, both of them eager to slip them back on their mother.

She stood, stretched, and tiptoed out, desperate for caffeine. It took but a few hours of her vigil to move from confused visitor to experienced member of the ward. The compassionate Jamaican nurse had showed her the coffee pot next to the head nurse's office. The Irish resident, brogue intact, pointed her to custard and gelatin tucked in a hidden corner of the fridge. An intern slipped her packets of saltines. Over the course of a few hours, the petri dish of medical horror became a bubbling cauldron of kindnesses, staffed by overworked people, mainly women, swimming through waves of broken patients.

Phoebe poured coffee, lightened it with chemical cream, and then carried the Styrofoam cup to her mother's room, where she leaned back into the rigid orange chair.

Time lagged. Everyone waited for something in hospitals: a doctor's visit, a bedpan, a wound to heal. She rummaged deep into her pocketbook until reaching a stash of striped white-and-red peppermints. After unwrapping one and then sucking hard to rid her mouth of the flavor of hospital coffee, her mother's eyes opened.

"Wahta," Lola croaked.

Phoebe found the cup filled with crushed ice, mostly melted, and then held the straw to her mother's lips.

"How do you feel?" She worked to keep tears from her voice.

"Where Daddy?" Tears fell down her mother's bruised cheeks. "Hurt? Worse than me?"

Phoebe hesitated.

Her mother tried to turn her head, winced, and then remained still. "He die, right? I feel it."

Phoebe's tears matched her mother's. "I'm so sorry, Mommy. I'll call Deb to come."

"Let Deb rest. You here." Her words revealed missing teeth, gaps her father would have made perfect. She gestured for more water. Tears ran in an unstopped stream. Phoebe didn't know whether to wipe them away.

After three sips, her mother pushed away the cup. "Hurts. Red. My sweet Red. Always."

"I know," Phoebe said.

"No life without him." Her mother touched the wetness on her face without wiping it away, almost caressing this proof of love.

"You have us," Phoebe said. "We need you."

Her mother ignored her words. "Where rings?"

"Here." She held up her right hand. "Deb and I take turns wearing them."

"And Daddy's?"

"Left hand," she said, lifting it.

"Good." She tried to raise her neck but couldn't. "Take off my necklace."

"Keep it on, Mom. If they have to operate, then I will."

"Want to see how it looks on you. Please."

Phoebe, trying to see through the tears, worked the worn gold chain clasp around to the front and undid it. She inched the necklace off carefully and held it in her hand. Her great-grandmother and then her grandmother had worn it before her mother.

"Put it on."

Phoebe fastened the locket. The chain was thin, the pendant warm.

"Take good care of that." Her mother gasped in pain as she fell back.

. . .

Phoebe laced fingers with Deb as the limo sped them toward the final good-bye. Their parents were dead. They were orphans.

Mount Lebanon. New Montefiore. St. Charles.

Cemetery signs lining the Southern State Parkway out on Long Island chronicled the future of all passing by. Phoebe wanted to blind-fold Kate and Noah, keep them walled off from jealous ghosts hovering overhead, seeking company.

She'd been on this road before: Grandma, Aunt Nanny, Uncle Sid, they were all buried in Beth Moses.

"Life goes by in a second." Her mother snapped her fingers each time she said those words. "Boom, and you're gone, yet every minute is so long. Your grandmother taught me that."

Boom. Phoebe had left Bellevue for a walk. When she returned, her mother had died—not lasting one night after learning of her husband's death.

Boom.

What had been the lesson? Phoebe should have panned for more nuggets of ancestral wisdom. Maybe Grandma warned them to weather the long pain of the minutes because otherwise joy rushed away? Pay attention? Do good? Love your family? Hold them close before they disappear into the ground?

Phoebe squeezed Jake's hand, grateful that he had known her parents for so long. He'd become flesh of her flesh, as her parents had with each other. Her mother touched her father often. Despite her sardonic nature and cutting words, she never stinted on showing Daddy love. The knowledge came in a torrent of memories. Squeezing her father's shoulder as she left the table at Peter Luger Steak House so recently. Leaning over and kissing the bald spot on top of his head, ruffling the bits of red hair remaining, still earning his nickname.

Her parents were gone.

The previous night, she and Deb had sorted through family pictures, making posters for the service and then holding objects you don't realize are the most precious until death do you part. The small blue and white delft box where her mother put her rings each night. The scrolled brass mail station in the hallway.

Death taught you that souls lived in the ephemera once surrounding the ones you loved. Families fighting over ancient decks of cards and leaking teapots struggled to be keepers of the past. Now she understood. Possessions mattered because they held your history.

They walked slowly from the limousine to the family gravesite, a spectral lawn with room for a hundred graves. Would she and Jake rest someday with her parents, or would he insist on majesty? Phoebe feared a lonely place of grandeur where she'd be alone with him until the children joined them.

Deb reached for her. They walked together clutching embroidered black handkerchiefs from their mother's drawer. Talismanic bits of her parents shielded them during the finality of burial. Phoebe wore the gold locket, Deb the wedding and engagement rings.

The men's and boys' black silk yarmulkes flapped against hairpins in the early December wind. The older women—her aunt Ruth, and many of her mother's friends—had pinned lace circles on their hair. They clutched black coats close as they huddled, a clutch of widows. Those with living husbands stood straight and a step behind, rejecting death, seeming unwilling to taunt the spirits.

Jake took her hand as they reached the gravesite opened for two boxes. Noah took her other hand. Kate leaned her head on Jake's shoulder.

Part 4

___

IT FALLS APART

CHAPTER 22

JAKE

September 2008

"How about some cupcakes with your coffee?" Jake faked a grin at the accountants. The two had been sent from the US Securities and Exchange Commission—otherwise known as the SEC—the goddamned federal overlords of money. "The best you'll ever taste. We bring in a few dozen from the Cupcake Project every day. It's my wife's company, by the way."

"The Cupcake Project belongs to your wife?" This was the young one of the duo, a woman who looked as though cupcake tasting were her second job.

Jake held his hand to his heart. "Love of my life. The softie of the family. All the profits go to Mira House, a community center on the Lower East Side. She's been working there since college."

"I read about that business." The balding accountant's stern expression broke into a vague look of admiration. "So, your wife started it?"

"Yup. We moved back to Manhattan a few years ago so she could oversee opening the store downtown. Right near Mira House. She's the bleeding heart, and I'm the head of stone." Jake leaned forward as though to tell them a secret. "Of course, everyone's a soft touch for their wife, right? It's not common knowledge, but I helped with the start-up costs."

Jake made sure to sound self-deprecating, letting them know he was severely lowballing his contribution to the Cupcake Project. "The connection? It's not a secret, but I don't spread that around. Phoebe gets full credit for this one."

He left the room and called his secretary. "Connie, bring a tray to the conference room. Stat. Pile up enough cupcakes to stun an elephant. Add bagels, coffee, tea, and anything else you can think of."

He raced up the stairs to the thirty-seventh floor.

The damned SEC had unearthed accusations from years ago, and today he might pay that overdue bill.

Jake might be the only man on Wall Street who'd been helped by 9/11—not something of which he was proud, just a truth. Hell, Jake lost friends. Solomon's sister died. Jake closed JPE so the entire company could attend the funeral.

Never would he wish that death and destruction on a soul—hell, he'd donated hundreds of thousands of dollars to helping victims' families—but in a strange shift of historical winds, 9/11 had blown away a sword of Damocles dangling over Jake's head. Earlier in the year, a small industry publication, *Funds Upfront*, had called Jake's lack of volatility almost impossible when paired with his constant incredibly high returns. Unnamed sources in the hedge fund world—and fuck them all roundly—were "baffled by the performance in Jake Pierce's fund."

He agreed to meet with the writer after the article had come out, Jake's avuncular smile showing how little the suppositions of ghosts concerned him. He ticked off his accomplishments: early automation and computerization programs, infrastructure, management, retaining staff—everything but the fucking enamel on his teeth that helped him legally and stunningly second-guess the market.

Two weeks later, a different reporter had written about the issues with a sharper pen. This author—some bitch who couldn't be more than twenty-five—questioned how his Club accounts returned a steady 15-plus percent for more than a decade, theorizing that the JPE brokerage "eased and supported his under-the-radar Pierce Fund," and then wove a scenario on how he might have done this.

When asked to go on record for the woman's article he said, "Each and every word is ridiculous on all counts and also impossible. Any member of my firm will tell you there's an iron curtain between my brokerage and my private fund. Those who've supposedly 'reverse engineered' my methods couldn't reproduce my profit? Well, let me say this: I sure as heck wouldn't invest with them."

But the bitch reporter wanted to hang him. She had ended her smear job by quoting from some supposed investment manager whose client inherited Club-invested assets: "When I called, trying to figure out his game, Pierce would only say, 'It's nobody's business what goes on. It's a private fund.' Honestly? It made me uneasy. I couldn't understand his reasoning on how they were up or down in any given period. In the end, I advised my client to leave."

After the article, his biggest feeder fund, those Wasp fucks Cook and Baylor, had called with concerns. Charlie's genius boys had cooked up some perfect design of a supposed "real-time" computer program to assuage them. The Cook and Baylor assholes came in, watched the show, and were convinced—because people were idiots at heart—but by then, rumors had floated to the SEC.

In a stroke of what-the-fuck luck, before the whispers built a head of steam, terrorists had brought down the World Trade Center with two hijacked airliners, flown another jet into the Pentagon, and crashed a fourth plane in a Pennsylvania field. Nobody cared about covering him anymore.

Jake unlocked the door to the Club offices. Laughter greeted him. His staff, these geniuses in charge of keeping the fund afloat, played catch with a huge stack of ledger pages.

"What the hell are you doing?" he asked.

Gita-Rae, the last person he expected to act foolish, tossed the papers to Nanci. Charlie stood smoking, shaking his head at the scene.

"Hold it, boss," he said. "They're cooling down the paper."

"And aging it," Gita-Rae added. "We can't give fresh-off-the-computer paper to the SEC."

"Your office, Charlie." Jake nodded down the hall with a quick jerk. He was telling, not asking. When they got there, he slammed the door and backed up against the steel file cabinets.

"What the fuck?" Jake, who'd last smoked in 1968, had an urge to bum a cigarette. "Do you think this is some kind of fucking joke?"

Charlie stared with dead eyes. "They've been working nonstop for two weeks, including two weekends. They're just blowing off steam while they age the report. We can hardly give the SEC perfect paper if it's supposed to be old reports."

Jake composed himself. "How does it look?"

"Our job is to show them we weren't front-running, right? Well, we have enough to bury them in proof."

The previous month, in Jake's first meeting with the man and woman from the auditing arm of the SEC, he'd asked what it was they were seeking.

"What do you think we're looking for?" the guy had retorted as though guest starring on *Law & Order: Accounting Division*.

Jake set the bait. "I assume you're looking for front-running." Front-running was this year's crime du jour, as brokers ran wild using information from their analysis department before sharing the data with clients.

The SEC hound neither confirmed nor denied Jake's supposition, but his expression told Jake he'd hit the right road.

"I can guarantee you, nothing like that goes on here," Jake said. "I'd stake my family, my honor, and my bank account on that."

Which was 100 percent true. Why the fuck would he need to use analysis for trades he never made? Sometimes he wished he were front-running, back-running—anything but juggling billions of pure lies.

. . .

The SEC flunkies bought the bullshit, studying the oversized paper as though he'd handed them the Magna Carta. They'd come expecting nefarious schemes, but the idea that the two years' worth of trading records they requested could be manufactured from whole cloth never made their radar. The Club was the purloined letter of Wall Street. Had they asked for the records from the NASD—the National Association of Securities Dealers—it would be game over.

Jake dripped with sweat under his suit by the time the bald guy and the fat woman left. Minutes after shaking hands and sending them off with cupcakes, joking about bribery by cupcake—ha, ha—he locked himself in his office. He pulled the shades and removed his jacket. As he walked to his large private bathroom, he unbuttoned his shirt with trembling hands.

His teeth chattered from pent-up fear; he was amazed the accountants couldn't read hidden panic on the nimbus surrounding him. Before getting into the shower, he splashed icy water on his face until it anesthetized his skin. Anxiety pounded through his chest. Every sound became the SEC returning after unearthing some oddity as it reexamined his numbers.

Who the fuck knew what Solomon and Charlie had told Gita-Rae to enter in the bullshit reports. Nanci didn't exactly have a sharp mind; her fingers were nimble on the keyboard, but not infallible by a long shot.

Jake turned the shower as hot as he could take it, washing sweat out of his hair and then using a rough loofah to scrub at the electric currents of fear flowing through his veins and itching at his skin. Leaning against the glass walls, he broke apart and slid to the tiled floor, his gasps muffled by the pounding hot water.

Once calmed, he closed the taps and stepped out. He'd give up a year of sex for one fucking Xanax.

He wanted out.

Phoebe asked him so often that her words had begun to scrape his soul: "When is enough, enough, Jake?"

When he insisted on buying the penthouse apartment in Manhattan, he thought she'd divorce him. Phoebe wanted him to close shop, promising that she'd turn the Cupcake Project over to Eva and Mira House. "Let's enjoy life, enjoy our money!"

"Kate and Noah would love to be in charge," she told him repeatedly.

All true.

Phoebe would never believe they wouldn't have enough money to retire—even if he liquidated every account, their houses, the boats, and damned watches.

Even if he believed finessing the Club closing was possible, the hopelessness of buying out member accounts held him prisoner, especially now. Everyone was demanding cash these days, looking to liquidate, terrified by the recent plunges in the market beginning with last year's Black Monday. Nobody wanted to ride the waves, stick it out. They all wanted the equivalent of mattresses to hide their money under.

"Jesus, Phoebe," he wanted to say, "getting out is my damned dream."

Every day, he wrote numbers in pencil, playing the same game: How much to make it right? The magic formula tantalized him and was always out of reach. There had to be a way. Sure, you heard about all the people who got caught, but he'd bet that more than one guy pulled it off.

The Club was his albatross, a blind, sucking maw of need. Every penny withdrawn meant bringing in another penny. He did nothing but shovel money into the monster's mouth.

Numbers marched across the pad.

The Club's cash accounts were dangerously low.

Which put him back on the fucking roller coaster to get more clients, because, for sure, tomorrow morning the telephone would ring with more people wanting to empty their accounts.

Nothing had changed since the days when Eli Rosenberg and his putzy cousins pulled out their money.

On the desk were the books he'd carried from the Bronx. He opened *Registration and Regulation of Brokers and Dealers* to a random page.

"We have seen that the effect of subordinating a liability pursuant to a satisfactory subordination agreement is to permit such indebtedness to be treated as part of capital for purposes of the rule."

Close to gibberish, that's how it read to Jake now.

Jake skated on the thinnest of knowledge these days. Years of spouting bullshit, along with turning over all operation of their legit business—the brokerage—had knocked out all stores of real information. He spent his days as a babbling brook of words meaning nothing, and yet nobody questioned him. How long before everyone saw he was a naked emperor? Jake almost hoped the SEC would find him out, allowing him to release his hold on the bulging bag of lies he carried everywhere.

Any day now, he'd burn his ledger.

CHAPTER 23

PHOEBE

November 2008

Diffuse morning sun lit the breakfast nook. Phoebe missed the brilliance of the ocean's reflection. Even in a penthouse, Manhattan rooms never flooded with the spectacular light that bounced off the water. She shook the *New York Times,* both to straighten the pages and get Jake's attention. "Listen to this, honey."

He made a humming sound from the back of his throat, which she took as permission to read aloud.

"The mortgage crisis hasn't merely caused millions of home foreclosures, cost big Wall Street firms tens of billions of dollars and forced layoffs." She leaned the paper against the coffee carafe.

"It has also made it harder to find willing participants for *Wall Street Warriors*, a cable television show that documents the lives of traders, brokers, bankers, and other financial professionals."

Jake twisted his lips into an expression of impatience.

"Insane, right?" she asked. "Did you know they were doing a reality show about Wall Street?"

"Jesus Christ, Pheebs, do you think I want to listen to that shit first thing in the morning?" He slapped the *Wall Street Journal* against the kitchen table. "A reality show? All the damned realism I need is waiting for me every morning when I walk in the office."

The beginnings of a Jake rant colored the atmosphere. Their mornings became worse daily. His clockwork schedule had fallen apart, and she didn't know why. Some days he left for JPE an hour late, almost as though he didn't want to leave the apartment; other days, he ran out to meet Charlie at dawn.

She scanned the paper for something calming, news he'd enjoy, but the headlines all contained dynamite:

Blame Not a Problem to Find in Mortgage Market and Credit Crisis
Wall Street Markets Tumbled the Most in Nearly a Month Yesterday Afternoon . . .

Finally, the word *optimistic* appeared in the business section. "Listen to this, Jake. From Athens: 'The European Central Bank claims havoc wracking global financial markets showed signs of lessening, leaving its benchmark interest rate unchanged at 4 percent.' Good news, right?"

"If we lived in Athens." He scraped up another piece of omelet. "Good eggs. How do you do it with all that fake shit?"

"It's real egg whites and low-fat cheese." Jake's talent for changing the subject rarely fooled her. "Athens should mean a lot to you. We're part of the world economy."

"The world economy? When did you become an economist? Give me a break." He shook his head. "You read your section of the paper, and I'll read mine, okay? Stop sharing every word. You're driving me nuts."

"Why are you being such a bastard?"

Jake looked up from the sports section with his lopsided grin. "You just read me the reason why. Right? The news."

Phoebe avoided smiling back. "Well, which is it? We're worried about the news? We're fine? Should I cut back? Are we in trouble?"

Half the people they knew wore pinched faces. She didn't want Jake carrying the burden alone.

He put down the paper and locked eyes with her. "I'd never let you down. No worries, but if you want to save money, you can start with this." He held up his last bite of toast—dry, no butter or jam.

Phoebe waved away his words. The older they got, the more she watched their meals. They were in their sixties. She had no idea of her natural hair color anymore. Appointments for Botox and wrinkle fillers were as regular as visits to her dental hygienist. Already Jake took Lipitor for cholesterol and Lisinopril for his high blood pressure, though he managed to forget his frightening numbers each time he left the house. Beyond her table, there was no controlling him.

"Thank your lucky stars I watch out for you," she said.

After folding his napkin and placing it next to his plate, Jake came up behind her. He leaned down and kissed her neck. "Pheebs, you're still the sugar in my coffee and the honey in my heart. Seriously. You know how much I love you?"

Maniac to mushy and sentimental again—male hormone surges? She should ask Helen if Alan was like this. "I love you too. Now go earn money for that dry toast I intend to keep serving. I have to check in with Ira and Eva about the incubator store." Eva's newest idea excited her more than anything they'd tried: a small space right in Mira House. They'd take advantage of the growing moneyed population around the settlement house, while training unemployed women to staff the in-house Cupcake Project.

"Got it," Jake said. "Toast money coming."

He left to shower. His scraped-clean plate wouldn't prevent him from barking at Connie for a bagel and lox within a half hour of arriving. No matter how many times Phoebe spoke to her about the heart problems in Jake's family, she ordered Jake his loaded bagel.

"I'm his secretary, not his doctor," she'd say.

What could Phoebe say? She knew how impossible it was to say no to Jake.

She cleared the dishes, brought them to the kitchen, and stacked them in the sink for Shirley, who'd be there soon. Getting the clean sponge from the dishwasher, she wiped down the counters and then carried a cloth over to the table, making sure to wipe every crumb. Jake's need for order, always strong, had bordered on obsessive since they moved to Manhattan. If she didn't have Shirley, she'd give up either the Cupcake Project or Jake.

Too bad Shirley couldn't clean up his tantrums along with the dishes.

After refilling her coffee cup, Phoebe walked out the door to the patio. Sixty-six degrees—warm for mid-November. Russian junipers in giant pots swayed. She imagined the hundreds of tulip bulbs planted behind a protective grassy screen blooming in the spring. Soft pillows and cushions covered the seating running the length of the terrace. Soon she'd have to pack them up for the winter. Owning two homes made her life twice as hard. She'd give up Greenwich, but the grandkids loved it there.

Phoebe pinched back dead bits of foliage as she walked along the perimeter. Recently she'd sensed something seriously wrong with Jake. His mouth had thinned to almost invisible. He drummed his fingers until she felt like chopping them off. The kids said his snapping at work had gotten out of control.

She tipped her head back and let the sun penetrate. Tall buildings surrounded them, but the sky was always available up in the penthouse. Blessings undisguised, blessing in the skies. Skyline of New York here, vast views of the Atlantic in their Greenwich home brought joy, but she'd give it up in seconds for calm.

He should retire. They didn't just have enough; they had too much. No matter how many charity checks she wrote, it didn't seem like she gave away enough. Jake had to stop. The pressure on him kept her up nights, knowing how he carried the entire family on his shoulders. Every one of their relatives either worked for Jake or had money invested with him. They couldn't all keep leaning on him.

His work remained as much a mystery to her today as it always had been. Phoebe was welcome at JPE by everyone except those who worked on the thirty-seventh floor. Nobody went there unless expressly invited. Not that she wanted an invitation. The one time she'd entered, needing papers for Jake, who was home sick, the people working there, especially Gita-Rae, looked at her as though she carried bedbugs, which could only improve the filthy place anyway. They'd be like pets up there.

Afterward, Phoebe asked Jake how he let the thirty-seventh floor stay so disgusting—stacks of old computers, piles of papers, battered wooden desks covered with tchotchkes—when he wouldn't let the rest of the company display anything personal except one photo in a silver frame.

"I don't give a shit as long as they do their business. Nobody goes in there," he said. "Just stay away from them. They're a bunch of animals— animals who work well. They should. I pay them enough. Case closed."

. . .

Noah grabbed Phoebe in a bear hug the moment she opened the door. As usual, he, his wife, and their daughters arrived before Kate's family.

"You're shrinking, Mom. Old age is starting already. Better get some Fosamax. Kids, come here! Holly, Isabelle, can either of you see Grandma?"

Phoebe reached up and ran her hand over Noah's smooth cheek. He had a heavy beard—like Jake he often shaved twice a day—although everything else about him screamed Phoebe, from his fine black hair to his slight build. "My comedian son has arrived. Grossinger's Hotel lost big when they lost you."

"Oh, poor Mom," Noah said. "The Catskill hotels closed so long ago. Is dementia starting?"

"Grandma isn't shrinking! And Daddy isn't a comedian!" Five-year-old Holly hopped on her right foot and then her left. "And she doesn't have dementa." She turned to her mother. "What's dementa?"

Before Phoebe's daughter-in-law, Beth, could answer, Isabelle, at nine, a been-there, done-that sophisticate, rolled her eyes. "It's *dementia*, not *dementa*. It means getting confused from being old."

Holly turned to Beth, stricken. "People get confused when they're old?"

Beth glared at Noah. "Daddy was teasing. Nobody's old or confused."

"Are you sure?" Jake came into the entry and swept up Holly in one swift motion. "This one's getting pretty old. Huge! Jeez, you're breaking my arms, kiddo."

"You're teasing, Grandpa. Right?"

"I don't know. You seem kinda heavy. Are you getting fat, or have I become weak?"

"I'm not fat! Am I, Mommy?"

"I'm teasing, babykins." Jake raised Holly's arm as he held her. "You feel like a little chicken. Are you sure you're not hollow?"

Kate and her family arrived as Beth comforted Holly and chided Jake in one long sentence. In the midst of their huge apartment, the nine of them crowded in the foyer. Phoebe's tension abated. Dinner would be fine. Nothing in the world made Jake happier than having the family together.

"I love this, Grandma," Amelia said. Phoebe's oldest granddaughter beamed as she held out her plate for seconds of chicken polenta casserole.

"Say 'please,' Amelia," Kate reminded. Amelia and Kate were almost visual twins, though Amelia had inherited Phoebe's father's red hair. Both carried Jake's don't-screw-with-me attitude.

"Grandpa, tell the story about selling the cookies," Isabelle asked.

"Not now, kiddo." Jake reached for a baking powder biscuit and then shoved it whole in his mouth. He looked at Phoebe with a "What? *What?*" expression.

"Tell it, Grandpa!" Amelia said. "Tell it."

The grandchildren loved the story—just as Noah and Kate once had—of Jake and his friend pretending to be Boy Scouts, going door-to-door taking orders for nonexistent Boy Scout cookies.

"Come on, Dad. Share your finest hour." Noah pushed his glasses up on the bridge of his nose.

"Tell us!" Isabelle shouted.

"Enough already with the stories." Jake's voice sharpened. "Must we go over old shit for the rest of our lives?"

The children reared back. No one spoke. Holly began crying. Beth swept her out of the chair and carried her from the room.

"Dad? Are you okay?" Noah asked.

"I just don't need any crap tonight." Jake papered over his obvious shame with pugnacity.

"All the girls did was ask for a story," Phoebe said. Amelia and Isabelle didn't say a word. "Don't worry, darlings. Grandpa's not mad at you. You didn't do anything wrong. He's just in a bad mood."

That was a bullshit excuse. Jake never turned on the grandchildren. She waited for him to do one of the head-spinning emotional shifts he'd been pulling lately, but instead he stood too quickly, knocking over his water glass. He slammed his chair under the table and stormed out.

"Girls, go in the TV room. Amelia, put something in, or—a DVD. Take the plate of cookies from the kitchen."

They waited in silence for a few minutes. Kate's husband, usually the quiet one, spoke first. "Is he all right?"

Zach was a doctor; perhaps he saw signs of disease.

"What the hell's going on with him?" Kate balled up her napkin and threw it at Jake's place mat. "This is what he's been like at the office. An asshole."

"He's a wreck." Noah removed his glasses and rubbed his temples. "When we ask him what's wrong, he bites off our heads. Last week, we asked him to go out for lunch, and he refused. 'Too busy, too busy,' he said. Half the time, he's holed up with Charlie or working the phones like a lunatic. If he pulls at his hair anymore, he's gonna start looking like me." Noah ran a hand over his thinning hair. "He darkens the windows every day."

Jake's office, like all the offices, was a fishbowl, with glass that electronics could turn opaque.

"I'm worried, Mom," Kate said. "Noah and I—"

Noah interrupted. "Let's face it, the market is shit. The brokerage is hurting—not layoffs bad, but tense."

"Funds are switching all over the place," Kate said. "He keeps taking money out of the brokerage and sending it up to thirty-seven. Or into the trust."

A fog of inexplicable fear seeped in. "What do you mean?" Phoebe asked.

"What I said, Mom." Kate rolled her eyes as though she were fifteen and reminding her mother to listen. "He's switching millions from the holding accounts into the family foundation and the Club. Accounting, he keeps saying. Bookkeeping. But it's hurting the company's numbers. He ignores everything we say. Can you talk to him?"

Phoebe pushed away her plate, the smell of meat revolting. She clenched her hands in her lap. "If you were worried about money, why'd you let him help buy you the house?" she asked. Three million dollars he sent to Kate's lawyer to speed the sale. "Chicken feed," Jake had said.

"Dad wanted us to buy it," Kate insisted.

"That's the problem." Phoebe crossed her arms to keep from throwing her own napkin. "How can he slow down if he keeps buying, buying, buying for everyone?"

"Don't worry, Mom. You know it's gonna be fine," Noah said. "Dad always finds a way."

CHAPTER 24

PHOEBE

Freezing rain beat against the terrace door. The world felt as if it were going to explode this morning. Knots twisted Phoebe's back. A vague apprehension suffused her every breath. Thanksgiving the previous week had been a subdued time, with everyone on best behavior and Jake nearly silent.

Last night, he'd ordered her to put money that he'd give her into her bank account, which made no sense with redemptions flooding in, but when she asked for his reasons, he wouldn't clarify the request.

"Just do it."

Two days ago, he couldn't eat supper. Not a bite. He'd tried to hide his lack of appetite by picking at the fish, moving vegetables around on his plate, and barking about her lousy, boring suppers. Last night, she had found him with a giant bag of M&M's, reaching steadily, hypnotically, hand in, hand out, while he watched some old John Wayne movie. He lived on sugar, water, and movies.

. . .

Phoebe slipped into the elevator and pressed the gold button for the thirty-eighth floor. She'd come for the money. Her hands trembled against the tissues and change in her pockets. December had turned so cold and wet that morning that she had put on her mother's old fur

212

coat. Jake said the same thing every time she wore it: "Why do you wear that ratty thing? Makes me look like a miser."

Jake would take her into Fendi tomorrow and buy her anything if she so wished, but she didn't wish at all. She hated fur and wrapped herself in this one only because it reminded her of Lola. Phoebe never would have imagined she'd miss her mother so much. In any case, her coat would be the last thing on Jake's mind today. He had verged on unhinged when he called at eight that morning to remind her to get the money *now!*

"What's the rush?" she'd asked, the phone crooked in her neck as she put together papers for a meeting with Eva.

"Don't ask questions." He sounded frantic. "Gig will have the check ready for you. Ten."

"Ten million?"

"No, Pheebs. Ten dollars. I gotta go."

She'd wanted to ask a thousand questions, but hearing the answers might have been worse than not knowing. Seeing Gig tempted her to dig—he took care of the Cupcake Project's books, so that gave her rights—but terrifying article after article in the paper locked away her curiosity. Bear Stearns taken in a forced sale. Lehman Brothers, bankrupt. Merrill Lynch sold. What if something happened to JPE? Only remembering that they were part of a crowd soothed her. Everyone in New York ran scared these days. Jake was bookkeeping. He had handled crises before and would again.

Light poured through the bank of floor-to-ceiling windows. She forced a smile at the receptionist. "Hi, Wendy. How are the kids?"

"Jesse finally got his braces off. He's thrilled and . . ."

Phoebe nodded, hearing nothing as the woman unrolled her life.

Jake's secretary waved as Wendy babbled. Phoebe waved back, but avoided eye contact with Connie. Ordinarily, Phoebe never came into the office without chatting with her, but Jake's insistence drummed. *The money needs to be there before noon. Got it?*

"Excuse me, Wendy." Phoebe interrupted midgush as the receptionist expressed her gratitude to Jake for paying for her son's braces. "Gig's waiting for me. We'll catch up later, hon."

Secretaries, drivers, data entry clerks—staff at JPE were always thanking her for operations funded, overdue tuition bills paid. In a field known for people leaping from one dangled carrot to another, at JPE, they settled in for the duration.

Phoebe headed down the corridor and entered Gig's office.

"Phoebe, doll." Gig came from behind his desk and pecked her on the cheek. "I have everything ready."

He handed over a thin envelope with her name. She didn't check it, simply tucked it in her purse. She didn't stop in to see Jake, whose words rang: *Get the fuck over to the bank, pronto.* When she reached the waiting Town Car, Leon put down the *Daily News* and hurried out from the front seat, but she had the back door opened before him.

"The bank on Fifty-Third, please, Leon."

"Pleasure, Mrs. Pierce."

Phoebe worshipped Leon's tendency not to make small talk. Being Mrs. Pierce meant providing smiles and sympathy, keeping up with births and deaths, bar mitzvahs and confirmations. Jake had pushed her years ago to become the maternal face of JPE. She carried the JPE employees around in her head: Wendy's son's crooked teeth, Connie's mother's breast cancer, Leon's kids' five college tuitions—they crowded her mind along with the people from the Cupcake Project and Mira House.

. . .

A pink-faced man materialized and ushered her into a hushed back room the moment she entered the bank. Perhaps the suited woman at the dais behind the security guard watched for clients with multi-million-dollar accounts, and then, when one appeared, summoned an executive with a stroke of a computer key.

"Mrs. Pierce, how nice to see you," he said. "Owen King," he reminded her without a hint of judgment about her memory.

"And you, Mr. King."

"How can we help you today?"

She patted her purse. "I have a deposit."

Owen King showed every one of his overwhite teeth, smiling as though Phoebe brought bliss into his life. Were banks so desperate for cash? The banker ushered her into his mahogany paneled office. "What can I serve you, Mrs. Pierce? It's so nasty out. Would you like something warm?"

Warm sounded wonderful. Tears of gratitude threatened. Phoebe blinked, humiliated at appearing so fragile. Crazy rich lady, he must think, reeling from her stock losses. No, Owen, it wasn't that. She didn't even know why she was scared, or what of.

. . .

A deep-green throw enveloped Phoebe. She rubbed the soft cashmere between her fingers as she read her sister's email.

> Ben and I have Charlotte for a couple of days. What is it with our kids—they have to reach back to the nineteenth century for their kids' names? Pheebs, if Mom were alive, she'd gobble up this little girl. Blond curls springing out all over her head. Remember how Mom moaned and groaned about your stick-straight black hair? Horsetail hair, she called it. No wonder you smelled like rotten eggs for so many years with those awful perms!
>
> Anyway, we want you and Jake to come down and rest. Sounds like you're both exhausted. No surprise, with everything going on. Our friends are terrified, watching their balances sink. Thank God for Jake. Even if he won't come, you get down here. But make him come.

Phoebe stopped reading, imagining a trip to Florida. Jake never relaxed there—not with clients everywhere. Maybe the only place she could take him to unwind would be the moon. But they could go somewhere with Ben and Deb. A cruise to Alaska. Ben never tried talking business with Jake. "What do I know from derivatives?" he'd say. "You take care of my money, and I'll make the golf dates for us."

Then he'd put an arm around Jake and squeeze. Sometimes Ben got so overwhelmed by gratitude that he'd grab Jake by the shoulders and kiss him.

"Such royalty, my daughter," her mother would say if she saw

Phoebe miserable while covered in cashmere. "My spoiled princess, are you feeling the pea? A little trouble and you fall apart? Your grand-mother came over on the boat by herself at thirteen. Thirteen! Do that. Then complain to me. Raise ten children on the Lower East Side. Then complain to me. Lose two little ones to the flu. Then complain to me. Your life is golden, Phoebe."

CHAPTER 25

PHOEBE

"Phoebe!"

Jake's scream startled her awake. How long had she napped? Hazy light came through the window. The rain had stopped. The clock showed 12:40. She swallowed. A sour film reminded her of the banker's warm latte.

"Phoebe." Jake leaned on the doorjamb of her study as though holding himself upright. His grey skin brought strokes and heart attacks to mind. "Wake up, Pheebs."

"I'm up." She threw off the light blanket and stood so fast she became light-headed. "What's wrong? Are you sick?"

"The kids are here."

"Noah and Kate?" She touched a hand to her chest. "Are . . ." She didn't know what to ask first.

"Come." He turned to walk away and then stopped. "I love you. You're the blood running through my veins, sweetheart. You know, right?"

Cancer. He'd brought them together to tell them. Please God. Give her strength. Let her hold up for him, for Kate and Noah. She took her husband's hands and held them tight, kissing each one.

"Of course I know."

They walked to Jake's study. Kate and Noah sat side by side on the massive couch. The contrast between the rich red tapestry and her children's bloodless, pinched faces tore at her chest. Jake fell into his chair, the soft brown leather worn to his shape, the matching hassock indented where he rested his feet as he read his endless thrillers. She took the wooden rocker. She sat slowly, feeling the easy ripple of the rocker moving with her weight.

Please live, Jake.

"Dad has something to tell us," Kate said.

"Right." Phoebe kept her face calm even as her stomach folded like origami.

"I have something to tell you," Jake repeated. He twisted his wedding band in circles. "You're not going to be happy."

"Rip off the Band-Aid, Dad," Kate said.

"This isn't easy." He looked out the window as though studying the skyline, avoiding Phoebe's eyes, the way he did when he'd screwed up. "Explaining is almost impossible."

Phoebe crossed her arms. Forget cancer or a coronary, unless she tallied another woman under heart problems. If he thought he'd marry some mistress, a young trophy bitch, he'd better get rid of every knife in the house. Bastard.

"Stop scaring Mom." Noah turned to her. "The problem is business. We went into Dad's office. Uncle Theo took us in after we went to him—"

"We were worried, Dad." Kate made a calming motion with her hand. "We wanted to talk to Uncle Theo about you taking money out of the brokerage account to—"

Noah intervened. "We're not questioning your authority, but—"

"Enough." Jake raised his hands, but instead of the flood of recriminations Phoebe expected, he covered his face and began sobbing.

No. Dear God. Cancer was making him act crazy. Or another woman. He thought he was in love with some girl thirty years younger than him. Forty.

Oh, but I also love you, Pheebs.

She could just fucking hear him now.

Noah put a hand on his father's shoulder. Then he sank down and placed a hand on his knee. "Dad, you can talk to us."

Jake covered Noah's hand with his own. "You're a good boy. You've always been a good boy."

Cancer.

"I . . ." Jake breathed deep enough to restart his heart. "Jesus, this is hard."

Kate perched forward. "Just say it, Dad."

Jake leaned back and looked up at the ceiling, his eyes not meeting theirs. "There's no money," he said. "Everything is gone."

Kate and Noah squinted as though Jake were crazy.

"Gone?" Noah repeated Jake's declaration as a question. "We lost our money? We—"

"Not our money. Everybody's money. Not lost. Not exactly. It was never there. I mean, it was there, but I never did anything with it."

"You're not making any sense," Noah said.

This babbling—was prattling a stroke symptom? She tried to re-member the signs.

"I developed a . . . strategy. When things went south a while ago, I borrowed from Peter to pay Paul. I thought I'd catch up, but I couldn't. I didn't. Now almost nothing's left. A strategy . . ." His words drifted away.

"A strategy? Borrowing from Peter? Strategy? That's a scheme, not strategy. That's fraud." Noah paced to the window and then circled back to the couch and Kate.

"You raided clients' accounts?" Kate whispered.

"Not exactly," Jake said.

Someone had vacuumed out Phoebe's blood and left this husk. "Then exactly what?" She shredded the fringe at the edge of the pillow in her lap.

"There weren't any accounts anymore. Just one big chunk of money."

"One big chunk? Gone? The investments can't be completely gone. Those portfolios are packed with solid companies, Dad," Noah said. "Something's got to be there. I don't understand. You're not making any sense."

"Listen. There weren't any investments," Jake said. "Not anymore."

"You're not making any sense!" Noah repeated the words with more emphasis, almost shouting as he pointed at Jake.

"There were stocks once, but I sold them when things got bad. And then I covered them."

"Covered them how?" Noah asked.

"With what we got from new investments."

"How long has this been going on?" Kate's voice shook.

Phoebe shivered as she tried to make sense of Jake's words, the children's questions.

"I only need a few days. Next week I'm meeting with the lawyers—Gideon and his guys. He's the best in New York. We'll figure something out."

"How long, Dad?" Kate repeated.

"Too long." Jake bent over and mumbled to his shoes. "I'll put everything right."

Kate pressed between her eyes. She placed her cup on the coffee table, rose, and marched to where Jake sat. He appeared suddenly shrunken and old.

"Put it right?" Kate shook her hands at him. "Figure something out? You're talking about a Ponzi scheme. That was your fucking scheme, Dad? That was your secret recipe? That was how you made the money soup? Jesus fucking Christ, there's no making this right."

Forever she'd remember Kate swearing at Jake and him remaining silent.

"A Ponzi scheme?" Phoebe asked.

"A fraud. He paid his clients' so-called profits with infusions from new investors. There was no profit. He just gathered more people to fleece. He never invested anything," Kate said. "Dad's a thief."

Jake lifted his head. "We still have some cash. I wrote out checks already for the people that matter. Listen, plenty of people made loads of profit before this."

"Can you hear how insane you sound? They profited 'cause you gave them someone else's money!" Kate closed her eyes and shook her head before continuing. "Let's get this totally straight. You took people's money to pay other people. It was all made up."

Phoebe ripped at her palms with her nails.

Concentrate.

It was all gone?

He stole it?

Phoebe needed to focus. She forced herself to stare at the chair on which Jake sat. The needlework pillows her sister had made. "Why do you show that crap?" That's how Jake talked about presents from her sister. But she'd fought him. She put out the pillows.

Jake dredged up his in-charge face, trying to grasp control and retain his roar of ownership. "Not always. I'm not saying that. Problems came, and obstacles kept happening. I didn't set out to do this thing."

"So how long? A month? A year? A decade?" Kate asked.

Jake threw up his hands. "Not a month. Or a year."

"Longer?" Noah had been able to read his father since childhood. Jake remained silent until Noah repeated himself. "Longer, Dad?"

"Much longer. Don't you understand, Noah? Mom?" Kate shook her head in disgust. "He's a criminal. We'll be pulled down with him now that he's told us." She wrapped her hands around her upper arms. Her thinking posture. Phoebe tried to break free of her frozen coffin. Slivers of ice filled her throat.

They all watched, waiting for Kate the analyzer, Kate the problem solver, to conjure magic. Finally, she opened her eyes. Unwrapped her arms. She stood. "We're going, Noah. Come with us, Mom."

He stole money? He made it all up? Phoebe was locked in a conversation time delay as daughter Kate transformed into business Kate. Her daughter's mind raced incessantly—didn't Phoebe always say that about her girl?

Kate placed a hand behind Noah's back. Phoebe wanted to go with her competent daughter, her tender son. Walk away from this stranger.

But look at Jake with his shaking hands. He looked like ashes.

"I never meant for this to happen," he said.

"Who held the gun to your head?" Kate said.

"I'll make it better." He turned to Phoebe. "I can fix this. I promise. Gideon's the best lawyer in the field. He'll know what to do."

"Mom, if Noah and I stay here, we'll be accessories. Please. Come with us."

"You won't be in any trouble, Pheebs. You're my wife."

"How much did you put in her name, Dad?" Kate asked.

"You think I'd hurt your mother?" Jake asked. "I never involved any of you." He wept again, the sounds torn from his throat.

"How can I leave your father all alone?" Phoebe choked out the words.

Kate tipped her head. "Did you know about this?" she asked Phoebe.

Phoebe touched her chest. "Oh my God, of course not."

"How could you think that?" Jake said.

"How could I think it of *you*, Dad?" Kate put her arms around Phoebe and whispered, "Don't take his side. Please."

"Oh, baby," she murmured, "there are no sides."

Kate drew back. "There are *only* sides now."

Noah seemed lost. "This isn't possible. How could you do this?"

"I'm sorry. I'm so sorry."

Noah went to Jake and took his hands. "Dad . . . Oh, Dad."

"Noah. We're leaving now."

Tears ran down her son's cheeks.

Kate's voice softened. "Come on, baby brother. Let's go."

"Kate," Jake said. "Please. Wait. Phoebe, talk to them."

"There's a hurricane on the way." Kate tugged Noah's arm. "And we're getting out of the path."

Phoebe didn't move. Didn't say a word. Kate was smart—smarter than any of them.

Jake rose and came to the rocking chair. He clamped a hand on Phoebe's shoulder, linking them, revolting her. His hand anchored her to horror.

"I need a few days, that's all. Just a few days," Jake insisted. "I already called Gideon and made an appointment," he repeated.

He called a lawyer before he told us. Before he told me.

As though reading her mind, Jake squeezed her shoulder. "I couldn't tell you until it was under control. If Theo hadn't brought the kids in, I wouldn't have said anything."

"Theo knew?"

"I told him yesterday. He said he'd wait until Monday."

"Wait until Monday?" Kate asked. "That's what you told Uncle Theo? Might as well get him his own lawyer right now."

Phoebe began to speak and then pressed her mouth shut. She didn't want to understand any more.

"We're leaving," Kate said.

Jake continued to press her into the chair. She shrugged his hand away and went to her children. Kate raked furrows through her hair in harsh wounding movements. Phoebe reached up and pulled down her girl's arm. She wiped Noah's tears. "Shah, shah," she said as though speaking to an injured toddler.

"This is a crucial moment, Mom." Kate's voice cracked. "Don't put your head in the sand."

Her savvy daughter would protect Noah. Zach would watch out for Kate—her son-in-law would never abandon his wife.

Jake slumped on the couch, a million years old.

How could he do this? Who would take care of him?

She stared at her husband. They'd been together since she was practically a child. She'd married as a girl. For better or worse.

"I'll call you later," Phoebe said. "You'll bring the girls for dinner."

"Mom, listen to what I'm saying. We're never coming back."

Phoebe hugged her rigid daughter. "No. You can't make such a decision just like that." She tried to gather Noah in her arms, but he backed away to his sister, and together they walked out.

The front door closed.

She turned to Jake. "What did you do? God in heaven, what did you do to us?"

CHAPTER 26

PHOEBE

Jake left the room without a word.

Phoebe wandered through the ornate rooms, trying to think. She folded and refolded stacks of sweaters, her hands buried in drifts of soft cashmere. She cleared coffee cups and scrubbed the stain of Kate's red lipstick from the china. On the terrace, she lifted her face to the stinging wind.

Next came bourbon. For courage. For deadening. To face the next minute of her life.

When Phoebe had finished the drink, and another, she found Jake. "You stole it all?" She hovered at the entrance to his study, gripping the edge of the ivory-colored doorjamb.

Boxers sparred on the screen. Jake lay on the leather sofa, arms dangling, his fingers scraping the rug. He kept his eyes on the television, watching sweat-oiled men pound each other, and answered without looking at her. "The money you took out this morning was to cover all the checks I wrote. There's almost nothing left after that."

"Checks? To whom?" She tightened her fingers around the crystal glass filled with ice and bourbon. Thin crystal. Expensive. Baccarat. Simply squeezing too hard might shatter it. Yesterday, if she so wished, just for fun, she could have thrown the entire set against the wall. Just to hear the crash of splintering glass could have been her pleasure for the day. Replacements were always available.

What had she paid for this one glass? Two hundred? Three?

"Checks for the people that matter," Jake said.

"Don't they all matter?"

"Sure. Everyone," he muttered.

Lies. All he told were lies.

"What am I supposed to do?" He still spoke without looking at her. "Should I write a check to the richest clients, like Louis Klein, or your sister and Ben?"

Her sister. She lowered herself to the edge of the leather chair with shaking legs.

"It's over." Jake still wouldn't look at her. "We can only help a few people."

She remained mute, at a loss for a frame of reference.

"People like Louis made plenty off the company, believe me," he answered himself. "They're not losing a thing."

Louis Klein treated Jake like his fourth child. He called Phoebe on her birthday and sat at the family table at their kids' weddings.

"I wrote checks to your sister, bonuses for all the people in the office. People like Leon—that's who I'm taking care of. The money will go out tomorrow morning. I'll make sure." He spoke as though doing something worthy of pride.

Waves of faces flashed. Uncles. Cousins. Eva. Linh. Zoya. Ira. Mira House. She might as well separate molecules of water as isolate family and friends not in the Club.

"I'm seeing Gideon on Monday. Don't worry. I'll put everything in order."

"How?"

"Don't worry."

"My sister's money is gone?" she asked. "Eva and the others? Ira? Mira House?"

Jake struggled to a sitting position and placed a hand on each of his knees. "Are you not listening? Almost everything is gone. I'm slicing up what's left; too many people need a piece of the pie. The Club's gone, Pheebs. You gotta stay quiet for now. Don't call Deb, or the money could disappear before she gets it. Do you understand?"

"How did this happen, Jake?"

He raised the television volume. "Like a house burning, one stick of furniture at a time."

. . .

Now they faced going to the party.

The holiday celebration.

JPE's bash was always held someplace fancy enough for the women to glitter, while allowing the men to wear nothing dressier than sports jackets and fresh shaves. A place where they could let down their hair, receive expensive gifts selected by Phoebe, drink endlessly, gorge all night, and live up to the family touch Jake infused into the company.

This year's "family touch" was Jake's fingers snaking into the staff's pockets, pulling out their salaries, and channeling the money to the thirty-seventh floor—where most of the staff had invested their life savings—smashing their trust until it was no more than particles of dust.

She would skip the party and let Jake claim whatever illness he wanted for her, if not for the tiny hope that some miracle would bring Kate and Noah to the celebration.

Extravagant fabric shimmered from Phoebe's closet. She stared at dresses, evening skirts, and palazzo pants until they blurred into a Picasso of her wardrobe.

Bouclé.

Crepe.

Silk.

Red.

Beige.

Blue.

White.

Black.

Black.

Black.

She could take a knife and slash every piece.

Or slit Jake's throat.

Thief.

Crook.

Pirate.

Plunderer.

Jake walked in, his charcoal suit too clean a contrast to his blood-shot brown eyes, dense with misery. He'd combed back his thick hair but skipped the second shave he usually took before a party. His tie knot appeared clumsy.

"You're not dressed," he said.

"When did it start?" she asked.

Silence.

"Why did you do it?"

Still as dirt.

"Nothing makes sense."

"Just get dressed. We'll talk later."

When he left the bedroom, she rummaged in her dresser till she found a prescription bottle under a pile of silk camisoles, shook out a Xanax, and swallowed it dry. Once the pill was down safely, she grabbed a long black skirt and a grey blouse. She'd match Jake. Sack cloth and ashes. Two clichés of penitence.

A car service driver picked them up. No one worked during the holiday—especially not Leon. He could drink his favorite Chopin vodka, which Jake always made sure was on hand, all night if he wished—he'd be the driven, not the driver. The night of the party, Jake sent a car for Leon.

Connie rushed over, hugging Phoebe first and then Jake. "I was so worried about you!" she said to Jake. "Where'd you go? You disappeared. You didn't answer your calls; I was going crazy wondering what happened. Some questions came up about the party and I—"

Jake patted Connie's shoulder. "Phoebe's sister took ill." Jake tapped his chest as though the problem lay in Deb's heart. "She's in the hospital. West Boca Community at first, but we arranged transportation to Cedars."

His lies rolled out like lush carpet. Smooth and so thick that you sunk right in. He'd use anyone, wouldn't he? Her sister. His brother.

"My goodness!" Connie's hand went to her heart, mirroring Jake's gesture. She tapped her oval red nails—lacquered so shiny they resembled valentines—against her blue satin dress. Her gaze shifted to Phoebe, reaching for her hand, which Phoebe reluctantly gave over. "Is your sister going to be okay?"

"She'll be fine." Her words traveled through broken glass lining her throat.

Jake put an arm around Phoebe shoulders. "It's a party. She doesn't want to talk about it, so can you keep it under your hat, sweetheart?" he asked Connie. "I'll catch you up tomorrow. For now, smile."

Connie obeyed with a toothy grin. "Anything. Everyone's been wanting to say thank you. The room looks fantastic, huh?" She held out her right hand, pointing casually and shaking her wrist a bit. The peridot and diamond bracelet Phoebe had picked out as a gift—the green stones matching Connie's eyes—were magnificent against Connie's olive skin.

"The bracelet looks lovely." Phoebe felt sick as she added the prices of the bracelets and watches she'd bought for the staff.

"How do you know exactly what I love? Thank you!" Connie admired her outstretched wrist. "It's gorgeous."

Phoebe stretched her mouth into what she hoped resembled a smile more than a rictus. "You deserve that and more." How much had Jake's secretary invested in the Club? Had she brought in her family's money, like most of the JPE staff? "Have you heard from Noah? Kate?"

"No. Why?" Connie's face tightened. "Are they in touch with your sister? Do you want me to try calling?"

"No, no," Jake broke in. "Not to worry. Only a few crossed wires. It's all under control." He scowled at Phoebe. "No work for Connie tonight."

On the ride over, she'd tried Kate and Noah every ten minutes, then five, repeatedly pressing redial until Jake grabbed the phone and turned it off. "Enough," he'd said. "They'll be at the party."

Phoebe peered through the dimly lit room, but she didn't expect to see them. She snuck into the ladies' room and turned her phone back on, first checking for messages and then calling both children again. She sat on the closed toilet seat, pressing Noah's and Kate's numbers until, finally, she gave up. Lipstick reapplied haphazardly, she returned to the party.

Kate's words came back. *There's a hurricane on the way.* All those people out there were right in the path.

Fairy lights shimmering in fresh ropes of evergreen reflected off crystal stars hanging from the ceiling. They hurt her eyes. A waiter walked over carrying a silver tray covered with filled wine glasses. Phoebe reached out, but Jake clamped a hand on her wrist and waved the jacketed young man away. "No drinking. I need you compos mentis."

She pulled away from him and stopped the waiter, touching his shoulder and then gesturing for a drink. Jake's glare and his hard jaw meant nothing to her.

Theo sat in a corner with his wife, both gripping glasses filled with amber liquid. Glenfiddich, she knew. Had Theo told Ellen? His wife always stuck inseparably, almost insufferably, close to him, so seeing her glued to him provided no clue. Jake's brother appeared as though someone had tipped him over and emptied his soul.

Phoebe pulled her sweater tight. Jake had used her as part of his making things right. Sending her to Gig, to the bank. Was she now liable?

As if she couldn't feel worse, Charlie, the consigliore of the thirty-seventh floor, walked toward them. She could imagine him with a cold handgun tucked under the leather jacket he wore all winter. Top staff dressed corporate, as ordered by Jake, while Charlie marched around the office in muscle-hugging black jeans and black shirts.

At best, the folks from the thirty-seventh floor unnerved her; most made her skin crawl. Gita-Rae's low-cut blouses highlighting her bony chest made Phoebe feel as though she were examining X-rays. Connie had confided that the girls up on thirty-seven shook visibly upon Gita-Rae's approach, and her supervision style included voice-cracking

screams. Her obsequiousness toward Phoebe smacked of behind-the-back nastiness. Those who spat down, often licked upward.

Jake put a hand around her waist and pulled her close. He reeked of need. His caress repulsed her.

"Hey, boss." Charlie pumped Jake's hand. "Mrs. Boss." He kissed Phoebe on the lips—she'd been too slow to offer her cheek. Waves of cologne attacked her. "Terrific party." He held up his arm. "Great timepiece."

"Wear it in good health," Jake said.

"How you holding up?" Charlie moved in too close. "Everything good?"

"Everything's fine." Steel embedded in Jake's response pushed away the question.

"Ya need anything?" Charlie persisted.

"Get me a Coke," Jake said.

Charlie's mouth tightened. Obviously, he hadn't been offering his services to personally fetch something. "Coming right up, boss."

As employees descended, Jake squeezed her hand as though it were a life preserver, while nodding and accepting thanks for gold pendants, cashmere shawls, and leather briefcases. Jake insisted on presents people wore and carried. He liked seeing his generosity at work.

CHAPTER 27

PHOEBE

The digital clock clicked from 5:59 to 6:00. Thin light crept into Phoebe's study. Ridges marking the sofa's tufts divided her back into individual squares of pain. Questions raced in a hamster wheel of repetition throughout the sleepless night.

What are the kids doing?

Deb—should I tell her, despite Jake's warnings?

Who, who, who in the world is this man I married?

Jake fell into an Ambien-induced coma soon after they returned from the party—suddenly he found drugs wonderful and fine. She, on the other hand, couldn't take one. Not after all the wine and Xanax. *I Love Lucy* played all night as she lay in front of the droning television.

Phoebe couldn't bear lying next to Jake. Even when she'd dozed occasionally during the long night, her subconscious wormed another reminder of the looming abyss and woke her. Questions blurred as Lucy and Ethel tumbled from antic to frantic in their attempts to fool and please Ricky and Fred.

She dialed Kate and then Noah on autopilot. Painful pressure in her chest screamed heart attack, terrifying her in one moment and, in the next, bringing a coward's comfort as she imagined the relief of lying in the hospital.

Phoebe tipped back her head trying to get a bead on her blindness. How much had she missed? Was there a single genuine particle in

Jake? She continued wondering while setting up the coffee, showering in the guest bathroom, and throwing on a terry cloth robe from the guest room closet. She poured two cups of coffee, unable to break her habit of carrying a cup to him, adding half-and-half and sugar to his, leaving hers black and bitter, not certain that even skim milk could slip past the knot clenching her stomach.

Fuck what he'd said. At eight, she'd call Deb. Eva.

Phoebe caught sight of the photo rendered to art hanging in the hall. Crystalline water and turquoise sky served as a backdrop for the family portrait from Greenwich. Phoebe took the silver frame off the wall. She fixated on Jake's eyes—bringing the picture so close the image pixilated—searching for a clue. The kids were barely out of diapers when the picture was shot. Were Jake's crimes already in motion?

She appeared love struck. In two dimensions, she gazed at Jake as though he were God, while he stared at the camera.

"You know what your problem is?" her sister had asked whenever Phoebe seemed surprised by some Jake transgression in those days. "He put stars in your eyes when you were too young, and you still haven't shaken out the glitter. Sweetheart, the gold's supposed to fall out by the end of the first six months. Eighteen tops, and that's only if he's away in the army."

Deb had been right. Phoebe always stayed the girl who'd sinned and been rescued by Jake.

Phoebe, steaming full mugs in her hands, banged the bedroom door open with her knee.

"Wake up." She placed Jake's coffee on the nightstand, centering it on the oversized bronze coaster.

He blinked as she opened the curtains. "What time is it?"

"Six thirty."

"Did the kids call?"

"No." She sat on the wing back chair facing his side of the bed. "I need to tell Deb."

Jake drained half the cup as he always did with his first swallows and then threw back the covers. "No." He stomped to the bathroom.

"She has to know!" Phoebe yelled through the door. "So she can sell her shares."

Jake stormed back into the room, his face red and tight. "Don't be a moron. There's nothing to sell. There aren't any 'shares.' It would be a withdrawal from a dry account. I can't handle the redemptions already in line."

"How about the main business? Can't you handle a withdrawal there? What will Deb and Ben do? Everything they have is with you."

"You really aren't getting it. There is no money. Nothing, except for the checks I wrote. She'll receive one, but I can't give the full amount to—"

"We'll sell the Greenwich house. Give the money to—"

Jake sank on the bed. "Phoebe. Houses aren't spare gold bars you can turn in for cash, and even if we could, what do you think? That Deb and Ben will keep this secret? That they won't call their kids, their friends—"

"She'll stay quiet if I ask."

Jake sat beside her, taking her hands until she pulled away. "No one keeps a secret like this. Don't worry. I only need a few days. Deb and Ben are on the list for a check. When I meet with Gideon, he'll help me figure out the next step."

"Why, Jake? What was this for?"

He avoided her eyes. "I always thought I could make it right."

"Why would you even start? So we could buy shit? Expensive furniture?" She strode to the walk-in closet and flung open the doors. "Shelves of shoes and racks of dresses? You became a thief for this crap? You sold your soul for houses?"

"I'm taking a shower," he said.

"You're really going to work?"

"Of course. What did you expect?"

"But . . . the kids?"

"Kate and Noah will be at the office."

"You think so?" Against all odds, she was ready to believe him.

"I'm positive," he said. "I promise. I'm gonna fix this. There's gotta be a way out."

Phoebe dragged herself to make Jake's breakfast as he showered. Would the kids be at work? They were so close, the four of them. Unusually so, seeing or speaking to one another daily. For Kate and Noah not to answer her calls indicated disaster.

She reached for her favorite red bowl—once her mother's—cracked two eggs and tried to calm down, whisking beat by beat.

Dissociate.

Heat the omelet pan.

Using the paring knife, she sliced a pat of butter directly into the stainless steel. Screw the Pam spray. Once the butter melted to the perfect edge of sizzling, she slipped in the beaten eggs.

She stood immobile as the edges of the eggs thickened and turned puffy. Water stopped running in the bathroom. No matter how expensive the paint or thick the old plaster walls, pipes ran through them, and sounds bled out.

She lifted the corner of the omelet, impatient to fold it. Toss the eggs on a plate. Throw herself into a second shower and wash off her fear with stinging hot needles of water.

A buzzer startled her as cheese bubbled from the fold. She looked at the clock as though it might provide an answer. Almost eight.

Noah!

Kate would be getting the kids ready for school, but Noah could leave the house early. He'd always been the forgiving child. "Don't be mad at Mommy," he'd plead when she and Kate had their mother-daughter fights during the teenage years.

She pressed the speaker button for the intercom to the lobby. "Yes?" She smiled, anticipating hearing Noah's name.

Anthony, the weekday man on the desk, announced himself and then said, "Two gentlemen are on their way up to see Mr. Pierce."

"Men?" She clutched the edge of the counter. "Who? You let them up?"

"Um, they're with the law, ma'am. They had badges." Anthony's typically even voice rose. "They didn't ask; they just went."

She released the speaker button. "Jake!" she called. When he didn't answer, she screamed full blast, *"Jake!!"*

Within moments, he ran into the kitchen, wet hair slicked back, thin bare legs peeking from beneath his robe. "What's wrong?" He looked around as though expecting an explosion or fire.

"The police." Fear blocked her throat and chest. She struggled to speak through the thickness. "The police are here."

"Police?" He whipped his head in both directions, as though men hid behind the stove, under the counters. "Where?"

"On their way up. Anthony just called."

"What the—"

The front bell chimed, followed by a rap on the wooden door.

"Get the door," he ordered.

Phoebe pulled her robe tighter. "They're here for you. You answer it." She ran toward their bedroom, hearing muffled words float up as Jake opened the door. Phoebe listened as she yanked jeans and a sweater from the closet. *Please God, let the children be all right. Tell me what to do.*

She picked up the phone and dialed Jake's office.

"Connie, it's Phoebe."

"Hey, hon. You guys left so early last night I didn't say—"

"Are the kids there?" Phoebe rubbed the edge of the bedspread.

"Haven't seen them. Want me to check?"

"Please. And if they're not there, could you find Theo?"

She waited for what seemed like hours until her brother-in-law came on the line.

"You okay?" Theo asked. "Connie said you seemed panicky. What's wrong?"

"Are the kids there?"

"Not since they left with Jake yesterday."

"Have you spoken to them?"

"No." He sounded beaten.

"I can't talk," she said. "Police are here. I'll call as soon as I know more."

"What—"

"I gotta go." After hanging up, she forced herself to walk with calm control, following voices to Jake's study. A man stood on either side of her husband.

"Mrs. Pierce?" The taller of the men addressed her. He held himself as though in charge and was dressed so soberly his clothes frightened her. Between his somber expression and dark suit he'd brought a funeral into the house.

"Yes."

"Agent Todd Hynde. This is Agent Ryan Forsyth." In place of a handshake, they each flipped open a black leather cardholder and showed identification.

"We waited for you," Agent Forsyth said. "At the request of your husband."

She nodded as though his words contained a single nugget of normal. Terror trickled down her spine.

"Why don't we sit down," Agent Hynde said, pretending that choice existed. She curled her shaking hands into balls.

The agents each took one of the two chairs, leaving Jake and Phoebe to sink side by side into the couch. Hynde, the black agent, took the leather chair. The white one sat on the upright needlepointed bench, the red-and-blue pattern incongruous against his funereal suit.

"We're here—"

Jake held out his palm. "No need to explain."

Her husband's hair, thick and grey with a memory of dark brown, was drying into the thatch she'd loved. She'd always been inordinately proud of Jake's full hairline.

"I know what this is about," Jake said.

"Then you're aware that we're looking for explanations." Forsyth, that was his name. His skin held the ravages of teenage acne. His low voice sounded midwestern.

"There are no explanations," Jake said. "Or, I should say, there's only the truth. There are no excuses. I'm guilty. The important thing is this: I did it all myself. Nobody else was ever involved." He looked at Phoebe with intent so hard it hit her chest. "Just me."

Phoebe could take in only pieces of Jake's answers to the agent's questions.

"The funds are gone."

"I paid investors with money that wasn't mine."

"It went on for a few years."

Agent Hynde stood when Jake stopped talking. "I'll be right back," he said, more to Forsyth than to them.

They sat in silence. Waiting. Phoebe brought in coffee but couldn't open her mouth.

Agent Hynde returned. "Sir, we'll be going in. You'll need to get dressed. No belt, no tie, no shoelaces, no jewelry. If you remove them now, you won't have to do it there."

"Not even his wedding ring?" A lake of putty surrounded her.

"No, ma'am."

"They said no jewelry," Jake said at the same time, as though she'd embarrassed him in front of his friends, his colleagues.

Phoebe sat with Hynde and Forsyth while Jake dressed, somehow thinking she wouldn't be allowed to go with him to the bedroom— but also not wanting to. The two men sipped coffee, acting out a charade of polite society.

Jake came back wearing a pressed blue shirt and grey slacks.

"We'll be putting on cuffs," Agent Hynde said.

"Get my raincoat," Jake said to her. "To cover them."

She ran out and grabbed his coat, taking off the belt before bringing it to him, feeling proud that she remembered to do it and then ridiculously stupid for her pride. How did Jake know to ask for the raincoat? He met her eyes as she draped the beige fabric over the steel bracelets. She examined him for some hint as to the horror ahead of them, but he seemed like a kid turning over the reins to his parents.

She shook the thought from her head. He was in shock. They both were.

"Call Gideon," he said. "Get him down there now. Do whatever he tells you."

"There? Where is there?"

Jake turned to the two men at his side for the answer, resembling Noah at six. Adulthood tumbled off Jake's shoulders.

"The federal courthouse, Mrs. Pierce." Agent Forsyth reached into his wallet and withdrew a card. "Call this number."

"Should I come down?" Phoebe prayed the answer was no.

For a moment, they appeared to be three men linked by their embarrassment at not knowing how to answer a woman's question.

What do women want?

"Just do what the lawyers tell you," Jake said finally. "They're in charge now."

CHAPTER 28

PHOEBE

The wheels set in motion by calling Gideon's office felt more like a runaway train than the logical legal progression that Phoebe had expected.

"Someone will call you back. Stay there," a youthful male voice ordered when she called to ask if they needed her.

So she stayed.

An hour later, she phoned again. This time the receptionist connected her to a harried-sounding woman who didn't introduce herself. Phoebe didn't ask, tumbling into the role of supplicant without rights.

"I've been waiting quite long." She tried to sound even: not frantic, not entitled. Stable. Calm.

"Be patient," the woman said. "This isn't like standing in line for a restaurant table. I can't tell you any more than what Jerry said before."

Fuck you.

Who's Jerry?

Take care of me.

"Got it," Phoebe said. "I wanted to be sure I didn't miss anything. A call. Or something I should do. If—"

"We'll let you know when something involves you." Phoebe couldn't read the woman's sigh. Disgust? Pity? "I promise. We'll contact you. Do something to relax. It's a long road."

Drugs and alcohol were ready answers for relaxing in this circumstance, but she needed a clear head. Water therapy, the only option available, led to a shower, the second shower she wanted earlier, leaving the stall door open in case the phone rang. She lathered lavender-scented gel, praying for the promised aromatherapy of calm. Water splashed over the marbled sill on the floor. Phoebe imagined Jake screaming, "You're spotting the granite!" She opened the glass door wider, dried off with puckered fingertips, and dropped the towel into the puddles.

Shirley-sounds came from the kitchen. Poor Shirley must be shocked seeing dishes on the counter. Phoebe never left a thing out. Did Shirley realize Phoebe's compulsive cleaning came from managing Jake's mania? No doubt. She and Jake were undoubtedly far more transparent than they imagined.

Transparent? Her husband was fucking opaque.

She should tell Shirley before the television did it for her, but the people in Gideon's office repeated Jake's order to keep quiet. Eva, Zoya, Linh, and her family—they'd all find out via media unless she acted in split-second timing. In an act of cowardice, she'd left an early-morning message for Eva, alluding to a family problem as a reason for missing work, promising to speak soon.

Oh God, what was she thinking? Her sister needed to hear this from her, not as breaking news on TV. After locking the bedroom door, she pressed Deb's number into the bedside phone on Jake's side. Her sister, as always, picked up immediately. She and Ben were up by seven, dressed and out by ten.

"You caught us!" Deb answered as though Phoebe made her day simply by calling. "We're on the way to Bed Bath & Beyond. The kids are coming down, and I want to get new sheets for the guest rooms. We were going to get a new mattress, but—"

"Deb. Stop. I need to tell you something."

Her sister inhaled. "What's wrong?"

Phoebe pictured her sister clutching her chest just as their mother had always done. "Is Ben there?" she asked.

"Why?"

"Please. Put him on the extension."

After a moment of silence Deb said, "Hold on."

Phoebe wanted to break their sisterly intimacy, praying that if Ben absorbed the news with her sister, it might dilute and thus soften the blow.

"Okay. He's on. What's wrong?"

"I'm here," Ben affirmed. "What is it?"

Their voices held the tension of people expecting death, anticipating awful truth. They'd make reservations. Fly to the funeral. Get out the black dress, the somber suit.

"Phoebe." Ben snapped her to attention. "Don't keep us waiting."

She snaked a hand into the drawer and under a mound of scarves, feeling for her emergency cigarettes. She fingered the cellophane wrapper. Unopened, of course. About three times a year, she'd smoke one cigarette, throwing out the pack right after.

"This isn't easy," Phoebe said. "Something awful happened."

"Just tell us," Deb said.

"The money is gone."

"What money?"

"Yours. Everyone's."

"What are you talking about?"

How many conversations like this were ahead? People would call asking for reassurance, "Not me, right?" She imagined the faces of her friends, cousins—even the rabbi who'd performed the ceremonies at the kids' weddings.

"Jake totally . . ." Phoebe couldn't think of a way to frame the enormity. "He lied about the investments. All the investments. Everyone's."

"What? How?"

"In every way possible. There are no investments. Nothing. It's all made up. It's paper." Jake had said that. Paper.

"Paper? What do you mean 'paper'?" Ben's voice rose.

"Please don't yell," Phoebe said. "I'll tell you everything. I just found out."

Ben took two loud breaths. "What about the statements? The money we take out every month? Where does it come from?"

"I don't understand anything." She tried to relax her fingers before she squeezed the cigarettes so hard she'd crush them. "He said it's all just paper."

"What the hell does 'just paper' mean?" Ben asked. "Has he gone off his rocker?"

"The kids. Ben's family!" Deb said. "Them, too?"

"Of course them, too," Ben said. "What? You think he only screwed his family? What the fuck, Phoebe? Is he insane?"

Crazy, insane, psychotic, I don't believe it, how, why, what the fuck—so many words doomed for repetition.

"Don't scream at her," Deb said. "You don't think she's dying from this?"

For a few moments, no one spoke.

"You knew nothing?" Ben asked. "Are you sure?"

"How dare you ask that," her sister said.

"It's not such an impossible question, Deb." Anger crackled through the phone. He'd obviously raced ahead to the consequences of Jake's actions faster than Deb. "They live together. She has an office there."

Phoebe pulled at the cellophane strip locking away the pack of Marlboros. "I use the office for convenience. That's all. To take care of Cupcake Project business. The only thing I do for JPE is wrap presents. This was as much of a shock to me, to the kids, to Theo, as it is to you."

"Of course." Deb sounded dazed.

Ben kept quiet.

"Nothing's left?" Deb spoke so softly that Phoebe had to strain to hear. "Nothing?"

Phoebe thought of Jake's checks, waiting to be sent out. Then she thought of the FBI. "I only know Jake wanted you to be first in line for what he still had. He planned to write you a check today, but the FBI took him."

"Jesus," Ben said.

"I don't think he'll be sending those checks out." Fuck it. She'd smoke right here.

"What's going to happen?" Ben sounded stunned.

Her sister began weeping, her tears starting Phoebe's, until both of them were sobbing.

"I'm clueless," Phoebe said between gulps. "I'm waiting for the lawyer to call." She ripped open the pack of cigarettes and lit one.

After disengaging from her sister and brother-in-law, she splashed icy water on her face and then reached Theo on his cell. "They're already here," he whispered. "I'll talk to you soon."

She held a match to the end of another cigarette and called Noah, then Kate, again and again, repeatedly, until finally her daughter picked up.

"We're not supposed to speak with you," Kate said without preamble.

"According to whom?" Phoebe asked.

"Our attorney."

"You have a lawyer? Did you have Daddy arrested?"

Kate didn't answer.

"You didn't give Daddy the weekend?"

"Have you lost your mind, Mom?"

Crazy, insane, psychotic.

"Do you realize the scope of this scheme?" Kate asked. "This isn't a mistake or a lapse in judgment or Daddy's usual bullshit. This is billion-dollar fraud. Do you have a clue what kind of risk he put us in? Hasn't the impact of what he's done hit you?"

"He only asked—"

"Asked us to give him the weekend? For what? To make us coconspirators? You're very lucky our lawyer made this move."

"But . . ." But what? "We don't even know why he did it," she said finally.

"Who the fuck cares why! Get your head out of the sand and leave, Mom. Now. Stay with him, you lose us. Stay with him, everyone blames you along with him. Get out."

"I'll think about it. Really. I promise. But not when—"

Kate hung up.

Phoebe put the phone back in the cradle. She turned the television on low, tuning into CNN in case the story broke.

What do you wear to a courthouse? A suit? A dress?

Just then, Ben's words came back: "Did you know?"

If her own brother-in-law asked her that, what would the rest of the world think? Her hands shook as she pulled on beige wool pants and a plain black sweater.

Who knew what this sweater cost—she couldn't remember. Five hundred. Eight hundred. Two thousand. Phoebe still looked at tags when she bought things—nobody grew up in Brooklyn without checking prices—but the theory of relativity crept in and then tipped so far she threw cashmere sweatshirts over Gap jeans while gardening.

Now, more than anything, she wanted to be invisible.

After dressing, she smoked another cigarette before calling Eva at the store. Her stomach turned at the prospect. As she took her last puff, the phone rang. Phoebe jumped at the shrill tone.

"Gideon wants you at the courthouse. Now. Bail, everything else. This will move fast. Someone will meet you in the lobby."

The woman said this as though Phoebe understood what "everything else" and "bail" meant beyond what she'd gleaned from years of watching *Law & Order*.

"Right," Phoebe said. "Can you tell me who I'm speaking with?"

A beat or two later, the woman answered, "Luz Aguilar. I'm on your husband's team."

"Can I ask you a question?"

"Go." The woman spoke as though the entire world waited for her. "A fast one."

Phoebe adjusted her tone to match Luz's. "Dress code?"

"For you? Now?"

"Right," Phoebe said.

"Doesn't matter. No difference. Sorry, but you don't count. Just get here now."

Luz Aguilar disconnected without saying good-bye. Apparently Phoebe had sunk so low that not only did she not count, she no longer rated courtesy. She peeled off the expensive wool pants and pulled on black jeans.

. . .

Hurry up and wait.

Phoebe sat for hours, uncomfortable, anxious, and angry, and with no one to call. No one to complain to, no one to ask to keep her company. Calling to say what?

"Waiting in a court lobby is awful, you know."

"Yes. I'm here because Jake's been arrested."

"And, oh, all your money is gone."

If someone died, support flowed like water. For this, there were no friends.

They'd stuck her on a bench, occasionally running out to make demands and ask questions. Houses to sign over. How much in her private checking account? Turn it over. She made a series of phone calls under orders from Gideon's staff. Banks. Real estate lawyers. Maybe Jake moved that money to cover his legal ass. Paying her sister, friends, and family was probably more of his bullshit.

Luz's heels clicked on the hard stone floor as she approached. Phoebe recognized the shoes. Red soles. Black leather. "We've hammered out an agreement. Now we'll see if the judge takes it."

About nine hundred dollars for that particular pair of Louboutins. Phoebe's latest pair cost more than twice that.

Luz got up, began clicking away, and then turned to where Phoebe still sat. "What are you doing? Gideon is expecting us."

"Sorry, I thought you were filling me in."

"This isn't a hospital where you're waiting for someone to give birth, Mrs. Pierce."

Phoebe blinked away angry tears. More than anything, she wanted Noah and Kate. Alone, she'd become paralyzed and humiliated, letting this bitch teetering in low-end Louboutin heels treat her like an addled old lady.

. . .

The moment she walked into the stuffy courtroom, she recognized the back of Jake's head. He turned as though sensing her—no surprise

after a lifetime together—and gave a wan half-smile. If he'd shaved that morning, it wasn't apparent. The agents must have come just as he'd lathered up. His hair stuck out in grey tufts. The wrinkles in his face and creases in his shirt stood out with such sharp sadness that she wanted to close her eyes. Loose skin hung from under his chin. The word *elderly* might be attached to his name at that moment.

Phoebe touched her neck.

All the Botox and other poisons she'd injected, keeping herself perfect for him. The tweaks she'd gotten to look younger. Jake smiled a little wider. Words from his eyes burned across the courtroom. The noose tightened.

. . .

A lifetime later, Jake and Phoebe staggered from the courthouse. They slipped into a car provided by Gideon. This would be the moment she'd remember her life rebooting. Her old life ended when Jake told her and the kids his version of the new truth. FBI agents in their home heralded limbo. When she signed over everything to keep Jake out of jail, she entered hell. The houses, boats—everything they owned— Jake had put in her name. He'd always said it was for tax purposes.

She floated in an unfamiliar world, her new life, unaware of customs or language.

Grilled cheese, the way she'd made it when Kate and Noah were small, seemed like the only desirable thing to eat. She used the American cheese she kept for her granddaughters, mild and soothing, pressing it between slices of Arnold Country-Style white bread. Large, fat slices. She dropped both sandwiches into the pan of sputtering butter, hypnotized by the edges crisping and sealing, turning them over and using the spatula to weigh them down to melt faster.

They ate the butter-tight sandwiches in front of the television, avoiding each other's eyes, saying little more than "Pass a carrot" or "Make it a little louder." Episodes of *Criminal Minds* stuffed their TiVo, which, despite the irony of the title, they watched. The show rarely left the world of murder. At least Jake hadn't killed anyone.

. . .

Friday morning, the two of them sat like orphans without a friend in the universe. The phone rang repeatedly, but they'd lowered the volume and screened calls.

Phoebe poured coffee for Jake and remained standing, the pot in her hand.

"What?" His weary, victimized voice turned her stomach.

"Why? Can you give me one reason why?"

"How many times an hour are you planning to cross-examine me? I don't need this now."

"This isn't something happening to you alone." Phoebe let out the fishwife screech clawing at her throat. "You're aware of the rest of the world, right?"

He glared. "Who almost went to jail yesterday? Was it you? Was it my brother? The kids? Who, damn it? My assets are all in a voluntary freeze. I can't do a thing without the court's permission. Did you know that?"

You made your bed, now you lie in it, blared in her head, but she didn't want to offer him a fight, conscious of how much he'd welcome the distraction.

"I only know what you tell me," she said. "Are my accounts all frozen?"

"Not yet."

She imagined packing her bags. Walking out. Taking a cab to Kate's. She should do it.

Now.

Phoebe picked up the paper. She turned it so the headlines faced him.

Bull S—T on Wall Street
Sins of the Father: Children Turn In Jake Pierce

The *Post* composed the most hurtful banners. The doorman bought it for her. Along with the *Daily News*, and every other paper that hadn't been waiting as usual at their door. She picked up the front section of the *Times*, still pristine from delivery, the headline visible above the fold.

Disaster Unfolds on Wall Street

"Why must you torture me?" Jake asked. "Do you think I'm not in enough agony?"

"Who are you feeling sorry for? Yourself?"

Jake shoved away his plate of toast and dropped his head in his hands. "I'm sorry beyond what you can imagine. I never wanted to hurt you or the kids. I made sure you were above reproach. Do you think I don't know this affects other people?"

"People aren't 'affected.' " She pushed the paper closer to him. "They're ruined."

"Don't you think I'll pay for this for the rest of my life?"

"We're all going to pay for this—"

"I'll be put away. My price is freedom."

Hateful words formed. The list of lives he'd smashed rolled till an infinite number of people snaked through every crevasse of her brain.

And, still, she didn't possess the coldness to walk out.

Dissonant thoughts and anxieties sparked until they drowned one another out and the noise exploded into a screen of hot-red worry.

The kids. Her sister. His brother. Her friends. Almost every single one, except Helen, had given Jake their money to invest. All their relatives handed over their life savings. Jesus fucking Christ almighty, what had he been thinking?

All his employees. Thousands of faceless people. More? She ran her hand over the newspaper as though the answers would seep into her skin.

Jake cradled his head in his arms. His hair, always so impeccable, so perfectly tended, stuck up in pieces, so suddenly grey it seemed that any remaining brown had disappeared in the courthouse.

Without her, Jake would be entirely alone.

With him, Phoebe would only have but him.

Maybe he was mentally ill. She prayed it was true. She left the kitchen, ready to call Eva. After pulling on a thick sweater and boots, she went to the screened-in portion of the patio, wanting the privacy afforded only by the outdoor space with Jake home, a portent of the days facing her.

She dialed the phone.

"Phoebe." Eva's even tone gave away nothing. Had Phoebe called Zoya first, shrieks would have greeted her. "How are you holding up?"

She'd walk on the thinnest of ice answering that question. Sympathy seemed the last thing to expect. The Cupcake Project necessitated calling Eva, but she was also the first friend Phoebe had called.

"I'm about as bad as you envision. I can't lie."

"I hope that's true," Eva said. "That you can't lie."

"Do you mean did Jake tell me?"

"Not asking is impossible. I'm certain you're devastated, but we're ruined. Everything. We put everything with your husband."

Phoebe struggled against crying. Forcing Eva into any sort of sympathetic position shamed both of them. Not only had Eva lost all her savings, her work, she was now supporting the daughter of her cousin, who she'd managed to get out of Rwanda years ago, along with some of her husband's family.

"I knew nothing," Phoebe said. "Linh and Zoya?"

"As you can imagine. Zoya is swearing in Russian, Yiddish, and English. Her son is ready to come and kill your man. Linh hasn't stopped scribbling numbers since we read the papers." Eva paused for a moment. "Thank you for calling." The words were clipped and cold.

"Did you doubt me?"

"Certainly you could have left it to lawyers. Calling took fortitude."

"I'm planning to sign the Cupcake Project over to the three of you," Phoebe said.

"I don't think that's going to be possible."

Eva understood more about the nuts and bolts of the Cupcake Project than Phoebe ever had. Of course, this idea of transferring the business, conceived in a flash, wouldn't be straightforward.

"The papers are complicated, but I think it ultimately belongs to me. Jake's assets are all frozen, but not mine."

"Phoebe, I don't think you are aware of the implications. Are you in shock? Everything you possess will also be frozen in moments, if it isn't already. You no longer have the ability to transfer anything."

"Don't I own the business?"

"Soon, I think, nothing will be yours." Eva's voice became iron.

"We will run things until someone tells us otherwise. The receipts always went to the accountant. Where should we send them now?"

The business end of the Cupcake Project had drifted over to Gig Baumer, Jake's accountant, more each year. She virtually gave him the keys to the business, paying no attention to where he put the money.

"Can you use the cash to pay the staff and vendors?" Phoebe asked. "No, never mind. I'll ask—" But there was nobody to ask but Jake, and how could she ask him? "Send me your bank account information, and I'll transfer twenty thousand dollars to you immediately."

"Phoebe, we've already locked the shops for the weekend. Ira is getting us a lawyer from the Mira House board. You can't fix this. You don't want to see the truth. You think you're in hell. That Jake's crime is your tragedy. But it's not. You have no idea where you'll end up. My guess? Someplace decent."

CHAPTER 29

PHOEBE

Three weeks later, New York showed through a scrim of white as light snow fluttered over the city.

Phoebe and Jake settled in to reread soothing books—him, a Lee Child thriller; her, a Susan Isaacs novel—as Christmas Eve dusk fell. Phoebe read constantly. An unoccupied mind meant wrestling with perseverating choices: Did she lack the courage to leave or was it staying the course that revealed bravery?

Jake was in virtual lockup despite being out on bail. He was allowed on the streets within a prescribed radius until seven o'clock in the evening, but the barrage of screaming reporters, photographers, and furious investors waiting outside kept him marooned at home. Phoebe was the one who fetched supplies, braving the glare of the world. She might as well be considered under paparazzi arrest.

Revulsion poured in acid waves each time she left the house.

"*Phoebe! Phoebe! Phoebe!*" the reporters screamed as though calling a runaway dog. "Over here!"

"How much did you steal?"

"Where's the money?"

Their home and cell phones rang with tearful and raging messages from the bilked: strangers, friends, and family.

"I hope you and your evil bitch wife die."

"We have nothing now. We can't even afford Paul's cancer medicine."

"Jump out a window, why don't you!"

They spent their days in bathrobes or sweatpants; Jake with his eyes locked on the television, hers on the computer or a book. They slept by Ambien; Phoebe stumbled through on Xanax.

Their apartment held the grim presence of a family in mourning. No sheets covered the mirrors, but Jake and Phoebe sat a solitary shivah, where no one visited except lawyers, who brought papers to sign instead of casseroles.

Jake offered his proffer the previous week, which meant little to her. Luz described it as a confidential meeting, with Jake receiving limited immunity for the day, regarding what he said. Luz's words only confused Phoebe. The moment she hung up with the clipped lawyer, she looked the word up on the US Legal website:

> In the context of criminal law, a proffer agreement is a written agreement between federal prosecutors and individuals under criminal investigation, which permits these individuals to give the government information about crimes with some assurances that they will be protected against prosecution. Witnesses, subjects, or targets of a federal investigation are usually parties to such agreements.
>
> Proffer agreements are not complete immunity agreements. Although the government cannot use actual proffer session statements against the individual in its case-in-chief, the information provided can be used to follow up leads and conduct further investigations. If those leads and further investigations lead to new evidence, the new evidence can be used to indict and convict the individual who gave the information in the proffer session.

As Phoebe understood it, the legal system tried to obtain information it could use against Jake and others, while he worked toward getting some leniency. But all outcomes led to prison.

"What if he were mentally ill?" she'd asked Luz. "Would that keep him from jail?"

"Nothing is impossible." The attorney bit off each word. "In such an improbable case, he'd be put in a facility for the criminally insane."

Phoebe still waited for details from Jake, who swore that he had managed the scheme alone. Not one person had helped him. Somehow she was supposed to believe that Jake, who asked her for help turning on their home computers, had pulled off this insanity himself. She'd stopped asking, no longer willing to bang on a locked door.

They remained caged in their luxury jail, speaking with almost no one but each other, lawyers, and whichever doorman was on duty. Helen and Deb checked in daily, though the strained conversations added more stress than not. The children refused to talk. Noah, however, sent an email, again urging her to leave. "Don't stay on a sinking ship," he'd written.

When guilt overwhelmed her, Phoebe reminded herself that Kate had her husband, and Noah, his wife. They'd be all right.

She wrote both kids long emails every day, filled with attempts to make them understand her position. None bounced back, so at least they hadn't blocked her address.

Today's words probably blended into those from yesterday:

My sweet children,

I hope you are all well, even as you go through hell. Daddy and I are locked in a combat-free war, where he refuses to talk about anything more than the television schedule for the night. I do consider leaving hourly. How can I not? At the same time, incomprehensible questions plague me. What if someone learns that their child has, God forbid, murdered someone? Did they stay there for a loved one—even as they hated the act?

Hate the sin and still love the sinner. Phoebe's emails sank under the need to explain herself and her stubborn loyalty. The children wanted her to stop caring about Jake, but how fast could one fall out of the habits of love? The caretaking? Few understood the experience of being married to someone you met when you were fifteen. Jake was as much brother, father, and sometimes even child, as he was husband.

Phoebe prepared a feeble version of Christmas Eve dinner. The television played while she cooked. When she returned ten minutes later, Jake glanced up from an ancient episode of *The Twilight Zone*, evidently the only thing he'd found that didn't touch on Christmas, family, or happiness.

She placed a platter of bagels with cream cheese and lox—delivered by Zabar's, paid via *knippel*—on the coffee table.

"Can you at least tell me the outlines of what they asked and what you said?"

He sliced a bagel, slathering the surface with cream cheese before covering it with oily orange lox. "Let's be peaceful, sweetheart. For tonight," he said.

"Help me figure out how I can stand by you."

"Are you questioning your choice?"

"Of course."

"I never thought it would go this far," he said. "That's the truth."

"What do you mean?"

"It started . . . The problem started because I never wanted to see it happen again—what happened with your father."

"I don't follow."

"It got out of control. Everything seemed so good, and then it wasn't. Everyone wanted their damned money, like I was a bank . . ." His words trailed away.

"When?" she asked.

He looked up from his knees, and she saw wheels turning, decisions being made.

"A while ago. Not that long. I always thought I'd fix it."

"Why didn't you?"

"The problems became worse." He put down the bagel and wiped his hands on a napkin. "I couldn't figure out how to stop."

"Or step up," she said.

"Should I have ruined our family? Lost everything? Gone to jail?"

"But that's what's happening," she said.

"Does the past matter at all, those long years of success?"

Insanity now seemed Jake's proper legal defense. She stood on an eroding beach, digging in with her toes as raging waves washed away the sand.

She'd thought Jake a god; an original iconic deity of Wall Street.

"That's madness. All that ever mattered was you and the children. Now the kids are gone, and you're a stranger."

"Why do you stay?" he asked.

"Who would even talk to you if I left?"

"You're a good woman, Pheebs. No one knows that like me."

"I always thought you were a good man."

"And now?"

"Now? Now I think you're a criminal. A weak man." She reached for his hand, his palm so familiar she might be holding her own flesh. "They claim you're evil, a monster, but I hope that's wrong. Maybe you just lack courage. Maybe you're filled with hubris. A greedy man."

Another moment breathing the same air he'd expelled from his lungs threatened to choke her. Maybe standing by him was possible if she saw Jake through a lens of his being pathetic—her limited child.

Phoebe tried to imagine the bravest choice. She filled two glasses of wine. "Might as well drink it, Jake."

He picked up the glass, swirling it for a moment before taking a few gulps. She drank hers more slowly, but finished first. She topped off his and then refilled her own.

"There's nothing in front of us," he said. "Nothing good faces us."

Jake was right. Their life was effectively over. They might as well make it easier on everyone. No trial or lockup or shame spilling over to the children. They'd be devastated, but they'd grieve, and then it would be over.

He offered his arms, and for the first time since his confession, she let herself collapse into him.

. . .

They pooled their Ambien. They would go together. Phoebe put both bottles in the kitchen and then joined Jake in the living room. He held a pen above a pad of paper. "I don't know what to say." His watch collection gleamed from the coffee table.

"Write about love. Apologize."

Phoebe took a sip from the brandy snifter, sifting through her jewelry as Jake wrote. She slipped an antique diamond bracelet into a baggie with the rope of pearls Kate treasured.

She held the engagement ring Jake had bought to replace the tiny diamond chip she'd originally worn. Gleaming, from Tiffany's, and perfect. She didn't add it to the pile, nor did she put it on. Only things from long ago seemed appropriate to send.

She picked up everything her mother had once owned. The locket she'd removed from her mother in the hospital with the familiar clouded pictures of her and Deb. After the funeral, Phoebe hadn't taken it off for months, rubbing the worn gold as though her attention might alleviate her guilt at having loved her father more. The cool metal heated in her hand.

She took out her own pad and began writing letters, first to her son and then her daughter.

> *Dear Katie,*
>
> *Most of all, I want you to remember I'm not angry. You shouldn't even think I could consider that, but guilt can haunt a child, even a child as adult and capable as you.*
>
> *You made the right decision. Take good care of Amelia and Zach. Most of all, take care of you. I've treasured you since the moment I held you, my sweet child. You and Noah are first in my heart always, though I suppose, if that's true, you're wondering why I'm here, and not with you and your brother. This will probably not seem like enough justification—considering what he's done to everyone—but I just couldn't bear the idea of Daddy being alone. For better or for worse, right? And does it get worse than this?*

Phoebe went back and crossed out the last line with a heavy hand. Of course it got worse than this. Death. Illness.

> *Daddy and I have been together since we were practically children. I don't know how to walk away. Believe me, if I didn't*

*know you and Noah had each other and your families, I'd never
leave you alone.*

*Okay, enough. Sounds like I'm asking you to feel sorry for me,
right? But, sweetheart—I had a wonderful life until now. You
and Noah are anything and everything a mother could dream of
having for their children. Being grandma was the second biggest
joy of my life—having you and Noah, was, of course, number one.*

What else could she write to her girl? How could she say good-bye
without making her sad forever? Phoebe didn't want to send Kate
paper so tainted with shame and self-pity that her daughter's only option would be burning the letter.

*You and Noah can start over. You're both young and smart.
There is nothing so big here that you can't make a good life.
This is all new and awful, but the horror will pass, no matter
how hard that is to believe. You got a raw deal, but what is, is,
at this moment. Your children are treasures. Zach is more than
wonderful. The skills you possess are beyond pride-worthy. Hold
your head up. You did nothing.*

Don't wear your father's sins.

*Love always and forever,
Mommy*

CHAPTER 30

PHOEBE

Phoebe slid her mother's locket into a padded envelope. Tears blurred her vision as she picked out a few more meaningful pieces from the pile of gold and silver jewelry. She reached back for the necklace, scrabbling for the gold as though searching for a lost limb to touch it once more. For one moment, she prayed her daughter could gather comfort from these trinkets and, in the next, she questioned her sanity at the thought.

Was this what Jake stole for? Shiny relics? Baubles to hang around her neck, dangle from her ears?

Look at me! Look at my wife! I made it! I'm a big shot! Jake obsessed about hitting the big time since high school—and he'd spun stories just as long. How many dinner tables did she decorate while watching guests drink up his bullshit about catching a giant fish or the time he spent a summer building houses in Haiti?

Haiti? Jake would have added air conditioners to the deck at their Greenwich home if it were possible. That's how much he hated humidity. And he loathed fish.

Phoebe squirmed at his performances, rolling her eyes when they got home, but everyone loved his jive. The more powerful he became, the more they wanted his stories. "Pretty soon, you'll have them believing you discovered America in a past life," she said as they drove home from some event.

Turned out he'd reeled her right in with all the others.

Jake came in and dropped his box of watches on the kitchen table. "Are you going to give them to Manny to mail?"

Phoebe finished the inch of brandy left from the generous amount she'd poured before writing the letter. "I'll mail the jewelry myself. The letters we'll leave here for the kids."

"Let me know if you need anything. I have a little something put away."

So Jake kept his own *knippel*. Maybe he stuffed his old shoes with thousand-dollar bills.

They had not spoken about money since his arrest. He never asked how she paid for groceries or the cable bill, or if they cut off her credit cards—which they hadn't, but they could. Not that she used them. Hate and naked curiosity from shoppers drilled her with every can of tuna she put in her cart. Better to transact fast using crumpled *knippel* bills.

Sometimes the exhaustion of making herself as small as possible made her want to walk into D'Agostino's and fill a basket with tins of lobster and caviar. Imagine those headlines.

Jake handed her the letters he had typed on his old IBM Selectric and shuffled back to his study. The television came on. Phoebe didn't worry about what he'd say to Kate—always considered his perfect child—but she needed to read what he wrote to their son.

Dear Noah,

What can I say that would make any sense? I have no excuses, no good reasons. I fell deeper and deeper, while convincing myself I'd find a way out. I never meant to hurt anyone. I don't know how it got so bad. I'm surprised I didn't have a heart attack from worry. At least I held to my vow to always keep you and Kate (and, of course, Mom) out of it. Of course you can't forgive me, but please, don't ever blame your mother.

I love you very much. You three were the most important things in my life even if you can't believe that now. I simply boiled myself a little bit at a time—slow enough that by the time I became red hot, it was too late to jump out. Though I tried. Believe me, I tried.

This wasn't what I wanted. You are a good boy, and I am so proud of you. I wish you could have gone until forever being proud of me.

Love,
Dad

Hate and caring mixed in her throat until breathing seemed impossible. She took his letters and hers, placed them in a white envelope, and labeled it *Kate and Noah.* After licking it closed, she placed it on the empty mahogany hallway table, weighing the envelope down with a heavy glass paperweight.

After encasing Jake's watches in bubble wrap, Phoebe slipped them in an envelope. She taped both envelopes tight and addressed the one with watches to Noah and the other to Kate. After throwing on her baggiest coat and jamming on an old ski hat, she wrapped a dull grey scarf around her neck, pulled it up to her nose, took the service elevator, and slipped outside into the snowy darkness.

Occasionally, a smart reporter hung out at the back, but she assumed that on Christmas Eve even the paparazzi would be on skeleton staff. She came out the back into the alley, grateful for the thick Uggs boots covering her feet. Too bad they weren't thigh high. Garbage cans, recycling bins, and snow equipment crowded the narrow space. Feral cats and rodents lurked in the corners.

Manny had shown her this way out a few days before, after seeing how the reporters hounded her. Weaving through the alley, expecting to step on an animal carcass or worse, horrified her. She stared straight ahead, walking on tiptoes, clutching the plastic Whole Foods bag containing the overstuffed envelopes.

She grabbed the handle of the grated door leading to the street, releasing and pulling the way Manny taught her, trying to be quiet—an almost impossible task with rusted, creaking iron.

The door exited about a half block from the building's main entrance, where the dogged cadre of paparazzi stood hunched against the cold. Their heads swiveled, seeking signs of her or Jake escaping via the front door, back, or even perhaps leaping from their terrace, considering how one guy peered up toward the top of the building.

"Hey, Phoebe, where ya going?" a reporter yelled, his words meant to stop her.

A thin layer of ice covered the sidewalk. Walking on the slickness took a concentration difficult to achieve with them panting like a pack of dogs behind her. Running now, she raced toward the mailbox on the corner, almost blinded by the fast-falling snow. Barely keeping her balance, she fell on the blue metal box, pried open the iced opening, and stuffed in the two envelopes. Stamps of every denomination nearly covered the front of the packages.

"Whatcha mailing, Phoebe?" she heard behind her.

"Christmas cards?" The broad New York accent asking the question matched her own.

She swallowed the Brooklyn "Fuck you!" jammed in her throat. Six men of varying heights hulked around her.

"Where's Jake?"

"What are you guys doing tonight?"

"Where's the money? Is that what you mailed?"

Tears of rage and fear threatened as she edged away.

"What did you do? Why are you staying? What do the kids think?"

Questions assaulted her as she tried to escape. She turned sideways, attempting to make a wedge of her shoulders.

"Move, damn it," she finally spit out. "Move the fuck away from me."

And there, she'd given them the morning headlines: "Phoebe Pierce Potty Mouth."

"Enough!" Manny pushed his way in front of the crowd of men, holding an umbrella out as though it were a lance. "*Gusanos*. Maggots."

Phoebe slipped as she worked to get away from the reporters, falling to one knee, her bare hand landing on the gritty iced pavement. Pain shot through it as she attempted to stop her slide. Manny grabbed her elbow with a strong hand and pulled her up. She tucked her hand into his arm, and he steered them away from the men shouting questions.

"What the eff, Phoebe? Nothing to say?"

"What's in the envelope?"

Words blurred behind her as they walked back to the building.

"They're just messing with your mind, Mrs. Pierce," Manny said. "Stay cool. They're waving a red flag, like bullfighters. They're just trying to feed off you for tomorrow's paper. Bottom-feeders, all of them."

Phoebe squeezed Manny's arm, attempting to put her overwhelming gratitude into the touch. If she spoke, she'd fall apart, and those bastards would never see her cry. Manny was her only protector—a man to whom other than being polite and handing him generous tips, she'd never given a thought.

. . .

"How was it?" Jake asked when she returned. He tried to peel her wet coat off her shoulders, but she shrugged him away.

"Fine," she said.

He pointed to her leg, her torn pants, her skinned knee. "Doesn't look fine. What happened? Are you okay?"

"Fine, I said." She moved away from his outstretched hand.

"Come on. I'll bandage you till you're good as new."

She bit her lip against the flood of softness opening in her chest. Jake was the expert at taping up the kids after they slipped on the ice or twisted something. Her stomach would drop, but he stayed calm. When Noah lacerated his scalp on a tree limb while skiing in Aspen, Jake pressed the huge piece of flapping skin in place until the ski patrol arrived. He'd studied the doctor's hands as he wove the needle in and out of their son's flesh. Phoebe averted her eyes, able to hold Noah's hand as the stitches went in, but unable to watch.

Jake led her to the guest bathroom. He rolled her pants above her knee, pulling the wool fabric away from the clotting blood. She winced as he uncovered the fresh wound.

"Sorry." He touched his lips to the skin above the gash. "Kiss and make better," he said, repeating the words he'd once said to the children.

Jake bathed the torn flesh and covered it in Neosporin. He tore open a large square Band-Aid with his teeth, peeled off the paper, and pressed it over her lacerations. After ensuring that it stuck, he used the pad of his thumb to smooth down the edges.

"There," he said.

Phoebe went into her bathroom without a word. She stripped off her clothes, stuffed them in the hamper, and walked into the shower. Water beat on her shoulders as she leaned both hands against the slick white tile. Tears mixed with suds as she covered herself with bath gel. She washed her hair with the same viscous liquid, wanting the smell of the lilacs, indifferent to caring for her hair.

Fuck texture. Fuck shine. Frizz, no frizz—who cared?

When the bandage steamed off, Phoebe balled it up and put it on the shelf with her shampoo and soap collection.

She wrapped herself in a terry robe. No lotion on her legs. No moisture for her face. Just a rough towel brushing her skin. She combed her hair straight back from her forehead, leaning forward to examine herself in the mirror. *See how smooth I kept myself? Always perfect, just like you wanted me.*

Jake's eyes were glued to the bedroom television where *Rio Bravo* played.

Phoebe handed him a glass of wine and then placed one on her side of the bed.

She imagined her family at the cemetery, standing before two caskets. The idea of death seemed selfish and punishing. She should stay to care for her children and granddaughters. Then Phoebe pictured all the hate now pointed at Jake aimed only at her. Rage already shot toward her as though she had nibbled on Kobe beef sautéed with babies' tears. If she took the pills, she could sleep. If there were some sort of heaven—an afterlife—God would see her heart and her deeds.

She'd been blind, she'd been stupid—but she'd not been greedy. She'd spent the money, but she'd never known of Jake's crimes.

Reincarnation might exist. She could start over. Come back as someone with an honest husband. A kind husband. Children who didn't have to spend their lives trying to win a monster's approval.

Phoebe wasn't a religious woman, but shouldn't she have prepared somehow? Made peace?

Leaving the kids would be a final act of selfishness. They'd asked her to come with them, but she stayed with Jake. Now she'd never be able to go to them. They'd hate her forever.

She couldn't do it.

"How many pills do you think it will take?" Jake looked at her as though she were some sort of suicide expert. He probably thought she'd Googled the question. Phoebe took care of everything in the home. Why not include researching how to die?

Of course, she had looked for the information and knew how many pills would kill them, but going through with this would be a deserter's way out. Any attempt to argue with Jake required a wrestler's strength—far better to use a sorcerer's wisdom.

"Four."

"Four?" he said. "So few?"

"These are the highest-strength pills." They weren't. They were only five milligrams each. "I'll only need to take three."

"You're sure that will be enough for us?" he asked.

"With the wine, definitely." Dying with that dose was near impossible. "Absolutely."

"Right. Down the hatch." Jake counted out four pills and swallowed them with his Chardonnay.

What if she told him to take more and only pretended to swallow hers?

"Your turn." He watched her as though she might cheat him in some way. "The kids will manage. Don't worry. If we're gone, they won't have to deal with all this. We're doing them a favor."

His silence was all she wanted. Phoebe swallowed three pills at once.

"I love you, baby," he said. "Always. From the first time I saw you."

"I know, Jake." She should say it back, to be kind, to be human. "Me too."

CHAPTER 31

PHOEBE

Phoebe woke to the sound of Jake retching. Seconds later, nausea overcame her.

After throwing off the covers, she stumbled to the other bathroom and dropped to her knees in time for her stomach to explode into the toilet and not on the floor. Half-digested pills spewed out in a brown froth.

Emptied, she curled up on the thick white bath mat. Her head pounded hard enough that she worried she might be having a stroke. Jake groaned from the master bathroom. She wondered if she should call 911.

Headlines appeared instantly in her mind. "Pierces Rushed to Mount Sinai: Pills & Alcohol Thought to Blame." The *Post* would be less gracious, more likely coming up with "Jake and Phoebe's Grim Reaper Investment Fails" or "Jake and Phoebe: Too Mean to Die."

Would the kids rush to the hospital? If she called them right this moment, decency would force them to come. Immediately, the thought of using this pathetic faux suicide attempt to bring Kate and Noah back to her disgusted her. She curled her fingers to keep from reaching for the bathroom phone and calling her daughter.

She tried to get up to go to Jake but couldn't. Finally, she heard him stagger to the bedroom and fall onto the bed. He'd gathered enough strength to do that—but not enough to come see whether she survived. Perhaps her husband wanted her dead, preventing him from witnessing her shame about him.

She reached up, slid a towel off the bar and pulled it on top of her, shivering until something resembling sleep came.

. . .

Christmas Eve seemed two years ago, but, in fact, only one long, crawling week had passed since the night of pills, and here they were on the couch, watching the Dustin Hoffman comedy *Tootsie* as 2008 clicked to 2009.

Obsessions with her and Jake doubled with each news cycle. Pundits and full-of-themselves essayists hammered the same questions: Did Phoebe Pierce know her life was built on fraud? Did Phoebe Pierce partner with her husband in hustling billions from investors? Friends and enemies debated for the world's curiosity about whether love and loyalty blinded her to his crimes, or if she chose to live in denial. People she hadn't seen since high school crawled out of the alleys to disclose Phoebe lore and photos.

Missing her children became sharper; shards of glass ripping at her.

She allowed herself to imagine, for one second, where they would all be in normal times. New Year's Eve, they went back to Greenwich—loving the feeling of being cozy in the house as the ocean frothed outside. The worse the weather, the more they loved it.

Kate and Noah and their spouses usually ate New Year's Eve dinner out while she and Jake stayed home with the girls. They built forts and slept in the pillowed fortifications. The two of them let the grandkids stay up late, all of them cuddled on the giant living room couches watching video after video curated by Jake. One of his joys had been planning the night's entertainment. He spent hours reading reviews, his face screwed up in concentration as he decided between one family film and another.

Jake hit pause to stop *Tootsie* and squeezed her knee. "How about a snack?"

"What do you want?" She concentrated on Dustin Hoffman, frozen in the act of applying lipstick.

"What do we have?" His hand weighed five hundred pounds.

"Sorry, my X-ray vision is on the fritz," she said.

"Hey, you do the shopping, you cook the food. Makes sense you keep stock of what we have, right? Do you need to make this a federal case? Could I have something to eat?"

"Open the cabinets. Acquaint yourself. I'm not hungry."

"So this is where we're going?" He frowned at her. "You're turning on me?"

"You want me to wait on you?"

He wrapped his hand around her forearm. "Waiting on me? That's what it is to you?"

She shook him off. "Stop."

"Now I can't touch you? It's been pretty obvious you don't want that."

"Sex? We're talking about sex now? Should I make sandwiches and then go down on you?"

"Would it be such a sin?" He pressed his lips together in disgust, the wounding expression designed to shame her into service.

He picked up the plates on the coffee table. Funny how Jake "helped" only when he wanted to hurt her. Was she supposed to be embarrassed that he was doing her supposed job?

She followed him to the kitchen, unable to resist his bait, itching for a fight.

He stood before the open refrigerator, staring as though a plate of roast beef might leap into his hands. Next he opened the freezer.

"Do we have ice cream?" he asked.

"Do you see any?"

"No. I don't." He glared at her.

"So why'd you ask?"

"Because I hoped I was wrong, and you took the time to buy some small piece of comforting shit, like ice cream or cake or a fucking box of cookies."

"Really, this is what you were hoping? Did you think of hoping the kids would call or the people you screwed all over the world might get some help? How about our family, every aunt, cousin, brother and sister—how about hoping they'll survive what you did to them?"

Jake slammed the refrigerator shut with the unsatisfying kiss of expensive appliances. He shuffled to the dining nook and sank into the edge of the curved booth. "When I think about it, I fall apart. Which is why what I want now is a piece of cake." His eyes appeared weaker than she'd ever seen. "I try to imagine a life without family. Us. Everything. I just can't."

If she were going to stay with him, shouldn't she be kind? She touched his shoulder with two fingers for a moment. "I'll make something."

He took her hand and kissed it. She forced herself not to pull away, to claw her way out of his hold. Tried to remember when this man's touch didn't disgust her. "Thank you," he said.

Fury gnawed her guts. "Watch your movie."

"What would I do without you?"

Pity flashed as he shambled out. Jake strode over the world like Zeus since the day they had met. She opened the pantry door and reached for the airtight containers holding shredded coconut and chunks of dark Valrhona. While the melted chocolate cooled, she beat egg whites with salt until they stiffened, slowly added sugar and vanilla, and whipped until it became a glossy meringue.

She dipped in a finger at each stage—loving the flavor of the sugary egg mixture, relishing the grit of coconut. The chocolate. Rich, dark, thick; she couldn't stop tasting as she mixed. After lining the cookie sheet with parchment paper, she dropped teaspoon-sized lumps in even rows. As they baked, she ran a spatula along the side of the bowl, scraping and licking until she tasted more rubber than chocolate.

The timer rang, and she slid out the tray, replacing it with a waiting one of raw macaroons. She put them on a rack to cool, eating one, two, and then a third and a fourth the moment she could touch them.

Phoebe crammed cookies into her mouth until the sugar sickened her. Then she opened the liquor cabinet and grabbed one of the ridiculously expensive liqueurs that clients showered on Jake. Glinting from the shelves, overdesigned bottles lined up like perfume flagons for giants. She pulled out the crystal-faceted stopper of the Courvoisier L'Esprit cognac, the Lalique glass cool in her hand, and tipped the bottle to her mouth.

She arranged a dozen cookies on the Limoges plate she hated most—stupid birds on a black border; yet another client gift—and carried it to her husband, along with the open bottle. Then she covered a never-used Flora Danica oval platter, easily worth a thousand dollars, even secondhand, with cookies for Manny's family, wrapped it in green cellophane, and used a butter knife to create curling cascades of silver ribbon.

"Keep it," she'd say when he offered to return it.

. . .

Jake's cell phone rang as she poured their first Monday cups of coffee. He peered at the caller ID. "Gideon," he said, pressing Talk.

"What?" he said after a minute.

Phoebe raised her eyebrows, and he motioned for her to stay quiet. His voice rose. "Bullshit! Family fucking mementos, that's all we sent. Christmas presents. We're not allowed to celebrate the holidays? Now that's on the list of things I can't do? Fucking feds."

Jake remained silent for a few minutes. Phoebe could imagine Gideon's deep, soothing voice sending platitudes equaling "You're fucked. Do what I say." Her husband seemed stunned when the conversation ended, the phone dangling from his hand. "The kids called the feds about the jewelry. Now they're going to try to revoke my bail. I gotta go in."

"They called? Kate and Noah?"

"Ungrateful—"

"Jake! Don't. Their lawyer probably told them to do it, to keep out of jail."

"They're not going to jail because we sent them a few presents."

"How the hell would you know?" She slammed a box of Cheerios on the table. "How would you know anything about what's wrong and what's right?"

"And you know so much? Why not look it up on your computer

with everything else you're so addicted to? Google 'ungrateful children' while you're at it. Everything they have is from me."

She should leave right now and never look back. Not unless she wanted to turn into a pillar of salt. But twisted remnants of her wedding vows kept her at Jake's side. She questioned her own culpability. If she'd paid more attention, would she have seen signs? Jake was the biggest storyteller of all time—she knew that. As a teenager, he'd once convinced a math teacher that an answer, which Jake's friend had inked on his hand and then shown to Jake, had been done in his head through a self-designed formula.

But he'd married her the moment he'd thought he'd brought harm to her. Now their eyes met, and she still saw that boy. Try as she might, she couldn't find a way to morph him from man to monster.

"I'll check your suit while you shower."

Part 5

———

AFTER

CHAPTER 32

PHOEBE

"Beware the ides of March" seemed a wholly appropriate quote for this day. Phoebe curled up on the bed with her laptop—her best friend—waiting for Jake to come in and say good-bye. Numbness fought with guilt. She wanted him gone for so many reasons.

Having her children back in her life.

No longer seeing him twenty-four long hours a day.

He'd begged her not to come to the courtroom, not to watch him plead guilty to crimes that would send him to jail for the rest of his life. Agreeing came easy.

Jake's complete house arrest—his punishment for sending presents to the children—had been carved out of time, an unreal period of suspended animation where they ate, read, and inhaled television shows.

Lovemaking, of course, disappeared. Intimacy with this Jake would be like making love to a stranger. He never asked, either out of knowing she'd turn him down or his own disinterest in anything but film and food. He consumed prodigious amounts of candy, bagels, and chips—things she never allowed in the house—ice cream, cheeseburgers, and worse, which they washed down with alcohol as they worked their way through their wine collection.

Phoebe acted as enabler and short-order cook. Why deny his only pleasure? If he dropped dead of a heart attack, it would be the kindest outcome for the family. She researched life in prison online, but after the third time that Jake rejected her reports, she let it go, especially with Deb reminding her that she'd better start worrying about her own future. With Jake's accounts frozen, they used her funds for all expenses—though spending anything over one hundred dollars required a report to their monitor from the feds.

Not that she bought anything but food. The trail of paparazzi kept her as housebound as Jake. It took until February, when her long grey roots became a visual band of stress against her dyed dark hair, impossible to cover with mascara, for her to call to schedule a color and cut.

"Hi, Claudia, this is Phoebe Pierce," she said to the receptionist. "Can you get me Kevin's first opening? I can come anytime."

Awkward silence hung until Claudia squeaked, "Please hold."

No chirping of "Hello, Mrs. Pierce!" Years of generous tips guaranteed the response. Phoebe wasn't naive. Awkwardness didn't surprise her, but she was shocked by this full-on pretense of nonrecognition.

After about three minutes, Claudia returned. "I'm sorry, but Kevin isn't accepting appointments at this time."

Phoebe waited a beat for her brain to connect the words and then said, "Who *is* accepting appointments?" Her need to get rid of grey measured against pride turned out to be a sad formula.

"I can't say that anyone is." Claudia's desire to end the call leaped through the wires.

"Can I speak with Kevin?" Connecting with her hairdresser became a wretched harbinger of her entire life—acceptance representing any hope of being less than a fugitive from polite society. "Please, Claudia. Ask him to come to the phone."

"I'm sorry," Claudia said. "He isn't available."

A mirror hung above the dresser. No makeup. Her roots climbing out more each minute. She wore an oversized worn shirt of Jake's. Her image appeared old as dirt.

"Fine. Thank you," Phoebe said, offering gratitude to the woman for wiping out her last remnants of pride. Self-punishment had become her raison d'être, as she devoured every story she found in the newspaper and online and read every angry email sent by friends and family blaming her for drawing them into the Club. This morning she had received one from Ira, his sympathy making his anger all the more painful.

Dear Phoebe,

No doubt you are at the moment worried about far more than Mira House, or me, but yet, here I am.

Am I reaching out? Yes and no. We've been friends too long for me not to worry about you. I think of how awful your life must be now, even as I wonder if it's a life of your own creation. Let me be blunt. Did you know? Yes, I suppose I sound like the newspapers, but there is some difference here. I am not assuming you were connected to this horrendous crime, nor can I assume you were not.

Perhaps it was a failing on Phoebe's part not to understand, but why couldn't he assume she might be innocent?

I keep asking myself, could you not have known what Jake did? Was he that good an actor?

Jake had fooled millionaires and captains of industry—why not her? Did other spouses quiz their husbands and wives each night as to the veracity of their lives? Of course she accepted Jake's accounting of his days, his business, his world. Why the hell wouldn't she? Did women usually spend nights poring over spousal contracts and bank accounts?

If you were fooling me, then I am the sucker, and I suppose we're both the worse for the fraud. You knew, I think—despite my never speaking about it—I sat on deep feelings, which I never thought I deserved. How could I ever hope to compete with your husband: Rich! Brilliant! Though I did wonder how you were happy with someone who worshipped success over all else.

Do you think he ever truly loved you? I don't believe anyone who loved his family would do that.

The question haunted her. Love and lying coexisted, she supposed; she had begun her marriage based on a lie, yet had always loved Jake. She had spent her life making up for her sins, by being a good wife and mother.

"It's time." Jake's entrance startled her. She slammed the computer shut, not wanting her worlds to collide. "Gideon is downstairs with the car."

"You know I'll come to court if you need me." Phoebe fixed a piece of Jake's hair sticking up from where she'd trimmed it. She'd become his barber after the arrest, learning from an online video and using shears ordered from Amazon, haven for the homebound. Now it was time to order hair dye.

"I don't want to put you through that. Here." Jake held out an envelope. "It's what I'm going to say in court. There's also a letter for you." He stopped her as she began to slit it open, gripping her wrist too tight. "No. Not until I'm gone."

She let him hold on. "Should I walk you down?"

Jake stroked her cheek. "We'll say good-bye here. Gideon will call and let you know everything." He pulled her close. "We've barely talked about you. Where this will leave you. I've spoken to Gideon about your future. He's working to keep you from harm."

She let Jake retain his belief even as she knew that ship had sailed long ago.

"I love you and always have." Jake's voice shook as he began sobbing.

Who are you crying for? Once again the question drummed.

She pushed him away, reached for a tissue, and pulled one out. "Here," she said, not unkindly. "It's time for you to go."

. . .

After, she lay on the couch in a daze. No computer, no television, getting up only for the bathroom and to answer Deb's call, not wanting her sister to worry, but begging off the phone almost immediately. Jake's envelope waited in a radioactive glow on the coffee table.

At two o'clock, Luz called.

Phoebe asked the expected question. "What happened?"

"You know, of course, that he pled, yes?"

"Yes." Phoebe matched Luz's staccato.

"By now, he should be at Metropolitan Correctional Center. It's federal. I emailed you the address, all the relevant information for visiting, phone calls, etcetera. All the rules are there. You only need his inmate number, which we'll get you as soon as possible. He'll need you to fill his account."

"With money?"

"For the commissary. I sent you an item-and-price list."

"Gideon didn't take care of that?"

Kudos to Luz for pulling off silent annoyance and patronization at the same time. "That's the family's responsibility," the lawyer said finally.

A wake-up call of bricks fell. Apparently her new job would be the prisoner's wife.

"We have a recommendation for an attorney for you."

"A lawyer?"

"Gideon can't represent you." Luz didn't present this as open to question. "It's time to concentrate on the problems in front of you."

"Why can't I just give everything back?"

"It isn't even appropriate for me to talk to you about this. We promised Jake we'd put you with the best lawyer."

"Jake is not in charge of this decision."

"I'm sorry. You didn't earn that money."

"Neither did he." She slammed down the phone and ripped open the envelope with Jake's letter.

Dear Pheebs,

And now I'm gone. Good riddance? I suppose you're feeling serious relief, having me gone. Holding back from killing me has been hard, eh?

You kept asking me why. Why? Why? Why? As though there were some bible of reasons I followed, but it is sadly simple. My work with the Club became a rolling stone gathering no moss. Makes no sense, right? This is what happened: I did it to make

some money to make up for losses. I needed cash so I got some "extra" clients. Their deposits came in, and I made payouts for others. And I always thought "tomorrow" I'd make it up.

I guess I became Scarlett O'Hara. (Now you understand my weird addiction to that movie you hated.) I identified with her. Tomorrow is another day.

Don't laugh!

Like Scarlett, I longed to be good like Melanie.

Like Scarlett, I would do anything to hold my Tara: JPE & the Club.

And, as Scarlett wrapped herself in curtains and convinced people she wore haute couture, I waved statements in front of people and convinced them I did what no other could: give them an ever-upward financial journey.

Pheebs, am I alone to blame? Sure, people like your sister, or Eva, of course I understand how they believed in me. But those big shots like Louis Klein who invested with me? The fund managers who sent people? Aren't they liable also? How did they convince themselves that miracles were possible? Constant ups? No downs?

Listen: The kids will come back to you and me. I know they will. Eventually they will understand I always meant to make this right. I'd find a way to score big, cover the entire nut, and shut down the Club (after paying everyone). Or JPE would make enough that I could shave off enough to make things right.

I thought I might sell everything and we'd fly off to paradise.

I'd get an insurance policy that covered suicide.

I'd invest in something different—movies—and make a new fortune.

I never thought it would end this way. I thought I had more time.

Nobody thought I'd make it so big, including me.

Now, it's almost a relief to have it over. Trust me, Pheebs. The burden has been heavy. You have no idea how much I wanted it to be over.

Now it is.

I am so sorry I've hurt you and the kids. I need you. Now more than ever. You are all I have in this entire world.

I love you. Forever and beyond.

Jake

The sun mocked her. Phoebe stumbled over to close the drapes and then took Jake's letter to the shoebox in her closet where she'd hidden their suicide letters to the children. She tucked them together and resealed the box with scotch tape.

In the kitchen she poured a tumbler full of scotch and grabbed a sleeve of saltines from the box. For months, she had pulled her Gristedes food orders from childhood lists. Oreos. Campbell's tomato soup. Ingredients for tuna noodle casserole. Phoebe had turned from the *Silver Palate Cookbook* to *Betty Crocker*.

She stuffed saltines in her mouth to absorb the scotch, alternating alcohol and crackers until she emptied the glass.

Drunk, but steady—proud of her crafty move with the saltines—she lurched into the bedroom. First she stripped the linens and threw them into the laundry room. Then she took Jake's pillows, redolent of his scent, and stuffed them in a trash bag.

Luz had warned her against "divesting" of anything, reminding her of the papers she signed promising not to sell or remove "goods, tangible or otherwise." She tried to imagine someone wanting pillows reeking of Jacob Pierce.

After rolling a suitcase to the bedroom, she threw Jake's clothes on the bare mattress. She swept everything off the top of his dresser. Ties— she grabbed his millions of fucking ties—ripped them off the mechanized rack. Shirts, handmade, stitched with stolen money; armfuls went on the pile. Suits. Pants. Thick, absorbent robes. Silk pajamas. Cashmere socks. Pair after pair; a fortune used just to cover his feet.

She threw them in one suitcase and then another and then two more, and then shoved them into his study with the trash bag of pillows. His Lee Child, James Patterson, and Brad Thor books piled on the nightstand, she tossed to the floor, lusting for a huge torch with which to light them.

In the kitchen, she pitched boxes of Sugar Wafers, bags of M&M's. The rye bread Jake liked, the Ritz crackers he crumbled into soup, the Philadelphia cream cheese he smeared on bagels, the orange juice he drank: she threw all his favorites into the trash bag and lugged the overloaded plastic to the garbage chute.

She looked around the family room for evidence. A crystal bowl of nuts Phoebe first emptied and then, holding it between her fingers as though it were toxic, flung into a study, grateful for the sound of shattering.

Phoebe needed breakage, to throw and heave and pound, and the goddamned FBI wouldn't let her touch a thing. They hated her. They all hated her, Jake's handmaiden.

She circled the den, prowling Jake's cage until she came to his earphones dangling by a chair—his favorite, overstuffed and built for comfort with a matching ottoman—plugged in to music as he read. Drawn and unable to stop, she sat in Jake's indentation and jammed his headphones on her ears, adjusting the band before they slipped off.

She went back three songs in the playlist Kate helped him set up—his last Father's Day present. She threw back her head, Jake's soft charcoal sweater against her hair. Waves of the past washed in, beginning with Harry Connick Jr. singing "It Had to Be You." Each time Connick's version of the song, their songs, played, he'd croon along, his awful voice leaving her breathless with laughter.

Phoebe's heart caught, and tears poured down at the first sounds of "Let's Stay Together." Jake holding her tight at Solomon's wedding, dancing to the Al Green song, her hand on his broad shoulder, the feel of the wool suit, the scent of his starched white shirt, his smooth cheek when she reached up to stroke him.

Fuck you, Jake.

Fuckyoufuckyoufuckyou.

CHAPTER 33

PHOEBE

August 2009

Phoebe wandered the halls of the penthouse one last time, as agents tracked her every move. They'd been in and out of the apartment for weeks, tagging every item to enter in a master list so that she wouldn't take off with what was now property of the US government.

She'd become inured to the insanity of what they'd tagged, wondering who'd bid in the planned auction of all things Pierce. Of course, the rare Vacheron Constantin watches, some more than a hundred years old, and her Van Cleef & Arpels diamond earrings, worth over seventy-five thousand—and so heavy she rarely wore them—would bring salivating buyers. But Jake's boxer shorts and her yoga pants? Her colander?

Phoebe steeled herself against the humiliation of having her life displayed in a hotel ballroom where people judged her by cloth and jewels. All she wanted were a few things from her mother, her grandmothers—things not bought with blood money—for Katie, for her granddaughters, but no. They wouldn't let her choose anything from before Jake's crimes. Even the 10K gold ring worn to a sliver of gleaming metal by her great-grandmother's fingers was added to their list of items for sale. She begged to keep the red Pyrex mixing bowl from her mother's set—Deb had the blue one. The bowl was no collectible. Fork scrapes marked a thousand beaten eggs. But apparently someone might want to pay for the privilege of owning the homely bowl. Like everything else, by order of the feds, she'd leave it behind.

The feds thought everything the Pierces owned was valuable enough to auction off. She tried to imagine what pleasure or revenge someone could derive from Jake's underwear or her kitchen appliances. Their infamy must be far larger than she imagined if owning her mother's bowl provided cachet.

Today she'd leave with a small cloth suitcase so old it lacked wheels, filled with the few things her lawyer had won in the battle for bras and belts. Some jeans. A few sweaters. A lined raincoat. Harriet Joyner, the woman Gideon chose as Phoebe's counsel, fought harder than Phoebe thought she deserved. She sat in Harriet's office, nodding as the steel cable of a woman drew up paperwork that paid no attention to Phoebe's innocence, guilt, or desire to divest herself of anything related to Jake's crimes, including all the money he'd put into accounts in her name.

"It's your last chance to come out with a penny," Harriet had drilled into her. "I don't care what the world says. You worked, you started a business, and you raised a family. You never had a clue what Jake did. You were another one of his victims."

Harriet came from Brooklyn, middle class, same as Phoebe, although her version of growing up Brooklyn was as a black girl in the Canarsie neighborhood. The connection united them enough for Harriet to still Phoebe's objections with a glance. After fighting for the whole enchilada, knowing the end product would be a fraction of her request, if anything, Harriet had shocked the legal community with a million-dollar deal. This number, which to the average person sounded like an unimaginable fortune, would be considerably shrunk by the time Phoebe paid Harriet and gave half to Deb.

In the end, she might have a quarter million, which she'd leave untouched, hoping she could bring in seven thousand to eight thousand dollars a year in interest while she lived on Social Security. She'd be more secure than most retirees in the country, though a pauper by previous standards.

And then there was the theory of relativity. No more having to report expenses over a hundred dollars. Her minders from the feds had previously turned down her requests to subscribe to the *New York Times.* Basic cable was all she was allowed. Her prescriptions for Ambien and Xanax were scrutinized, but in the end, Harriet fought for her right to have the pills while Phoebe remained under federal control. Now it was over. She could fill morphine prescriptions if she so pleased. If she walked out with nothing but her jeans and raincoat, freedom was hers, if only from the government's oversight. However, Jake still swung from her neck like the millstone he'd become.

Phoebe removed from the fridge curling pictures held with magnets, grateful that Harriet secured her personal photo albums, starting with her three granddaughters, none of whom she'd seen since November, nine months before. Then she leaned her fingers on her antidote for tears, the decidedly different item on the refrigerator: rules from the Federal Bureau of Prisons.

Dress Code

Wear clothing that is appropriate for a large gathering of men, women, and young children. Wearing inappropriate clothing (such as provocative or revealing clothes) may result in your being denied visitation.

The following items are *not* permitted:

> revealing shorts
> sundresses
> halter tops
> bathing suits
> see-through garments of any type
> crop tops
> low-cut blouses or dresses
> leotards
> spandex
> miniskirts
> backless tops
> hats or caps

sleeveless garments

skirts two inches or more above the knee

dresses or skirts with a high-cut split in the back, front, or side

clothing that looks like inmate clothing (khaki or green
military-type clothing)

Visiting Duration

By law, an inmate gets at least four hours of visiting time per month but usually the prison can provide more. However, the Warden can restrict the length of visits or the number of people who can visit at once, to avoid overcrowding in the visiting room.

General Behavior

Because many people are usually visiting, it is important visits are quiet, orderly, and dignified. The visiting room officer can require you to leave if either you or the inmate is not acting appropriately.

Physical Contact

In most cases, handshakes, hugs, and kisses (in good taste) are allowed at the beginning and end of a visit. Staff may limit contact for security reasons (to prevent people from trying to introduce contraband) and to keep the visiting area orderly. The Federal Bureau of Prisons does not permit conjugal visits.

Phoebe folded the list and tucked it into her jeans pocket.

The world wanted her to suffer, and she would. Punishment felt deserved. Why the hell should she benefit in any way, including the amount Harriet managed?

A good girl to the end, Phoebe locked the door as she left, knowing the men and women in FBI jackets would change the locks within the hour. She pressed the elevator button and then traveled down, hefting the suitcase her mother had carried so long ago.

Manny hugged her with undeserved warmth.

"You've been so good to me," she said, as she leaned her head into his shoulder. "Why?"

"They pushed you down so far that it's impossible not to give you a hand up."

Shit. How did she not see him before? How many people did her ascension blind her to? "I'm sorry for whatever asshole stuff Jake or I did."

Manny dropped his mask enough for Phoebe to see the person, not the doorman. "Nobody wants to see us, Mrs. Pierce. Hell, we work for tips; we hide deep. Now you have no more money to give, and I have nothing to lose with you, but honestly, you were never an asshole with me. There's that."

"That's quite a gift." She kissed him on the cheek, inhaling his warm cologne. "You saved me more than anyone, and I did nothing to earn it. Thank you."

For the last time, she walked out the labyrinth leading to the rusty gate at the back. One lone paparazzi smoking a cigarette spotted and followed her as she headed toward the street a few blocks away, where Helen waited to drive her away. Determined to get out of Manhattan without being tailed, she flagged a cab, knowing a photograph would read something along the lines of "Phoebe's Still Riding."

Dollars ticked as she rode the short distance to the rendezvous spot Helen had chosen, a longer trip by car than by walking, not unusual in New York.

"There," she said to the driver. "The silver Camry."

He slid into the illegal space behind Helen's car. Phoebe's wallet held five hundred dollars, the last amount approved by the faceless FBI budget master—apparently the sum on which a person could begin a new life.

She handed the driver a twenty for the eight-dollar ride, waiting for her change, multiplying by twenty percent and then some for the tip. After a moment of receiving nothing, she leaned forward and angled her head into an inquisitive pose.

"Yeah?" The driver's mustache moved under his drinker's nose, as he chomped on an unlit cigar.

"My change?"

"Really, Mrs. Pierce?" He drew her name out as though sharing a dirty joke.

Phoebe glanced at his identification. "Yes. Really, Mr. Kane."

"Ya know, you and your husband got plenty to make good on, but he's locked up. And you're here." The scratched plastic shield separating them muted his voice. "So you can start with twelve bucks for me and go from there."

Rage blindsided her. Months of waiting in the background, hand-maiden to the most despised man in Manhattan, added to months of the press painting her as a money-grubbing accomplice to Jake's crimes, balled up in a white flash toward this vile man.

"Give me my money." Phoebe's frenzy of anger built till she thought it would consume her. She could barely control her impulse to scream as an elevator of hatred traveled up her chest.

She bit her lip and forced herself to look outside, calm herself. Window boxes filled with bright red geraniums decorated the white town house behind Helen's car.

This man.

This prick.

He thinks he knows me.

They all think they know me.

They think they know my life.

She took out her phone, switched it to camera mode, and, zooming in, she snapped a picture of his hack license.

"Hey? Whaddya doing?"

"Keeping tabs and keeping track, Mr. Kane."

Slamming the door shut as she left the taxi, she stepped out into the August heat.

She'd lived like a mole since December and now, like a mole, she blinked, trying to take in the idea of living in the sun.

CHAPTER 34

PHOEBE

Living in Poughkeepsie, New York, was so far outside anything Phoebe ever planned, that waking each morning still surprised her four months after moving there. The moment she opened her eyes, she'd look around in confusion, straining to orient herself to her new surroundings.

Poughkeepsie provided anonymity while remaining just a two-hour train ride to New York City. Her apartment complex boasted a quiet drug trade, a pool rumored to open a few weeks each summer, and carpeting that appeared to be made of recycled plastic supermarket bags.

A view of the Hudson River afforded a bit of pleasure, but otherwise her cramped one-bedroom's only advantage was cheap rent and neighbors who didn't give a shit.

. . .

Phoebe readied to see Kate. Already swathed in winter layers for the ten-block walk to the restaurant where they'd meet, she wrapped on a final touch—a scratchy but warm scarf—and then glanced in the entry mirror.

She'd hung the mirror a few weeks ago, thinking its red oval frame would detract from the two locks and chain on the black metal door and chipped mushroom-colored paint. Instead, the vivid shade played up the dinginess like fuchsia lipstick on a toothless woman. Few of her improvements made a difference in her melancholy of estrangement.

But today was different. Elation rose with a yeasty delight at seeing Kate for the first time since Jake's confession.

She peered in the mirror more closely. The color of her hat should have been named is-this-navy-or-black?—the shade, endemic to companies who skimped on using adequate and proper dye, could flatter nobody. Her longer hair required fewer cuts. She also changed her appearance by pulling it back and up. Not becoming, but the style served her purpose: invisibility. People barely noticed women her age anyway—with her hair, she guaranteed it. When she truly needed to hide, Phoebe wore brown contact lenses. Today she applied two coats of mascara and kept her eyes blue.

Phoebe slipped on sunglasses and left the house. The street where she lived might appear threatening through her daughter's eyes. Industrial lineage haunted the area, bringing to mind thoughts of shadowed murder and leg breakings.

. . .

Poughkeepsie Slices provided decent pizza, red leather booths, and a beer and wine license.

Kate waited in the back of the restaurant.

Phoebe rushed over, cognizant of not drowning her daughter in need and love, but not able to hold much back. She drank her in, absorbing her through her eyes.

"Baby." She held out her arms. After hesitating, Kate fell into her. Phoebe enveloped her daughter, whose familiar scents overwhelmed Phoebe with sadness at the extraordinary length of time without seeing her and the joy at finally being together.

Kate's hair no longer framed her face in perfect waves but hung lank and dry, pulled back by the sunglasses pushed on top of her head. In a year, Kate had passed from thin to scrawny. A burgundy sweater drooped in folds over her angles. Her cheekbones had sharpened to knife-edges.

They held hands across the table, taking comfort in touch before talk. Phoebe's chipped nails matched Kate's. Without manicures, facials, and all the other niceties they'd previously had on tap, the polished veneer of the moneyed lucky melted away mighty fast.

"How are you doing?" Phoebe dove in, needing to start somewhere. "Amelia? Zach?"

"Amelia's almost fine, but she misses Grandma and Grandpa. Most of this goes over her head. Zach and I are holding on. He's putting up with a lot."

"You offer plenty. Don't downplay your worth."

"Look at me!" Kate wiggled her fingers as she outlined her body. "Not just me. You too. We're mother-daughter 'after' portraits, except our makeovers went in the wrong direction."

"Nothing like a scam to bring you from Saks to Target."

"What's to worry about, I guess? That we look like shit when the paparazzi catch us?" Kate noted. "I can actually feel *schadenfreude* hitting me as I walk down the street. It's a physical thwack."

"Your father's locked away. We're the only punching bags available."

"Missy Ross turns the other way when she sees me. Literally, Mom, she turns her head as though I carry a stench."

"Missy is hardly one to talk. She has the morals of a rat. Isn't she the one who slept with three of her personal trainers?" Falling back into this mother-daughter rhythm with Kate provided balm so unfamiliar it just about knocked Phoebe over. Reconnection wouldn't all be this easy, but she drank the moment's available comfort.

"Her husband works twenty hours a day. He wouldn't know if Missy blew her trainer on their bed while he slept."

"I guess I'm the last one to talk." Phoebe took a napkin from the stainless steel holder and brushed crumbs off the table. "About not seeing things."

"You? Come on, Mom. If anyone should have seen something going on it was us. Noah and I were the idiots."

"Not true. What did you and Noah think was going on up there?" The box opened. Doubtless they'd pound on this for years. Phoebe imagined repeatedly picking at the same scab until she finally uncovered the answer.

"We thought Dad performed some old-school shit that he was both embarrassed by and proud of. The computers were a hundred years old; he didn't use any of the new technology. We figured he sat around with Solomon and Charlie—'cause everyone knew he was a moron around computers—and used some sort of Daddy voodoo they translated into the computer."

Phoebe said nothing, not wanting to interrupt their delicate connection.

Kate rubbed the edge of the laminated menu card. "Truthfully, we kind of believed he was an idiot savant when it came to stock picking and buying and selling."

Phoebe examined the approaching waitress for any sign of recognition, but the woman shuffled as though the only thing on her mind was getting off her feet.

"Get you girls a drink?"

Phoebe's and Kate's eyes met in a moment of yes.

"White wine, please," Phoebe said.

"Red for me."

Phoebe shook her head at Kate's words. "Um . . . the white is better." She widened her eyes, hoping her daughter understood the message about the horrors of the tannic-ridden Carlo Rossi red served here, without Phoebe having to spell it out in front of the waitress.

"Uh. Okay." Kate nodded at the waitress. "And a Greek salad. Dressing on the side, please."

Phoebe shook her head again. "Not just that. Bring us a small pizza. With extra cheese. And pepperoni. You're going to eat at least one piece, Katie."

Kate shrugged the same way she had when forced to taste broccoli years ago. "I can barely get anything down."

"Start trying. How's Zach? Really?"

"A rock, but shaken, like all of us. His parents approach me as though I'm toxic." She laced her fingers and brought them to her mouth. "They were invested with him too. Of course. Jesus, Daddy Voodoo spread his fucking tentacles everywhere."

"Everyone keeps asking if I knew, if I suspected." Phoebe groped in her purse for the cigarettes she rationed out like sticks of dynamite. "Who suspects their husband is operating a Ponzi scheme? I barely knew what the word meant. You and Noah worked with him, and you never mistrusted his honesty, right?"

"We wondered about his connections," Kate confessed. "Noah and I worried that insider trading was how he kept those Club returns so high. We worried someone was giving him information."

"Did you ever ask him?" This blunt analysis of Jake, mincing his actions without fear, soothed her, creating the connection provided only by family conversation.

"Once. Boy, oh boy, never again. Noah and I asked to take him out to lunch. Our dime. Like that was some proof of us being adults."

The waitress placed small, thick-walled wineglasses in front of them.

"You might as well get us each a second one now," Kate said.

The woman turned to Phoebe, who nodded. "And a plate of garlic bread, please."

The moment the waitress left, Phoebe returned to the topic. "What happened at the lunch?"

"Daddy exploded," Kate said. "He went nuclear. Some of it was the same as always. You've heard it: 'This is my business. When I want to invite you in, I'll tell you. Stick to what I assign.' The usual, Mom, but also very different."

"Different how?"

"I suppose it's because we actually asked him, directly, about things like insider information. He went ballistic. 'What, I can't be smart enough to manage the Club without using bullshit methods? You think I'm playing the fucking edges somehow?' Then he became scary calm: that thing where he's wrestling with his temper—you know how he gets.

"He was like a machine spitting out orders," she continued. "'You will stay away from the Club. I've built up years of exacting methods—whether you think I'm capable or not—to make that place what it is. Nobody fucks with it, including my nosy kids.'"

"I'm so sorry," Phoebe said.

Kate stared at her mother with pleading eyes. "Mom, stop seeing him. Noah needs you. He's falling apart. He's drinking. Noah thought he was honoring our fucking father by not drinking. Now that he figured out why Dad didn't touch alcohol, he's making up for lost time. He told me you're emailing, but you need to really be in his life, which means cutting off Dad."

Emails with Noah were lopsided conversations, with him writing lengthy tirades about Jake and having given up his life for his father, and Phoebe answering with attempts to apologize for Jake and then steer her son to a healthier place.

"I contact him every day. Like I do with you," Phoebe said. "Each time I email or leave a message, I ask him to meet me. I don't want to pressure him to the point of adding to his pain. He refuses to get together."

"He won't see you until you stop visiting and talking to Dad."

"All I do is force myself to visit him once in a great while. Trust me, I hate every—"

"It doesn't matter if you hate it," Kate said. "As long as you keep going, you're attached. It reflects on all of us when you give him some sort of forgiveness or tacit approval."

"Approval? I fooled myself into thinking it took courage, standing by your father simply so he'd have one person in this world, but you think it makes you and Noah somehow complicit? That's the opposite of—"

"Mom. He doesn't deserve your courage."

. . .

Phoebe didn't ask Kate to come back to the apartment. She wasn't ready for her daughter's sympathy. The cracks in the wall, a few sticks of furniture ordered from Bob's Discount, carpet soaking up spilled wine like a drunk on holiday. Economic changes provided an education in why poor people's houses seemed rickety. Cheap furniture retains value for about two weeks. The polyester blanket she bought only a few months ago already appeared diseased with pills.

The things Phoebe missed mostly represented sentiment, but occasionally comfort took center stage. It was for emotional connections that she'd wanted her mother's red bowl and the handmade mugs that she and Deb had found in Vermont. But her sheets? Pratesi cotton felt so much better than Kohl's polyester that Phoebe felt ashamed for not realizing it before.

She thought about her favorite art, especially the quirky copper mosaic she'd bought in North Carolina—an ache she admitted to no one, because it only added to her Phoebe Antoinette persona, and, anyway, who the fuck cared about art after losing her children and grandchildren? Sheets and copper meant shit after Jake robbed the world.

But damn it, she sometimes missed beauty.

And comfort.

Most of all, she was lonely.

Phone calls were the highlights of her day. Along with haunting Noah and Kate, she called Helen every day, careful not to be unremittingly depressing—a difficult job while her existence included keeping her bare feet from touching the rug and scouring Goodwill for books to read. She put off joining the library, afraid of being recognized. These were things she told nobody. People hated whiny victims, reserving their admiration for those who suffered nobly, so she acted as though she lived a plucky sitcom.

At the end of every day, she called Deb, both of them working overtime to sound chipper, Deb making the fact that Ben now bagged groceries at Publix into a series of funny stories.

Mail cheered her. Friends who hadn't been struck down by Jake snuck out of the past. They weren't ready to meet or call, but they'd pen occasional emails, inching their way toward, Phoebe hoped, a closer connection.

She stood, still wobbly from the wine and hopeful that the postman had left his delivery. Her apartment, on the first floor, was just steps from the bank of mailboxes, the kind that had been in Jake's building growing up, where the mailman had the key to unlock all of the boxes from the top.

People, Time, and *Newsweek* were jammed into the box. She subscribed to more magazines than any one person should, but along with the *New York Times,* they were her links to the world—plus, subscriptions were far cheaper than the newsstand price.

A cable bill. Her daily letter from Jake, announcing to the world, or at least to the postal carrier, that her prison pen pal was the most notorious financial criminal in the United States. The return address gave his name, what they called his identification number, and the words *Federal Correctional Institution Ray Brook* along with the post office number and address. Jake wrote her name in his sprawling style, usually bigger than the space allowed, forcing him to cram in the final letters at the end.

A package for Phoebe sat in the open area. Helen probably sent it. The return address read "Offprint Books." Small presents of books and magazines arrived from her often. Phoebe grabbed the box and headed back to the apartment, ready to fortify herself with one more glass of wine before opening Jake's letter, hoping that a soothing new detective novel waited afterward.

She stood on tiptoes to reach her one decent wineglass, having splurged at the Crate and Barrel outlet, and poured a hefty serving of Riesling.

> *Dear Pheebs,*
>
> *How are you, my love? Did you speak to the kids this week? News—anything at all will be welcome, but you know that, right? And the little ones? Did you send them my love? I'm getting good in the woodworking shop. My plan is to make dollhouses like the other guys are doing for their kids.*

Her insides twisted at the thought of the girls getting Grandpa's love, and yet she hurt just as much at the idea of them thinking he didn't care. Noah and Kate told the girls that Grandpa stole money at work, a lot of money, and he'd be in jail forever. And when they asked why he did it, their parents told the truth: nobody knew.

> *Believe it or not, my skill with the saw gets better every day. They have me making stools now. I told the guard the other day*

that if he let me sign it, I bet they could charge a hell of a lot more money.

Phoebe laughed before she could catch herself. Moments like this knocked the wind right out of her; times when she responded to Jake's twisted humor and fell into an old pattern of connection.

My canteen account has sunk pretty low. If you could give me a little replenishment, I'd be grateful. I continue to think of ways to make it up to you, any small thing I can do. This for better or worse thing isn't exactly going in your favor, huh?

Gideon told me that Charlie, Gita-Rae, Nanci, and Solomon were arrested. I'm putting my money on Gita-Rae to fold first, but we'll see. Not that anyone but me did anything at all.

Jake had become a junkie about himself. Rather than avoiding articles about his crime and punishment, as had been his habit before his sentencing, he immersed himself in media, becoming his own biggest fan and defender. His blindness stunned her as he retold how much money his early investors made from the Club—intimating that their guilt matched his.

Descriptions of prisoners watching football followed, along with chummy games of cards they played. Jake had escaped to a strict summer camp, while she bore the brunt of his criminal aftermath. He'd bragged to her in the past about how the inmates admired him, even asking for financial advice.

She dreaded the onerous weekly phone calls with Jake. At least during the visits, he worked at amusing her, probably for the benefit of his nearby buddies. On the phone, all she heard was his relief at having the huge weight of keeping the Club going lifted off his shoulders.

Jake might not love prison, but he prized being free of the burden of his awful pretense. She put aside the letter to file with the rest. Why she kept this record was a question for Freud, she supposed. His letters were toxic and irresistible all at the same time. Sympathy for and fascination with the man one had loved forever didn't vanish in a puff of smoke, even at the worst of news about him. Repeatedly, she tried to understand her disconnect: hating this Jake; still locked into the man she married.

CHAPTER 35

PHOEBE

A dozen monkeys could crash through the window and jump on her head, and Phoebe would still be reading *He Stole More Than My Money* by Bianca Miller. The sky darkened as she squinted to read the last few pages of the book.

The package, most definitely not from Helen, contained an advance copy of a tell-all memoir by this Bianca person, this mistress of Jake, who'd slithered into her mailbox to reveal sordid details of a story costarring Phoebe as an unknowing and now horrified participant.

Pain throbbed from her teeth to temples. No amount of aspirin would touch this headache. Bianca Miller owned truths about Jake that Phoebe never suspected, further fracturing her misaligned memories. Again and again she chastised herself for caring so damned much: how dare it matter if Jake cheated their entire marriage? He had stolen the blood of her family, friends, and more strangers than she could count in ten lifetimes. Who cared if he'd bedded this woman?

She did.

Decades of love and marriage couldn't be wished away. It turned out she could be hurt repeatedly. Knowledge of Jake's hideous crimes didn't inoculate her against his personal corruption. Fuck you, Bianca Miller, for taking your own humiliation and splashing it over me.

Offprint Books had obviously sent this advance copy of Miller's book for a response, but what kind? Fighting Bianca Miller in public? Most likely, a publicist hoped the shock of the book would send Phoebe to the nearest tabloid for a media version of hair pulling with Bianca and give her trashy book a sales bump.

Fat chance. Photos of Phoebe along with cruel theories about her were splayed across every continent already, and she had never responded. She'd been analyzed and found guilty in the court of public opinion. There wasn't much Phoebe took pride in anymore except for sewing her mouth shut from day one. She owned herself, if nothing else.

Shaking with hunger and rage, but unable to put down the book long enough to even make a sandwich, she grabbed a jar of peanuts from the kitchen and continued plowing through.

Jake came to my bed at least once a week (sometimes more), never getting what he needed at home. Yes, I was ashamed of sleeping with a married man, but it seemed clear that his wife couldn't care for him as I did. He was a father with still-youngish kids, so he couldn't leave, but though his responsibilities lay with them, his dreams were about me.

I prepared for him body and soul. In the morning, I cooked dishes she refused to make. Eggplant parmigiana was his favorite. I'd dream of our night to come as I dipped the thin slices (the way he liked it, layer upon layer) into an egg bath, coated them with seasoned cornmeal (my special touch), and then do it again. I call it twice dipped. Then I dropped the slices into bubbling oil. She refused to fry anything. Jake said she hated the smell because it clung to her silk dresses! A new kind of selfish invented by Ms. Stuck-up.

I planned and made our meals ahead of time, wanting to devote every minute to Jake when he arrived. The eggplant. Pasta drowned in homemade sauce, covered with fresh-grated parmigiana. I put pats of butter in the hot pasta before smothering it with the cheese. Asparagus tips with pepper and butter. Plum tomato slices, salted and drizzled with oil.

The first dessert was something like ice cream with homemade fudge sauce or chocolate chip brownies. The second dessert? A piece of me.

Jake's "special desires," all rejected by her, really cemented him to me. Listen, if a wife doesn't take care of her man's needs, he's bound to stray. Jake said she was a lazy lover (the worst kind!). I guess at her age that happens. (He seemed young, but women get older much faster than men. So they got to work to keep their men interested and happy.) Jake told me that just once he wished she did more for him in the bedroom. (But she never did, and I was glad.)

I'd open the door dressed just the way he liked, wearing tight, low, and slutty (yes, might as well call it what it was) outfits. Sometimes my black lace bra poked out of a sheer pink shirt; the top three buttons opened. Trampy and see-through, which the salesgirl called diaphanous. A push-up bra, of course, with me spilling out.

Total truth: I am a 38D. She's a 32B, if that. Hardly a handful, he'd tell me, and believe me, this man likes breasts. Looking. Touching. Blush coming on . . .

Perfume meant a lot to him. He bought me a huge antique atomizer filled with my favorite perfume, Poison, and begged me not to wear any other.

Okay. If I'm going to tell it all, I will. 'Cause I think Jake Pierce's kinks explain him. That's what a shrink friend told me. What did he like? Having his hands tied up while I "took care" of him. In all sorts of ways, and I think you can picture it, yes?

Phoebe threw the book across the room. Yes, she could picture it, all right.

. . .

Phoebe woke up sure of a few things:

1. She'd break all connections with Jake.
2. She'd get on her knees if needed to see Noah and her grand-

daughters. She'd stand in front of his house twenty-four hours a day if that's what it took.

3. She'd call Ira.

Phoebe began her program by calling Kate, leaving a message when her daughter didn't pick up. "I loved seeing you yesterday, though I hate seeing you so sad. We need to reconnect: you, Noah, and I. I'm severing connections with your father. I promise this with all my heart, though it might take a tiny bit of time. Not more than a month. I need to confront him in person, and getting up there is tough. Please tell Noah. I want to address this as the family we still are."

. . .

The next day, Phoebe reached out to Ira. She didn't lack insight into her timing. Miller's book, no matter how full of half-truths, bequeathed permission.

Attraction to Ira had churned in the past—not with the knife of sexual pull Jake held over her, but with a more dangerous appeal for a married woman: the draw of a good man.

Before calling Ira, she examined her motives for all her actions. The truth didn't put her in the best light. Jake's cheating and Bianca's book drove her into an emotional anger that offered permission to break ties with him. Why that and not his far graver crimes? This personal fraud missile was a direct shot, waking her from the comfort of melancholy. No more wallowing in self-pity.

Time to say good-bye, Jake.

Phoebe needed to find out the condition of the things she left behind, beginning with Mira House.

. . .

Phoebe pulled it all out readying for Ira. Her extended period of barely using makeup meant that her bag had remained stocked—she didn't expect to own potions like this again. That the feds let her take her cosmetics without discussion testified to the FBI hiring too many men; they'd never imagine that the sum total of her sack of creams and makeup added up to nearly two thousand dollars. Certainly someone would have paid at least that to try the beauty routine of Phoebe Marie Antoinette Pierce.

Serum. Moisturizer. Primer. Foundation. Highlighter. Colors for her cheeks and lips. She'd forgotten the sensuous pleasure of smoothing these creams on her face. Phoebe wasn't fooling herself that romantic glitter would return to her life, but damned if she couldn't enjoy covering her lips in vermilion.

They'd meet in Rhinebeck, the town Manhattan folk loved, only a thirty-minute drive from Poughkeepsie. Dicey for Phoebe—it would be an easy place to be recognized—but screw it. She wasn't a criminal on the run.

. . .

She arrived early enough to pick a private table. Aroi Thai Restaurant served all her purposes, with excellent food, a location at the end of the street—farthest from the main drag—and though a popular spot, nobody chose it for people watching.

Phoebe sat with her back to the entrance. "I'll be the woman wearing a greying bun," she had warned Ira.

"So it's longer," he'd said on the phone. "Your hair."

"Among the many changes."

"Is your heart intact?"

Without thinking, she had put her hand to her chest. "I guess I'd describe it as mildly defrosting, though I'm not sure that's good. Sensitivity isn't a blessing right now."

Ira's kindness made waiting less nerve wracking, but her pulse still raced. This was her first time seeing anyone other than Helen, Deb, and, more recently, Kate since Jake's arrest.

A slim young man refilled her water glass. "Is your companion coming?"

Her heart slipped. For a moment, the waiter knew her and wondered if Jake would join her. Then she realized he was politely probing whether she'd been stood up.

"He's coming." She tried to sound sure, but anything could happen. Pretty Phoebe of Erasmus Hall died long ago.

"Something while you wait? A drink?"

"No, thank you." No drinking and driving, thank you. The law remained in the front of her mind. Always. Plus, alcohol equaled relaxing. Phoebe didn't know if Ira maintained his crush, but being vulnerable frightened her. Friendship. That's the only thing she wanted.

"Phoebe." Ira slipped in and placed a hand on her shoulder, providing the simple gift of touch. He put out his hands and pulled her to her feet. They stood for a moment, just looking, and then he drew her into him.

"I'm sorry." He held her tight.

Phoebe raised her head. "For what?"

"I should have called. Waiting for you to reach out was wrong."

She shook her head. "No. I understand. How could you know—"

"I know you." He hung his coat on the back of his chair and then pulled out her seat. "I should never have questioned you."

Phoebe half grinned. "I thought I knew Jake, and we were married since I was a teenager. How can I blame you for being unsure about me?" She stopped and put her hand to her mouth. "Don't think I haven't thought about Mira House. And the Cupcake Project. Calling that an understatement is an understatement. That *I* haven't contacted *you* before now is wrong."

"Now that we've determined we're both truly awful, let's say hello and enjoy a meal." His hazel eyes radiated compassion. She'd devalued that trait during her life. Sconces above the white fireplace built a glow over his thick salt-and-pepper hair. The thought made her laugh: in her desperation for connection, she made Ira into a momentary Jesus.

They ordered as though this were the Last Supper, keeping their conversation light as they waited for food. Rhinebeck: beautiful and expensive. Weather: decent for December. Obama's first year as president: excellent. When their meals arrived, they nodded as though readying to reach the next level.

Crispy salmon infused with spicy mango, Thai spring rolls crunching in her mouth—for the first time in months, Phoebe didn't eat like an animal crouched over her kill.

"Yes. Mira House lost a lot. True, true," Ira said, picking up the trail of the serious conversation for which they were fated.

"An enormous amount. I'm amazed you survived." The surrounding couples made her feel like she fit in and as though society had opened its arms for a night. "Credit probably goes to you. Your calmness."

"Mira House is doing fine for a number of reasons. I figure it like this: the money we invested with Jake, well, we'd never expected those funds to begin with. That came from the Cupcake Project, and not everything went to Jake. We bought things, durable goods for all the programs. Sent kids to college on scholarship. Got new computers. Redid the gym. Hell, Phoebe. We're ahead."

Phoebe wanted to touch his worn and winter-dry hands resting on the table. This kind, kind man. "You're a good man for thinking like that, Ira."

"And you are a good woman, Phoebe, despite your determination to punish yourself. Do you even know what happened to the Cupcake Project? Do you want to know?"

She examined her ragged fingernails. The last thing that should matter, but still, she wanted to hide the fraying skin, the dry brittleness. "I didn't call anyone after the one time I spoke with Eva. I didn't think they wanted to speak with me. Shit. I'm lying. I was afraid of everyone's anger: Zoya shrieking, Linh crying—"

"Stop. Before you rend your clothes, listen. The woman in charge of the . . ." Ira put his hands in the air, lost.

"The aftermath. Senda Dempsey." Phoebe had read the name online.

"Right. Her. She appointed someone as overseer for the Cupcake Project, and that person allowed Eva, Zoya, and Linh to remain as managers. They're making money. My guess is Dempsey is going to have it valued and then sell it."

"Maybe the three of them can buy it."

"I doubt it. They're living check to check like the rest of the world."

"Maybe I can help figure something out. Maybe—"

"Maybe you can. And maybe you can't." A stern expression appeared on Ira's face. "But you can call Eva. Connect and find out how they are. You weren't sent to jail. Undo your chains."

CHAPTER 36

PHOEBE

The rituals of entering Ray Brook prison never failed to terrify Phoebe: long lines of cheerless women, restless children frightened into good behavior, and a few stone-faced men waiting to visit, the lack of anything bringing optimism or dignity—color, art, music—and guards pushing all limits of hierarchy as they inspected every scrap of identification offered.

Phoebe compulsively checked to make sure she'd not worn an underwire bra. The website Prison Talk provided too many threads where women described being turned away if the metal in an underwire set off the metal detectors.

Her identification checked, her clothing approved, and having proven she carried nothing but her ID, Phoebe entered the visiting room. Staking out a spot required thought, not because one molded plastic chair might be better than another, but because corners provided a modicum of privacy. Her drab tweed sweater blended with the furnishings.

Phoebe nodded at an older woman waiting at the next table: a sister member of the sorority of sad wives, one she'd seen before. The tired-looking woman, her roots an inch long, returned the nod with her lips pressed tight. Maybe she had dental problems; maybe she wanted Phoebe to mind her own damned business.

The prisoners lined up and, five at a time, entered the visiting room.

Some searched the tables with desperation; others emanated a lack of concern so seemingly forced they belied their casualness. She saw Jake before he found her. Thinner than last time, his green prison uniform somehow pressed and impeccable. His thick hair, cut short, almost buzzed, gave him a rough appearance.

He spotted her and gave her a tough-guy smile, as though they were on the playground, and he couldn't appear weak in front of his buddies.

She remained seated.

"Where's my permitted contact?" He held his hands in askance, waiting for her to rise and hug him.

Phoebe debated refusing his touch until she saw the guard, the pockmarked one, staring as though wondering if a situation was developing, what with Jake standing over her. Getting up without a smile, she allowed an embrace, while averting her head to keep his lips away.

"Something wrong?" he asked as they sat. "Kids okay?"

"It's been a long time since the kids were okay."

"You know what I mean." He glanced around as though checking to see if anyone listened in. As though his life was so interesting that someone might sell their conversation to *People*.

Which could happen.

Fine. Let some drug dealer make money off them.

"Are they healthy?" he asked finally.

"Noah's drinking. Kate looks like she hasn't eaten in months."

Jake poked his head forward in question, unused to this attitude. She usually kept things light, wanting only to skate along the surface until she could escape from him and prison.

"Deb and Ben drive people back and forth from the airport, schlepping their bags, so they can pay for groceries, and Ben became a 'rental husband.' They're trying to sell the condo."

"Rental husband?" Jake leaned in just enough not to get called out over the loudspeaker. "Did you bring quarters?"

Vending machines, the highlights of the visiting room, lined one wall. Chips, candy bars, even yogurt.

"Rental husband, meaning he rewires retired women's lamps for ten bucks. On weekends he bags groceries. And no, I forgot the quarters."

"Christ, Pheebs. I have little enough as it is. You know how much I look forward to this."

"Really?" she asked. "As much as you look forward to, um, eggplant parmigiana?"

"What are you talking about?"

"As much as you wanted asparagus tips with pepper? Softened ice cream with cake? Big breasts?"

Jake glanced around as though expecting rescue from those surrounding them. Maybe the pink-swaddled baby held by her daddy. Perhaps the woman so heavy her arms draped over themselves. Or maybe the woman to Jake's right, Ms. Tight Lips—perhaps she'd give him a way out.

"Keep your eyes on me, Jake. Me." Nothing would stand between her and this low-pitched confrontation, this end to her marriage.

When he fully concentrated on her, she asked, "As much as you looked forward to Bianca?" She lowered her voice more. "Playing games?"

He flinched. Never underestimate the surprise factor. Phoebe couldn't say any more; she wouldn't repeat the bedroom practices described by that woman or be the one to give him the book. Let him wonder. Let him worry. Let him find someone else to fetch and bring quarters for him.

Jake remained silent, holding out for a loophole. A coward here, like every place else. He'd make her do the heavy lifting, wait her out. Rage gnawed and grabbed her head.

"Say something. Tell me. Give me back my life. All of it was a sham. Give. It. Back."

"What do you want?" Desperation to calm her poured like sweat from Jake.

"What do I want? I just told you. Truth." She shook her head. "No. I want nothing from you. How could I believe a word out of your mouth?"

"You know I love you."

"I don't know anything about you." Pain sliced through her head and neck, clusters of nauseating spasms, sharp and then thudding. She pressed the heel of her hand to her forehead.

"What's wrong?"

"An advance copy of your Bianca's memoir came in the mail," she said. "She wrote an entire book about you."

"She wrote a book about me?"

That he didn't deny it, that he immediately went to "she" and "me" shouldn't have surprised her, but it did.

Calm down. She needed to calm down right fucking now. Jake, in his pressed prison pants, worried because one of his whores wrote a book about him, and the pain in her chest and the flickering, long fluorescent lights and stale air and the woman's fat hanging off her chair and the smell of pent-up men and the vibrations of violence and the shaking hands and knife in her head and the pains in her arm and the feeling her heart would explode out of her body and—

. . .

She lay on the cold concrete floor. A concerned guard knelt beside her. "Stay still. Medics are coming."

She moved her eyes from side to side. Everyone had been pushed back, visitors on one side, prisoners on the other. A line of guards separated them.

Jake stood to the side with Pockmark.

"Do you want your husband?" the guard asked.

She closed her eyes, but the room spun, forcing her to open her heavy lids. "No."

. . .

"Mrs. Pierce, you have too many signs of severe stress for me to enumerate." The doctor perched on a padded blue stool with a stethoscope hitched around his neck. Bearded, burly—they'd given her some sort of Paul Bunyan mountain man doctor. "It's atypical for panic attacks to cause fainting, but it can happen."

"Just lucky, huh?" She plastered on a smile while trying to figure out how fast she'd be able to leave this community hospital and drive home. Adrenalized anxiety had compelled her to race straight to the Adirondacks without stopping, leaving early in the morning to be on time for the last hours of visiting, planning to drive back home that night. Now someone had sewn rocks into her body and soul.

"My guess is that you hyperventilated, constricting the blood vessels to your brain. Then this, combined with adrenaline, and anxiety and panic, overpowered you. Some parts of your brain actually shut down during a panic attack, while others rush into coping mechanism mode. In other words, your body said it couldn't go on and shut down by fainting."

Hearing this, Phoebe never wanted to leave this sterile emergency room cubicle. She wanted to remain here with Dr. Paul Bunyan and the angel-nurses who'd brought her apple juice and crackers, safe in this disinfected room.

"Do you have someone to call? Someone who could help you?"

. . .

Helen steered Phoebe's car with ease. When Phoebe had called, after hearing the initial garble of words, her friend said simply, "Give me the name of the hospital."

"I'm sorry you had to rescue me again." Phoebe leaned against the cool window glass, her headache still throbbing, though at a softer beat. "Kate wanted to come, but there was nobody to watch the girls and Noah . . . well, Noah isn't doing well and—"

"Let's not call it a rescue, and please don't apologize. It's friendship. Hey, Alan and I got to listen to an entire audiobook on the way up. After all these years, that's practically sex for us."

"Eva spoke to me the other day. She's not that angry at me."

"Why would she be?" Helen's hands tightened on the wheel. "Jake's the bad guy, remember?"

Helen, not having lost anything through the Club, didn't understand how anger at him fell on her. But that worked out well, giving Phoebe one friend with whom she could be the same person as always. "The woman appointed to oversee the bakery isn't that awful, apparently. She let them stay on as managers, but eventually the feds want to sell the place."

"Why don't you get involved?"

"How?"

Helen squeezed her arm. "There's your first step. Figuring it out."

A wave of interest came through for the first time in too long. Swift adaptation saved you, not wallowing in the muck. Bianca had freed her.

"I left Jake," she said. "Although considering he's in prison for his next two lifetimes, that's a tough one for me to claim."

"No. Prison or not, you were still tied to him. Strangle-tied."

Phoebe opened a sleeve of Oreos, handing two to Helen before stuffing one into her mouth. She crunched the brittle cookie and comforting cream, grateful to be shooting down a dark road. Highways were built for confessions.

"Noah is locked in the past," Phoebe said.

"The past isn't far away. You shouldn't be surprised."

"I don't think he's trying to get out. I don't mean he's enjoying it, but an undertow of depression is pulling at him. I'm worried about him. About Kate too, of course, but Noah is drowning in everything. Kate says he's online all day, seeing the awful things being said, worrying about the case against them—"

"Is that going anywhere?"

"The lawyers are confident criminal charges won't be filed, but public perception is killing him. All their money is tied up. Kate's also, but it's worse for Noah. They only had his income. His wife is back to teaching, but they can't live on what Beth brings in."

Drifting thoughts floated on the Valium cloud where Doc Bunyan had sent her. "Jesus. The book! I have to get in touch with Kate and Noah."

"Call. Now. From the way you described it, they'll need as much preparation as possible. Call Kate first." Helen didn't have to say why.

Kate answered the phone saying, "How are you? Helen called."

"Did you realize your father had mistresses?"

"What?"

"I'm sorry," Phoebe said. "That came out just awful. Can I blame the drugs they gave me at the hospital? Baby, we'll have to hunker down for another humiliation."

When she finished telling a G-rated version of Bianca's story, Kate sighed. "He's humiliated himself, Mom, not you, but this will be bad for Noah. He confronted Dad about other women in the past. Guilt ate at him, as though he hid something for Daddy. When is the book coming out?"

"Next month," Phoebe said. "I need to see Noah. Help me."

. . .

Bloat obscured Noah's fine features. He wore rumpled chinos and a too-small sweatshirt she recognized from college. Nevertheless, he was there, and the sight of him meant everything.

"When are you going to tell him you'll never see him again?" Noah asked. "You're not going there again, are you?"

"I went there to tell him, honey, but that's when I fainted. I'm not sure—"

"Did he get the message?"

Phoebe thought of the letters still coming daily. The phone calls she didn't answer. "Sort of."

"What does 'sort of' mean?"

"It means he heard, but didn't accept it."

Noah paced in a small circle. The Metropolitan Museum of Art seemed like a good place to meet when she proposed it—Beth thought they shouldn't be at their house, not with the kids still so confused—a neutral space where they could sit and not be faced with Noah having to say yes or no to alcohol, but it had been a horrible choice. They avoided the museum restaurant that served booze, leaving only the cavernous cafeteria or sitting on uncomfortable benches, facing first the sentimentality of American impressionist Mary Cassatt—a reminder of just how shitty their lives were in comparison to her subject—and then Salvador Dalí's *Crucifixion*, a message of life's cruelty.

She tucked her arm in his. "Walk with me."

They strolled past a wealth of brilliance, seeing nothing.

"Just write him and say fuck off," Noah said as they waited for the elevator.

"I'm tempted."

"Why wouldn't you?"

They walked a bit farther, until she'd found her way to the Chinese courtyard. They settled on one of the graceful benches, Phoebe grateful to sit someplace peaceful.

"I'm not joking, Mom." Noah twisted on the wooden seat, straddling it so he could face her. "You don't owe him a thing. Just send a short letter. A note. 'Fuck you; leave me alone.' Tell the prison you don't want to hear from him. Get off the list of people he can call, or write. Damn it, Mom. Don't offer him another ounce of kindness."

She wanted to gather him into her arms, her poor son, his sweetness eaten up with shame and bitterness. "It's not about him, honey. It's about doing it right for me."

"That's a lie." He swung his legs back around and rested his head in his hands.

"How am I lying?"

"Writing means you're trying to do one last thing for him. Same with seeing him or calling. Do you still think something can get through? He's fucked up and useless."

Noah moved closer, and she put her arms around him. He leaned toward her, coming to rest his head on her shoulder. "Everything hurts."

"Oh, baby," she murmured. "Sweetheart, let me help you find your way out. You can do it. For you, for Beth, for the girls."

He shook his head as though telling her he was lost. "I feel as though I'm being crushed."

"By who? By what?"

"By the hate directed at us. Don't you feel it? Have you seen what people say about us? The cartoons? The comments? I want to stand up to it, answer them, tell the truth—but I don't know how."

"You can't take on the world one person at a time, Noah. Especially not when you're like this."

"Like what?" he asked.

Phoebe wasn't sure if he'd become truly disconnected or if he was in denial about how low Jake had knocked him. "Baby, your drinking is out of control."

"Beth told you?" He drew away. "She doesn't understand."

"She didn't tell me, and, by the way, she understands plenty. She's the one taking care of the kids, of you."

"You're right." He blew out a large sigh. "Remember the last time we were here?" he asked.

She put a hand to her chin, rummaging memories. "No. I don't."

"We took the girls to F.A.O. Schwarz, and you bought half the store for them. Then you felt guilty about buying toys instead of giving them education and values, so we came here. When they got tired, which was pretty fast, since they were far too young for the Met, you took us to the Patrons Lounge. We didn't have to sit on benches that day. Jesus, how much did you and Dad pay for that privilege?"

"Do you miss it so much?" she asked.

He shrugged. "It's just a memory of when we were somebody. Let's go upstairs and find someplace they serve drinks."

Phoebe wanted to say no. Bring him to his senses. Nurse him back to health. How did you do that with a grown child—what could you offer to heal them?

"Please, Mom. I know you want me to stop. And I will. But for today, let me pretend to be happy for one afternoon. And I don't know any other way."

CHAPTER 37

PHOEBE

March 2010

Phoebe divided her possessions into "keep" and "Goodwill," covering the fragile items first in plastic supermarket bags and then wrapping them in newspaper. The donations covered a wide swath of floor; the "keep" stack filled only a few cartons. Noah would come later today to bring a few boxes to her new apartment. The place was empty, and the owners were fine with her bringing things in early. If she moved a little each day, with Zach and Noah transporting the heavier stuff on April 1, she'd save the cost of hiring a mover.

Her new space was half the size of this apartment—which wasn't much to begin with—but she'd be in Montclair, New Jersey, with her children and grandchildren nearby. The train to Manhattan would get her to Noah's apartment quickly. Kate's house was a ten-minute drive.

Phoebe swathed the last white Ikea mug and placed it with the rest of her service for four. In her before life, she'd owned multiple sets of china: the treasured Rosenthal lapis, blue edged in gold; the expensive and gaudy Flora Danica—so overpriced it embarrassed her—that Jake had insisted they buy; and others that she could barely remember. What else had she left behind in the penthouse? Though the feds had banished her only seven months ago, she'd forgotten so many of her things. Still, visions arrived at odd times. The cashmere throw in which she'd wrapped herself for comfort. Densely woven wool socks.

Did some woman wear them now, or were they displayed like the pelt of a captured animal?

Sometimes she dreamed her objects all returned, stuffed in every corner of her tiny apartment. She'd wake smothered by the memory of things. With her children back in her life, with being able to hold her granddaughters, she didn't care if she drank out of Ikea for the rest of her life. Though there was something to be said for fine bone china touching your lips as you enjoyed a perfect cup of coffee and not the gritty edge of cheap ceramic.

She imagined the field day the press would have if a thought like that got out: "Phoebe Purses Lips Against Cheap Pottery."

The phone's shrill ring shattered the quiet. Phoebe dropped a half-wrapped water glass, watching as it rolled on the rug.

"Mom." Kate's panicky voice held no tone Phoebe wanted to hear. She clutched the receiver. Dread spiraled down her throat.

Tears muffled Kate's words.

Noah.

Blood alcohol.

Motorcycle crash on 95. Near Greenwich.

· · ·

Beth barred her from Noah's funeral.

Kate brought the message: Phoebe would attract the paparazzi, Beth said.

Hordes of media would follow Phoebe, allowing Jake's apparition to mar the ceremony. He was forbidden in body and spirit—even if the prison system had allowed him a compassionate leave.

Phoebe knew that Beth blamed her for not helping Noah more. She couldn't disagree. She charged herself with her son's death.

"We might be able to talk her into letting you come, Mom," Kate had said. "Right now she's so angry she can barely form words. I took Holly and Isabelle to my house."

Phoebe visualized the three little girls huddled together in one bed. She ached to hold Noah's daughters, bury her grief in being there for them. "No," she said. "Let her lash at me. What else can I offer?"

All previous pain meant nothing. Jake's crimes fell away, diminished in importance. But she blamed him. The misery he brought Noah. She blamed herself. Staying by Jake's side.

For brief moments, she imagined Jake. Him tortured. She questioned so much about him—their marriage—but never his love for Noah and Katie. The part of her still unbelieving of the tornados in her life, those vestigial emotions that hadn't yet caught up with the unraveling of her life, of knowing her husband was a crook, a cheater, and a bastard, that part of her ached for Jake's arms.

But only for seconds, until she pushed away the feeling.

Anguish hollowed her into a brittle vessel holding nothing but Noah's specter. Death seemed reality and life an apparition. Nothing could staunch this grief except draining her body of all blood, all life.

. . .

Phoebe was alone the day Beth buried Noah.

Neither alcohol, food, nor pills passed her lips. No coffee. Only sips of water. She wouldn't satisfy her needs. Allowing relief after ignoring Noah's desolation for so long, after months comforting herself with the belief that Beth could care for Noah, seemed obscene. Jake alone wasn't responsible. Phoebe owned the blame and welcomed laceration.

Mortification seemed vital that day: suffering in mind and body until nothing but pain filled her. Jake tried to reach her, but she refused his call, afraid the hate would overwhelm her—more frightened that he'd offer comfort and that, in her anguish, she'd clutch at his consolation.

They'd killed him, she and Jake.

Cold metal pressed against her forehead, splintered wood from the edge of the sill ground through her black pantyhose as she knelt against the door. Her wet cheek took on the imprint of the rough mesh grid covering the door panels.

Security measures. To keep the thin door from being kicked in. Phoebe wanted that protective barrier knocked in and gone, that steel, the mesh. She prayed for the roughest of thieves to break in and steal

her life, end what she lacked the guts to do. She wanted the thud of a
boot against her face.

A clutter of half-packed boxes surrounded her. She wore black, an
ugly dress woven of smothering polyester that made her first hot and
then cold. How did you not put on a black dress the day of your son's
funeral? That morning, she carefully inched on black pantyhose, new,
from CVS, and too-tight black shoes from Target.

Tomorrow she'd throw them all out.

Helen, Ira, Eva, and Deb all implored her to accept consolation, to
let them come to her, but she refused everyone. They didn't understand. Their comfort would bring only more pain, reminding her she
was alive. They were alive.

If she were brave, she'd have accepted their offers, let herself feel
the agony of their love working to fill the space where Noah should
be. Instead, she pressed harder on the mesh and tried to feel nothing
but the metal grinding against her flesh.

Part 6

——

GOOD-BYE, JAKE

CHAPTER 38

PHOEBE

More than six months passed before Phoebe rose from the metaphorical steel mesh on which she'd leaned since the day of Noah's funeral.

Until August, her new apartment remained as Spartan as when she'd arrived; the moving day had been so close to Noah's death that the events merged in her memory. Upon arrival, she'd unpacked some clothes, a few dishes, and essentials such as toothpaste and soap. Decorative items—the very few she'd bought after everything she owned was sold at auction—remained buried in cardboard.

The nights she didn't have dinner with Kate, Zach, and Amelia, she numbed herself with curated television as she ate a Lean Cuisine with about as much pleasure as she would have received from intravenous feeding. Anything remotely connected to emotion cut straight to muscle. She set her DVR to record *Jeopardy!*, *Wheel of Fortune*, and *Who Wants to Be a Millionaire*. Nothing with families, happy or troubled—families broke her in half. Reruns of *Friends*, showing carefree young adults, were impossible.

Documentaries about animals, just animals, no humans, were best.

Now, reunited with Beth, each day she took the train to Manhattan to pick up Noah's girls from school. Isabelle and Holly unthawed her enough to unpack a few comforts, like the crochet hook and wool she'd bought but never used. Now she worked on creating afghans to give at the holidays.

In September Beth returned to work as a math teacher, traveling up to the Bronx and back by train each day. She needed Phoebe, who picked up the girls from school and stayed with them until Beth got home. She left hot meals for her daughter-in-law and granddaughters, freshly laundered clothes, and a clean house, grateful to be busy. Once a week, they ate dinner together, but no more than that, not wanting to give Beth a reason to tire of her presence.

Phoebe rose to the occasion with her fragile granddaughters, so needy, so reminiscent of Noah, and became stronger.

Today, with unseasonably warm October sun begging first for walking slow and ice cream, and then sand and teeter-totters, they stopped off at the playground on First Avenue. Swings and cones were the only tonic available for Phoebe's eleven- and seven-year-old granddaughters. She sat on the bench, smiling faintly as the girls pumped their legs, side by side, seeing who could swing higher.

A slice of peace.

A novel waited in her bag, a small paperback copy of *Jane Eyre*, her current speed these days, but the frenetic activity in the playground made her too nervous to take her eyes off the girls for even a moment. Older children hovered over the little kids, anxious to take over the swings, looking for an opportunity to help a smaller child fall so they could grab the spot.

Within ten minutes, a familiar stare burned her neck. Sensing the eyes drilling into her before she saw them no longer surprised her. There they were: a clutch of women a few benches away, rubbernecking. A quick glance at their pocketbooks told her that these weren't nannies.

The blondest of them stared openly, her chin tipped up as though to say, "So what?"

Phoebe hoped they'd tire of gaping at her if she ignored them. *Don't engage* was her mantra when in Manhattan.

The blonde marched over, purse swinging on her arm. Why would anyone wear heels to a park? Granted, they were wedges, but Blondie swayed on the uneven, springy rubber surface—the wobble detracting from her aura of righteousness. She plopped next to Phoebe and crossed her legs, the leathery tan skin of her calves denying her smooth, injected face.

"You have a hell of a nerve coming here," Blondie said.

"Are you representing the Park Bench Committee, or is this your singular mission?" Phoebe tipped her head and smiled as though they were in the midst of warm negotiations.

"Grandma! Are you watching?" Isabelle screamed. "Did you see how high I went?"

"Me too!" Holly yelled. "Look at me!"

"Incredible, girls!" Phoebe called and then turned back to Blondie. "Well, which is it?"

Blondie shook her head as though clearing away Phoebe's words. "You don't belong here, Mrs. Pierce. Those women over there?" She pointed. "They know people who lost everything with your husband. The two of you are poison and—"

Holly appeared in front of Phoebe, tugging at her arm. "Grandma. Come push us!"

"In less than a minute, honey. I promise. Go, quick, before someone takes your swing! Go." Phoebe hugged her and then turned back to Blondie, replacing her smile with venom.

"You want to hate me, hate me. You want to believe bullshit about me, it's your fucking prerogative. But don't you dare talk to me. I don't give a damn what you think. And never again make my granddaughters uncomfortable in any way."

Phoebe gathered the girls' lunch sacks, stood, and flung her purse over her right shoulder. "Pray you always know exactly what your husband is doing, honey. And then prepare for the worst."

She rushed to the swings and wedged in next to two doughy women wearing uniforms: nannies pushing their small charges with strong arms as they spoke to each other in what sounded like Russian. Not seeming to recognize her was enough for them to seem like merciful angels.

Stretching her muscles eased Phoebe's tension as she moved from

Holly to Isabelle and back again. Sun warmed her shoulders. Gratitude for these lovely girls, for being needed, and for being able to offer help overcame her.

Phoebe said a silent prayer of thanks to her mother, who, she swore, had sent the right words to her from heaven at just the right moment.

. . .

Walking down the street in Greenwich, it seemed as though she'd never left and never been there, all in one shifting moment. The long-gone family who had lived in that house on the water, built on air and theft— were they real? If nothing from her marriage rested on a foundation of truth, what did it say about her life, her experiences? Who was Phoebe if the entire narrative of her life were lies dusted with fool's gold?

The closer she got to Le Penguin restaurant, the more determined she was to fight for Suzy Ramsland's support. Suzy of the Ramsland Insurance–husband-money always showed a willingness to walk on the wilder side. The first time that Phoebe met her, at the long-ago *Hair*-themed fund-raiser, Suzy had crackled with seductive energy. More important, the Ramslands never invested with the Club, leading to Jake calling Suzy "that crazy cracker bitch."

For years, Phoebe convinced people to invest in something she knew nothing about—why not try it with something she loved?

The restaurant was tucked on a side street. Inside the door, floor-length curtains blocked the entrance, keeping the October chill from the small room. Suzy, seated at a corner table, smiled and toasted Phoebe with a tall glass of pale-gold wine.

"So, here you are," Suzy said as Phoebe took a seat. "The center of the most gossip Greenwich has seen since the McKennas and Coddingtons played switchies."

"I imagine I rated a bit more conversation."

"Don't be so sure. Your dishonor had a lot less sex." Suzy paused and wrinkled her face as much as Restylane and Botox allowed. "Barring that sleazy little mistress book, of course."

"Which I'm certain sold well at Diane's Books."

"I'm afraid she couldn't ignore the demand," Suzy said. "But the library stopped short of bringing her to Greenwich for an author appearance. Out of respect."

Phoebe laughed more fully than she'd ever expected to laugh again. "Thanks for meeting me. And in public, to boot."

"Honey, you've done nothing wrong except marry a lying shark. If I stopped seeing every woman in that category, I'd be a lonely lady." Suzy placed her hand on Phoebe's wrist. "I'm so sorry about Noah. He was a beautiful boy and sweet as a ginger snap. What a hell of a scar you must be wearing on your heart."

Phoebe blinked. "If I weren't sitting across from you, I'd hug you so hard you'd break."

"You're the one who looks like she'll shatter. You've always been thin, girl, but now you're downright skinny."

Suzy beckoned for the waiter. His swift arrival testified to the size of her tips—never a guarantee in this town. More than once, Phoebe spotted miserly gratuities left by megamillionaires.

"Mrs. Ramsland," he said. "What can I get for you?"

"Bring Mrs. Pierce a glass of the Bordeaux and another for me." Suzy emphasized *Mrs. Pierce* enough to force a stiff smile from the waiter toward Phoebe. "With truffle fries to soak it up while we peruse the menu. And thank you so much."

He left. Suzy peered at her. "Happens a lot, that attitude, I bet."

"Let's say I'm not the prom queen anywhere."

"Must be tough after a lifetime of being pretty and popular."

Phoebe thought for a moment, dwelling on Suzy's true words. Her path had always been smoothed by someone else's efforts, whether her father or Jake. "Neither of those matters anymore."

"Of course—it's about Noah and wanting to keep Katie safe. Baby, that's motherhood, and it never stops. Jesus, we're only as happy as our unhappiest child. Truer words were never said. I understand. My sister lost her son. God sliced that loss right off her heart."

The waiter slipped in front of them a steel cone lined with paper; the parchment absorbed oil from a generous serving of crispy fries.

"A mama's station is always tuned to her child's well-being, no matter how old. And losing a child"—Suzy shook her head—"well, you might as well die yourself. That's what you think until your soul knits back together."

"I don't know if I deserve healing."

"Hell, you didn't kill the boy. Even Jake didn't do that. I'm not gonna insult you with a bunch of God talk, but some of us are too fragile for the journey, and we gotta go home. I really believe that. You're made of stiffer stuff, so you're stuck with carrying on, pain and all."

Phoebe bit into a fry, the salty flavor waking up taste buds deadened by a steady diet of Campbell's soup and crackers. "I need something huge from you, Suzy. I won't pretend that we were ever the closest of friends, but still I am asking you to share two of your greatest assets: your money and your name. Not personally, but to make a mark in this world."

"Okay. I'm intrigued."

Crossfires of murmurs bounced around the room. Phoebe had developed extraordinary hearing for the whispers. *Is that her? I'm sure it is. What a nerve!* Awareness of the Gap sweater she wore while surrounded by women wearing Brunello Cucinelli threatened to overcome her resolve.

Would she have been any more generous to a fallen friend than these former neighbors surrounding her? She scrutinized her ragged cuticles.

Worst-case scenario, Suzy said no. What the hell—Phoebe had already had so many doors slammed in her face, she'd barely feel Suzy's rejection. "How'd you like to help some terrific women, partner with one of the oldest settlement houses in New York, and become part of a women-only entrepreneurship? How would you like to use those two things I mentioned—funds and connections—and be the female version of Newman's Own?"

"Will it excuse me from the next ten charity balls?"

"A lifetime's worth and more. I can guarantee meeting three wonderful women and one terrific man. The only charity balls you'll attend will be the ones you decide to throw. Which you might, because you're gonna love working with us so damned much."

"Is it legal?" Suzy smiled to take the edge off her question.

"One hundred percent. You'll probably never make a dime."

"Better and better."

"But there are a bunch of women who've never had enough. You may well guarantee them rising higher than they ever dared hope."

"So what's this golden opportunity for being a do-gooder?"

"How'd you like to buy the Cupcake Project?"

CHAPTER 39

PHOEBE

After the meeting with Suzy Ramsland, Phoebe's life veered. Her world would always be deeply damaged from Noah's loss, but the hours of flagellating herself lessened more each month. She threw her heart into her family and her hours into work.

Twinkling blue and yellow lights decorated the Christmas tree guarding the Cupcake Project's entrance in Greenwich. Soft white cleaning cloths waited on the counter; brooms and mops leaned against the wall. Phoebe and Eva wore Christmas-red aprons emblazoned with the Cupcake Project logo. Hours of scrubbing faced them, but neither wanted to stop talking. Maybe they had poured just that much more brandy than usual into their tea, or maybe the full moon loosened their tongues—whatever the reasons, secrets flew like rare birds.

"Eleven of them rattled like glass marbles in a can." Eva clutched her mug as she spoke of her cousin's worst days in Rwanda, the girl Eva had adopted after she and other members of her family had made a rescue operation for the family left behind.

"One day she was home on college break, the next, hiding in their neighbors' basement—which was nothing like you think of a basement. She escaped there after watching men use machetes to murder her family to death. Her mother. Her father. Her brothers. My girl hid in a box after her parents and siblings were butchered. She had

326

escaped to a dirt hole where she lived for seven months. Eighty thousand people were killed in a hundred days. We all know people who hacked children to pieces."

Phoebe tightened her arms, gripping her elbows until the points dug into her fingers.

"My cousin's daughter arrived in America with images of her family during their last moments carved into her heart like initials in a tree." Eva reached for Phoebe's hand. "And still, she wants to return home. She wants to look at the people who killed them and see how they survived. Do they fall to their knees in shame each and every day? She wants to see how our country managed reparations."

"Is she truly planning to go back and visit?" Phoebe asked. "Would you go with her?"

"I don't think it can be just a trip. Most days my darling girl can't bear the thought of returning and other days she feels she must return and stay."

"She survived a massacre. How can life not be filled with impossible choices?"

"Survival isn't the only point, Phoebe. Afterward, you must endure with dignity and then you must learn how to live without your loved ones. Why be surprised you want closure with Jake?"

"What your cousin, your family, went through—was that part of why you could bear to connect with me after all Jake did that hurt you?"

"My life isn't a mythical lesson to explain your troubles."

"I didn't start this conversation." Phoebe slammed her teacup.

"Hey, we don't have much money backing us. Watch the damn cups," Eva said. "I snap around the topic of my country. We're not a made for television movie. And I am not an African fountain of wisdom for Americans."

"Duly noted." Phoebe poured more brandy in her teacup and then tipped it toward Eva, who nodded assent.

"The people who hid my cousin were Hutu. Their relatives most likely slaughtered Tutsi, our people. You and I both saw evil we can't make sense of, and it haunts us. Sometimes that malevolence exists in people who also hold strands of good. And I suppose there are some who are purely wicked. Which do you think describes Jake?"

Phoebe fumbled in her apron pocket for cigarettes and found the chunky beaded bracelet Kate had given her, with the note "Fidget with this when you want to smoke." Phoebe considered it her antismoking rosary. "I'm not sure. He writes me every day. Why does he do that? Are his pleas for forgiveness a sign of some hidden good? Or does he just want a caretaker? Someone to fill his jail bank account?"

"Do you read the letters?"

"Most I put in a box. Once a month, I open one, looking for changes." She stood and grabbed a broom.

"Do you find any?" Eva began refilling the napkin dispensers.

"No. His letters are repetitive. He recites his day-to-day routine, justifies his crimes repeatedly, and then begs for forgiveness, spotting the paper with crocodile tears as he writes of needing and missing me."

"No wonder you can only read one a month. Does he mention Noah?"

"Every time. He's waiting for me to forgive him for our son's death along with everything else. Kate shreds his letters the moment they arrive. Why can't I?" She swept debris and cupcake crumbs into the standing dustpan. "Keeping them makes me feel like I'm still caretaking him, still bearing witness. Still connected."

"Is that what you want?"

"*No.* I want to sever all ties, not just physical ones. I need to figure out how to make a final psychic separation."

"I doubt a complete break ever comes." Eva moved behind the counter and brought out the unsold cupcakes. At the end of each day, they boxed them up for the senior center. "I think of Jake's crimes as crueler than they even seem. He had so much; why did he need to steal more? He should be graded on a curve of most awful."

"Even worse. If we'd stayed in Brooklyn, living the way I did as a girl, we'd be doing fine." Phoebe sprayed organic cleanser. "I wish we'd never left."

"I dream of home every night," Eva said. "Do you dream of Jake?"

"I do. In my dreams, we're still together. I'm aware we're not supposed to be, that he should be in jail. He whistles around as though everything is fine, while I panic, trying to figure out why he's there and not locked up. It's never a happy dream."

. . .

Jake approached the visiting room table. Her breath stopped for a moment as she assimilated his image with the many Jakes she carried in her memory: the muscular eighteen-year-old; the young adult, bursting with ambition and chutzpah; the father twirling his daughter; the grandfather, happily surrounded by his girls.

This man in prison cloth, shorn of his thick hair, ropy from exercise; this man she didn't recognize.

Jake sat. He took her hand. She let it lay limp in his and then, unable to resist, she stroked his familiar skin—just for a few seconds—before pulling back.

"Pheebs. My God, you're really here. You didn't warn me. I've missed you. When they said I had a visitor, I was afraid to hope. Are you okay? Jesus. I missed you," he repeated. "Happy New Year, honey. I pray 2011 is a better year for us."

"Our son died," she said.

Silence sat between them for long minutes. Finally, he spoke. "I wish I had died instead." He reached for her again. "My poor Pheebs. How did you get through?"

She ignored his outstretched hand, his words. "I won't forgive myself for standing by you. For leaving Noah alone."

Jake buried his head in his hands. She remembered this: her awareness of his tactics hadn't been erased. More quiet surrounded them as he waited for Phoebe to fill the space, expecting the wife and mother who'd rush in and stitch up the family.

She remained still. Finally, he said, "You . . . you aren't responsible for his death."

"No. I am. You are. We both deserve blame. We were given this sweet, sensitive boy, this funny, quirky, brilliant boy, and you tried to shape him into the person you wanted as your son. And I let you."

"No, sweetheart," Jake said. "He rode his motorcycle drunk. He crashed. He was an adult. He made an awful choice, a wretched choice—but he made the decision."

"Life isn't simple like that," she said. "A choice. Boom. Done. I chose to marry you, not a crook. Noah didn't choose a thief for a father, and he certainly didn't decide to work for a criminal father, to be tied in so deeply with you that the world painted him with the same brush."

"That's the media, baby. How many times did I tell everyone you weren't involved, that the kids—"

"No! You said you did it alone. There's a difference between denial and honesty."

"What, you're a lawyer now?"

She clutched the edge of the table, feeling the cold rounded steel, imagining metallic odors clinging to her fingers. "Telling the truth would be admitting Gita-Rae and Charlie and Nanci and the rest of them were involved. Anyone could see they were. But you protected them. By denying their involvement along with ours, you lumped us right in with them. You know they're guilty. Maybe they didn't know exactly how much of a total scam it was, but they knew they were making false statements. They knew the investments were fairy tales. They knew they mailed out fiction. Their case comes up soon, and they'll end up right where you are and then—"

"This isn't about them," Jake said.

"Bullshit. You placed loyalty among thieves in line with fidelity to your family. Jesus, you could barely look up an address on the computer. Did you think anyone would believe you could carry off that scheme alone? Thus, what did it mean when you said that I wasn't involved? Or the kids? It meant nothing. Nobody could discern the difference between you being true-honest and lying-asshole honest. No wonder Noah fell into a black hole."

She stood.

"You're leaving?" Jake's panic became a palpable mass around him. "Already?"

"I'm going to the machines." She walked away gripping a roll of quarters.

The last time she'd been on the prison message boards, she'd become lost in a piteous discussion of vending machine choices, as wives and girlfriends advised one another on the best deals, tastiest snacks, and options for vegetarian boyfriends. Sinking into that world could have been her fate. She prayed she'd have stopped supporting Jake on her own—that it wasn't simply Noah's death that broke the final threads—but she couldn't lie to herself. Or deny that Bianca's tawdry book forced her eyes open.

A young, oh-so-young, woman stood next to Phoebe at the line of vending machines. Ten cultures seemed to have merged into this one beautiful, sad Madonna holding a baby, staring at the choices behind glass as though mentally adding figures.

"I swear they charge twice as much here," Phoebe said.

The baby whimpered. The woman shifted her to the other shoulder and bounced her in the manner every mother knew. "It's worse down in some other places, where they only have pop." She patted the baby's back. "Although I guess that might make life easier. You could figure out exactly how much money you'll need to spend to make your guy happy."

"They bleed the cost of prison right from our veins," Phoebe said.

The woman nodded, seeming grateful for a moment with a prison wife who understood.

"Let me help you," Phoebe said. "I need only one thing . . ." She took a quick glance at the machine in front of her. "Some M&M's. Then you take the rest of my change. Less for me to carry out."

"Oh no! Your man wouldn't like that."

"Trust me. He already possesses more than he deserves." Phoebe fed twelve quarters into the chipped metal slot and then handed the remainder to the woman.

"Are you sure he won't be mad?" She tipped her head in Jake's direction. Even here, everyone knew who he and Phoebe were.

Phoebe got a bit closer and whispered, "Honey, when they're in here, *we're* in charge."

The young woman's face brightened. "So there's an upside, huh? Thanks, Mrs. Pierce." Renewed hope showed in her shoulders as she turned back to the machines.

Phoebe carried the candy to Jake, dropping it in front of him.

"What were you talking to that girl about?"

She ignored his question. "See this?" Phoebe held up the pack of M&M's. "This is the last thing you'll get from me. I won't ever be here again."

"You're saying good-bye with M&M's?" Jake scoffed as though this was just one more marital spat.

"No. I'm leaving you with words." She pushed the small, shiny bag closer to him. "This is simply kindness."

"You are kind, Pheebs. Always have been. Feisty, but compassionate. You're also my other half, and I love you. Nothing changes that."

She wouldn't let this king of bullshit force her onto his field. "Our love is long gone. I'm destined to be known as your wife, a footnote to the biggest crook in years. I'll be considered either a stupid woman clueless about what went on beneath her nose, or a Marie Antoinette eating stolen cake. The world will think what it thinks without my insight. I wasted too much on you already." She laughed. "You deserved your mistress's words. Not mine."

"Do you realize how much shit I took for that?" he said.

"The breadth of how much I don't care is endless." She held up her hands to stop him from talking. "I'll never write about you. The more I'm in the background, the happier I am, but I'll offer you one last chance to unload. Right now. A one-day sale on bearing witness, and it's happening today. Tell me the truth, Jake. What, when, and for God's sake, why? Give me the honest narrative of the life I didn't understand I was living."

Jake broke away from her gaze, staring out the high window framing a clearing sky. "I hate looking back," he said.

"Yesterday is the only thing you can offer me."

He shrugged. "I kept thinking tomorrow. Tomorrow I'll make this stop, but if I thought about it too much, I choked." He looked up, tilting his head back as though retrieving the past. "The panic attacks? Remember? They're gone."

Perhaps his doctor should have prescribed prison long ago. "When did it start? The shortcuts." Phoebe used the euphemism with deliberation, hoping to lead him to the real story. She needed to know how far back his schemes started. Who he was then and who he'd now become.

He tilted his head. "It's hard to recall, but it began—just a little bit—back in the Bronx."

"When you were with Uncle Gus?" she asked.

"Yeah."

"Was he involved?"

Jake's eyes widened. "Jesus, of course not. Gus appointed himself my moral compass. No, it was only me. Then me and Gita-Rae. A shortcut here and there at first, but I needed to make more money, and then more, and before I knew it, the scheme took over and began eating me like a monster. I always meant to make it right. Always. I never wanted this." He gestured around. "How could I?"

"Why didn't you try selling everything? Right away. Lived small. Been content. Couldn't you be happy without the trappings?" For a moment, she became Jake's wife again, helping, working to make life better and grasping at what might have been.

"I thought I'd manage to climb out and still hold on to what I'd built. I always wanted to be the best, own the finest. Hell, it worked so long that I began to feel invincible. Fuck it. I loved being a big shot and having people hanging on my words. I constructed a kingdom. But when the bottom fell out of the economy and everyone wanted their money . . . I missed my time. I got screwed."

"Jake. You never built anything. You never got screwed. You screwed—"

"Don't you think some of those guys—like Louis, for instance—wink-wink knew?" he asked. "Big genius businessmen should remember there's no something for nothing. And guess what? They made a hell of a lot of money off me."

Their brief moment of connection ended. She finally accepted that this man, this awful, morally corrupt man, this was Jake. This had always been Jake.

"Perhaps some people, like Louis, convinced themselves to believe in the impossible, but that's more than irrelevant. Jake. I don't care how old you are—if you live to be a hundred, atone for your sins until you take your last breath. Face your crimes. Teach the illiterate prisoners to read. Write letters of remorse. Give away your organs. Sell your true story and let the money go to the victims. Make amends. Somehow. I can't offer you anything but that advice. And I can give you nothing more except the past."

Phoebe walked around the table. Aware the guards watched, not caring if they chastised them—sure this was their last time together—she took Jake's hand and without words, urged him up to stand with her. "I left a package for you with the guard. A box with the letters we wrote when we tried to kill ourselves. And all the letters you've written me since you've been locked up. You can hold all the sadness now."

Prison cloth scratched her cheek as she laid her head against his chest for the last time. Jake was thinner, but he still felt like Jake. That his essence endured foretold his future.

The day she'd removed her wedding ring and given it to the federal government, she thought her life had ended.

After Noah died, she had wanted to follow him.

After Jake's confession, Phoebe had become two-dimensional, a photo that faded more each day. Now, leaving the last vestigial remains of that hologram in prison with Jake, she walked out of the visiting room and didn't look back.

. . .

Twenty miles away from Ray Brook, Phoebe stopped crying. The scent of coming snow and pine drifted in when she rolled down the window.

They'd all experienced agony from Jake's sins: the children, the family, and every investor. But for the first time, she knew—not with forgiveness, but with the gratitude of knowledge—that he'd also suffered by spending a lifetime waiting to be uncovered. But then he became lucky. His unveiling brought torrents of hatred, but prison blessed him with protection from the stares of an angry public, the pain of his shattered family. In prison he held fast to his pretense of importance.

In Ray Brook, Jake was a big shot.

Being a hotshot, no matter the venue, remained his top goal. She'd find a resting place for her lost marriage. How soothing it would be if love died retroactively. What did her mother say? "If wishes were horses, beggars would ride."

Wallow enough, and you sicken of swimming in self-pity. Phoebe would stop indulging in heartbreak. She could choose to believe that Jake loved her in his limited fashion, or suppose that loving anyone was impossible for him. She'd select her reality, understanding it would be the most mutable of decisions.

Someday she'd allow remembrances to float in without chastising herself. She'd loved Jake before comprehending he was part golem, a self-created Frankenstein. He'd always built walls around his center, ensuring a place she couldn't reach. Now she knew that her frustration had been well founded.

Love didn't die with death. Noah would always be with her. She prayed the pain might lessen, making more room for the tender memories of her son. She'd always be his mother. Unlike marriage, with children, death did not part.

Jake had been her family, and now he wasn't. For too long, she considered him either a dominant father or an unruly child. Holding and caring for him as such had chained her to her vows. But a husband wasn't a child or father. He couldn't grip your heart forever.

Phoebe might mourn the chimera of Jake, like missing fairy tales and once-loved mirages. Feelings could remain, like phantom limbs after amputation, but she couldn't lean on recollections of love one more day.

Jake's success had led her to believe she'd secured the right to wear silk and cashmere, to spend twenty thousand dollars the way her mother might have spent twenty. But she'd learned that nobody was guaranteed anything; nobody earned the right to such enormous riches. Reaching that level usually meant you hit a fluke, were born to it, or cheated.

Jake thought he could straddle the world on other people's legs. He paid a price, but not high enough. No price could be high enough to pay for Noah's death. Phoebe wasn't sure what Jake's missing pieces were; she knew only what he'd squandered and the lessons he'd never learned.

Rich people thought themselves special, but in truth, they simply possessed extra layers of insulation against the winds of misfortune.

Perhaps Phoebe could allow herself thoughts of a life that held more than survival. Of a future where she'd be there for her daughter. Her granddaughters. The women of Mira House.

Phoebe could atone for her blindness.

Quiet overwhelmed her. She slipped a Leonard Cohen mix Ira had made for her into the CD player. The moment "Dance Me to the End of Love" began, she turned up the volume and allowed one more round of tears to pour forth.

When the song ended and "Hallelujah" began, she dried her tears. She thought of those who still surrounded her. The reasons she had to wake. She remembered the most important lessons of life.

Fortunate are those who can dry the tears of others.

Blessed are those who can hold their family and friends close.

ACKNOWLEDGMENTS

The Widow of Wall Street touches topics close to me, including knowing when to question that which seems too good to be true. Fighting to stay above water; balancing love, money, family, and friends; finding the line between trust and watchfulness; and then staying in line with what we know to be doing the right thing—these are struggles we all face at one time or another.

Thus, I thank my mother for teaching me dedication to work, and for scaring me with the warning, "Always pay yourself first!" Early on she learned the lessons of being alone and broke. I didn't always follow her rule, but at least I felt guilty when I ignored her. I thank my grandmother for teaching me the value of kindness. And I thank the books crowded on the shelves of the Brooklyn Public Library for teaching me right from wrong when I was a child and needed guidance. I tried to bring all these lessons together when writing this novel.

Many people supported me while writing *The Widow of Wall Street*, but none more than Stéphanie Abou, the best agent possible. She has been my wise, warm, and determined agent and friend from the beginning.

Atria Books provides a supportive environment for authors. Judith Curr's wisdom and love of books shines through, and I thank her for giving me a place in the Atria family. Rakesh Satyal is an extraordinary editor—he improves everything he touches, and I am grateful to be working with him. Loan Le is a fount of reliability, warmth, and intelligence. Lisa Sciambra and Tory Lowy's dedication is apparent daily.

Hillary Tisman might be the hardest-working woman in publishing. I appreciate all the Atria staff more with each book. Philip Bashe performed miracles with my mountains of errors and brought his special expertise to the pages.

Ben Bruton, from Ben Bruton Literary, is passionate in his work and with his support—how lucky I am to have found him! Artist Rodrigo Corral brought my dream to life with his astounding cover art.

Nancy MacDonald is a friend, a genius, and a rock of stability. She improves everything she touches. Rose Daniels built a website that makes me grateful for her every day.

I would be lost without my writing circles. Ginny Deluca provides faith when my own is lacking. Melisse Shapiro keeps me safe during my worst moments and laughing afterward. My life would lack a center without these women. My beloved and forever writing group— Nichole Bernier, Kathy Crowley, Juliette Fay, and E. B. Moore are four of the wisest, warmest (and when need be, strictest) women in the world. The ever-brilliant Ann Bauer read my work in full draft— offering not just phenomenal suggestions but belief when my own was lacking. Novelist and cookbook author Jane Green has been a dear friend since I met her—and now she's shared a beloved cupcake recipe to go out to the world with my book!

To my cherished and trusted writer friends—bless our virtual water fountain: my dearly loved Chris Abouzeid, Christiane Alsop, Robin Black, Jenna Blum, Cecile Corona, Ellen Meeropol, Becky Tuch, and Julie Wu—you are all way beyond talented and loving.

Heartfelt thanks to the GrubStreet Writer's Center of Boston— especially Eve Bridburg and Chris Castellani—for bringing writers together and making dreams come true. Real-life hugs to everyone in the fabulous online Fiction Writer's Co-op, with a special shout-out to Cathy Buchanan for putting us all together and Catherine McKenzie for keeping us that way.

Thank you Nina Lev for listening to me agonize and offering "walk" therapy; Kris Alden for telling me which authors I should be reading; and to Stephanie Romanos for being the best road companion possible. And special thanks to a group of writers who energized me when

I needed it: Gina Bolvin, Marshall Findlay, Jack Gleason, Thomas Hess, Liz Kahrs, Marlene Kim, Suzanne Lipsky, Ann-Marie Rothstein, Sherrie Ryan, Peter Scanlon, and Sylvia Westphal.

Deep love and thanks to my family, including sisters of my heart, Diane Butkus and Susan Knight. I bask in the love of my cousin Sherri Danny, sister-in-law Jean Rand, and brother-in-law Bruce Rand.

Thank you to those who own my heart, who offer comfort, joy, and understanding: my children, Becca Wolfson, Sara and Jason Hoots, my granddaughter, Nora Hoots, and my sister and best friend, Jill Meyers—you are all so sweet, loving (and funny!). And again, the love of my life, Jeff Rand, the very best man I know.